The Vets

'The plot blasts along faster than a speeding bullet'

Today

'The book has all the ingredients for a successful block-buster'

Sunday Telegraph

'If you feel a sleepless night coming cn, here's something to help you meet it head on; Stephen Leather's fifth thriller. His last was praised by Jack Higgins who couldn't put it down. The same goes for this'

Daily Mail

The Chinaman

'Will leave you breathless'

Daily Mail

'Plenty of visceral excitements'

The Guardian

'A gripping story sped along by admirable, uncluttered prose.'

Daily Telegraph

About the author

Stephen Leather has worked as a journalist for more than ten years, working for a number of newspapers, including *The Times* in London, the *Glasgow Herald* and the *South China Morning Post* in Hong Kong. He is the author of nine highly acclaimed thrillers, PAY OFF, THE FIREMAN, HUNGRY GHOST, THE CHINAMAN, THE VETS, THE LONG SHOT, THE BIRTHDAY GIRL, THE DOUBLE TAP and, most recently, THE SOLITARY MAN (available from Hodder & Stoughton hardbacks). Stephen Leather lives in Dublin.

Also by Stephen Leather and published by Coronet

The Chinaman
The Vets
The Long Shot
The Birthday Girl
Hungry Ghost
The Double Tap

The Fireman

Stephen Leather

CORONET BOOKS
Hodder and Stoughton

First published in Great Britain in 1989 by Fontana

Coronet edition 1996

10 9 8 7 6 5 4 3

A CIP catalogue record for this title is available
from the British Library

ISBN 0 340 67222 6

Typeset by Hewer Text Composition Services, Edinburgh
Printed and bound in Great Britain by
Clays Ltd, St Ives plc

Hodder and Stoughton Ltd
A division of Hodder Headline PLC
338 Euston Road
London NW1 3BH

For Lulu

The first sound would have been the sound of the naked and wet body hitting the glass, a dull, flat thud followed by a crack as the window exploded into a thousand shards.

Maybe she'd have screamed then, but fifteen floors above the ground it would have been lost in the wind as she followed the fragments of glass into space and began the long fall, arms and legs flailing for something, anything, to hold onto.

I saw an old newsreel once, black-and-white and grainy; it had started off with a helium-filled airship coming in to land, swooping down with long ropes trailing from the nose. A ground crew of eight or nine men ran forward to grab the ropes and anchor the giant balloon, but a sudden gust of wind sent it soaring back into the air. Half the guys were smart enough to let go immediately, one dropped about twenty feet and broke both ankles.

Three held on and rode the airship up into the grey sky, turning slowly on one rope as it climbed higher and higher. The guy filming was a real pro. He pulled back, showing all three of the men like lead weights on a fishing line, then followed them down as they fell, one by one, to their deaths. He tracked the first one down, then slowly panned back, showing just how high the remaining two poor sods had gone.

He almost missed the second fall, but got the guy in the centre of the frame a second before he hit the ground. Then, slowly, he moved the camera back up and homed in on the last man on the rope, close enough so you could see his

1

straining hands finally open and slip, so close you could almost feel the palms burn as they began to slide.

The camera followed the doomed man every foot of the way to his death, you could see the arms whirling, the legs kicking, the mouth opening and closing as he screamed, all the way down. It's not true what they say about people dying of shock, that your heart stops and you die long before you hit the ground. The fall doesn't kill you, the desire to live is too strong for that, it's smashing into the ground at one hundred and twenty mph that brings oblivion. Right up until the last moment you're conscious and screaming.

She'd have screamed as she realized that nothing was going to save her, that she was falling to her death in a shower of glass. She'd have screamed, but that high up no one would have heard her and once she'd started to move fast, once gravity pulled her down to her final bloody embrace, then the wind would have ripped the yell from her throat and dispersed it instead into the hot night air.

The next sound would have been the sickly crump as she slapped into the ground like a wet sheet. I guess horns would have blared, passers-by would have screamed and before long the sound of a siren would have cut through the night as an ambulance arrived, too late.

She'd have died alone in the road, a long way from home. I should have been there. She was my sister and I should have been there.

I love a good rape. A gangland killing can sometimes make the front page, but more often than not it'll be below the fold, or shoved inside in later editions. A robbery has to be into seven figures at least before it's worth a mention, and unless someone gets his head blown off it's not going to get any further than a page three lead. A hit and run isn't even going to merit a couple of paragraphs in the 'stop press' column. But give me a good juicy rape, preferably with a dose of over-the-top violence, and we're talking page one, possible splash.

The one I had in my notebook was a cracker of a tale, mother and daughter in a caravan on a site just outside Brighton. Husband tied up and forced to watch before being beaten over the head with one of his own golf clubs. Two youths, one black, one white, one of them carrying a shotgun, the other a kitchen knife. Jesus, the story had everything, sex, violence, a police warning that they could strike again. The only thing missing was an orphaned dog. So long as the Prime Minister didn't call a snap election or die of AIDS it was going on to page one. I'd picked up the story myself from a pal on the Serious Crime Squad, and I'd talked my way into the hospital room where the daughter lay bandaged and on a drip feed. It had been easy. OK, so I might have given the orderly the impression that I was with the police and not just a nosey hack, but I hadn't actually lied. I would have done, but I hadn't had to. I'd just said that we had a few more questions and that and the fawn raincoat did the rest. The girl had lost her front teeth and she didn't, or couldn't, open her eyes for the twenty minutes I spent interviewing her, but I could hear her clearly enough. Good quotes, too, or at least they would be after I'd polished them up a bit.

I was practically running to my desk when Bill Hardwicke's gravelly voice grabbed me by the scruff of the neck and jerked me back to his office. Office, that's a laugh. One of six glass-sided boxes tagged onto the side of the open-plan converted wine warehouse where we worked, it was more like a squash court with furniture.

Bill always reminded me of a hamster in a cage, looking in vain for his exercise wheel. I bought him a pack of gerbil nibbles once and left them on his desk, but he didn't find it funny. No sense of humour, but Bill Hardwicke is one of Fleet Street's best news editors. Not that there was anything left of the Street now that all the nationals had moved out to the East End, but you know what I mean. He looked like a balding boxer, squashed nose and all, but one who hadn't trained for half a dozen years and who'd developed a taste for the finer things in life, like high-cholesterol food and malt whisky. He was sitting in his ergonomically-designed desk. He was totally out of place in the hi-tech office, a relic of the days of hot metal, Linotype machines and 3 am deadlines.

'How did it go?' he growled.

'Magic,' I said, and I could feel myself grinning from ear to ear. I rushed the details past him and he raised his eyebrows.

'Then get thee to a terminal, my son. Now.' I turned to go, when he added: 'By the way, a call came for you while you were out. Switchboard put it through to my office, it was from Hong Kong.'

'Sally?' I said.

'No,' he replied, not looking up as he toyed with his page plans. 'It was some copper. Wouldn't say what he wanted, said he had to talk to you. You got a story going on in the exotic Far East?'

'Chance'd be a fine thing,' I said, and left him to it. I slung

4

my coat over the back of my own ergonomically-designed chair and sat down heavily. I logged onto the system using my three-fingered technique – first and second finger of my right hand, first finger left hand. It was OK for a thousand words or so, beyond that and my hands began to ache. What the hell, when was the last time a tabloid hack had to write a thousand words?

There was an air of gloom hanging over the office, dampening the electricity that you normally find sparking through a newspaper. The technology was partly to blame, removing forever the clickety-click of typewriters and the whirr of stories being pulled out to be thrust into the hands of waiting copy boys. Now it is all done electronically and the only time paper is involved is in the final product.

We'd been writing all our stories into the computer for about four years, and the subs were well used to working on the machines, but now we were trying to do full-page make-up on screen and traditional newspaper skills were about as useful as a rubber sledgehammer. Management had brought in a team of young, thrusting computer programmers in three-piece suits to do the business. Except that they couldn't. Now the silicon chip whizz-kids, headed by the chairman's son, a curly-headed bastard called Simon Kaufman, were working in tandem with the middle-aged shirt-sleeved grumblers who made up our subs desk. Tempers were getting frayed, young Kaufman had publicly humiliated and sacked two of the older down table subs and there had been one stand-up fist fight, but we were no nearer to getting the production fully computerized and it was starting to get everybody down.

I leant back and started to shuffle the facts and quotes into a coherent pattern that would get my name back onto the front page. I looked around the office as my mind got into gear.

There were four phones lined up along the gap where our desks met, Roger's and mine. Two were white, one was black and one was the same musty green you find on bacon that's been in the fridge for three weeks, hidden behind the bottles of Schweppes tonic. Roger and I each had a white one, both connected to the switchboard, one of those swish jobs that plays 'O give me a home where the buffalo roam' to waiting callers. The black and green phones were of the old fashioned type, both were direct lines and we'd taken the numbers off them. The number of the black one we gave out to our police contacts, the green one to anyone else we thought might give us a story. The white ones rang all day, – social chit-chat, the odd punter with a bit of gossip, hacks from the other papers ringing up for info, the odd obscene caller ranting about the politics of the paper or a mistake on the racing pages. We get more than our fair share of nutters on the crime desk, you either hang up on them or, if you've got the time, you can play with them, sitting back in your chair with your feet on the desk until you get bored with the game.

If the green phone rang it was more serious and more often than not we'd get a story out of it. If the call came on the black phone Roger and I would reach for it together because it would be a tip off, anonymous or otherwise, that could lead to a splash. Usually he'd beat me to it, maybe because he was six years younger, maybe because he was faster, or had longer arms, but mainly it was because that phone faced toward him. Rank has its privileges. He was the chief crime reporter, it said so on his business card, while mine just said 'crime reporter'. He got first crack at the black phone, an extra fifty quid a week on his expenses, and a car.

Roger the Dodger was sitting opposite me now filling in an expense sheet, and I knew he'd had a curry last night because his breath reeked of it. He was chewing the end of his felt-tipped pen.

'Go all right?' he asked.

'Not bad,' I said. Keep your pissy little hands off, I thought. This one's mine.

'Andy, any chance of a coffee?' I asked, and was treated with a contemptuous look that said there was about as much chance of that as of hell freezing.

There were two secretaries servicing the specialist writers' section, when they weren't doing the really important work like painting their nails, getting their hair done or typing out press releases for our motoring correspondent's freelance public relations operation. The better of the two was a squat little blonde with perfect skin and big feet, accurate typing and one hundred and ten words-per-minute shorthand. Her name was Katy and she looked after the two industrial correspondents, the defence/aviation writer, the motoring correspondent and our consumer affairs specialist.

The other girl was Andrea. We called her Andy, which she most definitely wasn't.

She was a looker, a stunner. Tall and willowy, blonde like Katy but with legs almost half as long again, breasts that you just ached to touch and a smile that made you want to grab her and kiss her. Half the office lusted after her, and the other half were women. Andy had an address book which was slightly smaller than the L-R section of the London telephone directory and a voice that was a cross between Sloane Square and a razor blade being scraped across a blackboard. She spent most of the day on the phone talking to her boyfriends, girlfriends, relatives, lovers; interminable conversations in a voice that set your teeth on edge and she had a laugh like a donkey's bray. She was supposed to look after five of us: two on the crime desk, our Royal correspondent, the education writer, and the medical expert. I had one fifth of her, and I had the fifth that answered back. She was unreliable and a pain in the arse.

Roger and I had spent the best part of nine months trying to get rid of her, ideally to swap her for Katy so that Willis, the motoring correspondent, could suffer for a change. We'd tried piling work on her, being sarcastic, being rude to her, Supergluing her desk drawers shut, loosening the casters on her chair. None of it had worked and we'd got to the stage where we were talking about putting ground glass in her coffee.

'Do you want a coffee?' I asked Roger.

He nodded. 'Yeah, cheers. Did Bill tell you about the call from Hong Kong?'

'Yes, thanks. Said he'd call back.'

'Something up?' he said, and he had the look of a fox after a chicken, the scent of a trip abroad in his pock-marked nostrils. I was glad to be able to disappoint him.

'Dunno. Could have been my sister.' He lost interest as his hopes of a freebie evaporated. I took his chipped Union Jack mug and the pint pot I'd nicked from the Bell pub. I walked over to Andy's desk and plonked them down on her magazine. 'Thanks, love,' I said and bared my teeth. She scowled and took them over to the sink where we kept the coffee machine – God, she had a sexy walk – and a couple of the subs leered over the top of their terminals as

8

she walked by and slammed the mugs down on the draining board. I bashed out the first couple of paras of the story on autopilot, as I thought about the days when I used to spend most of my time on the road, before I had to play second fiddle to the likes of Roger the Dodger.

I missed the adrenaline rush that comes with being a fireman. Time was when all I did was cover the big stories, the ones guaranteed to make page one. I was the guy always ready to get on a plane at a moment's notice, covering everything from hijackings to ferry disasters, but that was before I'd started to have the blackouts. If it hadn't been for Bill Hardwicke I wouldn't even be number two on the crime beat. It was Bill who'd pulled me back from Beirut after I'd gone on a bender and missed a suicide bomber who killed a dozen marines as I lay slumped over a table in some sleazy back street bar. It was Bill who sent me to an expensive private nursing home to dry out at the paper's expense. And it was his signature on the bottom of the letter in my personal file that said if I ever again let my 'drinking problem' get the better of me I'd be looking for a new employer.

I wasn't teetotal by any means, but I was managing to keep it under control. Sometimes I went for weeks without a drink, and I'd long ago stopped keeping a quarter bottle of gin in my desk drawer. I was doing OK.

I was about half way through the story when my white phone rang, the shrill warble of a dying bird.

Roger was deep in thought over his expenses sheet and looking up at the ceiling for inspiration. There was no way on earth he was going to break off from his work of fiction to answer the phone so I hit the 'Store' button, sending the magic words into the machine's mega-memory, and picked up the receiver.

A voice speaking broken English, the grammar all twisted and the tenses all to cock, asked me my name and then asked me to spell it and then told me to 'wait for second please for call from Hong Kong'.

My first thought was that it was Sally, and my God had it really been Christmas since I last spoke to her? But I realized that she would have dialled direct and not gone through the operator, at about the same time the clipped male voice came on the line.

It was an inspector from the Royal Hong Kong Police. He checked my name, and the spelling, and then he told me Sally was dead and the room sort of telescoped and Roger looked about a million miles away and I felt cold inside and I wanted to say, 'are you sure?' or, 'there must be some mistake' but I knew it was only on TV that they make mistakes like that and I didn't want to sound like a twat.

'I didn't catch your name,' I said.

'Hall,' he answered. 'Inspector Hall. Your name was down as next of kin. Are your parents still living?'

'Our father died some time ago, but our mother is alive. What happened?'

'Your sister died yesterday after falling from a hotel window. At this stage it looks like a suicide case, I'm afraid.'

My stomach lurched and the hand that held the phone was shaking.

'What?' I said in a voice that was no more than a whisper. 'That's not possible.' Roger was pretending not to listen.

'I'm afraid it's definitely her, sir,' said Hall. 'She has already been identified.'

My mind froze, there were a million things I wanted to ask, but my head seemed to be filled with a single thought. Sally was dead.

'Are you still there?' asked Hall.

'Yes. Yes, I'm sorry, what do you, I mean, is there anything I have to do?'

He coughed, with embarrassment I guess. 'There are arrangements that have to be made, sir. It would be a great help if you would come out to Hong Kong.'

'Of course, I'll be there, I'll be there.' He gave me a telephone number where I could reach him and then he hung up. Roger was looking at me strangely and I realized I was sitting there with the receiver pressed hard against my ear, saying nothing.

'You OK?' he asked.

My mouth was dry and my hands were damp with sweat, but I just nodded and said yes. I had to look up my mother's number in my address book, which gives you an idea of how often I rang her. We were a loose-knit family to say the least. She'd remarried five years after our father had died, and spent a couple of relatively happy years with husband number two, running a kennels outside Nottingham, before he was killed in a car crash. He'd been well insured and my mother took the money and went to live with her unmarried sister in a small village near Truro. I suppose I saw her about once a year now and spoke to her on the phone whenever I felt guilty about not keeping in touch which, to be honest, wasn't all that often. Sally was all the family I really had, or needed, though I didn't even call her as often as I should. And now I wouldn't get the chance.

My mother wasn't in but my aunt was, and in a way I was relieved because I didn't know if I'd be able to cope with breaking the news to her. It was bad enough explaining to my aunt that Sally was dead and that I was going to Hong Kong. I hung up on her tears because there was nothing else I could say. If I was distant from my mother I was even further removed from my aunt and the rag-bag of relatives I had scattered around Britain. I only saw them at weddings and funerals, and that was usually only because Sally had dragged me along out of a sense of duty.

I left my coat hanging on the back of my chair and went to see Bill.

'I need to go to Hong Kong,' I said.

'Sally?' he asked.

'She's dead. I have to go.'

He started to get up but only managed halfway before he dropped back into the chair with a thud and a jiggling of flesh. He looked as if he cared.

'Go,' was all he said. He didn't ask any of the questions they teach you when you're a keen, hungry cub reporter on the make, he didn't ask why, when, who, what or where, partly because he knew the answers to three out of the five, one didn't matter and one was the reason I had to go, but mainly because it didn't make the slightest difference to him. I was in trouble, I needed his help and he'd give it, no questions asked. Bill and I go back a long way, our paths had crossed on the *Mail*, the *Express*, for two fiery months on *The Times*, and we'd come together again on the 24-hour-a-day comic that we both poured scorn on but which paid us twice what we were worth. I'm not going to give you any crap about me loving him like a brother because I'd still stitch him up if it meant I'd get his job, and I'd leave him as soon as a better offer was waved in front of my nose. But he was a friend in a world full of colleagues and competitors. He opened his mouth and I thought for one horrible moment he was going to say something stupid like, 'I'm sorry', and I wouldn't have been able to take that, not even from him. Behind me in the cavernous office I could hear raised voices and then I heard Gilbert Fell, an old-time sports sub in a red cardigan, scream, 'fuck this stupid machine,' followed by the expensive crash of an ATEX terminal being thrown to the ground and stamped on.

'What the hell was that?' yelled Bill, at last managing to get to his feet.

'Only the sound of my heart being broken,' I said. I gave him a half wave and said, 'See you, I'll phone when I get there.' But he knew I would, anyway.

A few years ago I'd have had a travel bag in my bottom drawer, ready, willing and able to be sent abroad at a moment's notice, but that was before I was a crime reporter. Now the most travelling I got to do was up to Glasgow every once in a while if there was a good murder or a decent rape case. And I'd managed to swing a week in Portugal out of Bill on the back of a time share con that the paper exposed, but generally I was tied to the office and the terminal while Roger snaffled all the trips for himself. Rank has its privileges. And perks. And a car. Bastard. But old habits die hard and I still carried my passport in my inside pocket, and I had a walletful of credit cards.

Andy was gossiping with one of the prettier copy typists, but even if she'd been at her desk there's no way I would have asked her to arrange things. This was important, I had to get to Hong Kong and I had to get there now.

'Katy, do me a favour, love,' I said, and she looked up from her typewriter, keen and eager. She really wanted to be a reporter and if it had been up to me she'd have been given a chance, but there's no way on God's earth the unions would let her make the switch.

'I have to get to Hong Kong right away, fix it will you? I'll call you from the airport to find out which airline. Just get me on the first flight,' I checked my watch, 'after eleven o'clock.'

She was already reaching for her Filofax.

'Any problems, get Robbie on the case,' and I gestured a thumb at our airline correspondent, slumped in his chair reading *Flight International*, listening to the phone and drinking herbal tea at the same time. The ubiquitous Robbie Walker, two heart attacks down and one to go, reformed alcoholic and womanizer, he was now a committed health food nut and he would have been out jogging every morning if it hadn't been for his triple by-pass. He'd been around a good many years and his contacts in the Ministry of Defence were second to none, but that wasn't the reason he was kept on. Our Robbie's forte was being able to get free flights for the editor and, as long as he could keep on coming up with the goods, he had a job for life and the editor travelled the world free of charge. As nice a bit of symbiosis as you'd be likely to find in Fleet Street.

'Try to get me in Economy and Robbie can get me an

upgrade, but I'll pay the full whack if I have to. If the first flight is full tell Robbie it's urgent and get him to get me on the jump seat.'

'Will do,' she said, but I was already walking away from her. As I headed for the stairs Bill put his head out of his glass cage and shouted that the office car was waiting for me at the front door.

I was at Gatwick an hour later and I called Katy from a pay phone. She said she'd got me on the direct Cathay flight and that Robbie had fixed it so that I didn't have to pay. I could tell from her voice that she knew about Sally, but like Bill she didn't say anything. I wasn't surprised she knew. A newspaper office is the last place you can expect to keep a secret. I got to the desk twenty minutes before take-off and the British Airways guy who did the button pressing gave me a strange look when I said I had no luggage, but Robbie had got me on First Class so he had to bare his teeth and ask me to go straight to immigration please and have a good flight. The Asian smile would have to wait until I got on the plane. I wasn't thinking straight, I couldn't concentrate, all my thoughts had been removed and individually packed in cotton wool and sealed in polythene bags. I didn't want to think about Sally, not right now, so I left the bags alone, I couldn't risk opening by mistake the one that had her name in it. But I'd forgotten something and I was just about to walk through immigration when I remembered what it was. I'd run out of coins for the phone. But the paper accepts all collect calls so I rang Katy and asked her who our stringer was in Hong Kong.

'I'll check with Foreign,' she said and she went off to Nick Webber's glass box. Fifteen minutes to go before take-off so there was no rush but I was still tapping the phone nervously against my ear by the time she came back on.

'Howard,' she said. 'Howard Berenger.'

'Staff or freelance?' I asked, because stringers could be either.

'Freelance,' she said. 'Do you want his number?'

'No kid, it's all right. Just call him and tell him to meet me at the airport. Tell him what I look like, OK?'

'Sure,' she said. She sounded like she was going to add 'Good luck' and I was relieved when she didn't.

'Hell, I nearly forgot. Ask Roger if he'll finish my story. It's slugged RAPE23 and it's damn near finished so I want my name on it.'

'Will do,' she said.

I made the plane with five minutes to spare. I've flown on most of the airlines in the world at some time or another, and after a while they all seem the same. The service varies, so do the uniforms and the food, but a plane is a plane and time in them is wasted time. I took the freebie shaving kit so that I would look halfway decent when I landed in Hong Kong and I took the headphones and put them on right away because I didn't want to make small talk with the tweed-jacketed bearded guy with bad teeth in the seat next to mine.

A Chinese girl with an American accent and too much eye make-up asked me if I wanted a drink. Do bears shit in the woods? Of course I wanted a drink, I'd wanted a drink every day of the three weeks I'd been on the wagon, and I wanted a drink now more than ever because I needed something to keep Sally in the bag and out of my head. I'd promised myself that I'd stay off the booze this time, come what may, but this was different. I needed a drink and if I didn't have one I knew I'd go crazy, so I ordered a gin and tonic.

It came with a tinfoil packet of salted nuts which I treated with the contempt it deserved. I held the glass up to my eyes, watched the bubbles collect on the inside and smelt the lime that nestled among the ice cubes and then I sniffed it and felt the spray tingle against my nose and I could smell the gin and then I sipped it and let the coldness of it roll around my tongue and down my throat and then I drank it in three gulps and it was gone. Three weeks. Almost a record.

The stewardess took the empty glass and then we taxied to the runway. The engines went on and the seat kicked me in the back and we were up in the air with just sixteen hours, or however long it was, between me and Howard Berenger and Hong Kong.

I put the seat fully back and tuned the stereo into the jazz channel and while Grover Washington Jr did his stuff I slowly and carefully opened the plastic bag with Sally's name on it.

Sally is twelve years younger than me and I'll be thirty-eight next birthday so she had more of her own teeth and a lot less cynicism than I had.

She's a full head shorter than I am which makes her about five feet two and me the older brother she always has to look up to. Her eyes are blue and bright and her nose turns up just enough to be pretty without being cute and she has a habit of licking her upper lip with her catlike tongue when she's worried. Describing a sister's figure is tough because you're talking about a body that I'd grown up with and seen change over almost three decades, but she was slightly plump and I guess if I was eyeing her up in a pub I'd have said that her breasts were just a shade too full and her legs a bit too short, but there hasn't been a day when I haven't been glad that she was my sister. She's smart, very smart, smarter than I am, she can out-think most people she meets and five minutes into a conversation she's finishing their sentences for them. She'll grow out of it I guess, except that she wasn't going to because she's dead and I must get out of the habit of thinking of her in the present tense because now she's part of my past.

I last saw her about a year and a half ago, in London. Sally had a grasshopper mind, chopping and changing and job-hopping whenever she got bored. Her CV was a nightmare. She'd dropped out of teacher training college and went off to sell skiing equipment in some posh resort in the Alps. She did well but soon got bored and came back to England with a couple of thousand pounds in the bank and a suntan and got a job as a computer operator with one of the big City stockbroking firms. Three months later she switched over to programming and made section head before chucking it in and crewing a yacht being delivered to some property tycoon in Australia. She spent a couple of months in Oz selling advertising space on a daily and decided she'd like to be a journalist, wangled a courier flight back to England and hit Fleet Street, except that the Street hit back. No experience and no union card meant that she had as much chance of getting a job on the nationals as she had of winning the Grand National without a horse. She managed to get a few shifts on one of the Sunday tabloids but then the chapel found out she wasn't in the union and showed her the door. She got a few articles published in women's magazines, but that wasn't what she wanted. Sally had set her heart on seeing her name in lights, and what she wanted she usually managed to get.

How, she'd asked me, sitting cross-legged on the leather sofa in my flat, how could she break into the closed shop that journalism had become? Find a free sheet that'll take you on, or a trade magazine. Learn the business from the bottom, shorthand, typing, pick up the basic skills and the union card, then switch to a local weekly paper, covering the courts and the district council meetings, think of it as an apprenticeship, then move up to one of the regional evenings or dailys. Keep pushing stuff out to the nationals, spend your holidays haunting the pubs and bars where their reporters drink, keep pestering the news editors until they give you a few shifts just to shut you up and then prove how good you are. If you're good you'll get in. If you're not, you won't. That's how I did it and it took me five years. That's what I told her, big brother offering younger sister the benefit of his advice. It felt good.

'Fuck that for a game of soldiers,' she said, and flicked her hair sideways in annoyance. So much for brotherly advice.

'There's got to be a quicker way,' she said, and true to form she found it. In Hong Kong. The journalists there are a transient bunch at the best of times so it was fairly easy for anyone who can string a couple of words together to get a job on one of the papers. That guaranteed membership of the Hong Kong Journalists' Association which in turn entitled her to a union card back in London. Smart girl. She'd arrived in Hong Kong eighteen months ago and I'd spoken to her half a dozen times on the phone. She

19

was enjoying herself so much she'd decided to stay. Hong Kong was magic, do you miss me? How's London? How's the comic? Must go, bye. Crazy. I'd barely thought of her during the time she was in Hong Kong, I guess because I knew she'd always be there at the end of a phone if I needed her, but now she was dead and the feeling of loss was a dull ache that just wouldn't go away. I missed her, I wanted to talk to her, with her. Shit, she was my sister and I should have been there.

I realized with a jolt that I'd said the last bit out loud and I opened my eyes to the tune of Sadao Watanabe's 'Birds of Passage' to see a stewardess bending over me with a worried frown spoiling her little girl looks. She asked me if I was all right and I said sure, just a bad dream, and would she please get me another gin and tonic and make it a double. This time I didn't savour it, I drank it quickly, but it didn't do anything to make the ache go away. I hadn't expected it to, it would take more than a couple of gins. At the very minimum it would need answers to the five questions Bill Hardwicke hadn't asked. I was going to Hong Kong to get the five answers and then I'd take it from there. Sally wasn't a jumper, she was too full of life to have ended it by throwing herself through a window God knows how many storeys up. She was full of fun and pulled me out of black depressions more often than I cared to remember.

I was going to miss her sense of humour. She caught me with a belter one afternoon, chewing gum at the counter of an all night chemist in Hampstead where we'd gone to buy Alka Seltzer and anything else that might help relieve what I thought was an upset stomach but which turned out to be the first sign of an ulcer that's been playing me up for the best part of four years now.

20

'What's the date?' she'd asked.

'Fifteenth, I think. Why?'

'We'll be needing these then,' she replied, and picked up a handful of contraceptives from a display box. 'Pay the lady, then,' she said, opening her eyes in mock horror. I was stunned and it was a toss up who was the more embarrassed, me or the grandmother behind the counter. Sally just stood there looking as if butter wouldn't melt in her mouth, revelling in my discomfort. Bitch. Then there was the time she sent a dozen red roses to the office with a card that said, 'To the man I love most in all the world' and signed it 'Reggie.' She'd been pulling strokes like that on me ever since she was 13 years old and I could never get angry at her because she was the one bright shining star in a life that I found grey and bleak. If you think I'm cynical now, you can't begin to imagine what I'd be like if Sally wasn't part of my life.

'I'm going to miss you, Sally,' I whispered, and this time didn't care that the words came out.

The stewardesses served dinner and then the lights were dimmed and a film flickered on. I finished another gin and tonic (fourth or fifth? Maybe the sixth. Who's counting anyway?), and reclined the seat and slept.

The ever efficient stewardesses woke us up two hours before landing and gave us breakfast and then I used the freebie washing kit, dumping it in the bin in the toilet cubicle. I wanted to arrive in Hong Kong with nothing, and I planned to leave the same way, the only thing I'd bring back would be the knowledge of what happened to Sally. Anything I needed while I was there I'd buy and leave behind. Don't ask me to explain why, it just felt cleaner that way. I didn't want to arrive with a suitcase like a tourist, or with a briefcase like a businessman. I simply wanted to find out what had happened and then get back to London.

I read the Cathay inflight magazine from cover to cover and tried to absorb as many facts and figures about Hong Kong as I could. Population six million or thereabouts, ninety-eight per cent of them Chinese, Chinese and English the official languages, shops open seven days a week, principal exports clothing, toys and watches, a Crown colony due to be handed back to China in 1997. That sort of stuff. Then my ears popped and the seatbelt light was on and we were flying between, not above, the tower blocks and then the 747 banked sharply to the right and we were dropping down to the finger of reclaimed land sticking out into the harbour.

Fifteen minutes later I was standing in one of the immigration queues, waiting impatiently midway down a line of a dozen people. The speed the lines moved varied with the efficiency of the immigration officer who was stamping the passports and our line was being dealt with by a young Chinese girl who gave all the indications of having terminal sleeping sickness. Eventually I got to the head of the queue and she took my passport without looking at me, then scrutinized every page, every visa. My passport is nine years old and I'd spent most of them flying around the world for various newspapers so I had almost as many stamps as Stanley Gibbons. She checked every one, then she squinted up at me through a pair of lenses that looked like the bottoms of milk bottles. The girls in Hong

Kong are the prettiest in the world the man in the seat in front of me had said as we'd taxied down the runway to the terminal building. He should have seen this one, with her badly-permed hair and a dimple in her chin big enough to grow potatoes in. This girl was ugly; her eyes were too far apart, her ears stuck out like mug handles and her skin was marked with old acne scars. She probably had a great personality, was an absolute dream with children and small animals and would make someone a wonderful wife and mother, but I doubted it. I think her plainness was more than skin deep.

'How long will you stay in Hong Kong?' she asked.

'I don't know. As long as it takes.'

'Business or holiday?'

'Holiday, I suppose.' I reached for the passport but she moved it away.

'You have been to Hong Kong before?'

'Only in transit.'

She flicked through the blue and white pages at a painfully slow rate until she got to the personal details at the front.

'You are a journalist?'

'That's what it says.' I was starting to get angry at her time wasting. I was in a hurry.

'Where are you staying?'

'I don't know.'

She looked puzzled and studied the immigration card I'd filled in before landing. The space marked 'Address in Hong Kong' was blank. I gave her a warm friendly smile, showed a bit of teeth and crinkled my eyes, the smile that says what a great, honest, open chap I am.

'I'm being met by a friend. He'll have arranged a hotel for me.' If I'd been a woman and she'd been more of a man

I'd have undone a few buttons and fluttered my eyelashes. I just wanted to get the hell out of this airport.

She paused, and then she stamped my passport and banged it down on the counter which was level with her forehead.

'Next,' she said, and I blew her a kiss as I walked past.

I headed for Customs, past the crowds huddled around the metal conveyor belts awaiting their luggage. I went through one of the 'Nothing to declare' passages but a tall, thin Chinese waved me back.

'You must wait,' he said, and pointed to a thick yellow line on the floor. He was obviously a chief something or other, an organizer rather than a doer. His men were busy checking the baggage of passengers from an earlier flight, opening suitcases and unpacking cardboard boxes.

'I haven't got any bags,' I said, and held my arms out at my sides.

'You must wait,' he said emphatically, and started making small brushing movements with his left hand, the sort you'd use to shush away a cat.

'For fuck's sake,' I said and stood behind the line until they'd finished with the family of four holidaymakers in front of me, a husband and wife and two young children complete with four suitcases, three travel bags and a large teddy bear that was examined in as much detail as an illegal immigrant. Swear to God, he looked up the bear's arse and prodded it. The labels on the suitcase said Bangladesh so I guess they were worried about drugs, but even so.

Eventually it was my turn, and the chief whatever-he-was walked over to watch his junior question me.

'Anything to declare?' he asked. A 'Sir' would have been nice.

'Such as?' I asked.

'Spirits, cigarettes, perfume, electrical goods . . .' he rattled off a list.

'Where would I put them?' I asked.

'Huh?'

'I haven't got any luggage.'

'Where have you come from?'

'London.'

'England?'

'I'm glad to see that the education standards in Hong Kong are every bit as high as they are back in Britain.'

'I'm sorry?'

'That's all right, can I go through?'

I walked past, nodding at his superior. I turned left, following the sign pointing towards the greeting area, through a double door which opened electronically for me and down a ramp towards a sea of faces. There was a mass of people and I swept them with my eyes, not a difficult task because most of them were Asian and I was looking for someone called Howard Berenger. I saw my name in capital letters on a piece of white card, held at waist height by what appeared to be an off-duty monk in a light blue safari suit. His face was well scrubbed and as hairless as a young girl's, his eyes were bloodshot and his nose had a bluish hue. The hair on his head formed a thick ring and was as white and fluffy as cotton wool around a virtually circular bald patch.

His lips were thick and red as if he'd been rubbing Vaseline into them, and his teeth were pure white. He must have been in his early fifties but he'd run to fat which had smoothed out the wrinkles on his face and he had the glossy sheen of a freshly picked apple. He'd obviously come to terms with his expanding waistline because his trousers looked as if they'd been specially made and were held up with a thick brown leather belt that could have been used to saddle a Shetland pony. Our Howard obviously liked his drink, and his food.

He'd seen my look of recognition when I read the card and he dropped it into a bin and came over, hand outstretched.

'Berenger's the name, laddie,' he said, in a thick Scottish accent. 'Howard Berenger.'

'Pleased to meet you, Howard,' I said, shaking his hand. It was cool and coated in a thin film of perspiration. It felt like a piece of raw liver and I had to stop myself wiping my hand on my trousers when he let go.

'No luggage?'

'No.'

'OK, let's go. I've fixed you up at the Excelsior.' He led me through the waiting crowds, and within six steps he was three feet ahead of me, moving gently and surely, negotiating his way with practised ease, while I was bumped and jostled. His hips and shoulders moved independently and there was no effort in his movements, despite his bulk he just glided along. He stopped to let me catch up, but after a few more steps I was lagging behind again. No one apologized when they banged into me, there were no smiles, just mute acceptance of physical contact which could not be avoided. I slipped behind Howard and coasted along in his slipstream as he carved through the chattering, noisy crowd. We went through another set of electronic doors and the heat hit me like a wet towel. I sucked in humid air that immediately soaked my face and hands, and I gasped. I took off my jacket and carried it over my shoulder.

'God it's hot,' I said.

'You've come at a bad time,' he said, then looked away embarrassed as he realized what he'd said. Yeah, I guess it was a bad time. 'It gets better though, and then we hit the typhoon season.'

'This is like being in a sauna,' I said, and loosened my tie.

'You get used to it,' he replied as we walked towards a waiting queue of taxis, red Toyotas with grey roofs.

We got into the back and Howard leant forward and spoke to the driver.

'Mandarin?' I said as we drove off.

'Cantonese,' he said. 'But I only know a few words. I can speak a bit but I understand hardly any of it.'

'How long have you been here?'

'Hong Kong?'

I nodded.

'Twenty-three years, on and off. I spent a couple of years in Indonesia somewhere along the way. Oh, I see what you're getting at – why don't I speak more of the language? Because it's a bitch to learn, that's why. It's tonal, the meaning of the word changes with the tone you use, and it's damn near impossible for a gweilo to learn.'

'Gweilo?'

'That's what the Chinese call us Westerners. It means ghost man or white devil or something. It's meant affectionately. Unless they call you "Say Gweilo". That means dead gweilo and isn't quite as friendly.' He laughed. 'It's made harder by the fact that the written language is so different from the spoken. Look at the signs above the shops.'

The pavements were thronged with a seething mass of

humanity that ebbed and flowed from shop to shop like a living tide. I could see what Howard meant, the signs were in Chinese picture writing, strokes and lines that meant nothing to me, the only way I could find out what the shapes said was to look in the windows.

'Suppose you were in a French supermarket and you picked up a can of beans. You'd be able to read the French for beans on the label, and you've learnt another word. That doesn't apply here. The written and spoken languages are completely independent. In fact the written language is the same throughout China, no matter what they speak, be it Mandarin, Cantonese, Shanghainese, or whatever. They might not be able to understand what they say to each other but they can always communicate by writing. And the only way to learn to read and write is to commit several thousand characters to memory. It takes years.' He pointed out of the window at a crocodile of small children in matching white uniforms, all carrying big rucksacks on their backs.

'See those bags? They're full of school books. The sheer volume of information that's shoved into those brains is frightening. And that's just to learn their own language. They learn English too, and with 1997 fast approaching most of them are studying Mandarin as well. Just to be on the safe side.'

Despite several hours' sleep on the plane, I felt dog tired, and the weariness compounded the feeling of unreality that made everything seem like a dream. Sally's death still hadn't sunk in, part of me was sure that she was still in my life, that I was on my way to see her and not to find out why she'd died.

'Have you been to Hong Kong before?' asked Howard.

THE FIREMAN

'No, first time, though I've passed through the airport a few times. It's not the sort of place I'd come to on holiday and I've never been here on business.'

The taxi slowed at a line of toll booths before we drove down through the cross-harbour tunnel, the perspiration clearly visible on my hands under the harsh fluorescent lights as Howard continued his thesis on the difficulties of Cantonese.

'It's the tones that make it really difficult,' he said. 'Each word can be said nine ways, in a high, low or medium tone, rising, falling or level. And each tone gives the word a different meaning. Take the word "cheung", for instance. It can mean long, wall, window, rob, gun, or to change money. Gow can mean enough, dog, teach, nine or prick. In English it doesn't matter how you say the word, dog is dog is dog. But in Cantonese you have to be able to simultaneously hear the word and the tone in which it is spoken. It's almost impossible for a gweilo unless they spend months on an intensive training course like the cops do.'

He was nervous and talking too much. That could have been because I represented the paper that paid him a big slice of his income, or it could have been that it wasn't the most comfortable assignment he'd ever been given, shepherding a man whose sister had fallen to her death.

'Twenty-three years is a hell of a long time.' I said.

'Aye, I came out here just after I turned thirty. I was working for a local radio station in Devon and getting nowhere fast. I took two weeks' holiday, came out here and never went back. I got my first job on RTHK, the Government radio station, and spent a few years with TVB, the bigger of the two television stations here. I

STEPHEN LEATHER

even spent a couple of months in public relations for my sins.'

We burst out of the tunnel into the open air again, and cars started fighting for position now that they were freed from the constraints of the single file tunnel lanes. Towering above us was a tall white building with a convex façade, and atop in large blue letters was the word 'Excelsior'.

'I moved to the *South China Morning Post* about eight years ago as a feature writer, but knocked that on the head when the paper was taken over. Now I string for your paper and a couple in Australia. I do a monthly column that's syndicated to half a dozen Scottish papers, and the odd radio report for the Beeb. And if I'm really desperate I do a bit of PR. There's plenty of freelance work to make a decent enough living. Most of the papers just pay lineage, and there are plenty of slack periods when nothing much happens in Hong Kong, so I wish more papers were like yours and paid monthly retainers.'

'Yeah, well I heard that our Foreign Desk has been told to review its costs,' I said. Howard looked as if I'd stabbed him in the chest. 'But that's nothing new,' I added, 'they're always threatening cutbacks. You know how it works.' He didn't look any happier.

The taxi joined a queue waiting to pull in front of the main hotel entrance. The cars weren't going anywhere so I reached for the door handle but it was locked and when I unlocked it the driver started jabbering and pointing to the road. I managed to get the door open but he pulled a lever under the dashboard and it slammed shut again.

'I'm not going to sit here with the meter running, I don't mind walking twenty feet,' I said and put my shoulder against the door and pushed, but the little sod had managed

30

to lock it again. Now he was shrieking and stabbing a bony finger at me and then pointing to the road again. The nail on the accosting digit was black and rotting and flecks of spittle splattered onto my face as he shouted.

Howard put his hand on my shoulder. 'He can't let you out, laddie. We're on a yellow line. If a policeman catches him he'll be fined on the spot.'

'Well why didn't he tell me that?' I asked, and even before the words left my mouth I realized how stupid that sounded. He had been telling me – in Chinese.

'I'm sorry,' I said and the driver grinned, showing me a mouthful of teeth every bit as black and rotten as the fingernail.

We eventually reached the front of the queue and the door was opened by a turbaned Indian in a black and gold uniform. The lobby was nothing special, functional rather than inspiring, and packed with Chinese and American tourists with a sprinkling of British Airways crews. I signed in and the receptionist asked me if I had any luggage and I said no. She said she'd get someone to show me to the room and again I said no.

'Just give me the key,' I told her and she looked at me as if I'd stolen her puppy or her handbag or her virginity or whatever it was she prized most. I thought she was going to burst into tears but she held out the electronic key card. The room was on the nineteenth floor and Howard had already started to walk to the lift, dodging in and out of a minefield of suitcases. The lifts were like the lobby, clean and functional and packed with tourists, and we seemed to stop at every floor on the way up.

The room was OK, one largish bed and one single, a phone on a table between them, middle of the range television, and a fridge. The bathroom was small with marble and red granite and it had another phone by the toilet but even so it was comfortable rather than luxurious.

Howard stood by the door with his arms folded as I gave the room the once over. i'd obviously been given the executive package because there was a vase of carnations on the dressing table and three books of matches with my name embossed in silver letters. OK, so my name was spelt wrong, but the thought was there. There was a cushioned bench seat under the window which looked out over the harbour. The water was chock-a-block with ships, either sluggishly rolling at anchor or busily sailing through, freighters, tugs, junks, fishing boats. A real working harbour. Immediately in front of the hotel was a typhoon shelter and though the weather was perfect and the water calm it was packed with boats. To the left of the shelter the vessels were pretty white yachts, expensive playthings for the Hong Kong rich. But to the right was a different story, a flotilla of small, dirty, wooden junks, with washing hanging from rope lines and steam rising from cooking pots. The yachts were once-a-week boats, but the junks were homes, where families lived, loved and did the laundry. There must have been a hundred of them, moored tightly together. God knows where they got their water from but there was no doubt where their sewage went because on the prow of one of the scruffy boats was a stocky fisherman who had opened up the front of his denim shorts and was playing a stream of urine into the water below.

'Welcome to Hong Kong,' I said.

'Huh?' grunted Howard from the door.

'Nothing,' I said as I watched a white hydrofoil shoot

past leaving a white wake foaming behind it. 'Fancy giving me a geography lesson?'

Howard joined me at the window. 'That's Kowloon over there,' he said, and pointed straight ahead. 'Tsim Sha Tsui to be one hundred per cent accurate, where the best shops and bars are. Over on the left is the Regent Hotel, with the New World Hotel next to it. Over to the right is the airport. That's all on the mainland, behind Kowloon are the New Territories and beyond that is China. We're on Hong Kong Island, in Causeway Bay. The business section is called Central, you can't see it from here but it's on our left. Between Central and here is Wan Chai.'

'The world of Suzie Wong?'

'A long time gone, laddie. More's the pity. It's a wee bit more commercial now. The road below us is the harbour expressway, it runs from one end of the island to the other, from here it passes alongside North Point and then Quarry Bay and beyond.'

'Behind us?'

'The Peak, home to the rich and famous, and the other side is mainly residential. That's Hong Kong.'

'Not much to it, is there?'

'Not in terms of square feet, but there's a lot going on. This place hums, that's its big attraction . . .'

He fell silent as he realized that I wasn't really paying attention, just letting his words wash over me. Hong Kong still felt like a dream, my mind was still back in London and I guess the jet lag wasn't helping. We stood together, looking down at the ships in the harbour.

'Where did it happen, Howard?' I asked eventually.

'Kowloon side,' he said, nodding towards the mainland.

'A hotel in Tsim Sha Tsui. You can't see it from here.' He paused, but he didn't wait for me to ask for more details, he knew what I wanted to know, it was just a question of choosing the right words.

'She was in the swimming pool on the top floor. It was late evening and she was alone.'

I pictured her carving through the water with her lazy crawl, breathing every second stroke. She loved to swim, she could go on for hours, never tiring, never changing the pace. I was faster over a short distance, but I tired quickly whereas she was a stayer.

'She went through the window. No one seems to know what happened,' Howard said.

'She didn't jump,' I said. It wasn't a question but he took it as one.

'Nobody knows,' he said.

'No, I'm telling you. She didn't jump.' I turned to look at him. 'Did you know her?'

He nodded. 'It's a small place, everybody knows everybody else. And you know what journalists are like.'

Yeah, I knew. And a stringer like Howard would probably be scared shitless that somebody young and keen like Sally would steal some of his precious strings.

'Her copy was good,' he said. 'She was a hard worker, all right, she'd take any job that was going. Any job that would get her a by-line. Seemed happier freelancing, because there were plenty of people more than willing to give her a staff job.'

'You socialize with her much?'

'Occasionally. And she rang me up a few times for help on stories. She was relatively new so I was a good source of background for her.'

'Did she have any problems, anything that was worrying her?'

'Not that I know.'

'What about enemies?'

Howard didn't answer, just shrugged.

'What do the police think? Was it an accident?'

'They just don't know, laddie, they just don't know.'

'Where is she now?'

'Kowloon Public Mortuary.'

'I want to go there. And to the hotel. And I want to speak to the police.' I'd written down the name of the inspector who'd phoned me in London and I handed the piece of paper to Howard. 'That's the guy I'm to see.'

'I know him,' he said. He walked over to the bed and picked up the phone, dialling the number from memory. He fixed up an appointment for us and five minutes later the turbaned Indian was opening the door to a taxi. In flawless Oxbridge English he asked me where I wanted to go and Howard told him.

The Indian spoke to the driver who nodded and crashed the taxi into gear and we moved out into the traffic with a series of gut-wrenching jerks.

'Where do they learn to drive as badly as this?' I asked Howard, only half-joking.

'Practice, laddie. It takes years of practice.'

We were early, and the bastards made us wait. Howard and I sat on a wooden bench while a fan circled slowly overhead. I'd taken my jacket off and rolled up my sleeves and loosened my tie, but was still panting like an overweight Labrador.

An old man hobbled past and slowly lowered himself onto the wooden bench next to ours, using a rubbertipped steel walking stick to steady himself. His skin was as brown and wrinkled as an autumn leaf and what little hair there was left on his head was short, stubbly and white. His toes peeped through holes in his slippers and the nails were black with dirt or age. The face was a blank mask, thin bloodless lips and impassive eyes, the eyebrows had all but disappeared. He was clinging to life as tenaciously as a pensioner to a bargain in a church hall jumble sale. I don't know why he bothered.

'Probably a triad boss come to give himself up,' whispered Howard, and nudged me in the ribs with his elbow. The old man cleared his throat and then sucked up the phlegm from his nasal passages with a guttural sound like a drain being cleared. He rolled whatever he'd dragged up around his tongue, breathed in through his nose and spat noisily at the wall opposite. The green and white mass of saliva hit the plaster with an oily splat and began to dribble down slowly, fighting gravity every inch of the way. I felt sick but I couldn't take my eyes off, as it smeared itself to the floor.

'Jesus, Howard.'

'You get used to it, laddie. Just be glad he didn't aim at your foot.'

A door at the end of the corridor opened and a young Chinese in a green uniform and shiny black belt walked out, his well-polished boots clicking on the stone floor. He beckoned to Howard and me with his hand, and ushered us into the room.

'Very polite,' I whispered to Howard.

'He doesn't speak English,' he replied.

'How do you know?'

He pointed to the chrome numbers stitched onto the shoulders of the green shirt.

'The ones that can speak English have a red strip of material under the numbers,' he said. 'Not that that means anything – the little bastards will still send you in the wrong direction just for the fun of it.'

The youngster pointed to a pair of old wooden chairs in front of a rusting metal desk. 'Please wait here. The inspector will be in to see you shortly,' he said in accentless English, and left us alone in the room. A gun in a glistening holster bumped against his hip as he walked. From the size of it he'd need both hands just to aim it.

Howard was totally unashamed. 'Maybe his mother hasn't got round to sewing them on yet,' he laughed and flopped into one of the seats.

On the wall behind the paper-strewn desk was a map of Hong Kong, dotted with pins of various colours, and with police mugshots stapled haphazardly around it. The filing cabinets were made of the same grey gunmetal as the desk with identical rust stains. There was a carpet of indeterminate colour on the floor, dotted with small flecks of plaster that had fallen from the damp, peeling ceiling.

The window obviously hadn't been washed for years, it was streaked with grey and made the outside look as foggy as a winter's day on the Isle of Dogs. A small air-conditioner set into a hole in the wall next to the glass did its best to keep the temperature of the room below boiling point, but it was failing miserably and groaning like a sick horse.

Leaving a journalist alone in an office is asking for

trouble. I began idly flicking through the green folders and sheafs of typed papers, looking for anything interesting. Looking for Sally's name. I'd just started to open the top right hand drawer when the door opened and two men walked in, one Chinese, one European.

I gave them a winning smile and walked back to the side of the desk where I belonged, dropping into the chair next to Howard.

The European was Hall. He didn't offer to shake my hand so I didn't bother to stand up. I guess he was a bit pissed off at my attempt at breaking and entering. Hall was a shade under six feet, brown hair cut to regulation length and wearing a grey off-the-peg suit with trousers that were just a bit too tight around the groin. His tie was dark blue with a coat of arms on it.

He had the same wary world-wise look that plain clothes policemen all over the world have after they've been lied to so many times that they expect to come across the truth about as often as Halley's comet.

It was also a look that said that the last thing he wanted to do at the moment was to talk to the brother of a girl who'd just been scraped off a Hong Kong pavement.

His companion was harder to read, tall for a Chinese and well built, wearing faded jeans and a black leather jacket that was scuffed around the elbows. His hair looked as if it had been cut with a set of blunt shears and a pudding basin and his nose had obviously been broken a couple of times. The tie was a masterpiece of bad taste, bits of purple, green and Picasso-type shapes in black and white. He obviously had no mother, no girlfriend, and no sister, because no girl would allow someone she loved to dress that way. He wore a thick gold signet ring on the litt'e finger of his left hand

and a bulky gold chain on his right wrist and as he listened to Hall he toyed with the ring and studied me.

Hall didn't introduce him, but they both nodded at Howard. Hall had brought a file with him, identical to those already littering the desk, and he opened it as he sat down. He interrogated me for the best part of an hour, and he was good. He followed up several lines of questioning, checking the spelling of all names, cross-referring on times and dates, when I'd last seen her, who her friends were, former colleagues, present lovers. He wrote everything down, filling two A4 sheets with his small scribble.

When he'd finished he opened a drawer in the right hand side of his desk and took out a large polythene bag containing a leather shoulder bag, a navy blue dress and a pair of white shoes. Hall took them out, placing them on his desk top one item at a time. He opened the flap of the bag and took out a thin gold watch that I'd never seen before, a money clip, a Gucci purse and a set of keys.

'These are your sister's effects,' said Hall. 'We found them in the changing room.' He handed me a typewritten list and a cheap biro. 'Can you sign for them, at the bottom.'

I scrawled my signature and then he ripped off the top copy, putting it in the plastic bag along with her belongings. He pushed the bag over to my side of the desk.

'There should be a ring.'

'I'm sorry?' said Hall.

'A ring. A gold ring with a heart on it. I gave it to her on her twenty-first birthday.'

Hall looked over at his colleague, who shook his head.

'There was no ring,' said Hall. 'Perhaps it is at her flat. We haven't been there yet.'

'She swore she'd never take it off,' I said, and then realized how silly that sounded. 'Never mind,' I said.

'Is there anything else you can tell me, anything I haven't asked you that you think might be important?' asked Hall.

'I want to know what happened.'

Hall paused, studying a sheet of paper in the file.

'She fell from a high-floor window, dead on arrival. There was no note. You know as much as we do at the moment.'

'Sally wouldn't have committed suicide.'

'You sound very sure of that.'

'I knew her. She was my sister.'

'That may be, but she could have changed. Something could have happened.'

'Do suicides normally throw themselves through windows?'

'I don't follow you.'

'Look, I'm a journalist, I've covered more than my fair share of jumpers. The sort that jump are the ones that want to attract a crowd, to become the centre of attention for once in their lives. They usually sit out on a ledge and wait for someone to talk them out of it.'

Hall leant back in his seat and seemed about to speak. I pre-empted him by holding up my hand. 'Let me finish,' I said. 'Sally wasn't the sort to kill herself, period. But, and this is one fucking big but, if she was she wouldn't throw herself through a window. She talked tough, but she couldn't bear pain. You couldn't get her into a dentist's chair without pumping Valium into her. If Sally was going to kill herself she'd make sure it was perfectly painless and she'd make damn sure there wouldn't be any blood.'

I looked at the two coppers and could see in their eyes that they weren't listening to me, any moment now one of them was going to lean forward and say, 'there, there, it'll be all right.'

I banged my hand down on the desk. 'Why won't you just believe me,' I yelled, trying to shock them into action.

'There's no need to raise your voice,' said the Chinese guy in an American accent. Mid-West, I think. I ignored him.

'Suicide is not unusual in Hong Kong,' said Hall quietly, as if he was talking to an imbecile. 'It's like a pressure cooker here, one of the most densely populated places in the world. Not everyone can adapt to it.'

I closed my eyes and sighed deeply, he just didn't understand.

'If she'd had a problem she'd have called me,' I said wearily.

'Hong Kong is not an easy place for European women, the social scene for them isn't as, shall we say, fulfilling as it is for the men. You wouldn't believe how many expat wives are on tranquillizers, or how many just pack up and leave their husbands after a year or so here. Few marriages can survive this place.'

'Sally wasn't married.'

'I know, I know. But the pressures are the same.'

'She wouldn't kill herself. She'd just leave.'

The two policemen looked at each other and I could practically hear them thinking, 'he isn't listening to a word we say.' Yeah, well maybe they were right. But I knew Sally, and they didn't.

'What happens now?' I said.

'There'll be an autopsy,' Hall replied. 'Then we'll be able

41

to release the body. You can either take her back to England or make arrangements here.'

'You're still waiting to do an autopsy? But it happened three days ago. Why the delay?'

'It takes time,' Hall said, wearily. 'We don't have the facilities, or the manpower, that you have back in the UK. We've just lost two pathologists to Canada, part of the brain drain. I'm afraid your sister has got caught in the backlog. I'll do everything I can to speed things up, but . . .' He left the sentence unfinished.

'Well why bother with an autopsy, if you are so sure it was suicide? Are you telling me that there's some doubt about the cause of death?'

Hall shook his head. 'No, but an autopsy might tell us why she killed herself. She might have been drinking, or on drugs.'

'No,' I said. 'I'm the drinker of the family, and she never took drugs.'

'She might have been ill.'

'So ill that she'd throw herself through a window to end it all sooner rather than later? Christ man, you seem to be doing nothing more than trying to come up with reasons she would kill herself. I wish you'd put the same amount of effort into finding out what happened. Have you spoken to her friends? Her colleagues? Was she alone in the pool when it happened?'

'There were no witnesses. The pool was closed, locked up for the night.'

'So how did she get in?'

'We don't know.'

'The pool was just for guests of the hotel?'

'No. Members of the health club could use it as well.

42

Your sister was a member, but that doesn't explain what she was doing there after the place had closed.'

'And what was she doing there?'

'Swimming, it appears. Naked. We didn't find a swimming costume.'

'And what are you doing now?' I said.

'Doing?'

'About finding her killer?'

'At the moment we don't know if we are looking for a killer.'

'What sort of investigation is this?' I asked him. 'You haven't even searched her flat, for God's sake. By the sound of it you couldn't organize a piss-up in a brewery, never mind investigate a murder. Where the fuck is your boss? Perhaps I can get some sense out of him.'

'I am Inspector Hall's superior officer,' said the Chinese, quietly. 'And I can assure you that everything that can be done, will be done. It is less than three days since your sister died. You cannot expect miracles.'

'Maybe not,' I said. 'But I know enough about police work to know that if you don't have a suspect within forty-eight hours then the chances are that you're never going to have one. Come on, Howard, we're wasting our time here.'

I walked out with Howard behind me, past the spitter and back into the scorching sunshine, swinging the plastic bag by my side. A bag full of Sally.

This time I was the one walking fast, the anger burning through my system, and Howard had to jog a little to keep up.

'You must let me borrow that book some time,' he panted as we made our way towards a taxi rank.

'Which book?'
'The one about winning friends and influencing people . . .'
'Fuck off, Howard.'

We flagged down another cab and joined a line of traffic waiting to enter the tunnel that linked the island to Kowloon. It took the best part of fifteen minutes to travel the one hundred yards to the tunnel entrance and less than five to drive through it. We had to stop at the rank of pay booths to hand over the toll and then we were into the traffic of Kowloon once more, and on our way to the morgue.

'There's no need for you to identify . . .' Howard began to say, but I cut him short with an angry look. 'It's definitely her,' he finished lamely. 'One of her friends has already done the paperwork.'

I didn't bother even trying to explain to Howard why I had to see Sally one last time, to touch her and feel the cold flesh that would show me that she was dead. I would have had to have told him about a frightened little girl with a tear-stained face who'd climbed into my bed a week after our father had died. It was three o'clock in the morning and she was seven years old. Her hair was unkempt and her cheeks were flushed and wet and she was rubbing her hands together like an old woman. I put my arms around her and held her, feeling the tears trickle onto my shoulder as she cried.

'I dreamt Daddy was back,' she said, haltingly between the sobs. 'He came into my room and said he'd been away but he'd come back and he'd bought me a present. He kissed me. I could feel him kiss me. Then I woke up and he wasn't there.' She sobbed again and after a while her breathing steadied and deepened and I thought she was asleep, but she spoke again, whispering into my ear. 'Daddy is dead, isn't he?'

'Yes, love, he is.' There was no doubt about it, we'd watched the coffin slide along the stainless steel rollers and through a purple velvet curtain on the way to the furnace to the tune of some recorded hymn. We'd seen the coffin go but I knew what Sally meant. We'd said goodbye to a wooden box with a wreath on top, we hadn't said goodbye to him. He'd died in his office of a massive haemorrhage that flooded his brain in less than two seconds and which killed him before he even hit the floor. Click, like a light being switched off. Sally and I were at home when our mother got the phone call. It was the school summer holidays, I was waiting for my A level results and Sally was enjoying her seemingly endless break from primary school drudgery. Our mother walked into the room in a state of shock and put her arms around us. *The Saint* was on television, Roger Moore in black and white. It was 4.15 in the afternoon. It was a Wednesday. Our dad was dead and we never saw him again. He was cremated three days later and Sally started having the 'I'm back' dreams.

'I don't know if he's dead,' she whispered. 'They should have let me see him,' and then she fell asleep. She was right, of course. We'd last seen him at the wheel of his BMW, waving goodbye and promising to take us to the pictures that night. The memories were all of him alive, walking, talking, laughing, shouting. The memories didn't allow for the possibility of him not coming back. He was alive in our heads and our hearts. We should have been allowed to see him before they cremated him, but that wasn't the way things were done. He went from the office to a hospital to an undertaker into a sealed coffin and into a furnace. A wake would have been better, the Irish had the right idea, put the corpse on show, remember the good times, celebrate them, but be aware that they are over. It's not even a human thing. Take two dogs that have lived together for years, then one of them gets run over. The survivor will pine for weeks, searching the house, looking for its partner, ears pricking up hopefully at every night-time noise, just in case. But if you take him to the body of the dead dog, he'll sniff it, maybe nudge it with its nose, then walk away uninterested. There's no forlorn howling, no whimpering, no attempt to get the carcass on its feet, just a placid acceptance that what was once living is now dead. Acceptance, that was what I wanted, just the knowledge that Sally was dead so that she wouldn't walk into my room when I was asleep and say 'I'm back' and kiss me on the cheek. But how could I explain that to Howard? I couldn't, so I didn't even try.

The taxi stopped in front of a line of wreaths on the pavement. Before I could reach for the door handle it was opened by a swarthy youth wearing a red T-shirt and dark blue shorts. His hair was damp with sweat and in his hand he held a battered black clipboard. He spoke to me in rapid Cantonese and I shook my head. Howard was still sitting in the taxi, sorting green notes out of his wallet. The man pushed the clipboard in front of my face – it held a chart full of different designs of wreaths, circular, oval, square, plain and fancy. He poked at one of the varieties with his forefinger and spoke to me again. I shrugged, but by then Howard was by my side.

'What does he want?' I asked.

'He wants to know if you will buy any flowers.' He could see my confusion, so waved his hand, taking in the tower blocks around us. 'These are all funeral parlours. He just assumed that you are here to make funeral arrangements and he hopes you will buy one of his wreaths.

'Tell him to fuck off, Howard,' I said. Two more taxis had pulled up behind ours and more of the vultures descended, grabbing for the door handles before the wheels had stopped turning.

'Where do we go?' I asked Howard, and he led me down a small side road towards a high wall. There was a sign there which said Kowloon Public Mortuary with a row of Chinese characters below it. Across a tarmac car park was a building the colour of crème caramel. We walked to two glass doors at the entrance but they were locked and Howard had to press the bell by the side of the doorway until a young Chinese girl in a white coat came to open it. We walked into a cool hall tiled like an East End butcher's shop. There was a big steel freezer door to the left but we walked past it, Howard talking to the girl in English, slowly, pronouncing each word clearly and precisely.

'She's on the ground floor, this way,' he said to me. We followed the girl to another freezer door, which she pulled open with a grunt. Plumes of cold air billowed out and the temperature dropped a couple of degrees. I don't know what I expected, but this wasn't it. I'd visited mortuaries in Britain but they were as sanitized as a supermarket, bodies neatly stored away in oversize filing cabinets. This place was obscene. The fridge was filled with metal racks, like steel bunk beds, three high. Each was occupied by a corpse. Not one was covered, they were just lying there in the clothes they'd been delivered in. There was an old man in a pair of green and white pyjamas, his face twisted into a sneering grimace, a child with her throat cut, her head practically severed from her body, a young man in a safari suit who'd obviously gone through a car windscreen. All of them just lying there like broken robots.

'Why aren't they covered with cloths or something?' I asked the girl, but I'd spoken too fast and she just gave me a puzzled look. 'This is macabre, Howard. It's like something out of a cheap horror movie.'

At the far end two corpses, stiff with rigor mortis, had been stacked against the wall like planks of wood. They were both men, and both had been placed with their foreheads against the side of the fridge, arms frozen by their sides.

All the bodies had labels tied to their big toes, name, date and identification number.

The girl walked towards the two standing bodies, and then turned left and pointed at one of the racks.

'Oh God, I don't believe this,' I said. The corpses were all dressed in the clothes they'd died in, and Sally had been wearing nothing when she'd fallen from the hotel. Now she was lying on a sheet of metal as naked as the day she was born, her flesh as cold and white as a boiled chicken, frost collecting on the black triangular thatch of hair between her legs. Close up I could see she was covered in grey bruises and contusions and then I realized I was looking at the good side, the side that hadn't hit the ground first. Howard put his hand on my shoulder and tried to pull me back but I shook him off and stepped forward, my arms stretched out towards her. Her left side was crushed and mangled, the face, down the arm and hip and her leg, the blood congealed and hard, the flesh ripped and shredded from the impact, fragments of bone protruding through the punctured skin. I looked at Howard and his face said: 'What did you expect after falling fifteen floors?' and though the words were never phrased I said: 'I thought she'd at least have been covered. At least they could have covered her up.' I pointed at the girl in the white coat, my finger wavering before her startled face.

'Get a cloth, something to cover her with.' She didn't move, her mouth open like one of the frozen corpses. 'Now,' I shouted at her. 'I want her covered, now.' She ran from the cold room, coat flapping around her legs. I took Sally's hand in mine and it felt like wax. Her breasts wobbled grotesquely as I raised her arm and pressed her palm against my cheek. The ring wasn't there.

'I'm sorry I wasn't here,' I said to her quietly, then as an afterthought I added, 'Sleep well, love.' I put her arm back alongside her body and walked away without looking back. Howard followed me out of the fridge and closed the door behind us. I didn't even notice the heat as we stepped into the outside air, though within seconds I could feel the beads of sweat collecting on my brow. Condensation was starting to collect on the inside of the polythene bag. I'd forgotten I was still holding it.

'We're going back to the Excelsior?' said Howard, as he pushed me into the back of a cab.

'No,' I said. 'I want to see where it happened.' He didn't argue, just gave the name of the hotel to the driver and then settled back into the plastic seat, eyes closed like a Buddha in repose.

It was a modern glass and steel structure, flanked by shops filled with cameras and Gucci bags, places where tourists could be fleeced by professionals. The pavements were packed with people, moving slowly, knocking and banging gently into each other in the afternoon heat. Young Chinese couples walking arm in arm, sweating tourists in brightly coloured holiday outfits, schoolchildren in white uniforms with book-filled rucksacks on their backs, and a seemingly endless supply of old ladies in virtually identical flowery cotton shirts and trousers. There were old men in shorts and plastic sandals, fit young men in dark suits with slim briefcases, middle-aged men carrying birds in small cages, and women with babies strapped to their backs with strips of cloth, a tidal flow of humanity that coursed through the arteries of Kowloon.

The taxi door was opened by a youth in a scarlet outfit that looked like it belonged in the Charge of the Light Brigade. I left Howard to pay the fare and walked into the lobby through two huge frosted glass doors, each held open by a young boy. They seemed to go for door opening in a big way in Hong Kong, probably a combination of cheap labour and expensive automatic doors. The atrium seemed to stretch up forever, it was square with ranks of internal balconies crawling with ivy. Four cylindrical see-through lifts glided silently up and down while below them a bustling coffee shop was entertained by a gorgeous Chinese girl in a white dress playing a grand piano. I craned my neck back to watch one of the passenger-filled lifts soar up as Howard arrived at my side.

'Impressive,' I said.

'Aye, it's one of the best. Not up to the standard of the Mandarin or the Regent yet, but they're getting there. They've got the prettiest girls in Hong Kong in reception. Just look at the bonny wee lassies.' He was practically salivating as he ogled the rank of young girls behind the marble counter.

'You're a dirty old bastard, Howard,' I said.

'Aye, maybe you're right. But don't tell me you're immune to yellow fever. It gets us all in the end. They're soft and gentle, it's like making love to butterflies. Have you ever had a Chinese girl?'

'I once went out with a girl who had jaundice,' I said. 'Come on, leave it out.' The last thing I wanted right now was a session swapping sexual memories with a lecherous old hack. But maybe Howard was being kind, trying to take my mind off the hell-hole of a mortuary and the fall that had killed Sally. Christ, I needed a drink. We walked to the lift and went up to the top floor, the fifteenth. The label by the button said 'Health club and swimming pool'. I watched the girl in the white dress get smaller and smaller as we rose up. When the lift doors opened we were so high up that the sound of the piano was lost in the dull throb of faraway conversation. Howard pushed through heavy wooden swing doors into the health club's reception area where a girl in a bright blue leotard and navy leg warmers bounced up to ask for our membership cards.

Howard explained that we were thinking of joining and just wanted to take a look around to see what facilities were on offer. She nodded her head eagerly, long black hair jerking backward and forward across her shoulders. She was tiny, with flawless skin and a boy's figure, no make-up or nail polish, just fresh and new and young. I felt a hundred years old. Howard put his wrinkled and liver-spotted hand on her arm like an over attentive Father Christmas and gave her a look that would have alarmed her parents, even if it had come from a fat man in a red suit with a white beard. Like a lamb to the slaughter she offered to show us around.

'That's all right, dear. We'll just wander around on our own.' He seemed reluctant to let go of her arm and eventually she pulled away, eyeing him like a frightened fawn.

'Show me the pool,' I said, and he took me through the exercise room where young girls and overweight middle-aged men were torturing themselves on chrome and black leather machinery that wouldn't have looked out of place on a space station. A man wearing stars and stripes shorts puffed and sweated away on a jogging machine as he listened to a Sony Walkman while an attendant watched the dial that showed how fast he was running. I thought of getting one for Bill Hardwicke's office but it would have been an expensive joke.

The pool was a good size, about twenty metres by eight, I guess, with a diving board at the deep end. It was surrounded by bright green artificial grass and white plastic chairs which glinted in the sunlight streaming in through the glass overhead. It had the look of a greenhouse, as the walls too were transparent. The view was nothing special, just the tops of the nearby blocks of flats and shops, but it was bright and sunny and a good place to swim.

Without my having to ask, Howard walked over to the far end of the pool, empty save for a matron in a plastic hat swimming a stoic breaststroke. He stood by one of the big glass panes behind the diving board.

'Here?' I said, and he nodded.

I rapped it with my knuckles and it felt solid, more like wood than glass. There was no indication that it was a replacement.

'You'd need some force to go through that,' I said, stating the obvious. I pressed my nose against the glass and looked down.

'She fell into the road?' I asked and Howard said yes.

'She didn't jump,' I said.

'I know, laddie, I know.' It sounded as if he was humouring me.

'Did she use this pool a lot?'

'She was a keen swimmer. If she wasn't swimming here she'd use the pool at the KCC.'

'KCC?'

'Kowloon Cricket Club. It's a few miles from here. They've an open air pool.'

'Sally's a member?' The word 'was' still didn't feel right on my lips.

Howard laughed ruefully. 'Sally wasn't a joiner, but she could always find someone to sign her in. She had a lot of friends.' He was having no trouble using the past tense and I could have hit him for that, driven my fist into his face and twisted it so that his lips would split and bleed because I didn't want her to be dead.

'What about enemies?'

He shrugged. 'I don't know of anybody who'd want to kill her,' he said quietly.

We walked back along the pool side and the woman in the pool was Sally, her wet hair plastered to her head as she turned to float on her back and waved. I smiled and raised my hand but then the smile turned into a grimace and Sally turned into an old lady with a white plastic hat. My hand was half outstretched towards her. To cover my embarrassment I ran my fingers through my hair. 'Christ, I need a drink.'

* * *

The flight and the whistle-stop tour of police station, mortuary and hotel had taken more out of me than I realized, and though my eyes opened at nine o'clock I spent over two hours drifting in and out of sleep until Howard banged on the door. I wrapped myself in a large white towel and let him in.

He was wearing a similar safari suit to yesterday, but in cream. He was carrying a plastic bag and he emptied the contents onto the dressing table: three cotton shirts, a couple of pairs of socks and underwear. There was also an aerosol of deodorant. With a jolt I thought of the bag full of Sally's belongings, lying on the window seat, the silent proof that she was dead and this wasn't a dream.

'I thought this might come in handy,' he said, holding out the deodorant.

'Yeah, I was sweating a bit,' I said. 'I'll just take a shower.'

The water jetted out hard and fast, almost scouring the skin from my back as I washed and then I turned it on full cold and gasped as the icy water hit me.

'How far away is Sally's flat?' I asked Howard as I towelled myself dry.

'Fifteen minutes in a cab. Mid-levels, a block in Robinson Road.'

'Good one?'

'It's not the Peak, but it's a place for expats rather than locals.'

'Where do you live?'

'A place called Shek-O, there're a lot of journalists living there, mostly Aussies. It's on the south side of the island.'

'Flat?'

'No, two-bedroomed house by the beach. It's quiet, so quiet that it's easy to forget you're living in Hong Kong.'

I ripped the Cellophane off one of the new shirts and tried it on. 'Perfect fit,' I said. 'Thanks.'

As soon as I had finished dressing, Howard asked me if I wanted to eat. I walked over to the polythene bag and took out the keys.

'Never touch solids this early in the morning,' I told him. The air was suddenly split with the crump of an explosion, a dull boom that I felt as much as heard.

'What the hell was that?'

Howard looked at his watch. 'The noon gun,' he said. 'Jardines fire it at this time every day.' He took me over to the window and pointed down to a shining naval gun at the water's edge. 'The story goes that they fired it once to welcome a guest and the navy got pissed off so they were told they had to fire it every day as a punishment. Now it's a tourist attraction, a gimmick. And don't worry, they're firing blanks.'

'Aren't we all, Howard. Aren't we all.'

The heat caught me by surprise again as we walked out of the foyer. Shit, I'd forgotten to use Howard's deodorant. Already the sweat was collecting in my armpits.

A taxi pulled up in front of the hotel and we both climbed into the back. Howard spoke to the driver in Cantonese and the old man turned the air-conditioning down. For an expat who professed to be totally ignorant of the local language Howard seemed to be able to get his message across without too much trouble. He was a cunning old sod. A couple of times in the lift or when we waited in the police station I'd caught him eavesdropping on the Chinese as they chatted away in sing-song voices, and while I could quite believe he wasn't fluent I was certain he could understand a lot more than he let on.

'It's cold enough in here to freeze a polar bear's balls,' he said and rubbed his hands together. I was sweltering.

'You've been out here too long,' I said.

'Aye maybe you're right. Maybe you're right,' he replied. Crap. He was out here for good.

The taxi made its way up a hill, twisting in and out of the bends like a drunken rally driver. Out of the right hand window the Hong Kong and Shanghai Bank building danced in and out of view.

'Helicopter pad,' said Howard, and pointed to the top of the ultra-modern edifice. 'They're not allowed to use it, but it's there, just in case.'

'I don't follow you,' I said.

'1997, laddie, 1997. When the Chinese hordes come sweeping over the border the bank's executives will be picked up off the roof and flown to safety. That's the story anyway.'

'Are you serious?'

'That's just one of the rumours about Sandberg's Folly. They say there's an underground tunnel, big enough to drive an armoured car through, linking the building to the harbour so that when the shit hits the fan they'll be able to drive all the money out. And they say that the typhoon shields around the bottom of the building aren't there to keep out the wind but are there to be dropped if the bank is ever attacked.'

'True or false?'

'Act your age. These days money is shunted around the world at the touch of a button, you don't have physically to pick it up. And most of the bank's business is overseas now, anyway. If ever Beijing did decide to screw up Hong Kong the money would haemorrhage out in minutes, to Bermuda, Canada, America, the UK. All the banks have their own contingency plans drawn up and they don't involve armoured cars racing through tunnels.'

Dramatic though it was, the Hong Kong Bank building was dwarfed by a tall tower pointing to the sky like an accusing finger. It was of an order of magnitude bigger than the rest, towering over the Central office blocks like a schoolmaster surrounded by his pupils.

'And that one?' I said.

'Ah, the heir apparent,' he said. 'The Bank of China. They're already the real power in Hong Kong. The Hong Kong Bank and Standard Chartered might print the notes and make a lot of noise, but it's the little men in that building that will be running this place as soon as it's given back to China. That's the sixth tallest building in the world, and it put a few noses out of joint at the Bank when it was first announced. The Bank had gone and ordered the most expensive building in the world as a sign of their long-term faith in Hong Kong and then the Chinese went and built a taller building right next door. Massive loss of face.'

The road twisted again and Central was hidden from sight as we drove through Mid-levels, a mixture of new residential blocks and old low-rise buildings, lots of trees and greenery. As Howard had said, it was a place for expats, not locals.

It was a pink building, a dirty washed out pink like a block of soap that had been in the shower too long.

The block had been built on a slope in the fork between two roads. As a result the ground floor on the upper road was actually the third floor. I handed the keys to Howard and he unlocked a metal-grilled door, an ornate work of art that squeaked open as he put his weight against it. We climbed the stone stairs shoulder to shoulder up four flights to the top floor where there was another grille in front of the entrance to the flat. I was short of breath and my shirt was wet but Howard was relaxed, not a bead of sweat on his forehead. He had trouble with the lock, pushing the key in and out several times and jiggling it around until finally it slotted home and he pulled the grille outwards. There were two locks in the blue-painted wooden door but Howard had no problems with them and we were soon in the flat.

The door opened straight into the main lounge area, about eight paces wide and about fifteen paces long to a large sliding window. I walked across the perfectly-polished parquet flooring and pushed the window open. Beyond was a tiled balcony with two white wooden chairs and a slatted table. The balcony looked down across the harbour and over to Kowloon. To the right of the balcony were two towering green plants, palms or something, I couldn't identify them but they looked like they'd been growing for twenty years or more. A small, almost translucent, lizard scuttled from under one of the chairs, through my legs, across the floor and up a wall. There it stopped, feet splayed out like fingers, then it bolted across the ceiling and behind a rattan bookcase. I turned to look at Howard who was standing by a large mirrored bar built into the wall, laden with bottles of Scotch and gin and rows of glasses.

The flat was full of plants, in white pots hanging from the ceiling, standing in saucers on the bar, and trailing over the bookcase. In each corner of the room were circular clay tubs with small trees growing out of peaty soil.

THE FIREMAN

The furniture was all cane and rattan, a Habitat-catalogue of a room with large bulging green scatter cushions on the floor and a glass-topped coffee table covered in glossy magazines and crumpled newspapers.

Against the wall opposite the balcony was a dining table big enough to seat eight people, surrounded by high-backed chairs.

There was a television with a video underneath, and potted ferns on top, and by the bookcase was a racked stereo system with three feet high speakers that looked like a prize from a television quiz show.

'You look like you need a drink,' said Howard and I realized I was frowning hard. 'I'll get some ice,' he said and disappeared through a white louvred door that swung gently to and fro behind him. They were still moving when he reappeared with cubes of ice rattling in a crystal bucket.

'Gin and tonic?' he asked rhetorically, because he was already unscrewing the top of the gin bottle by the time I nodded. He made it strong and there was no lemon, but it was cold and I needed a drink, not to quench my thirst but to quieten the panic I could feel building inside, like awakening from a nightmare knowing, just knowing, that something bad, something terrible, had happened, but not knowing if the terror was real or the result of a bad dream.

I sat down heavily on the cane sofa and put my feet on top of a stack of Far Eastern Economic Reviews, pushing aside a set of car keys. Howard walked up to a free-standing fan behind the television and switched it on. It whirled and the draught ruffled the pages by my feet and cooled my face as I took another swallow of the tonic-tainted gin.

'This is one hell of a nice flat,' I said, more to myself than to him. He walked the length of the room, pacing like a wary old lion on a route he'd trudged a million times before.

'It certainly is, laddie.'

'How big would you say it is?'

'Three bedrooms, one of them's a study. About two-and-a-half thousand square feet in all, maybe a bit more.'

'She lived here alone?'

'That she did. She valued her privacy.'

'You've been here before?' I knew he had because he knew there was ice and he knew where to get it and he knew that one of the bedrooms was a study. But he wasn't stupid and he knew that I knew so he wasn't going to lie but I wasn't sure yet if I could trust this man.

He stopped pacing.

'Several times. We worked together on a couple of articles for the *Sunday Times* last year, and I helped her back when she'd had a few too many at the FCC.'

'FCC?'

'Foreign Correspondents' Club.'

I'd finished the drink and Howard stepped forward to take the empty glass and refill it. By now the ice had melted into pea-sized lumps which bumped against my teeth as I drank. A Singapore Airlines 747 climbed into the sky and then was lost behind a towering residential block and then I watched the wispy white clouds because I didn't want to ask the questions. I wanted to distract myself, I wanted to be somewhere else, up in the clouds looking down, not sitting on a rattan sofa with a lukewarm drink and a faded old hack who was going to tell me something that I didn't want to hear, like the policeman who knocks at your door in the middle of the night and says, 'you'd better sit down, I'm afraid I've got bad news.'

THE FIREMAN

Happened to me once, years ago, in Glasgow, when I was a young freelance trying to find the Big One that would get me noticed by London. I was on the graveyard shift for the *Daily Record*, from eight in the evening to four in the morning, the shift none of the staff men wanted to work. At least once a week somebody would phone in sick and the news desk would call me because I was young and keen, have notebook will travel and because I needed the money.

The high spot of the shift was organizing the curry run for the subs and a trip out to the main police stations delivering the first edition and picking up the details of the nightly stabbings and assaults. And at closing time there were the phone calls from the drunks, 'Hey Jim, can you settle a wee argument that me and my pal are having. In the 1972 cup final . . .' And you had to deal with the complaints if the compiler of the TV page had cocked it up again. That was a real pain until one of the subs gave me a tip. 'Ask them for the number of their TV licence. That usually shuts them up.' It worked every time.

I'd just got back with the curries for the lads when the news desk phone rang. It was a watchman at the British Rail works in Springburn ringing to say that a young lad had just got himself electrocuted at the yard. He was one of a group of neds breaking into carriages to steal the first aid kits. They weren't worth anything but it gave them something to do. This nutter had been standing on the roof of a train, using an iron bar to smash in the windows. He'd swung it too high, touched an overhead power cable and was lying in hospital with third degree burns over most of his body. The caller gave me the kid's name and address, and his own, not out of any sense of public duty but because he

61

knew I'd put him in the tip-off book and that at the end of the month a cheque would be winging its way to him. That one phone call would earn him almost as much as I got for a full eight-hour shift.

I dragged the late driver out of the photographers' rest room where he'd been watching a blue movie on their video recorder. He reeked of whisky and his flies were at half mast. Twenty minutes later we were in front of the grey tenement block where the boy lived and I told the driver to wait and went up to the second floor alone and rang the door bell until the lights went on and a small, pale woman in a yellow floral nightie and curlers opened the door and peered at me.

'What d'ye want?' she barked.

What I wanted was a quote from the tearful mother and a collect picture of her dying son, and then what I wanted was any other pictures of him so that when the *Glasgow Herald* and the *Express* arrived they'd be shafted. That's what I wanted, but first I had to get inside the house. I was English but I'd been north of the border long enough to switch into the Glasgow accent and I was young enough to give her the little-boy-lost-look and appeal to her maternal instincts.

'Oh, I'm from the *Record*, Mrs McNee,' I said. 'I'm terribly sorry to hear what happened to wee James. Could I come in and have a word with you?'

'What?' she said, and coughed like a rheumatic otter.

'Well, Mrs McNee, we thought if we printed what had happened to James it would serve as a warning to other children.'

A man appeared behind the yellow nightie, the same size as the woman, with a crew cut and several days' growth of stubble on his face. His chin was up in the arrogant pose of a small, angry man. In his greying string vest and baggy underpants he looked like an over the hill boxer that some up-and-coming champion had been using as a sparring partner.

'What did he say, hen?' he asked his wife.

'He said something's happened to Jim.'

The man opened the door wide.

'You'd better come in, son,' he said. And that was how they heard that their boy was dying in a hospital bed, from a young reporter who was only there for the story and the picture. She cried and he put his arm around her and then she went and made me a cup of tea and then there was the crackle of a two-way radio and a policewoman and a male colleague rang the doorbell. It happens that way sometimes. And yes I got the quotes, and the pictures, and the page three lead in the second edition. And I left my card on the mantelpiece so that when the guys from the other papers arrived they'd know who had beaten them to it. Things like that were important to me then. They still are.

It's funny how your mind does that, how it protects itself from facing up to unpleasant realities. Somehow my thoughts had got shunted away from Sally and her luxurious flat and I'd started replaying events of more than ten years ago, memories conjured up from the backwater of my brain.

'I can't understand why the police haven't been here,' I said.

Howard shrugged. 'They're not Scotland Yard, you know, and let's be honest, they're not investigating a murder,' he said.

'Not yet,' I said quietly, and drank from the tall, thin glass.

'Aye, not yet,' he said, and walked over to the balcony. He turned to face me and leant back on the green railing, arms outstretched as if he'd been crucified.

'This is one impressive flat, Howard.' He didn't reply, and I didn't look at him. Sometimes it's better that way.

'How much would you say a flat like this would cost?'

He paused, then cleared his throat like a head boy at speech day. 'That would depend on the length of the lease, whether it was furnished or unfurnished, the sort of deal she got from the landlord, service charges . . .'

'How much?'

'Anywhere between $20,000 and $25,000 a month, I suppose.'

This time I paused, and I could hear children playing in the street five floors below, shouting and shrieking. 'And how much did Sally earn, in a good month?'

'About the same.'

The yelling stopped and there was the sound of feet slapping on the road as they ran off. A dog barked and then I was looking at the clouds again and wishing. I kicked the key ring and it rattled off the magazines and fell onto the floor.

'What sort of car did she drive?' I said it quietly but I could feel the anger starting to grow, because this was like pulling teeth and that's not how it should have been because he was supposed to be on my side.

'A Porsche, a red one,' he replied, and we both knew the colour wasn't important. What mattered was that my sister was living in a flat she couldn't afford and driving a car she couldn't have bought. She was 26 years old, she was freelancing for a Hong Kong paper and a couple of magazines and stringing for one of the London quality Sundays. She should have been sharing a flat half the size with two other girls, taking the MTR to work and counting every penny.

'Where did the money come from?' I asked, and I still wasn't looking at him but I could sense him shrug.

'I don't know, laddie. None of us knew.'

'But you wondered? You asked?'

'Aye, we wondered. But we weren't asking the questions.' He walked in out of the sunlight and dropped into a white deck chair opposite me.

'So who was asking the questions? Who was asking why Sally was living way beyond her means? Who was digging?'

'The ICAC.'

'The what?'

'The Independent Commission Against Corruption. The colony's corruption watchdog. They were originally set up to clean up the Hong Kong police but they've moved on to cover racing, business, organized crime. It's probably the most powerful organization in Hong Kong, powers of search and detention the likes of which you don't see anywhere else. They're on a par with the Star Chamber.'

'And they were investigating Sally?'

He mumbled.

'What?' I snapped.

'That was the rumour. Hell, it was more than a rumour. They were on her tail like hounds after a fox. You can't even accept a free trip to Macau out here without clearing it with your editor first. Everything has to be above board. It's not like London where you get crates of beer and whisky every Christmas and free trips and God knows what else.'

'But we're not talking about a few bottles of Scotch here, are we?'

He shook his head and I finished the gin and tonic and stood up.

'I need to talk to someone at the ICAC, and soon. Can you fix it?'

'Aye, nae bother.'

I put the glass down on the bar and walked through the louvred door into the hallway beyond. There was a spare bedroom, obviously unused, and next to it a bathroom, the soap still wrapped and the towels neat and tidy and no hairs in the bath so she hadn't had visitors recently or if she had they'd stayed in her bedroom. The kitchen was square, a mass of gadgets, an electric rice cooker, an electric wok, two toasters, a huge green fridge that was empty except for three bottles of white wine and a half empty carton of milk that was two days beyond its sell-by date and starting to go off. There was a pile of dirty plates and pans in both sides of the double sink and I remembered how untidy she'd been as a kid and the rows she'd had from our mother for leaving her bedroom in a mess.

The master bedroom was nothing like the rough and tumble tomboy's bolt hole that she'd slept in as a child, it was a woman's room, soft and gentle – and tidy. A king-sized bed with an ornate carved wooden headboard, silk sheets and feather pillows. There was a thick blue rug by the bed that matched the cotton curtains and the pots of flowers on the large dressing table. The wardrobes were built into the wall and were big enough to walk in if they hadn't been bulging with clothes and shoes. The bathroom door was opposite the bottom of the bed and it was blue, too, and it smelt of talc and perfume that I didn't recognize. I couldn't believe she lived here, she didn't belong, it wasn't a place that Sally, my Sally, would have wanted.

Then I saw the large blue mongrel with a lolling tongue sitting by the side of the bed nearest the wall with its nose torn and one of its ears hanging loose. She'd been eight when I'd bought it for her when our mother wouldn't let us have the real thing because of the mess, the smell, the hairs, the trouble. So she talked to it and slept with it and called it Woofer and as she grew older she told him all her secrets. He was the one real thing in the flat, the one piece of my sister's life that I could recognize, and I saw her sitting on the bed and holding the silly blue dog and putting her nose against his and talking to him in a low, serious voice as his tongue swung stupidly to and fro and I held out my hand to stroke her hair but she wasn't there and Woofer was still on the floor looking at me through brown glass eyes. I found her ring in a crystal dish on the dressing table. The ring she said she'd never take off. The ring I gave her.

The study was closer to what I'd expected, a huge wooden desk surrounded by piles of newspapers and magazines, a battered old grey metal filing cabinet. There was a half-written story about diamonds as an investment in the electric typewriter on the desk. It was bland and needed a good sub and I could tell that her heart hadn't been in it. Freelancing is like that, you get given all the dross that the staff reporters don't want to do, the advertising features, book reviews and personal finance articles, but every now and again you come up with a splash, a story to get the adrenaline going and that's what makes it worthwhile, the kick that's worth waiting for.

There was a large multicoloured map of the world pinned to the wall and she'd divided it into time zones with a red felt-tipped pen and stuck flags into about a dozen major cities, London, New York, Toronto, Tokyo, and I guess they were places where she'd filed copy, or maybe she was just being optimistic because the merits of diamonds as a nest egg wasn't exactly going to make the front page of the *New York Times*. Next to the map was a dark brown cork notice board. Stapled to this was a scattering of newspaper cuttings in various stages of decay with paragraphs circled, story ideas for her to follow up in the future. Except that she didn't have a future anymore. There were three photographs on the board, all of the same man, a middle-aged Chinese with horn-rimmed glasses and slightly crooked teeth. One was a black and white head shot, a PR handout maybe, the other two were in colour. one of him laughing as he leant against the bonnet of a dark green Rolls Royce and the other of him in a karate suit and a brown belt, standing in the ready position as if preparing to bow, hands clenched tightly into fists either side of his groin, the effect spoiled because again he was smiling for the camera. I pulled one off the board but there was no caption on the back so I went back to the lounge and dropped it into Howard's lap.

'Lai Kwok-lee,' he said. 'Where did you get this?'

'The study. Three pictures of him pinned to the wall. What does this Mr Kwok-lee do?'

'Mr Lai,' said Howard. 'Surname always comes first. And Kwok-lee is his Chinese given name, he hardly ever uses it. Dennis Lai is the name he prefers. He's got fingers in more pies than Sweeney Todd. He's the boss of one of the big hongs here, property, trade with China, a small film studio, a few very lucrative franchise deals, a chain of shops, a couple of good restaurants, a couple of dozen taxis. It's easier to list the things he isn't involved in.'

'Rich?'

'He's not up there with the mega-rich shipping and property tycoons, but he's well past the stage where he actually knows his true worth.'

'And what is his true worth?'

'It would be impossible to pin down at any one time how much money he has. He's always got two or three deals on the go, opening up a company, shutting others down, taking over, selling off. He's not actually whiter than white either, there're whispers that he's the front man for Triad money.'

'So Sally was doing a story on him?'

'If she was I didn't know about it. But that wouldn't be unusual, we were both freelancers and Hong Kong is a small patch. We had our own secrets.'

'How can I find out what she was working on?'

'If she wasn't doing it here then she might have been using the system at the *Post*, she did quite a bit of work for them.'

'Can you fix it for me to meet someone there who could show me round, somebody who wouldn't ask too many questions?'

He nodded.

'Do me a favour and fix me another drink while I go through her files,' I said. Maybe I shouldn't have been so short with him but he'd spoiled it, now I didn't trust him because he should have told me about the flat and the car before he'd brought me here.

I spent two hours going through the desk drawers and the filing cabinet but it was all banal run-of-the-mill stuff, most of it background material that might come in useful at some time, cuttings about the political situation, a lot on the property market and financial services. The only thing with any bite was a file marked 'Drugs' but even that was just stories cut from the *South China Morning Post* and the *Hong Kong Standard*, nothing startling, nothing to set the hairs on the back of my neck on end, no tickle that would let me know I was on to something.

There were some typewritten sheets in the top drawer of the desk, a feature on a new shopping centre being built in Kowloon which judging by the way it was written was linked to some pretty heavy advertising, and underneath it was a brochure from the Diamond Bourse and some photocopies from a reference book about Hong Kong's importance as a centre for the sale of precious stones, and a swathe of Trade Development Council press releases bound up with a thick rubber band. The bottom drawer of the desk contained her cheque book, a scattering of keys, her bank books and a plastic file of invoices from the various newspapers and magazines she'd filed copy for. Assuming she'd kept them all, I calculated that over the last twelve weeks she'd been earning an average of $16,000 a month. Not bad, but not great. Certainly not enough to pay for the flat. Or the Porsche. Or to account for the $120,000 she had in the bank deposit books. Howard was lying back in the chair, eyes closed and breathing heavily through his nose but he wasn't asleep and he opened one eye as I pushed through the louvre doors.

'Nothing,' I said in a quiet voice before he could speak.

'Let's go.' I held out my hand and Howard returned the flat keys.

'Where?' he asked.

'A bar,' I said. 'With people. And noise. And drink.'

Howard had said something incomprehensible to the taxi driver and there were three letters over the entrance of the red brick and white roughcast building where we pulled up, but it wasn't until I saw the brass plate set onto the wall to the right of the wood and glass doors that I realized he'd taken me to the Foreign Correspondents' Club.

The air inside was cool and I sucked it in as we walked past man-size green plants and turned left into the tile-floored bar. A wire service printer click-clacked and a couple of guys in suits were looking at share prices on a TV screen set into the wall, muttering to each other.

The walls were white, with framed copies of newspaper and magazine covers dotted around, the ceilings were high and fans slowly turned above the heads of the fifteen or so people standing at the bar. The bar wasn't circular, oval, or star-shaped, more a combination of all three, like a vandalized bicycle wheel, surrounded by tall stools with brown plastic bucket seats. There was a dining area to the right, square tables with cream-coloured cloths, but it was the bar that was the obvious focus of the club. I'd heard stories about the old Hong Kong FCC, when it was thirteen floors up in Sutherland House, where the war correspondents refuelled before going back to Vietnam or Cambodia or wherever their foreign editors decided there was a fight worth covering. Where stories were told and arguments and old scores settled, where friendships and expenses sheets were forged. That it was a working club, where papers left threatening messages for errant reporters and herograms for star ones, where a journalist could be sure of finding someone who'd offer a bed for the night so that he could put in a claim for a hotel bill without letting go of his hard-earned money. I'd heard stories. I hadn't seen it, but the picture I had in my head was the sort of bar I'd have felt at home in.

This bar seemed to be aimed at expat civil servants. The only Chinese faces I could see were serving drinks, dressed like Cinderella's footmen in black trousers and dark orange waistcoats. At the far end were three gweilos in dark suits laughing like public school prefects at a caning, waving their half pints of lager and watching each other as they drank, verbal boxers waiting for a dropped guard, obviously colleagues and not friends.

To their left were three young women, Sloane Rangers a long way from home, with their shirt collars turned up in unison, regulation strings of pearls, pleated skirts and pumps. When they laughed they laughed together with their heads tilted back and it was the sound of wind blowing through a crystal chandelier.

'Welcome to the FCC,' said Howard, and we moved to the straightest part of the bar, to be met by a waiter who'd already poured Howard a whisky and placed a pink chit held by a black bulldog clip in front of him.

'Gin and tonic,' I said to the unsmiling barman. 'Let me get these,' I said to Howard.

'I'm afraid you can't,' he replied. 'Private club, only members can sign for drinks.'

My drink arrived and the tonic was flat but I didn't complain, just raised my glass to Howard and said 'Cheers,' and drank half of it. I was hot and thirsty, OK?

On the opposite side of the bar, perched on a stool like a vulture, was a hunchback with a greying beard nursing a pint of beer as he read what seemed to be a Chinese newspaper. Next to him was a barrel-chested balding giant of a man, drinking whisky and reading over the hunchback's shoulder.

The rest of the evening drinkers were uniformly middle-aged men with suits and ties, briefcases sitting at their feet like well-fed Labradors.

'So where are the foreign correspondents, Howard?' I asked.

'Long gone,' he said. 'No wars left to cover so they've all gone home. Few British or American papers keep anyone out here full time.'

'So who are the members of the club?'

'Local hacks, the wire services, journalists who write for the heavy magazines that nobody reads, the odd freelance. I guess they make up about ten per cent of the membership. The rest are civil servants, lawyers, accountants, bankers. A few public relations people. The beer's cheap and it's easy to get in – we're not as selective as the Hong Kong club, and nowhere near as expensive. 'Do you fancy another?'

I hadn't realized I'd finished the gin, so I said yes and the barman took the empty glass.

'How about a fresh tonic this time?' I asked him and he nodded curtly, just once, face impassive. Howard was sipping his whisky slowly. He raised his glass to the hunchback who nodded as curtly as the barman. The giant by his side grinned and growled. 'Evening,

Howard.' Together they looked like bit players in a Frankenstein movie.

'Who are Igor and Quasimodo?' I asked Howard.

'Two of the best journalists in Hong Kong,' he said. 'They used to be with the *Star* but now they freelance for one of the heavy magazines here. Old China hands, both of them.'

He told me their names but I didn't recognize them and that was hardly surprising – big fish in a small pool. Cancel that, small fish in a tiny pool and they weren't going anywhere because if they did they'd be eaten alive.

Hong Kong is not a journalists' town. There are precious few major media centres in the world – London, New York, Sydney – cities crammed with journalists fighting and clawing their way to the top of the pile and drinking each other under the table, competition sharpening wits and knives in the battle to be first with the news. Once you move away you're in the sticks and the pack soon forgets you, so you either leave for a short while and return or you forget about going back. The ones that stay away didn't belong anyway, so anyone who had been in Hong Kong for more than a couple of years was looking for a place to rest, or to hide. Burnt out hacks living on memories or chancers looking for a break. Or middle ranking nobodies who wouldn't get a job anywhere else. Yeah, all right. So I sound bitter and twisted. I'd had a rough couple of days, and being in the FCC made me realize how much I missed being a fireman. High salaries and ludicrous expenses put paid to most full-time overseas correspondents, it just wasn't cost effective to keep a man in a far-off country filing a couple of stories a week, so one by one they were called home or chopped. It started with the Far East, and then

Africa, then Europe, and now few of the nationals even bother with an office in the States. The wire services do a fair enough job of covering the world, and they can be topped up with local colour from stringers like Howard. Sometimes the stringers are paid a retainer, but usually they are on lineage plus expenses and they can make a reasonable living if they churn out enough copy. They're happy, they're earning, the readers are happy, assuming they're in the twenty-five per cent that bother to read the foreign pages, and the papers are happy because they're saving on salary, accommodation, school fees for the kids, flights home, medical fees and the rest of the bills that have to be paid to keep a full-time correspondent in place.

The system works for most of the time, but every now and again the big one breaks – a plane is hijacked, a hotel fire kills a couple of dozen people, a British teenager is raped, a dictator is deposed – and a stringer isn't enough. That's where the fireman comes in. The wire services don't provide personalized copy, there are no short, punchy stories for the tabloids or long, worthy in-depth profiles tailor-made for the broadsheets. They don't cater for individual styles, they push the same story out to everybody over satellite and through wires and into identical terminals in identical offices all around the world. And while the stringers can cope with the day-to-day news stories they're usually simply not up to covering the big ones. If they were that good they wouldn't be sitting in the back of beyond being paid by the word.

So on every national newspaper there are firemen, at least one, usually two and sometimes more. They're reporters who act as trouble shooters ready to be sent anywhere in the world with next to no notice. They're usually in their late twenties to mid-thirties, male, single, and first class operators, the best in the business. They move into a situation stone cold, get the story, sometimes stay for a follow-up feature, and then move out, fast, clean and efficient. They can be covering anything, from a war to a miracle at Lourdes, they spend most of their time in planes and hotels, and when they're back in the office between assignments they drink and pick arguments with the subs. They also have a flight bag in their locker, with a clean shirt, razor, washing kit and anti-diarrhoea tablets. They go to the company doctor every six months to keep their inoculations up to date. They tend to have two passports because some countries are stroppy about where you've been before. Taiwan doesn't like tourists who've been to mainland China, the Arabs don't like Israel and nobody likes South Africa. They carry their passports in their jacket pocket and credit cards in their wallet because sometimes they'll be out on a job when the shit hits the fan and they have to go straight to the airport.

Most journalists would kill for the chance of being a fireman on a national newspaper, of covering the big ones and getting splash after splash, of roaming the world's trouble spots and collecting visas like stamps, but eventually it's the job that starts to kill.

In the field you're on your own except for the local stringer, you've got to get the story while competing against the best in the world and then you've got to get the copy back to the office, and that's no pushover when you're with the paras in the Falklands or covering student demonstrations in Peking. After a while flying loses its glamour and one five-star hotel is very much like another. Soon the stories begin to look the same too, only the number of dead varies, along with the initials of the morons behind the latest atrocity.

The constant travelling starts to get to you, then you begin to get lazy, you take short cuts and before you know it you're relying on the stringers too much and you make less profit on your expenses because you're spending more on drink and then they pull you back to London and give you a desk job or make you industrial correspondent or number two on the crime desk to some snotty-nosed kid with halitosis. Then they send out someone young and keen that they've been grooming to be the new fireman and the cycle starts again only this time it's someone else's by-line on the front page.

Another drink appeared in front of me and the waiter half turned and pointed to Frankenstein's little helpers who grinned and gave Howard and me an exaggerated thumbs up. I winked and Howard said 'Cheers' and we drank. The tonic was flat but what the hell, you can't have everything you want in life, can you? But when I put the glass down I saw that the guy in the russet waistcoat was watching me as he polished a wine glass and I knew that he knew that I knew so I was damned if I was going to let him get away with it.

I pushed the half-full glass towards him and told him quietly that I wanted to feel little bubbles bursting against the back of my throat, that I'd like a fresh tonic water and not one from a bottle that had been opened twenty minutes ago, that I'd like it fairly quickly and that if it didn't appear PDQ I'd ram the glass up his arse. I'm not sure how good his English was but I think he got the message because he stopped cleaning the glass and changed my drink, watching me all the time through unblinking brown eyes.

Howard had gone decidedly frosty and I suppose he was starting to regret having brought me to his precious club so I gave him a winning smile and put my hand on his shoulder. 'I'm sorry,' I said. I was grinning but inside I really didn't give a toss whether or not he was unhappy, other than that I needed his help. He'd give me that anyway, because he wasn't doing it for me he was doing it for the paper, but he'd try harder for a friend. They always do.

'Howard, I insist you let me buy the next round.'

'Members only,' he reminded me.

'In that case old lad, I insist that you buy me a drink,' I said, and he did. And another. And before long we were both laughing and joking, but while he was relaxed and open I was weighing up the man, trying to calculate how best I could use him. I knew how to get people to talk, how to get information without them even realizing they were being tapped, I knew what questions to ask but the one thing I didn't know was who to ask, and for that I needed Howard and if it meant sitting in a bar with a bunch of no-hopers and the sounds of tinkling chandeliers and rugby club bellows then what the hell, I'd got drunk in worse places.

The Sloanes and their providers left after an hour and they were replaced by a group of five young men in jeans and fake Lacoste T-shirts. Sports subs from the *Post*, said Howard, just finished their shift. As they studied the menu chalked onto a large blackboard on the wall, they were joined by a tall, anorexic-looking Indian in a grey suit that was too short in the sleeves and too wide around the chest, a grubby white shirt with a frayed collar and what looked like a Guards' tie but obviously wasn't. The body was a gangling collection of limbs that belonged to an adolescent, and the rash of pimples on his forehead below a greasy mop of hair marked him as a teenager, but even

78

under the subdued lighting of the bar you could see the lines etched into the corners of his eyes and the furrows that ran from the side of his nose down either side of his mouth that gave his age as being thirty-five plus. There was a cigarette burning in his right hand and when he moved it up to his face to inhale I saw that half of his index finger was missing, and what was left was yellowed with nicotine. The man was constantly moving, shifting his weight from his left leg to his right, scratching his head, shrugging his shoulders, tapping his foot, all the time reading the menu and talking to the subs. An intravenous shot of Valium would probably have done him the world of good.

I realized I was staring when Howard leant across and whispered in my ear, 'John Healy, news editor at the *Post*.'

'Under a lot of stress is he?' I asked, only half joking.

'He's been like that as long as I've known him,' he said. 'Overactive thyroid or underactive pituitary or something.'

'It looks like he's on something.'

'Only adrenaline. You know what it's like being a news editor.'

Too right – caught between the devil and the deep blue sea, above him an editor with his eye on the budget and a knighthood and the opposition and below him chancers and freeloaders perpetually trying to stab him in the back. Living on a knife-edge isn't half of it, it's a balancing act that causes more ulcers and heart-attacks than alimony and high blood pressure combined. And it's a road to nowhere because the only way up the hierarchy of modern newspapers is through production, the nuts and bolts manufacturing of the product, selecting the stories, editing them, choosing the pictures and making the headlines fit. The down table subs graduate to the back bench and if they're good, and lucky, and brown-nose their way into the boss's good books then they get an office of their own and a title and maybe one day a shot at the editor's job. Maybe. But at least they're in with a shot. The subs can get to the top, news editors either die or are pensioned off. Healy looked closer to death than to a monthly retirement cheque.

'How did an Indian get a name like Healy?' I asked.

'English father – a major out here on attachment with the Gurkhas. Mother is the daughter of one of the wealthiest merchants in Hong Kong.'

'They marry?'

'I think she was quite keen but his wife and kids weren't too happy with the idea.'

'And she still had the baby?' Try as I might I couldn't picture the gangling, hyperactive Indian as a child in a pram.

Howard shrugged. 'She loved him. Like they do. Her father was all for having him floating face down in the harbour but she stuck to her guns and insisted that she be allowed to keep the baby. Her father disowned her, threw her out of the family home and she brought John up on her own. She died a couple of years back.'

'Sad story.'

'It happens, laddie.'

'I guess he's what you'd call a major problem,' I said and we giggled like a couple of schoolboys.

'He'd know what Sally was working on?' I asked. I was rapidly realizing how everybody in this town seemed to know everybody else's business. Small town mentality, I guess.

'Aye. I suppose you'll be wanting an introduction?' I drained the glass and said yes and when Howard ordered another round he called over to Healy and asked him what he wanted.

'San Miguel,' he answered, but the barman already had a can in his hand. He ripped off the ring pull and handed the lager to him without a glass. My gin came with a fresh tonic and another surly look. I was starting to like this bar.

'First today,' said Healy and drank from the can, his Adam's apple bobbing up and down furiously.

'Same,' I said, but I'd already lost count of the number of gins I'd had.

Howard introduced us and we shook hands. I could feel the stub of his index finger pressing into my palm and I shuddered. He didn't seem to notice, or maybe he was just used to it. Or maybe he did it on purpose.

'I'm sorry about Sally,' he said. Sorry didn't sound right, but what else could he have said? Sorry implied pity, I'm sorry to hear that your dog was run over, sorry about the mess, sorry I broke your pencil. Sorry wasn't a word you could use to describe a fifteen-storey plunge out of a hotel window, not when it was your sister. I didn't feel sorry. I felt angry. I wanted to know why and I wanted to know who.

'Can I help at all?' he said, fingering his collar with his left hand and swirling the can with the other.

'Sure,' I said. 'I need to know what she was working on.'

'No problem,' he said, and now he was adjusting his tie and his right foot had started tapping to a tune that only he could hear. He flicked his head to one side to clear the greasy hair from his eyes. 'Come round to the office tomorrow.'

81

'Cheers,' I said, and then added I'd better go because I was still jet lagged.

'I'll see you tomorrow,' I said to John, who had slid into one of the bucket seats and was bouncing his knees up and down as if bumping a toddler while scratching his chin. He waved farewell with his can of lager.

Howard walked me to the door. On the way out we passed the club's office where a young girl with shoulder length hair held back in a pony tail with a red ribbon was typing a letter. Behind her on the wall was a display of FCC souvenirs.

'I want to have a tie,' I told him.

'You what?'

'I want to buy a tie. An FCC tie. Or are they for members only, too?'

'OK, I'll buy you a tie,' he said patiently. 'Red or blue?'

'Blue, it'll go with my eyes.'

Howard bought the tie for me, dark blue with a yellow crest and yellow stripes. I took mine off and clumsily tied the new one around my neck as I leant against the wall for balance. I ceremoniously handed my old tie, black with blue dots on it, to Howard. He took it and sighed. I think he was humouring me.

'I'll help you get a cab,' he said.

'Howard old lad, I'm quite capable of calling myself a taxi,' I told him.

'Aye, that's as may be,' he said. 'But you might not be able to tell him where you want to go.'

'There can't be that many Excelsior Hotels in town,' I replied.

'Just the one, but the Chinese call it . . .' and I missed the rest because it sounded something like a George Michael chorus played backwards.

'Point taken, Howard. Call me a cab.'

'You're a cab,' he said and we both laughed out of all proportion to the bad joke. A taxi with its roof light on screeched to a halt and Howard opened the rear door for me. He chattered to the driver who grunted and nodded.

'John's a good lad,' he said to me as I climbed in the back. 'Go easy on him.'

I closed the door and wound down the window. 'I will do,' I said. 'But I've never trusted Indians. Not after what they did to Custer.' Then the taxi screeched away from the kerb and I fell back into the seat chuckling. He wasn't the only one with a sense of humour. Shit, I was pissed again.

It was Sally, but not the cold, dead Sally I'd seen lying on the steel tray in the mortuary with a brown label tied to her big toe. This Sally was warm, and smiling and tossing her head. 'Wake up,' she whispered, and nuzzled my ear with her nose. 'I'm back.'

I blinked and rubbed my sleep-filled eyes, then sat up as I realized it was her.

'I thought you were dead,' I gasped.

'Don't be silly, do I look as if I'm dead?' She put her hand on my forehead. 'You look terrible. Were you out on the razzle last night?' She sat on the bed next to me.

'Yeah, I was in the FCC with Howard. It's a terrible place.'

'Did he lead you astray?'

'I'm not sure who was leading and who was following.'

'You drink too much.'

'I'm better than I was.'

'It's still too much.'

'I can handle it. Where have you been, Sally?' The phone started ringing.

'I'll tell you when you've answered the phone.'

'Tell me now. I have to know where you've been.'

'Answer the phone first.' She bent her head down and kissed me lightly on the cheek. I woke up. The phone was still ringing but she wasn't there anymore. The 'I'm back' dreams had started.

It was Howard, ringing to see if I was OK.

'I'm fine, Howard.'

'Do you need me this morning?' he asked.

'No thanks, John will look after me.'

'OK. Look, leave this afternoon free.'

'For what?'

'A junk trip. Courtesy of the Hong Kong and Shanghai Bank. Lots of booze and great food. But more importantly, there'll be a lot of VIPs there, people you should meet. This place is a village, everybody knows everybody else's business. We might find out something.'

'You've sold me the idea, Howard. What time and where?'

'The junk leaves Queen's Pier at 4 pm, but I'll meet you under the Hong Kong Bank building at 3.30.'

'All right, I'll see you there.'

I replaced the receiver and lay on my back, left arm across my eyes to shield them from the bright morning sunlight that shafted in through the window and across the double bed. I was still dog tired, partly because of the previous night's drinking session but I told myself the jet lag wasn't helping, my mind accepted the fact that it was ten o'clock in the morning and I was in Hong Kong, but my body still thought it was 2 am and that I should be asleep. I rolled onto my side, flopped my legs onto the floor and wrapped myself in a hotel robe. My tongue was thick with fur and I wiped it on the towelling belt. God I hate mornings. I could just about manage to look out of the window without heaving, but I had to squint to do it. Something was missing, and it took me a while to realize what it was before it hit me with a jolt – the bag containing Sally's belongings had gone, the window seat was bare. I checked behind the chairs and under the bed and then I opened the dressing table drawer. Her watch lay there, with the money clip and the purse, next to a hardback New English Bible and a sewing kit in a white cardboard folder. Of course, the room had been tidied and I'd been too drunk to notice the night before.

I found the bag, the dress and the shoes in the wardrobe. I slipped the dress off its hanger and held it up in front of me, imagining her wearing it, standing in front of me, looking up with laughter in her eyes. I held the blue material scrunched up against my face and breathed deeply, filling my nose and my throat and my lungs with the smell of her. The dress was cool and soft and felt like silk and I rubbed it gently up and down my cheeks. 'Sally,' I said out loud and then it suddenly hit me how perverse I must look, standing there kissing my dead sister's dress. I screwed it up and threw it in the wastebin, along with her shoes, the money clip and the bag. The purse contained a couple of Hong Kong Bank credit cards and several hundred dollars. The money I left on the dressing table but the cards I tore in half and threw on top of the dress. The watch I'd have to think about. I didn't want her things, I didn't want my nose rubbed in her death, to know that all I'd ever have of Sally would be the objects she'd touched. Maybe I'd keep the watch for our mother. Or maybe I'd wear it. I dropped it into the inside pocket of my jacket in the wardrobe, remembering as I did that I still had to phone Mother. I'd been in no fit state last night, but now it was too late, she'd be asleep. Tomorrow.

I showered and dressed and drank three strong cups of coffee and ate a Danish pastry with chopped up bits of green stuff on the top, but it didn't make me feel any better.

It was Sunday so there was hardly any traffic on the expressway and I was in the *Post*'s office with Healy long before Jardines were firing their gun.

He met me in reception on the second floor, a cigarette in his hand and ash down the front of his shirt. The shirt was dirty enough to have been the one he was wearing last time I saw him, and it was certainly the same tie. He'd shaved, though.

He shook my hand and again my stomach turned as I felt the stub of his index finger press into my palm. The *Post*'s office was pretty much the same open plan tomb as I worked in back in London, though here the glass cubicles were gathered together in the middle. There were about half the number of terminals around and most were unoccupied. All the windows had been blocked off and filters fitted over the fluorescent lights so that the VDUs wouldn't give the journalists eye-strain by the end of an eight-hour shift.

The desks were piled high with old newspapers, stacks

of press releases and reference books. So much for the paperless office.

An old Chinese lady in blue jeans and a purple apron was emptying the waste paper baskets into a plastic barrel on wheels that was almost as tall as she was. She pulled it after her on a piece of thick rope.

Healy led me over to what I guess was his desk. It was covered in a thick layer of grey dust and there were cigarette burns all along the right hand side. An unhealthy looking china cup with a curved 'S' handle lurked behind an opened pack of Ritz crackers.

'You want one?' he asked, waving the box under my nose.

'No, thanks,' I said, and he took a handful and began slotting them into his mouth like coins into a vending machine.

I sat down in front of the grey and white terminal, as familiar to me as an old sock. I'd been using the sodding things for four years and my eyesight had suffered for it and there were times when I missed the old manual typewriters but the new technology was cleaner and faster and a lot easier on the fingers.

'Same system?' asked John and I nodded, sure, the good old Atex 6000, saviour of the newspaper barons and curse of the unions.

'What was her logon?' I asked.

'SALLY, I think, but she might have had a separate one for the Sunday paper,' he replied, so I keyed in OPT INFO and then called up the list of logon names. There were two, SALLYS and SALLYD, so I went for the daily.

I keyed in SALLYD and the VDU flashed once with ENTER PASSWORD. I looked at John and he smiled like a benevolent uncle. Passwords were supposed to be secret but most journalists knew each other's.

'STAR,' he said. 'She always was the modest one.'

I laughed at that because I knew what he meant and he was right.

I hit S-T-A-R, the screen flickered and I was through to her queue, a news queue with about a dozen stories in, none with her logon next to them.

The same went for SALLYS. Nothing. No stories, no notes, no contact numbers. As if she'd never worked on the paper. I flicked through her Save-Get queues, but they were empty, too.

'She was working on at least three stories that I knew about,' said John in answer to my unspoken question, lighting a cigarette and letting it dangle from the corner of his mouth.

'If there was anything in the system it's not there now,' I said.

He sat down heavily on a chair and back-heeled it over to mine, wheels skidding along the vinyl-covered floor.

His nicotine-stained fingers flashed across the keyboard and he called up queue after queue, holding queues for finished stories, queues that sub-editors used and then he went into the features department section but there was nothing.

'It looks as if everything she wrote has been purged from the system,' said John.

'Didn't you know?'

'How would I know?' he replied, crumbs sticking to his upper lip. 'I don't go through their personal queues.'

Like hell, I thought. Everybody did in London and I was damn sure things were no different in Hong Kong.

'Have you got back-up copies?'

'Not of the stuff in the personal queues, only what goes through the working queues.'

'Can you remember what she was working on?'

'A few things, sure, but Sally was a loner. I knew about the stories I'd given her but the rest of the time she worked on her own and just produced the copy when she was ready. She was freelance, remember, not staff.'

I leant back on the chair and put my feet on the desk, next to the VDU. John inhaled deeply and blew a tatty smoke ring towards the ceiling. Ash scattered across the keyboard as he waved his hand at me.

'She was working on a feature on drugs in Hong Kong, the cocaine scene, who was supplying it, where it was coming from, the damage it was doing. She was chasing up a couple of leads on the triads being involved and getting a lot of help from her contacts in the police.

'The advertising department had asked her for a couple of articles on the diamond exchange for a supplement we've got coming out next month. I think she'd started on that.

'And I'd given her a cracker of a story to chase up about the thousands of Vietnamese refugees being held in the camps here.'

'Nothing new about that,' I said.

'Don't you believe it,' he replied, dropping ash over his trousers as he leant forward. 'Seems one of the reasons the Government is taking such a long time to let the poor buggers out is because they reckon the North Vietnamese are using them as a cover for getting agents into the West. Once they get through the holding camp they can be sent to Britain, Canada, the United States. We've heard that the government is putting its own men into the camps to try to sniff out the spies. Great story.'

'If it's true,' I said.

'It's a great story whether or not it's true,' he laughed, spraying biscuit crumbs over the VDU.

'But there's nothing in the system at all.'

'Doesn't look like it.' He leant forward and used a page from a notebook to wipe the gunge off the screen, but he just smeared it across the plastic.

'How come?'

He shrugged. 'Maybe somebody has beaten you to it.'

'Who could have done it?'

'Security isn't exactly watertight here. There's a whole pool of freelances with access, on top of a couple of hundred reporters and subs. The advertising department aren't supposed to get into the editorial queues but it's not exactly unknown. And there are always strange faces wandering around. They've even locked the toilets because of the number of people who were wandering in off the streets for a pee.'

'Did she have a desk here? Or a locker?'

'No. She kept everything in her briefcase.'

'Briefcase?'

'A big leather fake Gucci case she brought back from Bangkok a few months ago. She carried everything in it.'

'There's no sign of that either,' I said.

'What's going on?' he asked.

'I wish I knew,' I said. 'I just wish I knew.'

* * *

THE FIREMAN

The doorbell chimed twice and then there were footsteps and the door opened, a smiling Filipina face and a flash of white teeth, cute and curvy in a flowery print dress and working for peanuts for a Chinese family because peanuts in Hong Kong was better than nothing in the Philippines.

'Yes, sir?' she asked, rolling the 'r' like a West Country burr, smiling naturally, little lines crinkling at the corner of her eyes so she was older than I'd first thought.

'I'd like to see Mr Lai,' I said and she said, 'Follow me, sir,' and led me through the hall and left into a lounge with a huge picture window that looked out over Central and across the harbour, a view similar to the one from Sally's flat but with no tower blocks in the way. The view from the top. A view that only money, real money, could buy.

'Wait here, sir,' said the maid and the eyes crinkled again and she smiled and walked out of the room, long legs taking their time because she knew I was watching her go. The room was light and airy and expensive, a room that could have featured in any upper crust glossy coffee-table magazine without a single alteration. It was a room to look at and to admire, not to live in. It was like being in a film set. The discreet wallpaper looked like silk which meant it probably was and the floor was made of a wood that I didn't recognize, a brown so dark that it was almost black. At least twenty cows had given their lives to make the leather sofa that ran along one side of the room with enough space to seat a football team. The reserves, a referee and a couple of linesmen would have had no problem finding somewhere to sit, from the obviously antique Chinese wooden collectors' pieces to the leather armchairs either side of a Victorian metal fireplace, not just for show because even Hong Kong gets cold in winter.

That's what it had said in the Cathay Pacific guide to Hong Kong, anyway. Above the fireplace was an oil painting, I didn't recognize the style but I knew the name in the bottom right hand corner and I whistled gently. At one end of the room, to the left of the picture window, was a baby grand piano and I recognized the name on that too, and the man in the photographs in solid silver frames, with his family, arm around his children, a pudgy teenage boy and a gangly girl, a wedding photograph, a graduation picture, Lai Kwok-lee at work, rest and play.

Footsteps behind me, the click, clack, click of high heels on hard wood and I turned to see a middle-aged Chinese woman walk into the room, chin up as she measured me through inquisitive eyes and I gave her the professional smile, the one that puts them at ease and makes them think you're on their side, the one that lulls them into a false sense of security so you can get in close and get what you want. She was the one in the wedding photograph with Lai so it wasn't hard to work out that she was his wife.

The professional smile was having about as much effect as if I'd waggled my ears, I was looking into a cold, placid round face with narrow lips and hard eyes, hair short and permed, a wide nose and a large dimple in the middle of her chin. Not ugly but far from pretty, the body stocky and rectangular, clothed in a little something Chanel had thrown together for a few thousand pounds. The gold and diamond Rolex on her thick weight-lifter's wrist wasn't the sort they sell for $200 in Temple Street when the police aren't looking, and the necklace would have kept a family of four in relative luxury for about a decade.

I couldn't see her teeth because she wasn't smiling but I would have bet a month's expenses that any cavities she had were filled with enough gold to send a prospector running to the saloon shouting, 'drinks all round, I'm gonna be rich.'

I told her who I was and who I worked for and I gave her the boyish smile, the one that says I'm only doing my job and I'd really appreciate any help you could give me because I'm not really sure what I'm doing. I raised my eyebrows expectantly but she still didn't speak and the idea of pretending to throw a fit and trying to win the sympathy vote crossed my mind.

'I was just admiring the photographs,' I said, and nodded towards the baby grand. Get her talking, break the ice. 'You have a lovely family.'

A slight smile, a curt formality for a compliment paid. No warmth.

'Who is the photographer in the family?' I asked, throwing her a question that was going to need an answer so I could at least see if she could talk.

'My son,' she said, and there was a glint of gold from the corner of her mouth. 'He wants to be a professional photographer when he is older.'

I was in. Always works with mothers, the boyish smile and ask about the kids. 'What was he doing on the roof of the train, Mrs McNee? Where did James go to school, Mrs McNee? How do you feel, Mrs McNee?'

'He's very good,' I said. 'Does he want to work for newspapers, or magazines?'

'Advertising,' she said, and I thought he's probably right, there's more money in it and probably as much integrity. My face was starting to ache. She was weighing me up and I got the impression she ranked me slightly higher than the man who came round to spray against cockroaches. She hadn't offered to shake hands, she hadn't asked me to sit down and she hadn't smiled. Maybe she had oil on her hands, maybe the chairs weren't made for sitting on, maybe she was on the sort of diet where they wire your jaws together. Maybe she just wanted me to get the hell out of her house.

'How can I help you?' she asked eventually.

'Actually, it was your husband I wanted, Mrs Lai,' I said. 'Is he here?'

She made an impatient clicking noise behind her tightly closed lips and I could see that when I finally got the hell out of her house the maid with the 'come get me' smile and the long legs and the flashing eyes was going to get a tongue-lashing that would make her wish she'd stayed in the Philippines.

'No he is not.' The click again. The accent wasn't English, it had a hint of Canadian so I guess she'd studied there or more likely spent a few years there to establish residency and get her hands on a passport while hubby kept churning out the money in Hong Kong. They'll take anyone, the Canadians, providing they've got the money or the entrepreneurial background to set up their own business. Then when the lifeboat is ready they move back to Hong Kong to milk it for as much as they can before 1997, knowing that they can jump ship whenever the going gets rough.

I couldn't hear the hum of an air-conditioner and I wasn't likely to in a house like this, but I was starting to sweat so maybe it wasn't switched on. I could feel dampness between my shoulder blades and at the back of my legs and I wanted to wipe my forehead but I didn't have a handkerchief and even if I had I wouldn't have given her the satisfaction of seeing my discomfort.

'Oh, I'm sorry to have bothered you. Perhaps I should have phoned first.' Bullshit. Rule number one of the doorstepping game – don't let them know you're coming. Rule number two – don't give up. They'll weaken eventually and ask you in so long as you're polite and keep smiling. Rule number three – when you're inside keep them talking so they don't get the chance to ask what it is you want, because you can't say you're after a page three lead or a picture of their dead son or a chance to prove how good you are.

'What is it you want?' she asked. Shit. So much for doorstepping rule number three. I widened the smile and told her I was doing a series on Hong Kong tycoons and as her husband was obviously one of the territory's (I nearly said colony but I knew how sensitive they get about that) most successful businessmen obviously I wanted to include him but I'd obviously called at an inconvenient time and obviously I was saying obviously too much. Obviously.

'Do you think he would be interested? I wouldn't need too much of his time?' I asked.

'I'm sure he would be,' she replied, and managed a half smile. It seemed I'd moved up from pest exterminator to drain unblocker so I asked her if she'd mind giving me a bit of background on her husband. I kept dropping in the word successful because her weakness was vanity and I could see her mentally preening herself, bathing in the reflected glory of her man. The man who'd paid for her Rolex, her house and her passport.

Of course, she said, sit down, she said, would I like a cup of tea, she said, still no smile but I'd got around her defences, found the weak spot. I took out the notebook from my jacket pocket and rested it on my knee, looking for the general question that would keep her talking and give me a chance to think.

'Where did you first meet?' I asked, pen poised like a heron about to stab a fish. It's easier if you know what you're looking for, if there are a few simple facts to slot into a story that you've already written in your head, the who, why, what, where and when. You know what you want, it's just a matter of the approach, meek and mild, aggressive, subtle, press the right buttons and get the information. Sometimes it's just a quote you want, a tight paragraph to put colour into a story, 'I warned him not to go to the depot at night, I knew something like this would happen one day.' Sometimes all you want is confirmation that the schedule line you've given the news desk is close enough to the truth to stand up as a story.

But sometimes you don't know what you want, you fix up an interview and you go along with eyes and ears wide open, antennae twitching because you know there's an angle there and you don't want to miss it. It's not such a problem for the features boys, they can write a colour piece about a paper clip or a postage stamp and they're so good at it they have you clamouring for more. But hard news is different – you're looking for the angle, the human interest, the tickle at the back of the neck that lets you know you've got the splash or a page lead at worst.

I did six months on an evening paper in the Midlands and blotted my copybook by getting pissed one night and turning up three hours late for my early morning shift. The punishment dreamt up by the rat-faced news editor, who spent most of his time selling his reporters' stories to the nationals, was to send me along to the inspector who ran the local police horse training school. I sat with the guy in his pokey little office for an hour chatting about horses and crowd control and dressage and my smile was wearing thin and my backside was numb and then I hit paydirt.

'See what you can get out of it,' Rat-Face had said. 'I see it as a spread with lots of pics.' Like hell he did. He saw it as a way of teaching me a lesson.

'Where do the horses go when they retire,' I asked the inspector and his eyes hardened a little and he said they didn't retire.

'We keep them until they're too old to work,' he said and adjusted his tie and I left it at that because the hairs on the back of my neck were tingling, I had the story and I wasn't going to blow it by cross-questioning the guy with a notebook on my knee so I changed the subject and talked about temperament and feeding and led him by the nose for a full twenty minutes until he'd forgotten what he'd told me.

Then we went out with a photographer to the training field, and while the inspector rode stiff-backed between flagwaving and shouting constables I stood next to a hardbitten sergeant in jodhpurs and chatted, gave him the rueful smile and said, 'It's a pity the poor buggers can't be put out to grass,' and shrugged. No notebook, no pen, no looking at him as we spoke, just talking as we watched the horse being trained to intimidate football fans and striking miners.

'Too bloody expensive. And where would we keep them?' he replied as the wind ripped the flags through the air, snapping and cracking either side of the horse and rider. 'These horses are trained to work, they'd go mad grazing in a field somewhere.'

'So what happens? The vet puts them down, I suppose.'

'You're joking, man. The guy from the knacker's yard does it, and he pays for the meat too.'

He turned to look at me, suspicion aroused. 'This is off the record, right?' he asked.

'You think I'd use this in the paper?' I laughed and slapped him on the back. That got me out of saying yes it was off the record because no it wasn't, I was going to use every word. I changed the subject and before long the inspector rode up, followed by the red-faced and slightly out-of-breath photographer, and asked did we have everything we wanted and I gave him the winning smile and sure we did and thanked them both for all their help.

'Anytime,' said the inspector, and I thought sure, and I winked at the sergeant as the photographer and I climbed into the company van. Lambs to the slaughter, I thought. I was twenty-four years old and as cocky as hell.

It took me half an hour back at the office to track down the abattoir where the horses were slaughtered and I went round and chatted with a man in a blood-stained apron who, for a few quid and the promise of a few more, gave me the name of the pet food company where the horse-meat went.

Back in the office again I went through the picture files and came up with a handful of black-and-white shots of horses who'd been honoured for bravery and long service and had presumably ended up in cans of dog and cat food. Two phone calls to rent-a-quote animal lovers, another to a local MP and a call to the police press officer for an official statement and the story was in the bag.

The paper splashed it – 'Hero horses killed for Pet Food' – and we spilled it over to the centre spread. I could see Rat Face's eyes light up with pound signs but I beat him to it, sold it to the *Express* for more than I normally earned in a month and two months later I got my first job in Fleet Street. I'd burnt off a couple of coppers but what the hell, I wasn't going back.

So I sat in an uncomfortable leather armchair and let Mrs Lai's words pour over me like syrup over a pancake, thick and clogging and sickly sweet, while I nodded and smiled, doodling in the notebook because I wasn't after his life story. I was looking for the angle.

They'd come across from China together in a leaky boat thirty years ago, a couple of teenagers with their belongings in a canvas bag, and five taels of gold in a leather pouch tied around his neck.

The money was the life savings of his peasant parents, given to them so that they could start a new life in capitalist Hong Kong, she said, but with a downcast look and a lowering of the voice that gave her away – he'd stolen it and given them and the poverty of mainland China two fingers. He'd looked after the money then and that's how it had always been. They'd married in Hong Kong and used the gold to rent a small room in the New Territories and to buy half a dozen manual sewing machines, paying shifts of illiterate young girls with nimble fingers and simple minds to run them twenty-four hours a day, churning out dresses and T-shirts or whatever the buyers from the UK or America wanted.

Mrs Lai kept the books, Dennis cracked the whip, and soon they had a small van and then a bigger factory and more machines and more exploited teenagers and then he'd gone into plastics, making cheap toys to put in Christmas crackers and then manufacturing practical jokes, fake dog shit and rubber chickens and then the calculator boom took off and he was into injection moulding and started making the plastic cases that surrounded the chips and liquid crystal displays from Japan and then he'd moved into transport and at one point during the heady days of OPEC lunacy he'd owned a couple of oil tankers.

He moved out of textiles as the EEC and the United States began to build trade barriers, taking over a string of restaurants and a small construction firm. He was marked out as a coming man then and found the banks were falling over themselves to lend to him and he borrowed heavily on the back of a couple of high-profile contracts he'd managed to snatch from under the noses of the big boys and then he bought a small parcel of Central land at a Government Land Auction and put up his own building, taking over the top three floors as his headquarters and renting out the rest to one of the minor hongs. Dennis Lai, local boy made good. Long before he'd reached the top and got his house on the Peak Mrs Lai had stopped keeping the books, had got pregnant twice – a boy and a girl – had spent three years in Canada to get her citizenship and now devoted herself to charitable works and expanding her wardrobe and jewellery collection.

She told the story reverently, like she was laying out a treasured dress in front of me, at times looking like a little girl begging for approval, a pat on the head and a smile, yes, you did well, you got out of the fields and away from the insects that scarred your bowed legs with bites that the Chanel skirt couldn't hide, you escaped from the poverty that you hated so much that you ran away from your family and now wear your wealth on your wrists and round your neck and hang it on the wall so that you always know it's there. I was starting to feel sorry for the overweight and not particularly attractive Chinese lady with bad skin as her gloss gradually rubbed off but I pushed thoughts like that away and concentrated on her story. There were things I needed to know about her husband, about how he really made his money because the rags-to-riches story she'd paraded in front of me was straight out of Fantasy Island, who his business contacts were, why my sister had his picture on her wall and why one of the same pictures was in a silver frame on top of Mrs Lai's grand piano.

It was practically a speech, a story she'd obviously delivered before, and she told it without pausing for breath, refusing to give me a chance to ask any questions. She didn't even stop while the maid served tea. The Filipina was flirting outrageously, and she leant forward when she handed me the blue and white Wedgwood cup and saucer so that I could see down the front of her dress. She wasn't wearing a bra, and she gave me a smile that said she knew that I knew she wasn't wearing a bra. She offered me a tray with a sugar bowl that matched the cup and solid silver tongs but I said no thanks, sweet enough, but she didn't get the joke. All the time Mrs Lai was speaking, and she didn't even look round as the girl left the room.

Eventually she finished and clasped her hands together in her lap. 'And that,' she said, 'is our story. We have had a tough life, but through hard work and diligence we have done well. We have much to thank Hong Kong for. And now, if you'll excuse me, I have many things to do.' She rose to leave, but I held my hand up to stop her and asked her: 'Could I just ask you a couple of questions first, Mrs Lai?' She sat down again and reclasped her hands, fingers rubbing together. The atmosphere was starting to get chilly again, and it wasn't the air conditioning.

'Your husband is obviously very well-known in Hong

Kong,' I said, trying to appeal to her vanity again. 'I suppose the newspapers here are forever bothering you for interviews.'

She gave me a curt smile, a quick flash of teeth and the glint of gold. 'From time to time, yes,' she said.

'I was wondering if you could tell me the last time he was interviewed so that I could get a copy, it would help me with the background.'

'But I have given you all the background,' she said firmly, and I heard the click behind her closed lips.

'It would help me to check that I don't make any mistakes,' I pushed. 'Can you remember when he gave his last interview?'

'I can, but it will be of no use to you, I'm sure. He was interviewed by the *Hong Kong Economic Journal*.'

'I'll try to get a copy, what date was it?'

'It won't do you any good, it is a Chinese newspaper, and I am quite sure you are incapable of reading Chinese.' She got to her feet. 'And now, I really must . . .'

'What about the English language press?' I said. She shook her head and walked to the door.

Oh well, all or nothing, I was leaving anyway. I asked her if Sally had interviewed Lai recently and I could see by the look in her eyes that I'd pushed her too far.

'The girl who died?' she asked quietly, and then realization dawned and her mouth fell open.

'I should have realized,' she hissed, venom in her voice. 'I should have realized when you told me your name. You are her husband?'

'Brother,' I said. 'She interviewed your husband?'

She flung open the door and click-clacked across the hall

to the main entrance where the maid already had the door open for me.

'I shall inform my husband of your visit,' said Mrs Lai, and it sounded like a threat.

'Did she come here?' I pressed.

Her eyes hardened and the lips drew back in a canine snarl, and for one moment I thought she was about to spit in my face.

'Leave my house now,' she whispered. 'You have over-stayed your welcome.' Then she turned her back on me and click-clacked back down the hall.

'Goodbye, sir,' said the maid, smiling brightly.

'I love the way you roll your r's,' I said, and winked. She was still giggling as she closed the door behind me. At least I'd made a good impression on somebody.

I started walking down the Peak, heading for the harbour. There were no other pedestrians, and as I sweated along the pavement the cheapest car that drove past me was a very large Mercedes with a liveried chauffeur in the front and a child with a BMX bicycle in the back.

My shirt was soaked and I was dying for a drink by the time I'd gone a hundred yards and after half a mile I leant against a stone wall in the shadow of a leafy tree that wouldn't have been out of place in Kew Gardens. A taxi dawdled along the road and I plunged back into the sunshine and flagged it down. The shirt felt even damper in the refrigerated air of the cab and I leant back and closed my eyes.

I'd just about recovered when the taxi stopped at the back of the towering metal edifice that was the Hong Kong and Shanghai Bank headquarters. Howard was standing in the middle by two escalators which climbed up into the building. I craned my neck back as I walked over to him. The base of the tower, some fifty feet up, was transparent perspex criss-crossed with grey metal struts, and above that were tier upon tier of offices, illuminated by shafts of sunlight that seared through the huge atrium.

'How did it go?' asked Howard. He was wearing a light blue safari suit, not the same as the one he'd been wearing when he met me at the airport, this one had short sleeves.

'I didn't find out much,' I said. 'There was nothing in the computer, nothing to show what she'd been working on.'

'Was Healy any help?'

'He gave me a few pointers, but without her notes I'm not going to get anywhere. I need to know who she saw, what she was doing. You're going to have to help me, Howard. You're going to have to put me in touch with everyone she was working with.'

'I'll do my best, laddie. You seemed to have spent a lot of time with Healy and got very little out of it.'

'Yeah, I went for a trip to the Peak.'

'Sightseeing?'

'You can stop fishing, Howie. I went up to see Lai.'

'Where did you get his address?' he said, and he sounded angry. He flapped his handkerchief out and mopped his brow. Maybe our Howie was starting to lose his cool at last.

'He's in the phone book, it wasn't difficult.'

'Damn it,' he exploded, 'you should have told me.'

'Why? What the fuck's it got to do with you? You're just the hired hand.' His eyes narrowed when I said that and I could see that I'd struck home. What the hell, he asked for it, but I tried to soothe his feelings anyway.

'It was a spur of the moment thing, and anyway, he wasn't there.'

Howard seemed to relax then. 'I'm supposed to be looking after you, that's all,' he said. 'This is my territory, and it makes me look stupid if I don't know where you are . . .' he trailed off lamely. I thought it was probably best not to mention the run in I'd had with Mrs Lai in case he threw a fit.

I smiled and he smiled and I slapped him on the back. Friends again.

'OK, now where are we going?' I asked.

'Queen's Pier. It's a couple of hundred yards away.'

'Let's go then. It's some building this.'

'Aye, but it's a bit of an acquired taste. It grows on you after a while. The staff love it, though inside it's more like an electronics factory than a bank, sterile and metallic. The only things that they brought from the old building were these two bronze lions.' He nodded towards two magnificent metal animals lying on blocks of stone. At the base of one sat two girls eating sandwiches from a paper bag as they talked.

We waited by the roadside until a red-painted tram rattled past packed tight with passengers and then we crossed, stepping over the metal tracks and dodging an open truck piled high with boxes of oranges.

For the first time I noticed the noise, a high-pitched babble of voices like thousands of swallows preparing to fly south for winter. We walked into a square, green and cool with fountains playing, but the sound of the water was masked by the chattering of hundreds upon hundreds of girls and women, most dressed in brightly coloured dresses, standing in groups or sitting on benches sharing lunch boxes.

They were Filipina, all of them, skin the same as the girl who'd opened Mrs Lai's door, the colour of well polished mahogany.

'What is this, Howard? A demonstration?'

'It's Sunday, most of the Filipina amahs come here on Sunday afternoons to meet their friends. It's their one day off.'

'I didn't realize there were so many of them.'

'They're the biggest expat community in Hong Kong, by far. And generally they're treated like shit.'

'By the gweilos?'

'No laddie, by the Chinese. The Filipinas are tied to contracts, paid a salary which is about one third of the national average here, and if they quit they have to go back to the Philippines. A lot of them are beaten and sexually abused by their bosses. There was a case a few years back of a lawyer who got locked out on the roof garden of his flat with his maid. He made her climb down the outside of the building to get in through the window.'

He fell silent then as we weaved in and out of the gossiping groups of women, all dolled up in their Sunday best.

'What happened, Howard?' I asked.

He was still silent, and from his embarrassment I knew the answer – she'd fallen to her death. Nice story, Howard, shame about the ending. I let the question lie unanswered, and covered his *faux pas* by asking about the junk trip.

'We're on the bank's number two boat,' he said. 'Most

of their PR department will be there along with a few of the lads from their merchant banking side.'

'What's the reason for the trip?' I asked.

'No reason,' he said. 'Just a chance for them to meet the press. But that's not a kosher reason because they know us all anyway. It's just one of their social get togethers and they usually turn out to be a right royal piss up.'

We left the square and the sing-song clamour behind us, and walked to the harbour's edge to meet a group of gweilos standing by concrete steps that led down to the water. Fifty yards out bobbed a wooden-clad boat, built like an old-style junk but with two powerful engines in place of the traditional sail. Howard did the introductions and I got a series of earnest handshakes from the dozen or so bank staff and uninterested world-weary smiles from the press corps.

The journalists were a mixed bag. Healy was there, twitching and chain smoking, there was a young stringer from an Australian paper, a Commercial Radio reporter, a spotty English girl from the *Standard* and a tall, cadaverous China watcher from the *Far Eastern Economic Review* who looked like an off-duty undertaker. There was a handful of Chinese reporters, uniformly dressed in open-necked shirts, baggy jeans and training shoes, a sharp contrast to the immaculate suits and twin sets of the Bank.

As we stood around and made small talk another group of a dozen or so wandered along from the other end of the pier, shepherded by one of the suits.

'I think we're all here now,' trilled the middle-aged PR lady with too much make-up who was masterminding this little voyage into the unknown. She waved her guest list at the junk and it turned towards the pier in a lazy circle before coasting to a stop. It was held steady by an old woman and a man using long wooden poles, him at the sharp end and her at the back like almost matching bookends. They looked like elderly brother and sister, with lined, weatherbeaten faces and grey hair and they both wore black trousers and white nautical shirts.

'Mr and Mrs Fong, they're absolute darlings,' said the PR lady as she guided me onto the heaving deck. 'They've been with us for years, simply years.'

I was going to make some crack about it being time the bank bought them shoes but maybe they just preferred to go barefoot.

I found my way to a drink-laden waiter with the unwavering instincts of a homing pigeon and I had a G and T in my hand before the last guest was on board and we were growling through the waves. The small talk of the bankers held my interest for about ten minutes and I stuck it for another five until the conversation about rising rents, the cost of school fees and the problems of finding a decent amah got too much to stomach. The bar seemed to offer the nearest thing to sanctuary and I made it back there without throwing up. The man standing there ordering a drink had a head of thinning red hair scraped sideways in a vain attempt to cover his baldness. He had the look of a rugby player going to seed, muscle turning to fat, the skin ageing and slackening. He handed me a fresh gin and tonic without even asking what I was drinking. Instinctively I liked him. His name was Dick Graham, he was something to do with security at the bank and this time I lasted twelve minutes before I was bored to tears with his views on why there would always be a place for expats in Hong Kong. Over his shoulder I could see Howard looming over a pretty young Chinese girl with sleek black hair. He was gently stroking her shoulder as she looked up at him, her hand covering her mouth as she laughed at whatever it was that the lecherous old sod was telling her.

I made my excuses to Dick, telling him I wanted to look at the view, leaving the bar to stand on the deck, savouring the cool breeze that blew in from the sea. The sun was beginning to set and was turning the water blood red. I hadn't realized it was so late.

Healy detached himself from the clutches of the PR woman and walked over, a can of Fosters lager in one hand and a half-finished cigarette in the other.

'How's it going?' he asked, flicking ash over the side. The wind caught it and blew it back, smearing it across the knees of his trousers. He didn't seem to notice.

'Not so bad,' I said. 'Thanks for your help this morning.'

'I wish I could have done more,' he said. 'Sally was a good kid.'

He took a mouthful of lager from the can, and a thin dribble of amber fluid trickled down his chin. He wiped it with the back of his hand, which he then rubbed on his thigh.

'I'm still not sure what it is you're looking for.'

'For answers, I suppose. I want to know why.'

'Sometimes people just get to the stage where they can't take any more.'

'Take what?'

He shrugged. 'Life, I guess.'

I shook my head violently. 'No,' I said. 'Not Sally.'

'When was the last time you saw her?'

'That's not the point,' I said. 'I knew her, she was my sister.'

'People change.'

'You don't understand,' I said.

'Maybe you're right,' he admitted, and dropped his cigarette to the deck, stubbing it out with a scuffed shoe. 'But be careful you don't make too many waves.' He wasn't looking at me when he spoke, but I could sense that he was waiting to see how I'd react.

'What do you mean?' I said, keeping my voice as level as possible.

'Well, for a start, I understand you gave Simon Hall a hard time yesterday.'

'Where did you hear that?'

'Friend of a friend. I don't think you appreciate how small a place Hong Kong is. The story I heard is that you had him pinned to the wall and were threatening to castrate him with your bare hands.' He laughed, and nervously pulled the lobe of his ear. 'You'll get yourself a reputation,' he said.

'I just lost my temper, they didn't seem to be doing anything.'

'Why should they? To them it's a clear-cut case of suicide.'

I snorted. 'She wouldn't have killed herself. I know she wouldn't have killed herself.'

'They'll need more than a hunch to go on,' said Healy, and I knew he was right. What I needed was proof and so far all I had was a photograph of a Chinese businessman.

A couple of suits walked over, earnest young men with army haircuts and fox-hunting voices who wanted to know what 1997 would mean to press freedom. I said I was going on to the upper deck to get some sea air. I climbed the white wooden stairs alongside the main cabin and dropped into a deck chair. An observant white-jacketed waiter spotted my almost empty glass and came over with a refill. There were no Chinese on the upper deck, except for two waiters, and one by one the suits drifted upstairs to where I was, seeking their own kind. Healy and Howard stayed with the Chinese reporters, and both seemed to be drinking heavily.

The young Chinese girl with shoulder length hair, high cheekbones and large, almond-shaped eyes whom I'd seen with Howard earlier, climbed up the stairs and sat down in the chair next to me, slowly crossing one long leg over the other. She was wearing a knee length charcoal grey skirt and it rode up her thighs. Nice thighs, too. Her shirt was clean and white and she'd turned the collar up at the back. Around her neck was a string of pearls that were so small they had to be real. Her lips, when she opened them, curved upwards in a knowing smile.

'Eighteen months, Happy Valley, researcher with Business International,' she said, eyes flashing. The voice was soft and very American.

'I'm sorry?' I said.

'They're the answers to the three questions everybody asks. How long have you been in Hong Kong, where do you live, what do you do? I thought it would save time. My name's Jenny.'

'Nice to meet you,' I said, and clinked glasses with her. She looked like she was drinking gin too. 'Three days, the Excelsior Hotel, journalist.'

'You're Sally's brother,' she said, suddenly looking serious. 'I'm sorry to be so flippant, I didn't realize.'

'This is one hell of a small town,' I said, and took a

111

mouthful of gin and tonic. She looked hurt so I gently nudged her shoulder. 'It's OK, really. Are you a friend of Sally's?'

'I liked her a lot,' she said, nodding eagerly. 'Though I'd only known her for six months or so. She was very, how shall I put it, lively. Things seemed to happen when she was around. I'd no idea she was so unhappy.'

'Unhappy?'

'To have killed herself. I suppose she must have been depressed.'

'When was the last time you saw her?'

'Two weeks ago, I think, at a disco in Tsim Sha Tsui East.'

'Did she look depressed then?'

Jenny laughed, tossing her head back and showing me a set of perfect teeth that were every bit as white as the pearls. 'No, she was having a great time.' She frowned. 'You mean, you don't think she killed herself?'

'No, I don't. But at the moment I've no idea what did happen.'

We sat in silence for a while, and watched the guests fill their mouths with food. The party began to split into two, the gweilos moved onto the upper deck leaving the Chinese jostling around the buffet. We were looking down on the heads of two Chinese girls, reporters I guess, who were arguing fiercely in Cantonese.

'What are they so riled about?' I asked her.

'How should I know?' she asked.

'No, I mean what are they saying?'

'I can't speak Chinese, I'm an ABC,' she said.

'ABC?'

'American-born Chinese. Also known as a banana.'

'You'll have to explain that one.'

'Yellow on the outside, white on the inside,' she laughed. 'You've more right to be here than I have. You're a Brit, you can come and go as you please. I'm a Yank and have to get a visa.'

'And you don't speak any Chinese?'

'Not a word. Well that's not exactly true, I can say please and thank you, but that's about it. I went to a small school in San Francisco and Cantonese wasn't on the curriculum.'

'Your parents?'

'They were born in the States, too. I'm a second generation American. And it doesn't make for an easy life in Hong Kong, I can tell you.'

'Because everyone treats you like a Chinese?'

'That's it. The gweilos think I'm a local, and the Chinese think I'm stupid because I can't speak Cantonese. A lot of my friends are in the same boat and it can cause all sorts of psychological problems.' She saw me smile. 'Seriously.'

'I believe you. But you can always learn, surely?'

She raised her glass to her lips, and licked it sensuously, like a snake testing the air.

'There's nothing sadder than a group of Chinese Americans taking Cantonese lessons,' she said. 'I don't have to go in search of my roots. My roots are in San Francisco.'

'You mean your heart, as the song goes.'

'Yes, my heart, too.' She looked serious again, frown lines appearing on her forehead. 'I really am sorry about Sally. I liked her a lot. I still can't believe she's dead.'

'I know what you mean. I keep thinking she'll phone, or I'll bump into her on the street.'

'What's going to happen about . . . I mean, is there

113

going to be a funeral or something? Will it be here, or in England?'

I shrugged. 'I hadn't even thought about that. There's going to be an autopsy first, that's all I know.'

'Oh God,' she said, and closed her eyes.

Without realizing it I'd taken Sally's watch from my pocket and was playing with it in my left hand, twisting the strap around my fingers. It was still going so it must have been battery operated but I couldn't see how the makers could have fitted one in because it was so thin.

'Is that Sally's?' asked Jenny. She'd opened her eyes and was leaning forward, her chin resting on her hands.

I nodded.

'It's lovely. May I?'

I handed it over and she laid it flat in the palm of one hand. 'It looks very expensive. Well, I suppose it would be. Sally loved expensive things.'

'What do you mean?'

'She had good taste. And in Hong Kong taste doesn't come cheap.'

She turned the watch over. 'I should have known,' she said, and handed it back. 'Dennis bought it for her.'

I'd missed the engraving on the back. 'To Sally,' it said. 'With love,' it said. 'From Dennis,' it said.

'Dennis Lai,' I said, under my breath.

'You know about Dennis, then?' she said.

'Not really,' I replied. 'Boyfriend?'

'And some. He's loaded. And smitten with Sally.' She made it sound like a disease, Christopher Robin's gone down with Alice.

'Have they been going together for long?' I asked. I couldn't stop using the present tense.

'As long as I'd known her,' said Jenny.

Did she know he was married? I wanted to ask. One of the waiters had appeared with a trayful of smoked salmon and triangles of brown bread and butter. He moved into the centre of a circle of the bank people, four men and two women, one of them the PR organizer, deep in conversation about whether there was more money to be made investing in the yen or the Deutschmark. Money had been their sole topic of conversation since I'd sat down.

The engines stopped with a splutter and the husband and wife team anchored the junk about two hundred yards from a thin strip of sandy beach. There were no lights on the wooded hillside beyond the beach, no buzz of traffic, just the chirping of unseen insects coming alive and the sound of water sloshing against wood.

Loudspeakers hidden around the boat suddenly came alive with Dire Straits and I shuddered at the typical Hong Kong style – find a vacuum and fill it, find a need and service it, find a plot of vacant land and build on it. Come across a bit of peace and quiet and murder it. I'd have felt worse if it hadn't been Dire Straits. I hate boats, I hate the movement, the cramped spaces, the dampness, the smell. Give me an aeroplane every time, but if you had to go to sea then there were much worse ways of doing it than on a Hong Kong Bank junk.

Beads of condensation were trickling down the crystal cylinder and soaking the paper napkin so I drank it in one and placed it empty on the wooden deck.

'Where did you meet Sally?' I asked.

'One of the discos in Lan Kwai Fong, I can't remember which one,' she said. 'Sally was as high as a kite.'

'Drunk? Doesn't sound like Sally.'

'Not drunk, high.'

'She didn't do drugs.'

Jenny laughed, and then stifled it when she saw the look on my face. She reached forward and put her hand on my knee. 'I'm sorry, I didn't mean to laugh.' She leant back as a waiter walked over and handed me down another gin and tonic.

She waited for him to go before speaking again. 'Perhaps there were some things she didn't tell her big brother,' she said, handing back the watch.

'It's beginning to look that way, isn't it,' I replied. 'Did she often get high?'

'When I first knew her, but recently she'd slackened off. Hey, she wasn't into anything heavy, I know that much. She sniffed a little cocaine, but who doesn't these days? That's as far as it went. She wasn't an addict or anything.'

I got to my feet and patted her gently on the head. 'Jenny,' I said, 'it's been nice meeting you, but I have to get something to soften the impact of all the gin I've drunk. I'll catch you later.'

She smiled but her eyes were full of concern, for me or for what she'd said, I didn't know which. Maybe both. I went down the stairs backwards, feeling for the steps one at a time, one-handed because I was still carrying my drink.

The Chinese reporters were still attacking the buffet *en masse* like hyenas after a wounded gazelle, elbowing and pushing and piling their plates high with expensive food. Howard and Healy moved in for their share of the kill, Howard holding onto the arm of another young Chinese girl as if afraid that she'd try to escape. Beyond the buffet at the rear of the boat was a large U-shaped seat, upholstered in blue and white striped leather and I flopped onto it.

Healy had bent his head close to Howard's ear and was saying something to him, something that made him shake his head furiously. I wondered if it was true what Jenny had said about Sally taking drugs. Of course it had to be true, she had no reason to lie.

Dick came down the stairs and joined Healy and the two of them came to sit by me, leaving Howard to his food and his girl.

Healy drained his can of lager, flipped it over his shoulder into the sea and took a replacement out of his jacket pocket while he balanced a plate of food on his knees.

'Keep the harbour clean,' said Dick, shaking his finger. 'That's the slogan the government is trying to push.'

'An uphill job, I've given up,' said Healy, and nodded down at the two plastic bags that were floating past, full of God knows what. 'The harbour here is practically a sewer, sacrificed, like everything else, to commercialism.'

'It's better than it was, but I'll grant that you'll never see salmon jumping here,' said Dick.

'They spoil everything, they pollute, they ruin whatever they touch. They show no consideration for the environment,' said Healy, and I could feel his fiery resentment.

'Why should they look after it?' Dick asked. 'Borrowed place, borrowed time. You're more careful with something you own than something you rent.' He chewed on a chicken leg.

'Hell, Dick. The people here just don't care, locals or expats.'

'It's hard to care when everything you're working on could be taken off you in a few years.'

'Bullshit. That's absolute bullshit. The people here are concerned with just one thing – to get as much as they can out of Hong Kong before it's handed over to the Chinese. It's asset-stripping that's got more in common with a West African dictatorship than a crown colony. It's always been that way here, fortunes earned and won and then shunted offshore as quickly as possible. Expats live here in rented flats and pack their kids off to boarding school in the UK. They've probably got a house in London which they've rented out and most of their money is sitting in a Jersey bank account. The firms are even worse.'

'You're an expat, too. You're not Chinese. You've got the sanctuary of a British passport.'

'I'm half British,' he said. 'And all I've got is a British Dependent Territory passport. And we both know that's going to be practically useless come 1997.'

I swirled the gin and tonic around in the glass and listened. Dick wasn't looking at Healy, his eyes were on the bank's people and the guests who were gathered around a buffet table. The clink of knives and forks against plates cut through Mark Knopfler's guitar playing and now and again he was accompanied by the shriek of girlish laughter or a loud, bellowing guffaw.

The wind caught Dick's hair and blew it across his head, undoing his cover-up job and revealing his bald patch like a pale piece of raw chicken in the moonlight. For a gut-wrenching moment my mind flashed back to Sally lying naked in the mortuary but I stamped on the thought. Hard. A full eight inches of hair now flapped in the breeze like the flag at the back of the junk.

'Even you guys can see which way the wind is blowing,' said Healy and I had to smile at that one, 'because more than three-quarters of your business comes from outside Hong Kong.'

'I can't see why it upsets you so much,' said Dick, pulling his hair back into place with his free hand. He'd have had more luck solving Rubik's cube with one arm tied behind his back.

'If you really want to know, it's because the whole place is run by amateurs, from the government down. People who wouldn't be able to cut it back in London living the life of Riley on the backs of five million Chinese. Civil servants who wouldn't have got above the rank of clerical assistant in an English tax office being able to make the sort of decisions here that at home they'd only read about in the *Telegraph*. Property developers with maids, houses on the Peak and Rolls Royces.'

'They have these in London too.'

'Sure, but they work for it there. They get it on merit, on skill. Here, it's because they're Englishmen abroad. Look at the sort of ponces you've got on this boat. What would they be back home? Deputy assistant manager of some piddling little branch in Clapham. Here they're Lords of the Manor, waited on and courted by all and sundry. Yet the bank is nothing. Nothing. Most people in England haven't even heard of it.'

'We're big in Hong Kong,' said Dick. He'd swayed to his feet and was standing like a punch-drunk boxer waiting for the bell to sound.

'And what's Hong Kong? Nothing. A pimple on the backside of China and it's you and your kind who are squeezing it. A casino of a stock market with ideas above its station, a sprinkling of banks, a property market that makes its money solely on the back of scarcity of land, and a manufacturing sector that's ten years behind the times. What do they actually make here – clothes, watches and toys. Its one saving grace is its place in the time zone, and Tokyo's taken that advantage clean away, and the fact that it's a gateway to China. Before too long it'll just be a very small part of China, so what then?

'It's nothing, Dick. And so are you lot. Amateurs every one.'

Dick refused to be beaten and he waved his plate at me, looking for me to back him up.

'You're a visitor,' he said, 'what's the view from London?'

I sipped my gin and tonic. Most of the ice had melted but it still tasted OK.

'The view of what?' I asked. 'The place or the people?'

'Both.' Healy lit another cigarette and waited for me to speak.

'The place? I guess the exotic Far East, rickshaws and coolies. A place where they make plastic toys and cheap clothes. A town where sailors can get a little R and R. That's about it. The way its financial community acted during the stock market crash didn't do much for its reputation. It got a terrible press back in the UK.'

'Damn right,' said Healy, jabbing the air with the stub of his cigarette. 'Mickey fucking Mouse. The stock exchange just shut its doors for four days and fell through the floor when it reopened. And what did the British administration do? Sweet FA, just stood by and watched. And then called in an English merchant banker to help bail out the futures exchange.'

'Yeah, that got in the UK papers, too,' I said, and I could see that Dick regretted asking for my support. I suppose he thought we British would stick together. Pompous bastard, he'd asked for it.

Healy flashed me a smile. 'And the people?' he said quietly.

'One of the last bastions of the British empire,' I said. 'And the expats here are the same as everywhere else in the world. Has-beens and also-rans who couldn't make it back home proving that the mediocre can still thrive so long as you have another race to lord it over. Only in Hong Kong's case it's like the band playing as the Titanic went down.'

Dick missed the last bit because by then he'd turned his back on us and ambled to the stairs so that he could join the pals Healy and I had put such a lot of effort into slagging off.

Maybe he hadn't deserved it, though to be honest I didn't care.

'Twats like that really get up my nose,' said Healy. 'They act like they own the fucking place.'

'I know what you mean,' I said. 'I suppose he's going to sulk.'

'No doubt about it,' he laughed and we both sat there chuckling. When he stopped I asked him if he'd ever known Sally take drugs, and he squinted at me.

'No, why do you ask?'

'Dunno, just a feeling.' I nodded at the deck above us. 'Drugs just seem to go with this sort of lifestyle, you know, the moonlit cruise, the flash parties, fiddling while Rome burns, all that sort of crap. Drugs would just seem to fit in, that's all.'

'There's a lot of it going on, I can't deny that. But as far as I know Sally wasn't involved in it.' I wanted to ask Healy if he was a part of the drugs scene but he was hardly likely to say yes, and if he was, why had he put Sally on the cocaine story? 'Forget it,' I said.

'I'm going to get some fresh air at the sharp end. See you later.'

I weaved through the scavenging pack of Chinese reporters and walked up to the prow where I leant against the waist-high stainless steel railing looking down at the water lapping against the boat with the sound of a face being slapped.

Sally on drugs? Still didn't seem likely, not the Sally I knew anyway. I remembered a conversation we'd had three or four years ago when I'd called round at her flat and found it reeking of pot. I'd ended up playing the heavy elder brother, sitting on her sofa and lecturing her as she'd knelt by my side with her chin on my knee, dimples in her cheeks.

'You're angry,' she'd said and pouted, and I tweaked her nose.

'Of course I'm angry,' I fumed. 'I'm fucking appalled.'

'Don't swear,' she said, still smiling, but the dimples had disappeared.

'Don't tell me what to do,' I said, and stroked her hair, caressing the back of her neck.

'Somebody has to,' she answered, gently rubbing the back of my leg. I was close enough to see the pale freckles on her nose that she always tried to cover with a light dusting of face powder. There was spearmint on her breath. She was forever chewing gum.

'Are you taking any other drugs?' I'd asked her, and she'd given me her little girl lost face, and then raised her eyebrows in an exaggerated 'who me?' look. She pointed at her nose with her forefinger. 'Me?'

'You know what I mean.'

She'd raised her eyebrows even further, tilted her head

on one side and began drumming her fingers lightly on my knee. Cute.

'What d'you mean, brother of mine?'

'This flat reeks of pot. Do you use anything else?'

'No.' She was emphatic.

'Are you sure?' The fingers stopped drumming.

'I never lie to you. Ever.'

She did, but never seriously, just little white lies when she didn't want to hurt my feelings. But she didn't count them. And what the hell, neither did I.

'There's nothing wrong with pot, anyway,' she'd said.

'It's a drug.'

'So is alcohol.'

'Don't give me that.'

'Well, you drink too much.'

'I can handle it.' Huh, tell that to Bill Hardwicke. Or to the clinic where he'd sent me to dry out. That was only a few months after I'd sat there and lectured Sally on the dangers of taking drugs. 'Well I can handle pot,' she'd said to me.

'You can get addicted,' I said.

'When was the last time you had a gin and tonic?'

'Not the same thing,' I'd said defensively, because even back then I reckon I knew she was right and that it was big brother who'd needed looking after.

'It is, and look at the side effects. Think about the hangovers, the times you've fallen over dead drunk. The times your mates on the *Express* have had to carry you back from some all night binge.'

'Jesus, you've done it again.'

'Done what?' She'd looked genuinely puzzled.

123

'Changed the subject around completely, so that now I'm on the defensive. How do you do that?'

She smiled like a teenager being asked out for her first date, then put her chin on her shoulder and fluttered her eyelids like a '50s film star.

'I'm serious,' I'd said, and she'd stopped fooling around.

'I do not take heavy drugs,' she'd said. 'I never have and I never will.'

I believed her then and I believed her now. I turned to see Howard flip-flopping towards me, sucking something green through two bright red straws and carrying a fresh gin and tonic for me.

'I hear you and John have been winning friends and influencing people again,' he said with a grin.

'News travels fast,' I said and I grinned back because the anger had gone and because I couldn't afford to burn Howard off. I needed him too much for that. It was his city, he was the local and I had to have a guide.

'Too true it travels fast. By the time we get back to Queen's Pier everybody on this boat will know what you said, they'll each tell another five people by tonight, and tomorrow there won't be a gweilo on the island who doesn't know what you and John feel about Hong Kong. Take it easy, laddie.'

Laddie, for God's sake. The old faker had left Scotland more than twenty-five years ago. I shrugged and I could feel my sweat-dampened shirt sticking to my back. The anchors were pulled up and then the engines kicked into life again. It was starting to get dark, the water shifting to grey.

'Hell, I don't know. Sometimes I just get angry and say things without thinking.'

'Aye, you can get away with that in London, but not here. John can, he's always been a bit of a maverick and

THE FIREMAN

people are used to him by now. You're different, and if you're not careful they could all turn against you.'

I took a mouthful of the drink, just a sip because I was starting to get a little light-headed. I tried telling myself that I was drinking to deaden the pain of Sally's death but I knew that was only part of it. The problem was that I enjoyed drinking, I enjoyed it too much.

'In London it doesn't matter how many people you offend, you'll always find someone else to help you, someone to trust you,' Howard continued. 'It's a big place. But this is a village. If you upset the local school-teacher, the postmistress, the shopkeeper and the local bobby, then it's time to move on. The whole village will close ranks against you.'

He sat down on the deck and poked his legs under the railing and over the side where they swung backwards and forwards with the motion of the boat. He was surprisingly agile for a man of fifty and didn't spill a drop from his glass. My knees cracked and I grunted as I joined him. The back of my shirt was soaking now and I could feel beads of sweat trickle down between my shoulder blades. Howard showed not the slightest sign of discomfort.

'Think of them as sheep,' he said. 'A small flock of pampered sheep who want for nothing. Then along you come, a wolf who doesn't even bother to wear sheep's clothing. You frighten them. You're from the outside, you move too fast and you've got big, sharp teeth. They're going to run away from you and huddle together and comfort each other and tell themselves how lucky they are to be funny, fat white sheep and not lean and hungry wolves. They're not going to help you unless they think you're one of them. I learnt that a long time ago.'

125

'And which are you, Howard? Sheep or wolf?'

He looked at me and smiled and went 'Baaaaaa' in a long, low bleat that made me laugh out loud.

We sat together and watched the lights of Hong Kong island drift past, each office tower distinct in style and colour, small squat cubes, tall thin fingers of concrete, mirrored glass blocks, a plethora of designs so varied that they could have been assembled by a collector. And above them all towered the twisted knife of the Bank of China building, silently proclaiming the mainland's dominance over the colony. 'We are here already,' it seemed to say. 'And soon it will all belong to us.'

'Why do you stay here?' I asked.

He didn't answer immediately, just rested his chin on the railing. Above us, on the poop deck or whatever the raised bit in the middle of the junk was called, a small group had gathered around a young estate agent with a light green safari suit and an Oxbridge accent. Jenny was one of them. He was pointing out the buildings one by one, listing the tenants, the occupancy rates and the price per square foot. His party trick.

'I don't think I could work anywhere else, laddie,' Howard said finally. 'I love the place, the people, the climate . . .'

'The women.'

'Yes, and the women, I can't deny that. But it's more than that, there's something about the place, something that grabs and holds and won't let go.'

Fear, I thought. Fear of what might happen if he had to survive in the outside world, outside the village. Fear of being alone in a society where women didn't fall all over you because you were white or had money or a passport. Fear of having to compete in an environment where mediocrity isn't the norm, where only the good can succeed.

The black side of me wanted to grab him by the collar and rub his face into his fear to force him to confront it so that I could wallow in his discomfort, to shake him out of his self-satisfied contentment.

We sat without talking again, listening to the music and feeling the throb of the engines through the wooden deck.

'There are two sorts of people out here,' said Howard eventually. 'There are those who come in and try to change Hong Kong, to force it to conform with the rest of the world. They try to operate here in the same way that they do business in London, New York, or Sydney. They burn themselves out trying to wheel and deal here without ever realizing that the rules are different. They usually stick it for two years, maybe three. Then they leave. They don't realize that you can't change Hong Kong, you have to adapt to it.'

'And that's what you've done? Adapt?'

'The ones that stay accept the place for what it is, and the people for what they are. No matter how they dress, or how they speak, no matter how they adopt our lifestyle, these people are Chinese, with a culture that goes back thousands of years. Trying to change them means pushing against generations of inertia . . .'

'You've been here too long, Howard,' I interrupted.

'Maybe you're right, laddie,' he said. 'Maybe you're right at that.'

* * *

After the junk docked back at Queen's Pier and we'd said our goodbyes and I'd been given a frosty look and a limp handshake by Dick, Howard told me there was someone he wanted me to meet, so we caught a cab and it dropped us outside a nondescript office block in the middle of a shopping district. The aged watchman didn't even look up from his cubby hole, eyes glued to a girlie magazine, what little hair he had left on his peeling scalp blowing in the breeze from a large shuddering fan fixed to the wall. There were three lifts but even so we had to wait the best part of five minutes before one of the stainless steel doors slid back. Howard pressed the button for the fifth floor and when the doors opened again I followed him into a dark hallway heavy with the smell of incense. To the left was what appeared to be a Dickensian lectern, and behind it a middle-aged Chinese in a rumpled suit, chewing on the end of a cheap Biro. To the right was a leather-padded door sprinkled with bronze coloured studs, bolted top and bottom and guarded by a thickset man with his arms folded across a barrel chest.

'Ah, Mr Berenger. Nice to see you again. You have your card?' said the man with the pen in his mouth.

'Good to see you, Mr Lo,' said Howard, producing a green cardboard card from his wallet. 'Business is good?'

'Not so bad,' he replied, then bent his head down and carefully copied the details on the card into a large ledger. When he'd finished he looked up.

'Sign for friend, please,' he said, and handed the pen to Howard, bubbles of spittle stuck to the end he'd been sucking. Harold seemed not to notice and made his mark in the book. The heavy unbolted the door and as it opened the sound of an electronic organ oozed out like air from a leaking tyre.

The room was a large rectangle, with about fifteen or so small tables covered with red table-cloths surrounding a small metal dance floor. It was dark and humid, the only light coming from a bar to the right of the door we'd walked through and from the single candles burning in what seemed to be jam jars in the middle of the tables. Just half of the tables were occupied, by Chinese couples or groups of middle-aged men, and the air buzzed with conversation, some whispered, some shouted, all mixed in with the whining organ, the sort of out-of-tune wail that fakirs use to bore the pants off fangless snakes.

The organist was as close to death as you can get without being six feet under the ground, bald and wizened and curled over a tiny Yamaha organ on stainless steel legs. It was the organ that had the metal legs, though I guess his weren't much thicker. His hands were as crooked as a sports writer's expense sheet and he had trouble touching the keyboard with more than two fingers at the same time. He was sitting alone on a small raised stage, alone that is except for a drum kit minus cymbals and a couple of rusting music stands. Behind him on the wall were a line of foot-high silver painted letters that spelled out 'United Athletic Club' except that the A was upside down and hanging below the rest of the line. The door shut behind us with a resounding click and a waiter stepped out of the gloom to usher us to a table near the dance floor. The metallic floor glinted in the candlelight, it was about twenty feet across and made of large plates riveted together. There were drops of water near the middle. The waiter had pulled a chair out before I realized the table was already occupied, by a guy who looked the spitting image of Bluto, Popeye's rival. His beard was big and bushy and his eyes were virtually hidden behind sprouting brows that looked like giant caterpillars preparing to mate or fight to the death. Or both. The last time I'd seen him he was reading a newspaper over a hunchback's hump in the FCC. I was starting to realize just what a small place Hong Kong was, how everybody seemed to know everyone else and what they were doing. Howard's analogy of a village was a good one. Bluto almost got to his feet when he saw Howard approach, almost because as he rose his knees caught the table and it shook heavily and the candle and jar fell over and hit the floor with a crash. The organist didn't lift his head but we got a couple of filthy looks from some of the drinkers before they took in the full size and fighting weight of the man we'd come to see. He had a gut every bit as pronounced as Howard's but it was overflowing the top of his belt and barely restrained by a T-shirt that proudly stated: 'Bali-Island of Tits'.

'Meet Barry Fender,' said Howard, and waved towards the bearded hulk who was trying to settle back into his chair as a waiter scuttled around the table and retrieved the candle. The hand that gripped mine felt like five steel-filled sausages, soft but with a scarcely concealed strength. I wouldn't want to arm wrestle with this man. Hell, I'd think twice before sharing his toothbrush.

'Fender, as in bender,' he said in a gravelly Australian voice, and squeezed, not quite hard enough to need a trip to the casualty department of the nearest hospital, but close. 'Sit down,' he said, and ordered three beers. I didn't argue, just said that I was pleased to see him and retrieved my hand and nursed it on my lap, rubbing it gently to try to restore the circulation.

'You missed the show,' he said, more to Howard than to me, and waved his half-empty glass towards the dance floor. Some of his beer slopped over his hand and he licked it off with a tongue the size and colour of a breakfast kipper.

Now that my eyes were more used to the gloom, I could see just how seedy a place it was that Howard had brought me to. The tablecloth was liberally sprinkled with cigarette burns and the floor was dirty and unswept. The paint on the ceiling was flaking off in chunks and the walls looked and smelt damp. There were either large mouseholes or small ratholes in the base of the stage.

'She did amazing things with two ping-pong balls and a bottle of water,' he said. 'I got to hold the balloon,' he added, and winked conspiratorially.

'Thai?' asked Howard.

'No, Vietnamese, I think. Bloody good sort. And a great shot with the old blowpipe.'

The two of them laughed together. I didn't get the joke but I was fucked if I was going to ask them to explain. A curtain at the far end of the room was pushed aside and a small Asian girl in baggy jeans and a floppy pink sweater flounced out with a blue canvas bag thrown over her shoulder. Fender leant back in his chair and waved as she went past. She turned up her chin and then he spoke to her in a machine gun like chatter which stopped her in her tracks and seconds later they were jabbering away like a couple of monkeys until Fender obviously said something he shouldn't have because she hissed and drew back her hand as if to slap his face and then obviously thought better of it before cursing him and turning on her heel. Fender shrugged and watched her backside twitch prettily to the door. She kicked it impatiently until the heavy opened it to let her out.

'What did you say to her, you randy bastard?' asked Howard.

'Just chewing the fat,' laughed Fender. 'But the subject of what she did with the blowpipe did come up, I must admit.' He finished his beer and gestured for more. My glass was empty, too, though I hadn't realized I'd drunk mine. I could taste lager though, so it wasn't as if I'd been robbed.

'Were you speaking Chinese?' I asked Fender.

'Vietnamese,' he said, raising his caterpillar eyebrows as if amazed that anyone could be stupid enough to get the two languages confused.

'Where did an Aussie learn to speak fluent Vietnamese?' I asked him.

'Barry here used to be in the Australian SAS,' said Howard. 'If you think he's big now, you should have seen him twenty-five years ago. He was a good six inches taller and not so stocky.'

He could see he'd got my attention, so he paused theatrically and took a swill at his lager, replacing it carefully in front of him before speaking again.

'It was the training that did it. Barry signed up with the SAS, the meanest bastards in the Australian army. They fed him on raw beef, made him run hundreds of miles in full kit, and then they made him jump out of aeroplanes three miles up in the air, carrying a bazooka and a field radio. But because the Australian SAS wanted to show how hard they really were, they refused to use parachutes. That's why Barry here's the shape he is – it's the result of years of falling three miles and landing stock still on his feet. Bang!'

He slapped his hand down hard on the table and the two of them laughed like naughty schoolchildren.

'Compacted his spine like a crushed tin can,' spluttered Howard, and Fender leant over to slap him on the back.

'Get fucked, Howard,' I said, but I was smiling. To Fender I said: 'Seriously, where did the Vietnamese come from?'

'Vietnam, where else?' he said.

'Not strictly true,' said Howard. The waiter arrived and put three more beers in front of us then picked up a bowl of what looked like processed peas and placed them in the middle of the table. Fender motioned him to take them away. 'Not at these prices,' he said. 'It costs you an arm and a leg just to drink here.'

'Only if you watch the shows,' said Howard. 'They charge you for each show you sit through,' he explained to me. 'Fall asleep at your table and you can run up a hell of a bill.'

Something was moving underneath the stage, a small dark shape that glided behind the wooden planking, visible only when it passed by one of the holes, now you see it now you don't, like a duck in a shooting gallery.

Howard leant across the table and touched me lightly on the arm. 'Barry here is a victim of his own IQ,' he said in a low voice, and Fender sniggered. I felt like we were swapping dirty stories behind the bike sheds. I tried to use the beer to wash the taste from my mouth. 'I'll order you a G and T,' said Howard, and he caught the eye of the waiter and spoke quickly to him in Cantonese. The drink appeared while Howard continued his story. There was no lemon, but you can't have everything.

'They ran him through the standard IQ tests once he'd joined the SAS, and he scored 135.'

'Smart guy,' I said.

'Very smart, laddie. Well above university graduate level. But not smart enough, hey, Barry?'

Fender was sniggering again.

'If he'd scored above 140 they'd have taught him Mandarin, and that'd be a real asset now, no doubt about it. And if he'd scored less than 130 they'd have taught him Thai. And that would have been bloody useful bearing in mind his choice of women.'

'I like Thais,' admitted Fender.

'Like them? You collect them,' said Howard.

'Every man should have a hobby.' I was starting to get fed up with the Mutt and Jeff double act. My drink didn't taste too bad even without the lemon and I took a couple of gulps. It was hot and I was thirsty. I needed the liquid, the refreshment. OK, I needed the alcohol, so what about it?

'However, Barry scored midway between 130 and 140.'

'Neither here nor there.'

'They put him in a language lab, seven hours a day, six days a week, for twelve months, learning Vietnamese.'

'A year,' said Barry, shaking his head. 'Purgatory, purgatory.'

'During the day they kept him glued to a tape recorder, getting the tones right, teaching him the structures. In the evenings it was hours of book-learning, memorizing vocabulary.'

'It was hell, digger. You can't imagine it.'

'After a year he was fluent, perfect.'

'I still am.'

'He still is. Our Barry was then sent to Vietnam as an interpreter. He assumed he'd have an easy time, touring the camps, interrogating prisoners, slapping the odd VC around, enjoying the night life of Saigon. But that's not how it worked out.'

'Too fucking right,' agreed Fender.

A small pink nose appeared from a hole at the left hand side of the stage, followed by a sleek brown body and a tail and the rat boldly walked across the metal floor to the centre, where it sat and began grooming, scratching and licking, oblivious to the chatter at the tables and the ponderous organ music.

'Look at that wee bastard,' said Howard. 'He's got balls.'

'I can see them from here,' said Fender. 'Christ, now he's licking them.'

'I wish I could do that,' said Howard.

'Give him a piece of cheese and he'll probably let you,' laughed Fender, and the two of them fell about, the table juddering as their stomachs banged into it.

'The old jokes are the best,' I said, and I gestured with my empty glass at a waiter who was leaning against the wall. I pointed at it and then at the half empty glasses in front of Abbot and Costello and he nodded.

'I've never seen that before,' said Fender.

'Maybe it's part of the show,' said Howard.

'We'll find out when the bill comes, I suppose.'

The rodent's act came to an abrupt end then when a glass ashtray crashed to the ground six inches from its tail and slid off into the darkness. The rat leapt a full three feet into the air, twisted and landed on all four feet. Then it jumped sideways, and shot back under the stage. Howard and Fender clapped enthusiastically and cheered.

A woman in her fifties wearing a green dress a size too

small appeared at my right shoulder and bent her head down so it was level with mine.

'You want girl, sir?' she asked. Her breath smelt of onion and garlic, so overpowering that I turned my face away. As I moved she saw Howard and squealed in a little girl voice.

'Oh, Mr Berenger, long time no see. How are you tonight?'

'Not so bad, mamasan. Not so bad.'

'Do you or your friends require any company?' she asked.

'No thank you, mamasan, not tonight. Tonight we are here to drink and talk.'

'And watch the show.'

'And watch the show,' agreed Howard.

'Maybe next time,' she said, and wandered over to the next table, leaving behind a lingering odour of garlic and sweat.

'Was she offering us a girl?' I asked Howard.

'Just to talk to, laddie. If you want to take them out you'll have to pay the bar fine and pay the girl on top of that. It can get a bit pricey.'

'And most of them are slags here anyway,' broke in Fender. 'If it's a girl you want I'll take you down to the Makati later on.'

'Makati?'

'It's a diso-cum-pub down the Wanch. It's where all the Filipina maids go on their nights off.' He looked at his watch, a rugged stainless steel job that wouldn't have been out of place on a diver's wrist five hundred feet below the North Sea.

'At this time of the evening it'll be quiet, but give it a

few hours and the place will be jumping. And all it'll cost you will be a few drinks.'

The mamasan left the table next to ours and walked across the dance floor to a tape deck behind the organ player. She slotted in a cassette and as the little guy shuffled off the stage she pressed a button and the room was filled with the driving beat of a Cantonese pop song. A spotlight flashed on and a door opened at the far end of the room. Two Asian girls in short black skirts and silver halter tops ran out, weaved between the tables and posed in the centre of the steel circle, before starting an obviously well-rehearsed and oft-performed dance routine, bodies moving in perfect unison, faces equally blank and eyes with the same bored, uninterested look, just robots going through the motions.

Fender pushed the chair back to get a better view. 'Thais,' he mouthed to me, and clenched his fist tightly. 'I love Thais.'

One of the halter tops had disappeared already and then the other was removed with a flourish and thrown through the smoke-filled air to the mamasan who caught it nonchalantly with a practised wave of her arm. Her armpits were unshaven, hair sprouting from under her arms like the top of a coconut.

The girls were standing face to face, pretending to kiss, then they started to slide their left legs back, gradually dropping to the floor. One of the girls caught her high heel on a rivet and the leg locked and she pushed hard but it wouldn't move and for a moment the spell was broken and she smiled at me and the eyes glowed, dark brown and soft under long black false lashes, as her partner continued to slide to the floor. Then she managed to free her foot and the mask covered her face again and she began moving mechanically, rolling on the floor. From a distance they could have been twins, both with shoulder length hair, about five and a half feet tall in their black high heels, almond-shaped eyes and flattish noses, their skin the colour of those envelopes they send your tax forms in. But close up and without their clothes you could spot the differences, the one who'd smiled and who was now struggling with the zip on her friend's skirt had slightly fuller breasts and larger nipples and more cellulite at the top of her thighs. Her cheek bones were just a shade higher and her lips slightly wider, and they tightened as I watched her wrench the zip down and slide the skirt off before throwing it to the mamasan. Her partner repeated the actions with the same bored movements and soon they were both naked, except for the shoes. The music stopped abruptly and there was an awkward gap of a couple of seconds and then a slow soothing tune filled the air, all violins and woodwind, and the two girls began to stroke and caress each other as they lay side by side, with all the enthusiasm of an undertaker embalming an AIDS victim. They took it in turns to sit on each other and perform some pretty unconvincing oral sex. The whole thing was about as erotic as a St John ambulanceman demonstrating the kiss of life on a plastic dummy. Howard and Fender were entranced though, Fender was licking his lips slowly, rolling his tongue from side to side, slowly and sensuously, while Howard gently stroked his swelling stomach. Jesus, they were a couple of perverts. The girls switched positions and did a passable imitation of enjoying themselves in the old soixante neuf position and then the music stopped and they jumped up and held hands and curtsied like schoolgirls who'd just finished a poetry reading and ran off, buttocks jiggling and breasts bouncing. A couple of people clapped, but the girls got less applause than the rat. The spotlight winked off again and the organ cranked into life.

'I don't know about you, Howard, but I'd give them one,' said Fender, renewing his acquaintance with his beer and getting another line of froth on his moustache.

'Aye, they're a couple of bonnie wee lassies all right,' agreed Howard.

They both looked at me, wanting me to agree, to join their male fraternity, all boys together, nudge, nudge, wink, wink, know what I mean. I couldn't be bothered, I honestly couldn't be bothered, so I just shrugged.

'The shows aren't up to much,' said Fender. 'Not compared with what you get in Bangkok or Manila.'

'But you've got to take it where you can,' said Howard and Fender nodded, and motioned the waiter to bring over another round of drinks.

Fender leant forward, putting his elbows on the table and cupping his bearded chin in his large, labourer's hands.

'So what happened then?' I asked Fender.

'Huh?' he said, raising his refilled glass to his lips, leaving a thin film of foam on his thick black moustache.

'After they'd taught you Vietnamese.' This time there was something floating among the ice cubes but it wasn't lemon, it was a slice of lime. Things were looking up.

'They sent me to Vietnam,' he said, as if he was patiently explaining to a child that two times three is six.

'But he got more than he bargained for,' chipped in Howard. 'Instead of the easy life he was out on patrol, hunting for tunnels.'

'Tunnels?'

'The underground tunnels the North Vietnamese lived

in. They had whole towns ten feet under the jungle floor, complete with hospitals, ammo dumps, lecture halls. Rabbit warrens where they could disappear when the going got tough.'

'Almost impossible to find,' agreed Fender.

'But every now and again they'd find a way in, and that's where Barry came into his own. Twelve months of intensive language training paid off. They'd hold him by the ankles and lower him head first into the tunnels. It was his job to shout "come out with your hands up" in fluent Vietnamese. If the little bastards were there they'd start shooting, they'd yank him back up and throw in a handful of grenades and return fire.'

The two of them started laughing together, drawing a few hostile looks from the neighbouring tables.

It was a story they'd obviously told many times before, telling and retelling until all the rough edges had been smoothed off. It was as polished as a seaside pebble. There might have been a grain of truth left in it, but I doubted that. Then realization dawned and I put my glass down on the beer-stained cloth.

'You were helping Sally on the refugee story?' I said.

'Well, she sure as hell couldn't speak to them,' said Fender. 'She was a smart kid and could just about handle Cantonese, but Vietnamese is a whole different ball game. As soon as Healy gave her the story she was on the phone to me, offering to split the fee. She'd write the words, I'd do the translation and take the pictures.'

'Howard said you were a journalist.'

'Photojournalist. I do a bit of photography on the side. More of a hobby than anything, but I'm good with a camera.'

'Modest too,' said Howard.

'Come on, Howard, admit it. I'm one of the best.'

'You're not so bad. I've seen a lot worse,' agreed Howard reluctantly.

I wanted to ask him why he wasn't doing it full time if he was so good but there was no point in antagonizing him so instead I asked: 'How did it go?'

'Waste of time,' he said, stroking his beard. 'We spent the best part of an afternoon there but they wouldn't say a bloody thing. I got some great pics but we couldn't get it to stand up. Have you been round one of the refugee camps?'

I shook my head.

'There's a big one on Lantau Island, a ferry ride away. There are a few thousand refugees there, all Vietnamese. Some of the poor buggers have been there for six or seven years now. Hong Kong used to be a short stopover before they were taken in by Britain, Canada or the States, but they've virtually said that enough is enough. So they just sit there and wait.'

'Come on, laddie, it's not as if they're political refugees anymore, fleeing from Communism,' said Howard. 'The ones that are leaving now are economic refugees, they're just looking for a better standard of living.'

'You can't blame them for that.'

'Agreed, but you can't expect Britain to welcome them with open arms.'

'They could do more for them.' Fender looked at me. 'You know what choice they're given now? The Hong Kong government either patches up their boats and puts them back to sea with a week's provisions, or they can sit in one of the camps, with no guarantee of a place abroad.

Some choice, eh? Oh, what the hell, be still my bleeding heart,' and he emptied his glass.

'And the story you were on was to see if North Vietnamese agents were infiltrating the camps?'

'It would make sense from the Communists' point of view. South Vietnam is full of their agents, and all they'd have to do is pay for their passage on one of the boats and make their way to Hong Kong or the Philippines and from there to the West, assuming they don't end up rotting in one of the camps. Sally and I arranged to go on a tour of the Camp in Lantau, we told GIS we were doing a colour piece for one of the Sunday supplements.'

'GIS?' I said.

'Government Information Services – hear no evil, see no evil and tell them nothing. They're fine for shoving out press releases on trade figures but bugger all use for anything that even smells of a story.'

'And what happened?'

'Nothing, absolutely nothing. I got some great pictures, children behind the wires, men lounging in their dormitories, a woman with all her belongings packed into a small rucksack, all of it good stuff. But no story. I must have spoken to a score of refugees, and they all said it just didn't happen, or if it did they weren't aware of it. Sally gave it her best shot, though.' He guffawed, a deep-throated belly-laugh that had the table vibrating like an approaching earthquake.

'What do you mean?'

'She was practically pulling out their finger nails with pliers to get them to talk. She had spunk did Sally. She was a real trier. She'd ask the most goddamned impolite questions and I'd have to tone them down. Until we got to a face-to-face with one of the camp administrators, a middle-ranking gweilo civil servant called Barker. God, she went straight for the jugular, how many Special Branch officers were in the camps, how many North Korean agents had they found, how long were they going to keep the refugees behind barbed wire. The poor bastard didn't know what had hit him.'

That sounded like the Sally I knew, push, push, push until she got what she wanted, never mind whose toes you step on or whose feelings get hurt. Sometimes it works, you go in hard, question, question, question, until they lose their temper and give you the quote you need. Usually it's better to be more devious, to go around the houses, win their confidence and gradually pull out the information, but it's horses for courses.

It takes quite a while to learn the techniques. Your average cub reporter sweats up on an interview in advance, reads through all the cuttings and probably draws up a list of questions to ask. You soon learn that's not the way to do it, best to go in with an open mind, looking for the angle.

Sometimes, though, it pays to go in hard, to pretend you already know everything and antagonize them until they snap and you get lots of reaction. You can do it, but you have to know what you're doing and Sally didn't have the experience for that. It was just Sally being her usual impetuous self, head held high, leading with the chin. I remember her when she was six years old, riding her bicycle without holding onto the handlebars. 'Look Dad, no hands,' she'd yelled, until she lost control and grazed her knee and elbow on the ground, but she hadn't cried as our father picked her up and hugged her, her pride had steadfastly held back the tears.

She was a girl forever acting on impulse, but usually her instincts were right. What had gone wrong this time?

Fender had gone quiet and I suppose we'd both been thinking about the Sallys we knew, and I wondered how similar they were, if the girl who'd sat with her head on my knee in London had been the same cock-sure journalist he'd taken around the refugee camp. Had she changed since she'd come out to Hong Kong, or had I only seen one facet of her. No, I shrugged that thought off, I knew Sally, she was my sister.

'She was a good kid,' he said, softly, and Howard nodded in agreement. 'We could do with more like her in Hong Kong.' Fender's huge eyebrows knitted together as he frowned. 'If there is anything I can do . . .' he said, but he didn't finish the sentence, instead he banged his glass on the table, hard.

'Fuck it,' he shouted, 'she was so fucking young.'

Howard put his hand across Fender's arm.

'Relax, Barry,' he said. Fender shuddered all over and for a brief moment a flash of jealousy sparked through my mind but I ignored it, Sally and he were friends at best, nothing more.

Fender seemed to want to talk about her, so I coaxed him a little.

'What sort of journalist was she?' I asked him.

He thought for a while, and I knew I'd get an honest answer from him. 'She was a quick learner,' he said. 'When she first arrived she hadn't a clue, but she'd spend all night in the FCC picking our brains and she'd keep bringing in stories she'd written and asking for our opinions. She was a real trier, and she didn't mind being told. She just agreed with you and asked how she could improve.'

That was Sally, all right. She used people, but used them in such a way that they were grateful for being used. People got a warm feeling helping her, in the same way that you're grateful to the cat who sits on your lap and allows its ears to be tickled.

'Then she started getting some good stuff in the papers, mainly business stories,' Fender continued. 'She'd obviously got herself some good contacts and they began feeding her with top rate information, real Deep Throat stuff.' He nudged Howard. 'Remember that Securities Commission report on that toy manufacturer? Christ, that was a good story.'

Howard nodded. 'Yeah, we never found out where she got that from.'

'That's right,' said Fender. 'That was something else about her, she was so bloody secretive. She'd quite happily spend hours asking me questions, but she'd never ever let on who her contacts were or what she was working on, unless it was general knowledge or unless she needed help.'

'Like the Vietnamese story?' I said.

'Case in point,' agreed Fender. 'I'm sure she only told me about that because Healy had given her the story and she needed me to translate for her.' He fell silent again.

'But the story didn't stand up?'

'Despite all Sally's pushing, no. The Government clammed up and the Vietnamese we spoke to said they knew nothing about it, just gave us the same old crap about how they wanted a new life in the United States.'

'Maybe they were lying.'

'No, they'd sell their own grandmothers for a way out of the camps. If they knew anything they'd talk in the hope that it would get them a passport.

'We'd heard stories that Special Branch had put their own men into the camps, but we couldn't get that confirmed either. But that didn't surprise us, they wouldn't tell you the time of day. So what did we have? Sweet F.A. A fair enough collection of pics, but not the news story we'd hoped for. We decided to cut our losses and do what we'd told GIS we were doing – a general feature piece. Sally was going to write a couple of thousand words but then she lost interest and then she went to China for a few days. Shortly after she got back she died.'

'China?' I looked at Howard. 'You didn't tell me anything about China.'

'I didn't know. This is the first I've heard of it.'

'Why did she go?' I asked Fender.

'Something to do with a story she was writing about diamonds. She went to Zhejiang province, there's some sort of mining operation there.'

'Did she go on her own?'

'No, she went with Tod Seligman, he's fluent in Mandarin and he's always going in and out of China.'

'When did they get back?'

'About a week ago, maybe less. You should go and talk to Tod, I saw him in the FCC a couple of nights ago.'

'Tell me a bit about him.'

'Mid-thirties, good looking all-American boy. Looks like your typical CIA agent, light grey suits, steel framed glasses, short blond hair, blue eyes.'

'CIA?'

'Not officially, no, but you'd be hard pushed to find an American who isn't out here, especially working in the media. He's a copy editor on a financial paper but he keeps disappearing for a few days at a time and when he gets back it turns out he's been to Korea, Taiwan or the Middle East. He never writes a word and he's always vague about what he's been doing.'

'Have you got a number for him?' I asked Howard, and he pulled out a battered black address book from his jacket and copied two numbers onto the back of one of his business cards.

'Top one's his home number,' he said.

'Cheers, Howard.'

'Where are you off to, laddie?'

'Sally's flat, there's something I want to check. I'll call you tomorrow.'

I stood up and as I did the spotlight came on and the organ dried up in mid-chord. As I walked out a Filipina dancer in a red dress and a long white feather boa started to undress and Howard and Fender settled back to watch. I was glad that Howard hadn't offered to come because I wanted to be alone, to try to sort out the jumbled mass of data swirling through my brain and to assemble it into some coherent pattern. I reckoned that I'd be able to think more clearly in Sally's flat, and besides, I wanted to go through her files and check 'D' for diamonds.

Outside I caught a taxi, beating two Chinese couples to the doorhandle. I had to say the address four or five times before the driver nodded and pulled away with a lurch.

The lounge was the same as when I'd last been there, my empty glass was still on the coffee table. Howard had left the fan on and it was still ruffling the papers on the glass topped table and the plants on top of the television set were swaying gently.

Something was missing and I couldn't pin it down. It was like one of those kiddies' puzzles where you have two cartoons, side by side, and you have to work out what has changed, compare and contrast, spot the differences in the two pictures. Pictures. The photograph of Dennis Lai had gone. Howard had left it on top of the magazines on the coffee table and it wasn't there anymore and it hadn't been blown on to the floor by the fan. In its place were the Porsche keys.

I stood in the middle of the room and looked around slowly but nothing else seemed to have gone. There had been no sign of forced entry, both the grille and the door had been locked and the sliding window leading to the balcony was firmly shut.

The bedrooms were just as I'd left them but I stopped dead when I walked into the study. It had been stripped clean of every scrap of paper and photograph, even the map had gone from the wall. There was no mess, no overturned desk or drawers strewn over the floor, there were no ripped-apart cushions, no torn up books, no signs of violence. All the drawers of the filing cabinet were closed but as soon as I pulled one open I could feel it was empty. Even the piece of paper that had been in the typewriter had been taken and there was nothing in her wastepaper basket.

There was something else wrong, something different, the room had changed, subtly, but it had changed. I was sure the typewriter had been on the left side of the desk, not in the centre where it was now. And the wastepaper bin was right in the corner of the room instead of by the filing cabinet. The filing cabinet had been moved too, there were scrapes in the polished wooden flooring. It was as if the room had just been spring-cleaned by a careless maid.

I went into the main bedroom again and was hit by the smell of Sally's perfume as I sat on the bed and held Woofer close to my chest and rested my chin on his head.

'What happened, Woofer?' I asked, 'who's been here?' because the last time I'd been in Sally's room the daft blue dog had been sitting next to the wall with his tongue hanging out, not lying on his side by the pillows. I stayed on the bed for about five minutes but then I needed a drink. I had been sitting in the dark so I switched on the light in the lounge before filling a glass with a treble measure of gin and a dose of tonic. There was ice in the fridge in the kitchen but no room in the glass so I took a deep drink before dropping in a handful of cubes.

Drinking is part of the job, you learn that as a cub reporter on a weekly newspaper. People talk when they've been drinking so whenever you get the chance you take them to a pub and when you get to Fleet Street you graduate to wine bars. You keep the talk general and you make them laugh and you match them drink for drink and eventually you ask them the questions you really want the answers to and ninety-nine times out of a hundred it works. Sure, some stories come from press conferences and door-stepping, and there are plenty of contacts ringing in because they think you're a mate or because they want a tip-off payment. But when it comes to meeting a stranger, someone who doesn't know and trust you, or even a friend if you're running the risk of touching a nerve, then alcohol helps, it smooths the way.

You have to learn to handle it though, and when you're

young and drinking pints of lager you often screw it up
and end up being sick in the toilets and waking up with
a hangover and no story. It doesn't take you long to learn
the tricks. Always eat before you meet a contact in a pub,
or at the very least drink a pint of milk. You don't drink
lager or beer, even if he does, you drink a spirit and always
take it with water or a mixer. Whenever you get the chance
you just order yourself a mixer, but you mustn't get caught
because then he'll know you're trying to get him drunk and
you've blown it. You stick to that drink, no having a gin
then wine over a meal and then a brandy, you choose a spirit
and stick to it. I drink gin and tonic and now I can drink it
all night long without falling over and usually I wake up
with a clear head and a settled stomach. Usually.

So you match him drink for drink, and usually you pay so
he thinks you're a great guy, and then you gradually nudge
him towards the information you want, coaxing it out of
him the way you'd fillet a rainbow trout, gently teasing the
flesh away from the bones. Then when you've got the story
you speed up the tempo and start drinking heavily so that
he forgets what he told you and then you're home and dry.
The only problem is to remember what you've heard.

My method was to carry small pieces of card in my top
jacket pocket, and at some point I'd go to the toilet and
scribble down a few notes. The first thing I did every
morning was to check the pocket to see if I'd written
anything, it might just be a few key words or a name but
it would trigger off the memories and I'd have the story.

Drinking helps get the stories, but after a while it becomes
an end in itself. You go to press conferences where the story,
like the smoked salmon and pâté, is handed to you on a
plate, and you still drink, after which you go down the

pub with the lads to wind down because the tension gets
to you and the only people who understand, who really
understand, are other journalists. And then after a while
it doesn't matter whether you're drinking with other hacks
or drinking on your own and that's the point when you
start buying a couple of bottles of gin in the supermarket
when you do the weekly shopping and that's when there's
always a six pack of Schweppes tonic in the fridge. I've got
to that stage and passed it, and Bill Hardwicke had pulled
me back and dried me out, but now I needed to drink to
help dull the pain. That's why I was sitting on the balcony
of Sally's too-expensive flat drinking a gin and tonic with
too much gin in it. I could have sat on one of the chairs
or one of the big plush cushions but I wanted to sit on
the waist-high ledge that surrounded the balcony so that
I could feel what little breeze was there in this God-awful
town and because I could lean my head against the cool
tiles that lined the wall. Woofer was sitting on my lap with
his head against my chest and I ran my fingers through his
artificial fur but I was past the stage of talking to him. The
gin bottle was close by but I hadn't bothered bringing the
tonic with me.

I was five floors up and it was two o'clock in the morning
but it was still noisy, cars were driving down the road below,
insects were rubbing their legs together or doing whatever
it is they do to make their chirping noise, dogs were barking
and I could hear a bus grinding its way up the hill.

Framing the view of the ship-filled harbour were two
tower blocks, tall and thin with just a couple of rooms
aglow in each. Between them glinted the lights of Kowloon.
I had trouble focusing and the orange dots seemed to move
left and right and blur and I couldn't tell if they were on the

land or the lights of ships prowling through the polluted water. A taxi stopped below and its doors opened and slammed as a man got out and I leant over the edge of the green railing and then there were two taxis and then they merged to become one. The light on its roof went on and it growled back down the road and then something blue went spinning through the air, falling, falling and I reached to grab it but Woofer was gone, and I watched him spin slowly around until he hit the road below. There was no sound, no breaking bones, no blood on the tarmac, just a daft toy dog on the ground and I rested my head against the cold metal railing and held on tight to my drink and closed my eyes. When I opened them she was sitting in the chair opposite me, a smile on her lips and concern in her eyes.

'What happened, Sally?' I asked her and the smile grew wide and she shook her head slowly from side to side and gave a slight shrug of the shoulders.

'Who did it? Who paid for this flat?' I waved my glass towards the window, to the plant-filled room, and gin and tonic trickled over my fingers and onto the floor.

'Who bought you the car?' I asked, and she flowed out of the chair to stand in front of me, her hair swinging gently as her head tilted to one side. She shrugged again but the smile had been replaced by a frown and she crossed her arms across her chest and folded them, defensively hugging herself.

'What happened?' I shouted and then she was gone and my forehead was back on the tiles and I was looking at the road far below and there was a rushing sound in my ears and the balcony felt as if it was tilting sideways and then a hand grabbed my arm and Howard was there, pulling me to my feet and into the flat where he sat me down on the sofa in front of the coffee table. The glass was still in my hand and I raised it to my lips but it was empty and Howard took it from me and shook me. He had the toy dog tucked under one arm.

'Jesus, laddie, how did you get in this state?' he asked and I gave him the winning smile and dribbled.

'Stay here, I'll get you a coffee,' he said and I watched two Howards walk out of the room.

I wanted to call something witty after him, like 'you saved my life and now I'm yours forever', but I couldn't form the words and by the time I'd worked out how to say 'you saved' I'd forgotten the rest and I just let my head drop forward on my chest and closed my eyes. I fumbled with my left hand in my top jacket pocket for a piece of card but it was empty and anyway I couldn't have focused enough to write so I concentrated as hard as I could before I passed out, tried to ingrain into my synapses one thought so that it would be in my brain when I woke up with a thick headache and a furred tongue. The one thought was that the front door had been shut and the lock was a Yale and I had Sally's key but he'd still got into the flat to pull me off the balcony.

Howard took me to the hi-tech coffee shop on the first floor of the Excelsior and forced me to drink three cups of coffee as I slumped in a state-of-the-art chrome-legged chair. He made me drink it hot, black and with sugar, which was tough going for someone who was used to his refreshment coming cold, clear and with a slice of lemon.

The coffee went some way to sobering me up but I was still more than a little light-headed and I had to lean against him as we rode up in the lift, squinting at the two of us in the mirrored wall. I looked rough, all right, and I just hoped that the wet stain down my left leg was gin. The room was about fifty yards from the lift and we only banged into the wall twice as we tottered along the corridor like poorly co-ordinated contestants in a three-legged race. I stopped Howard halfway along and looked him straight in the eyes. 'Howard,' I said, 'I must phone my mother.' Then my legs went and he carried me the rest of the way. When Howard fumbled with the key and swung the door open I knew instinctively that my room had been searched.

Maybe it was the fact that all the drawers had been pulled out of the dressing table and were lying on the floor, maybe it was the fact that the mattress was half off the double bed, or the fact that the stuffing had been ripped out of the cushions on the window seat.

I also had a pretty shrewd idea who'd been rearranging my bed and it wasn't Goldilocks or the three bears. I could lay the blame squarely at the feet of three guys, not because my deductive powers qualified me for MENSA membership, but because one of the pairs of feet was sitting cross-legged on the single bed while their owner was cleaning his fingernails with a foot-long switchblade.

Another pair of feet was standing by the lamp in the corner taking the shade apart, and as Howard and I stepped into the middle of the room the door closed behind us. I turned to see the third pair standing in the bathroom doorway.

'Howard,' I said, my head on his shoulder, 'there's a chink in the doorway.'

'Jesus, laddie, don't you ever stop?' he sighed.

'Never, Howard,' I said. 'Not when I'm drunk. Especially not when I'm drunk.'

I tried to stand up straight but I was still dizzy and felt like I was going to heave at any moment and then the bastard behind me kicked me hard in the middle of the back and I pitched forward, only just managing to break my fall with my hands and when I rolled onto my back I could see he'd grabbed Howard by the neck and I kept on rolling until I hit the wall and then I pushed myself up on to my knees.

The guy on the bed uncoiled his legs and rolled off it. He was young and looked fit with massive forearms and a strong neck. He had thick lips and a wide nose, it was as if he was pressing his face to a pane of glass, but he moved well. He had style, grace and a knife you could slice a telephone directory with. He made small, swishing movements with it and the blade caught the light, flashing like Morse code. I forced my eyes away from it, tried to concentrate on his face, to work out what he was going to do next, slash or stab or if I was lucky he'd throw it and maybe I could get out of the way. The handle was black with a chrome stud that flicked the blade out and I was watching the knife again and if I wasn't careful I'd watch it go straight into my stomach. Look at his eyes, watch the face, the deepening lines around the mouth that'll show he's about to strike, the intake of breath just before he moves, the pull back of the arm before he lets go with the knife. I knew the signs, I'd watched the slow motion bits in the Sam Peckinpah films.

He was making circular motions with the knife now, widening circles, clockwise, around and around, holding it loosely by the handle, thumbs pressed up against the base of the blade, the sharp shiny hypnotic blade. I had my back to the wall, between the fridge and the dressing table, and the guy with the knife moved slowly sideways so that he was directly opposite me, his thick lips opening into a confident smile. The one by the lamp just stood where he was, hands on hips, a lazy grin on his face, waiting for the show to start. Both were dressed in open-necked shirts, denim jeans and baseball boots. Maybe they had the same tailor. The grip around Howard's neck must have tightened because he grunted, but I couldn't look at him.

I put my hands out to the sides, palms holding onto the walls at about waist height. I was sweating and it wasn't the gin. Jesus, I needed a drink. Then the knife arm pulled back and I tightened the muscles of my stomach in a useless reflex action and then the guy by the lamp spoke quickly in Cantonese, jabber, jabber, jabber, hands still on hips, chin thrust up, legs apart.

The one with the knife kept his eyes on me as he listened, but the arm relaxed and I allowed myself to breathe out, slowly. I was shaking, and the more I tried to stop it the more my arms and legs trembled.

Howard shouted something in Chinese and the knife man looked at him, just once, a sideways glance, the sort I used to give Andy when she walked past my desk in a tight skirt, quick and furtive. The fear of what might happen if I did anything got the better of the fear of what would happen if I stayed still and I made a grab for the dressing table with my left hand, groping for something, anything, to throw at my attacker. I fumbled the can of deodorant and it clattered against the mirror, but by the time the knife man had turned to look at me I had it in my hands. I had some vague idea of squirting it in his eyes but I was shaking so much I couldn't get the top off and then the knife started moving towards me. I screamed and threw the can at his face with both hands and tried to get my body out of the way of the blade. Both his arms went up to protect himself and without thinking I kicked him between the legs as hard as I could, still screaming. I was so frightened I had my eyes shut tight, sure that my stomach was about to be sliced open.

The kick knocked me off balance and I fell back against the wall as the air exploded from his lungs through clenched teeth and he bent double, the knife dropping from nerveless fingers as his hands went to comfort his groin. His face was about six inches from the buckle of my belt and I brought my knee up hard. Again I closed my eyes just before I hit him but I felt his nose shatter and blood soak into my trouser leg. He flicked over and fell backwards onto the single bed, wailing like a banshee, the cries of a woman, not a man.

I was exhausted and I leant against the wall for support, chest heaving. The trembling was getting worse, even my breath was coming in short gasps and I could hear my pulse pounding in my ears.

The guy by the door released Howard, then pushed him into the bathroom. He shouted at him in Cantonese and pointed at his face then slammed the door. It wasn't locked, but if Howard knew what was good for him he'd stay put. I felt very alone, and scared.

'What is it you want?' I said, and I could hear the fear in my quivering voice. 'Just tell me.' I inched along the wall and felt the knife under my foot, but there was no way they were going to let me pick it up.

'What do you want?' I asked again, disgusted at the pleading tone, the whine of a frightened schoolboy.

They kept either side of me, hands swinging freely, legs slightly apart, the confident swagger of men who knew they were good and who weren't going to be taken by surprise.

I had no illusions about what was going to happen next, the kick in the balls had been a pure fluke. My stomach was churning and it wasn't just the drink, it was my body's realization that it was going to get hurt. I felt so bloody helpless that I wanted to cry. Both of the men were younger than me by a good fifteen years, and that was a decade and a half that I hadn't exactly spent looking after myself.

They stood still, and the longer they waited the more tired I felt. The guy who'd been holding Howard was better dressed than the other two, he had a cream linen jacket on over his shirt and he was wearing black leather shoes with gold buckles on. He was quite good looking, hair neatly brushed to one side and features that made one think that maybe he wasn't fully Chinese, the nose was longer and more pointed, the eyes weren't so slanted. He was completely calm and breathing softly through his nose.

They moved together as if in reponse to some unspoken command, both falling back into stances that could have been karate or kung fu or a paso doble for all that it mattered to me. I was stone cold sober now, one of the side effects of the prospect of getting the shit kicked out of me, I guess.

My head was clear, adrenaline coursing through my veins cueing my body for fright, flight or fight. Fright was already taken care of, flight was out of the question so that just left fight, and that was only seconds away. I'd lost the advantage that comes with a swift kick in the balls, now it was two against one and this time I wouldn't catch them off guard.

THE FIREMAN

They were carving strange patterns in the air with their hands and then the one on the right turned his back on me and then his leg swung round like a whip and his heel caught me under the chin and my head cracked against the wall. He was still turning and he flowed back to his original fighting stance, arms waving, poetry in motion. Then it was the other one's turn, he shuffled forward and stamped his front foot and I looked down at the baseball boot and then his right fist flew forward and smacked me on the nose, just a tap but I could feel blood flow and my eyes water and when he stepped back I could barely see him through the tears and then he kicked me in the stomach and I slid down the wall with a volcano erupting in my chest.

When I came to Howard and I were alone in the room and there was blood on the towel he had in his hand. I hurt, but not too much, I guess the drink was numbing some of the pain. My left eye was puffed up and closing and two of my front teeth felt loose and my tongue was bleeding, but it wasn't so bad. I could live with it. I'd have to. The screaming mass of nerves that was my solar plexus was making breathing an effort but that could have been worse, too, so I made a feeble attempt to give Howard the wounded soldier smile until I realized I'd got a split lip. He dabbed at it with the wet towel and made soothing noises. The daft old bastard.

'I'm sorry, laddie,' he said.

'That's OK, Howard. No use crying over spilt blood.' He'd managed to get me onto the double bed so I just lay where I was and closed my eyes and tried to forget the pain. I've been hit a few times in my life, not so often that it got to be a habit, but often enough so that I knew how to duck. Sometimes you have to ask questions that people don't want to answer and you have to help a photographer take pictures that people don't want taken. Usually you can get by with some fast talking, occasionally you just make a run for it, but every now and again some clever bastard takes a swing at you. If there are witnesses then you just have to take it, and hope that your button presser is quick enough to get a snap because gentlemen of the press don't go around thumping the public, no matter what the provocation. If there are no witnesses around then you've always got the option of hitting them back and forgetting all that crap about the pen being mightier than the sword.

The first time I ever got hit on a job was up in Scotland, doing a shift for one of the evening papers. It was shitty work because evening papers have wickedly early deadlines which meant starting work at seven o'clock, before even the sparrows had started coughing up their morning phlegm. I'm never at my best until after midday and intravenous doses of black coffee, but in those days I was busy making a name for myself. Oh yes, I needed the money as well.

The news editor was a bearded Aberdonian with a gut that looked like an eight-month pregnancy, and twins at that. His name was Malcolm Fraser but everyone called him Big Malky, to his face and behind his back, it was all the same to him, hide like a rhinoceros with certain facial similarities too. He was an ugly bastard, inside and out. I learnt a lot from him.

I was twenty-one, I had my proficiency certificate from the National Council for the Training of Journalists and a piece of paper that said I could do T-line shorthand at more than one hundred words a minute, and I'd got about half a dozen decent by-lined cuttings under my belt and I was hungry for more.

I'd poured down two cups of murky canteen coffee and a greasy bacon sandwich and I was halfway through the morning papers when Big Malky bellowed from the news desk like an elephant in heat. I scurried down the office, notebook and pencil in hand.

He wanted me to go and interview a hit and run driver who'd been given a five-month suspended sentence after killing a ten-year-old boy who'd run out in front of his van. The police had breath-tested him and found that he was over the limit but he'd managed to produce a doctor who swore that the hay fever medication he was on could have produced a false reading and now he was back in his flat in Paisley and the boy was in a cemetery outside Bishopbriggs. Big Malky waved a handwritten note under my nose and said, 'Read this yer bleedin' Sassenach.' He had a sense of humour, did Big Malky. That and halitosis and a large mole on the side of his nose from which sprouted a cluster of black hairs that he refused to clip.

It was written on lined notepaper and that's always a bad sign, only nutters and children write to newspapers on lined paper. Only nutters use crayons, but among the mis-spellings and the bad grammar and the obscenities was one allegation that needed checking. According to 'A friend' who'd scrawled the message, the doctor was related to the driver, cousins once removed, and if true that would put a different complexion on the evidence given to the court.

Big Malky leant back in his plastic executive chair and put his size twelves on the desk. The chair groaned and either it or Malky made a loud farting noise that everybody in the newsroom pretended not to hear.

'Margaret is chasing up the birth certificates in Edinburgh, I want you to go and interview the driver,' he leant forward and the chair farted again as he grabbed a sheaf of newspaper cuttings and settled back, flicking through them. 'Kemp's his name. Go and have a wee blether with Mr Kemp.' He gave me the address and I practically flew from his presence, not because I was keen to get on with the job, more to escape the sickly sweet smell that suggested it hadn't been the chair making the noises. Both the early shift button-pushers were out on jobs and the office car was out picking up the editor from his Kelvinside mansion so I phoned for a minicab and waited for it in the street, the collar of my sheepskin jacket turned up against the biting Glasgow wind that chills bones and breaks veins and chaps your skin. The driver looked about fifteen years old and so did his battered Cortina.

His leather jacket was the same colour as the rust on the wings and the gear stick jumped out of first as we headed towards deepest, darkest Paisley. I kept the collar up and my eyes closed because at that time of the morning I didn't want to talk to anyone, never mind a moronic minicab driver, but he started a conversation anyway. Turned out he had a degree in economics from Strathclyde University and enough 'O', 'A' and 'H' levels to play a half decent game of Scrabble. That's what twenty per cent unemployment does for you. The car was his and he hired the radio from the minicab firm for an extortionate sum of money and if he worked seven days a week he could just about keep his wife and kid in food and clothes. He told me what he earned in an average week and for a while I felt guilty because it was about the same as I got for one casual shift and that didn't include the expense sheet I filled in every Monday. The guilt lasted about three seconds before I stamped on it and killed it. I was training myself to be hard, not to care, to be cynical and callous and tough like the seasoned hacks I went drinking with every night. I was getting there. We arrived in front of a soot-stained tenement block, four floors high with slates missing from the roof and 'Celtic are crap' spray-painted under a cracked window. Spelt right, too. Who said standards of education are falling?

He pulled the handbrake handle up a good ten inches before the car stopped rolling forward and asked me if I wanted him to wait. I figured he could do with the money he'd get for waiting and the few extra quid for the run back to the office so I said yes. Yeah, I was real tough.

Kemp's name was under the bell on the right hand side of the third floor landing which smelt of stale piss and cabbage. Or stale cabbage and piss. I tried breathing through my mouth but it made no difference, Big Malky and his farting chair paled by comparison. I pushed the buzzer and it rasped like a dying wasp and then I heard the sound of two bolts being drawn and a latch turned. The door opened a full six inches before a metal chain snapped tight and a shirt button appeared at the point in the gap where I'd been expecting to see a head. I had to go up another button before I got to a neck and then a full-lipped mouth that should have belonged to a camel before passing a long blackhead-spotted nose on the way to a pair of coal black irises set in bloodshot whites. Kemp was a big one all right.

'Mr Kemp?' I asked, in a high squeaky voice that came from trying to keep my nostrils pinched against the stink in the hall.

'Aye, what d'yer want?' he asked.

I told him I was from the paper and wanted to talk to him about the court case. He grunted and closed the door. Two minutes passed and I still hadn't heard the chain being released so I rang the bell again.

This time the chain was released and the door was flung open and I was looking at Kemp's bared chest straining to get out of its white shirt covered in green shamrocks.

'I'll tell you this once, sonny,' he said. 'Get fucked.' Then the door slammed shut in my face.

'Yes, Mr Kemp, sorry Mr Kemp, I'll be going now, Mr Kemp, sorry to have troubled you, Mr Kemp,' I said to the door, feeling brave now that there was a two inch thick piece of timber between us. I even tugged my forelock. Scared? Me? Too bloody right.

I climbed back into the cab and we were halfway back to the office when I figured that I ought to call Big Malky and give him the bad news. The third phone box hadn't been vandalized or crapped in so it can't have been there long. I got Malky on his direct line.

'He doesn't want to talk to me, Malky,' I said.

'I dare say he doesn't, you soft bugger,' he replied. Did I mention his witty repartee?

'He looked like he might get a bit nasty,' I said, trying not to make it sound like a whine.

'Back you go,' he said, and hung up.

'Yes, Malky, no Malky, three bags full, Malky,' I said to the buzzing in the receiver. It was obviously going to be my day for speaking to inanimate objects.

We drove back to the tenement block and this time my feet felt like lead as I forced myself back up to the third floor. Seconds after I hit the buzzer the door was practically pulled off its hinges and then Kemp was out on the landing with me. He pushed me against a damp plaster wall and grabbed me by the throat with one giant paw. He shook me backwards and forwards in time with his voice.

'Don't . . . you . . . fucking . . . listen? . . . Leave . . . me . . . alone . . . or . . . I'll . . . knock . . . your . . . fucking . . . head . . . off.'

I felt sick and my head was ringing. I could just about focus but it was an effort and I wondered what would happen when he finally let go of my neck, would I be able to stand or would my legs prove to be as weak as they felt?

'Do . . . you . . . understand?' The final shake was the hardest and when I opened my eyes it was to see his broad back disappearing through the door which crashed behind him. 'Yes, Mr Kemp,' I managed to whisper but I decided to save my breath, bending double and massaging my aching throat.

There was no point in ringing Malky, I knew exactly what he'd say, both to my face and as he put the phone down. Shit. This time the door opened on my third knock and I was halfway to hitting the wood for the fourth time when his fist caught me under the chin and sent me spinning backwards. The door slammed shut at the same time as I was slumping to the floor, gasping for breath. At least I hadn't bitten my tongue or lost a tooth. It could have been worse. That's what Big Malky told me anyway. And, you guessed it, I was to go back.

'I don't want to see your ugly face in this office without an interview with Kemp. Margaret's already been on the phone to say that we've got the bastard bang to rights. All we need is a quote from him to tie the whole thing together. Get the fuck back in there.'

'Yes Malky, no Malky, three bags full Malky,' I said, but I wasn't being brave because he'd hung up on me again. I was getting used to talking to a dead phone. There was only one thing to do. I needed the work so I needed this story. So I went back to the all-too-familiar door and pressed the buzzer and Kemp came out and smiled and put his arm around me and said 'Jesus, kid, you've got guts' and invited me in and poured me a whisky and told me his life story. Yeah, and if you believe that you'll believe the bit where the cavalry came charging over the hill at the last moment or the one where the good guy gets the girl and the bad guy gets thrown into the slammer. I'd stopped leaving a tooth under my pillow years ago, and I knew full well that if I went anywhere near Kemp again all I'd get would be a sizeable dose of GBH. Malky had done me a big favour by letting me know that the tip we'd had was kosher, so I sat on the stone stairs oblivious to the foul smells that wafted around me and took my notebook out of my pocket. My throat ached like hell but I couldn't stop smiling to myself as, in my very best T-line shorthand, I wrote down a one hundred per cent fictional interview with Mr Kemp, along the lines of 'It's a fair cop, you've got me bang to rights.' It was the first time I'd made up quotes to get a story to stand up, but it wasn't the last. I was surprised how easy it was. Ethics? It's a county near Sussex, isn't it?

I got a joint by-line on the late edition splash and a slap on the back from Big Malky that rattled my teeth every bit as much as Kemp's punch. The delightful Mr Kemp made a few threatening phone calls to the office and once had to be escorted from the building by a couple of security guards but there was nothing he could do – he didn't have enough money to sue a newspaper, few people do.

I slept and dreamt of Sally.

I woke with a start and when I squinted at my watch it was noon so I guess it was the bloody cannon that had shocked me out of sleep. My head hurt, a lot, I couldn't breathe through my nose and my stomach felt as if it had been used as a trampoline by a couple of Russian shot-putters.

I suppose the fight could have had something to do with it but it was hard to tell because that's how I normally felt after a really hard night's drinking. I liked to think of the previous evening's encounter as a fight rather than a beating. It made my ego feel a little less bruised, though it didn't do much for my nose or stomach. I tried to sit up and the pain brought back memories of the kick in the back so I stayed where I was and listened to Howard snoring on the neighbouring bed. He looked a lot older in sleep, I found it difficult to imagine him frolicking with a young Thai girl, even flat on his back his private parts seemed practically inaccessible. I tried visualizing all the positions, all the angles, but I couldn't see any way that he'd be able to achieve copulation. I reached over to the bedside phone and ordered coffee and orange juice. A loud snore reminded me that Howard might want breakfast so I ordered the same for him.

I managed to get to the shower and ten minutes under hot water ironed out some of the wrinkles and once I'd cleaned my teeth and gulped down a hot cup of coffee I could swallow without grimacing, though it still felt as if a hamster had shat in my mouth during the night. I shook Howard awake.

'Some nursemaid,' I said, but I don't think he heard me.

He made some sort of snuffling, gurgling noise and groped his way to the bathroom like an elephant looking for somewhere to die. When he reappeared it was with a large, white towel wrapped around his waist. He had perfect feet, the toes straight and square and not a callus or lump to be seen.

'How do you feel?' he asked.

'Like I look,' I said. 'Like a train ran over me. Do you have any idea who they were?'

'I didn't recognize them. Did they take anything?'

I checked my wallet. There was nothing missing and my passport was still in my inside jacket pocket. Sally's watch was still there. 'No, it wasn't a mugging,' I said. 'What did they say?'

'I don't know, I told you my Cantonese isn't up to much. When they were talking to each other they spoke too quickly and they used slang. I couldn't catch what was being said. And when they pushed me into the bathroom all they said was to keep quiet or they'd kill me. That was easy to understand.'

'So what was it? A warning? Well, why didn't they say something?'

'Maybe they were going to before you kicked the guy with the knife. Maybe he was the only one who could speak English. I don't know. It could be they were going to say something before hotel security turned up.'

'Hotel security?'

'Yeah, they came up a couple of minutes after you passed out. Wanted to find out what all the screaming was about. They came haring down the corridor and the three stooges ran off. You were still unconscious so they went off to get a doctor. While they were gone you came round and I put you to bed. You were fast asleep when the doctor arrived, he gave you a quick once over and said no damage had been done.'

I fingered my sore lip. 'Fat lot he knows about it,' I said.

'Security asked me if we wanted to call the police and I said to wait until I'd checked with you. They seemed more concerned about waking up the other guests.'

'Hardly seems worth calling the police in, does it? Seeing how much effort they put into investigating a possible murder, I don't see them getting excited over a simple assault.'

'The fact you were attacked might persuade them that Sally's case needs a closer look.'

'No, fuck them, Howard. We won't get any help from them, I'm sure.'

'OK. Whatever you say.'

'I want to see this guy Slazenger,' I said as he sipped his glass of orange juice.

'Slazenger?' he queried.

'The American. The Mandarin speaker.'

'Seligman, you mean. Tod Seligman.'

'Can you arrange it? For today?' He sat down on the bed and sighed.

'I don't see why not. He works the night shift and sleeps until the afternoon, I'll give him a call now.'

'One other thing, Howard. The ICAC. I want to talk to someone there.'

'Today?'

'If you can fix it.' Of course he could fix it, that's what stringers are for. As he phoned I dressed, slowly because it still hurt to move. I retrieved the can of deodorant from the floor by the bed and liberally sprayed my armpits, my groin and anywhere else that was likely to sweat during the day.

'Tod's not working tonight,' Howard said, dialling again. 'He'll meet us for a drink in Wanchai, 9.30. Do you want me to go with you to the ICAC?'

'No need. Just fix up the meet for me.' He nodded, and then began speaking to the phone, idly scratching his thigh under the towel as rivulets of water dripped down the back of his legs and stained the carpet.

I was adjusting my tie in the mirror when he finished. 'You're to see an ICAC officer called Tyley at three o'clock. I'll drop you off on my way home, it's on my way. We've got time to eat first, do you fancy brunch at the FCC?'

I shook my head. 'I'll eat here.' I watched him climb into his clothes and still couldn't work out how he'd ever be able to have intercourse so long as the laws of physics and gravity applied.

Shit. I still hadn't phoned my mother. Today, I'd have to do it today. I'd have to phone the office, too, and then I figured that no, a telex would be better, in case they started putting pressure on me to go back. There was a telex form in the desk drawer and I drafted a message for Bill, explaining that there was a lot of bureaucratic paperwork to go through but that I hoped to be back in London soon.

Howard was on his way out and he had his back to me when I said quietly, 'Has the office been on to you at all, Howie?'

I saw the shoulders tighten and he said, 'London, you mean?' without turning. Of course I meant London. He was playing for time, I could practically hear the wheels going around.

'Yeah, London.'

Howard turned, forming a smile with his greasy lips. 'One of the lads on the foreign desk gave me a call, asking what you were up to.'

'Did you tell them?'

'Let's face it, laddie, I don't know what you're up to,' he said, which was as good a way of not answering the question as any.

'Why didn't they ask me?'

'You'll have to ask them that yourself,' he said, and opened the door.

'Next time, let me know, will you,' I said, my voice flat and hard.

'Aye, laddie, I will.'

'And Howie?' He raised his eyebrows expectantly. 'Let's keep what happened last night a secret, shall we? No telling the police, or your friends, about the fight.'

He chuckled. 'I'll not say a word, but I think you'd better take a look in the mirror,' he said, and left.

He had a point. My lip was still badly split and the left eye was bruised and there was a two inch long graze under

171

my chin. I was examining the damage in the mirror when the telephone rang. It was Jenny.

'Hi,' she said.

'Hi,' I said. A regular conversationalist.

'I wanted to apologize for yesterday.'

'I don't follow.'

'I thought I'd upset you talking about Sally.'

'No, it's OK. Honest. I'd just had a rough day, that's all.'

'And still jetlagged.'

'Yeah, I guess so.' I was trying to work out whether or not I'd told her where I was staying or if someone had given her my number. Then I remembered the three questions game on the junk when I'd told her that I was booked into the Excelsior. I suppose I'm naturally suspicious, judging people by my own standards. Feigning interest, attraction or friendliness as a way of getting to a story is second nature by now, so much so that I assume that anybody who tries to get close is after something. So what was Jenny after?

'I enjoyed the junk trip,' I said, just to prove that I remembered where and when I met her.

She giggled. 'So I gather. Turned out to be a case of strife on the ocean waves from what I heard.'

'Oh dear, have I got a reputation already?'

'I'm afraid so.' Talking to her almost made me forget the pain in my chest and my sore face. I was glad she'd called. But still wary.

'Have you eaten yet?' she asked.

'No, just got up.'

'Can I buy you lunch?' It seemed a real invitation, she wasn't just offering to be polite, so I said yes and she said

172

she'd meet me in the Dickens Bar in the basement of the hotel in half an hour.

When she arrived I was already sitting at a corner table, well away from the bar. A brown waistcoated waiter showed her the way and when she got to within six feet a look of concern crossed her face and she said, 'My God, what happened?' I guess I still didn't look too good.

'Cut myself shaving,' I said as she slid into her chair and ordered a vodka and tonic. Today she was wearing a pale blue shirt, but again she'd turned the collar up. She was wearing a long white pleated skirt so I didn't get the chance to admire her thighs, and she'd replaced the pearls with a thin gold chain.

'Seriously,' she said. 'What happened? You're a bit old to be getting into fights, aren't you?'

'Thanks a bunch,' I said, fingering my cut lip. It hurt when I smiled.

'Well?' she persevered. She'd have made a good journalist, she wasn't going to let me laugh it off.

'Howard and I were attacked last night.'

'My God,' she said again, covering her mouth with her hand. There was no wedding ring. 'Where?'

I nodded at the ceiling. 'Upstairs,' I said. 'There were three of them waiting in my room.'

'Is Howard all right?' she asked, and for a brief moment I felt a flash of resentment at her concern for him.

'He's fine, they just pushed him in the bathroom. I think it was me they were after.'

'Why?'

'I don't know. They didn't say.'

'Did they steal anything?'

'Nothing,' I said.

'What happened, they attacked you for no reason?'

'I don't know. It was as if they wanted something. Or to frighten me. One of them had a knife.'

'What did they look like?'

'Hell, I don't know. Medium height, black hair, brown eyes.'

'That covers about ninety-eight per cent of the population,' she said, and smiled. Lovely smile. Just goes to show what an all-American diet and medical care can do. She was gorgeous.

'Did they have tattoos?' she asked.

'I don't remember,' I said. 'That's a strange question.'

'Not really,' she said. 'I was wondering if it was the triads, that's all.'

'The Chinese Mafia? Do they all have tattoos?'

'Most of them,' she nodded, her hair brushing her shoulders. 'They're a sort of badge of office. But if it was the triads, I can't understand what they were doing.'

'What do you mean?'

'Well, it's not as if they really hurt you, is it?'

I was crestfallen. 'What do you mean?' I asked. 'What do you call these bruises?'

She laughed, a soft, warm sound that made me feel good as she put her hand on my arm.

'Listen, boy,' she said. 'When the triads want to hurt someone they do it with hatchets and cleavers and what they leave behind doesn't generally sit in the Dickens Bar knocking back gins. If it was the triads, it was probably a warning. But why?'

'Sally, maybe,' I said. 'Perhaps she'd come across them on one of her assignments.'

'But why attack you? It doesn't make sense.'

'I know. Sally's flat had been searched, too.' I shook my head. 'You're right, none of it seems to make any sense.'

'Perhaps it was a story she was working on and they think she passed it on to you.'

'About the triads? Well if that's what they think they're mistaken because there was nothing in her flat and all I got from the police was a dress, a bag and the watch.'

'But they wouldn't know that, would they? Maybe you should try to find out what she was working on.'

I explained that I'd already done that, and told her about my visit to the *Post*'s office. As I did I realized that she was now thinking along the same lines as me, that Sally hadn't killed herself. I had an ally.

'Another thing,' she said. 'If she had done something to annoy one of the triads, they wouldn't have gone to all the trouble of making it look like suicide.'

'What do you mean?'

'They're not afraid of publicity, far from it. Triad killings are as public and as bloody as possible so that they act as warnings.'

'You seem to know a lot about triads considering that you're not from Hong Kong.'

She laughed. 'They're not confined to Hong Kong, boy,' she said. 'There were triad gangs back in my old neighbourhood in San Francisco. Everywhere there are Chinese, there are triads.'

'Doing what?' I asked.

'Usually drugs, they handle a lot of the drugs business from Asia to Europe and the States. And they're into prostitution. The closer we get to 1997, the more they're expanding their operations overseas. Hey, have you reported this to the police?'

'No point,' I said. 'They didn't steal anything and, as you so succinctly put it, they didn't hurt me too much. And after what I've seen of the police here, I'm sure they'll think it was self-inflicted. Shit, I wish I knew what was going on.'

'You and me both,' she replied. A waiter came over and handed down the menus. Jenny looked over the top of hers.

'I'd like to help,' she said.

'You are doing,' I said.

'No, really. You probably haven't even thought of one tenth of the things you'll have to do. For instance, did Sally leave a will?'

'What girl her age makes a will?'

'Exactly. So someone will have to look after her estate, terminate the lease on the flat, dispose of her things. Look, I don't want to be morbid but there are a lot of things that have to be taken care of.' She was talking briskly, like a school-teacher organizing a nature walk, and I knew that she was making sense.

'And you're going to have to decide what you're going to do about the funeral.'

'Funeral?'

'Of course. Will she be buried here or back in England? And if it's here how will your relatives come over?'

'God, you sound so methodical,' I snapped.

She bit down gently on her lower lip and studied the menu. She kept reading as she spoke. 'I wanted to help, that's all. She was my friend, and I feel that you're a friend too.'

'Hey, I'm sorry,' I said. 'I didn't mean to snap at you. I suppose it's just that Sally is still a very sensitive area and I flinch when anyone presses it.' I reached over and nudged her hand softly, just enough to make physical contact, to touch.

'If the offer's still open, I would like your help,' I said quietly. She nodded, and smiled again, and I felt better. A lot better.

I had the shepherd's pie, she had a salad, and we both seemed to have a good time. When we parted she kissed me on the cheek.

When Howard had said 'Tyley' I'd heard it as 'Tai-lee' and so I did a double take when I met him in his office ten floors above a public car park in Central. I'd been expecting a Chinese.

'Paul Tyley,' he'd said and shook my hand firmly and then waved me towards a black leather chair opposite his desk. His office was more that of a civil servant than a policeman, the walls were bare except for a few tasteful prints and his degree in a pine frame. No rusting filing cabinets here, everything was teak veneer and the carpet went all the way up to the walls. There was a pen set on his desk, a grey telephone, a crystal ashtray and a grey folder that had a black and yellow tag like a tiger's tail. I couldn't read the name on it from where I was sitting but I knew it was Sally's file.

Tyley had a boyish face, lots of even teeth, smiling blue eyes and a mop of light brown hair that he kept brushing out of his eyes because it was just a bit too long. With the desk between us he looked to be in his early twenties, but when we'd shaken hands I'd seen the deeply-etched laugh lines around his eyes and there was loose skin around his throat and the forehead under the fringe was marked with wrinkles from years of frowning. Distance was kind to Paul Tyley, but what the hell, I'm no picture.

'I'm sorry about your sister,' he said.

'Did you know Sally?' I asked.

'I'd met her a couple of times.'

'Socially?'

'Not socially,' he said, fingers absently running up and down the tag. There was probably a colour coding for the files. I wondered what yellow and black signified. 'She came in for an interview. Twice,' he added.

'She was under investigation?'

He gave me a smile that said 'of course' and I gave him one back that said 'I knew you'd say that'. We sat there grinning like a pair of frightened monkeys.

'Why?'

'We'd had an anonymous letter pointing out that she was a journalist living well beyond her means, driving an expensive car and with a wardrobe of quality clothes.'

'And the flat.'

He nodded, and then turned it into a head flick to swing the fringe to one side again.

'And the flat,' he said. 'A very expensive flat and no accommodation deal.'

'You check every anonymous tip-off?'

'Most,' he said. 'Especially those concerning the police, civil servants, jockeys and journalists. All of them are in positions of influence, and all can abuse it. Corruption runs right through Hong Kong. Or at least it used to.'

He sounded like a government warning, 'taking bribes can damage your health'. He opened the file and looked down, the fringe hanging vertically, a curtain of hair that hid his eyes as he read the top sheet.

'I thought this place thrived on corruption,' I said.

'Not anymore,' he said. 'At least not as openly as it used to. We've pretty much cleaned up the police force, and business here is a darn sight cleaner than it used to be. And we sorted out the stock exchange.'

'But why Sally? Why check up on her?'

'Because of the letter,' he said.

'No, I mean, why would anyone bribe her?'

'We're not concerned with the why,' he said. 'Just whether or not it was happening.'

'And was it?'

He shook his head and looked down at the file as he spoke.

'No, she was clean.'

'So where was the money coming from?'

He looked up sharply, squinting slightly as he toyed with the tiger tag. Tyley was sitting with his back to a large picture window, but from where I was all I could see was blue sky, the colour of a five pound note, clear and cloudless.

'The money?' he asked.

'The flat. The car. The clothes.' I gave him the smile that said 'trust me' and he gave me the one that said 'go fuck yourself'. This was the sort of non-verbal communication that was going to get him a punch in the mouth.

'I'm not sure I should tell you.'

'She's my sister.'

He looked as if he was going to say 'was' but he didn't.

'You're a reporter,' he said.

'So was she. If it makes you feel any better we'll say this is off the record. Not for quotation, etc, etc, etc.'

'I'm more concerned about why you want to know.'

I hate it when they talk like that, playing hard to get. I knew he was going to tell me, he knew he was going to tell me, but he didn't want to make it easy. He wanted to be talked into it, they always do.

'She was my sister,' I said, leaning forward to rest my elbows on my knees. 'Now she's dead and I want to know why.'

'We're not investigating her murder. Our job is to investigate corruption.'

'You were investigating her.' I stood up and began pacing up and down, parallel with the desk. The view was better, the sky was just as blue but I could see a bald spot the size of a digestive biscuit in the middle of Tyley's head, as bare as an airport runway. He self-consciously reached up to touch it so I guess I was staring. I looked at his ashtray instead. The telephone trilled and he listened before saying, 'No, I hadn't forgotten, I'll call him now.' He replaced the receiver.

'I'm sorry,' he said. 'Just my secretary reminding me about a call I have to make.' He picked up the receiver again and rapidly hit a series of buttons. The phone was similar to the one on Sally's desk, same design, same colour. He shrugged. 'Engaged,' he said. 'Where were we?'

'Sally,' I replied. 'Where was the money coming from?'

I walked over to one of the watercolours and pretended to study it, to cut down on the eye contact so that he'd be more at ease. It's easier to speak to someone who isn't looking at you head on, ask any Roman Catholic.

'She had a rich friend,' he said quietly.

'Dennis Lai?' I asked, and turned to look at him.

He raised his eyebrows. 'I'm impressed,' he said.

'Yeah? Well I'm not,' I said.

'She told you about Lai?'

'What would she tell me?' This wasn't getting us anywhere, so I decided I'd better play the nice guy, for a while
at least, and I gave him a winning smile. 'She didn't tell me
anything about Lai, I saw his picture in the flat, that's all. I
just put two and two together.' Humility, that always goes
down well.

'Well, you came up with the right answer. Lai paid for
the car, the flat, and most of the things in it. She was quite
open about it, with us anyway, but she made it plain that she
didn't want it generally known. He's married, you know.'

'She didn't do that good a job of keeping it a secret,' I
said. 'I've already met one person who knew.'

'That's not surprising, Hong Kong is a very small place,
and it's certainly not a place for secrets.'

'But once you found that it was Lai who was helping
her, you dropped the investigation?'

'No, we kept the file open.'

'Why?'

Tyley shrugged and simultaneously flicked the fringe from
his eyes. 'That's the way we do it. We rarely close files, unless
we get a successful prosecution.'

'Did drugs come up at all?'

'Drugs?'

'Sally was working on a drugs story, something to do
with a cocaine ring among the gweilos here.'

'Drugs aren't part of the ICAC's brief. But no, we didn't
even touch on it.'

My mind was whirling, firing off in all directions, trying
to make sense out of what was happening, why Sally had
been killed.

I moved back to the chair and sat in it. The ice had been broken now, he was talking freely, the earlier reluctance had evaporated like sweat off a camel's hump.

'So who would hurt her, Paul? Who would want to kill my sister?'

He paused, still fingering the tag. 'Mrs Lai, maybe?'

'A woman scorned? Hardly likely, is it?' She hadn't looked the killing type, but maybe the thought of losing all that money would push her to the edge. And it wasn't as if she couldn't afford to pay someone to do her dirty work. 'Did you come across any enemies while you were investigating her?'

'Not really. Certainly no one who would want to kill her.'

'Somebody must have hated her enough to write that letter.'

'After you've spent some time in Hong Kong you'll realize that anonymous letters are nothing special out here. It's a pretty poisonous place. But writing a letter is one thing, killing is another.'

'I guess so.'

He looked at his watch. 'If you don't mind I'll try that number again.' He picked up the receiver, and this time pushed the recall button, and then waited as it dialled the number. He swept his hair back with his hand, listened for ten seconds or so, then put the phone down.

'Still not there,' he muttered. He looked at me curiously for a while. 'I've got to ask,' he said, 'what happened to your face?'

'I was mugged,' I said.

'Did you report it?'

I shook my head. 'No, they didn't take anything. Look, what do you think happened to my sister?'

'How would I know?' he said. 'The last time I saw her was . . .' he checked inside the folder, 'four months ago.'

'How did she seem?'

He sighed deeply, folded his arms across his chest and settled back in his chair. Talk about giving off defensive signals, Tyley was practically going into hibernation.

'Please, I have to know,' I said.

He seemed to reach a decision, ran his fingers through his hair and said, 'The first time she was here she was helpful, seemed very interested in our job here, she went out of her way to answer our questions.'

'About Lai?'

'Everything. She quite happily supplied us with bank statements, invoices, receipts. I wish all our investigations were as pleasant. But the second time was a completely different matter.'

'In what way?'

'She went for me, verbally. Called me all sorts of names, accused us of persecuting her. Said she'd splash my name across the front page of the *Post*.' He smiled. 'I had to tell her that it's against the law to report on an ICAC investigation and she hit the roof.'

'Maybe you'd touched a nerve during the second interview.'

'Or maybe she'd just got that much more attached to Lai. Or maybe at the time of the second interview she really did have something to hide. Or maybe I just caught her on an off day. Did she often lose her temper?'

'No,' I said. 'That doesn't sound like her.'

'Perhaps it was the wrong time of the month,' he said, and looked at his watch. Subtle.

'I won't take up any more of your time.' I was going to stick the word 'precious' in the sentence but I thought better of it. No point in antagonizing Paul Tyley, I might need him again. That's the name of the game, you nurture and encourage the contacts you need, the ones you have to go back to. The rest you can burn, like tissues, use once and throw away.

I smiled at Tyley, gave him a friendly wink and shook his hand firmly. He obviously wasn't fooled because he didn't offer to buy me lunch or let me marry his sister.

On the way back to Sally's flat, lurching from side to side in the back of an aggressively driven taxi, I thought back to his question, 'Did she often lose her temper?' When I answered no I meant it, but now I remembered one occasion when she'd snapped at me. She was a teenager and the argument was over a boyfriend. Ever since our father had died I'd regarded myself as the guardian of her morals, whether or not she liked it, and I vetted her boyfriends with more care than the Vatican choosing a new pope. Hell, I didn't vet her boyfriends, I chased them off.

I was staying at home over Christmas and I came back from the pub and found her in the lounge necking with a spotty-chinned sociology student from the local polytechnic. It was almost midnight and he had his hand up the front of her blouse when I walked through the door. I'd grabbed him by the scruff of the neck and thrown him outside before you could say 'interfering with a minor'.

She'd stood in front of me and glared defiantly up and told me to keep the hell out of her life.

I said that she should be careful who she let touch her, that he wasn't good enough for her and she shouted that I'd never approve of any of her boyfriends and I said I'd approve when she made a sensible choice instead of the deadheads she insisted on bringing home. And who was I to approve or disapprove? she yelled. Your brother, I'd said, grabbing her by the shoulders. Exactly, she'd screamed. You're my fucking brother, not my father, and not my fucking husband and then she'd slapped me hard. Hard enough to make my eyes water. We stood staring at each other for a solid minute, and there were tears in her eyes, too.

'I'm sorry,' I whispered, then she threw herself against me and flung her arms around my neck and stood on tiptoe to put her cheek next to mine. I could feel her warm breath against my ear. She smelt of spearmint. 'I'll always love you,' she said into my ear. 'Always.'

'I know,' I said. I can still remember the heat from her body as she pressed against me.

Woofer was where Howard had left him, alone and unloved. I knew how he felt. The phone hadn't moved either. I picked up the receiver and pressed the recall button. The phone clicked madly like a grasshopper calling its mate, then I heard the ringing tone, then a voice said, 'Lai Kwok-lee.'

That's all, just his name. A direct line, maybe even a portable phone by his side. Two possibilities, either the phone hadn't been touched since Sally had been in the flat. Or somebody who had been there after she died had used it. I thought the latter was more likely, Lai had wanted his pictures back. Or something else. I told him who I was.

'I suppose we'd better meet,' he said. The words came out slowly, like treacle from a can.

'I suppose you're right,' I replied.

'Can you come round to my office?'

'Now?'

'Certainly. Where are you calling from?'

'Sally's flat.' I don't know why I told him that because immediately he would know how I'd got his number. I guess I didn't care, he was going to see me anyway.

'You should be able to catch a taxi downstairs,' he said. 'Tell them you want to go to . . .' and he spoke a few syllables of Cantonese. 'Can you remember that?' he said.

I said no, and I asked him to spell it out phonetically and wrote it down on a notepad by the side of the phone. I repeated it back to him.

'Excellent,' he said. 'My office is on the thirty-fourth floor. I shall be waiting for you.' He hung up on me before I could reply. Arrogant bastard. I had that written on one of my school reports, third or fourth year. Not bastard, of course, the governors would never have stood for that, but in the box where the form master got to sum up your character in twelve words or less he'd written that I had 'yet to learn that arrogance is an unproductive posture'. Nice line, that. Always made me think of an Alsatian with its back legs crossed. I've never been back to school, never seen the teacher who wrote those pearls of wisdom. One day I'd like to see him again and compare salary cheques. I went into the kitchen and fixed myself a gin and tonic. I found a fresh bottle of tonic in the fridge behind a red and white carton of Dairy Farm milk and a pack of Tulip unsmoked back bacon. Well, it was hot and my throat felt tight and dry. The bacon looked fresh, sealed in plastic, but there was a cheesy smell from the milk carton.

'First of the day,' I said, and raised my glass to no one in particular. 'But not the last.' It tasted good. It usually did. I looked out over the balcony. The tiles on the floor looked like the ones on the wall of the mortuary corridor, cream with a green stripe, and with a shudder I thought of Sally lying naked in the freezer. Jenny had promised to take care of all the arrangements, but I had to speak to my mother first and I might as well do it now because it'd be early morning where she was.

I had to check her number in the small address book which I always carried. She answered on the third ring and she sounded dazed. I suppose the doctor had given her something to take the sting out of her grief, but she was perfectly lucid, just slow and tending to mumble. I asked her what she thought we should do about Sally and she said she wanted her back in England. I didn't argue because the alternative was a funeral in Hong Kong where she had only friends, no relatives. It made sense to take her back, so I told my mother about Jenny and said she'd get in touch at some point and would she get the name of an undertaker who would handle things in Britain. She said yes but I repeated it all again to make sure she understood. Despite her grief she started probing about Jenny, who was she, how had I met her, all the questions asked by a woman who wants to be a grandmother.

She'd had no children by her second husband and neither Sally nor I had married. I'd come close twice but each time the job, and the drink, had been the more persuasive mistress and I'd walked away, much to my mother's undisguised dismay. I told her not to be so silly and said I had to go and hung up.

Lai made me wait in reception for twenty minutes before seeing me. A receptionist with shoulder length lightly permed hair and pouting lips asked me if I wanted a coffee and I said no thanks. When she smiled I noticed she had steel braces on her teeth. There were a couple of magazines scattered on a low shiny black table and I idly flicked through them. One was a copy of the latest set of report and accounts of Lai's company. On page three was a photograph of the man himself, just a head shot, in colour, the face serious and unsmiling, and below it a thousand word chairman's statement about how well the firm was doing, how confident he was in Hong Kong's future, how grateful he was to all the staff for their hard work and loyalty. Standard grade-A bullshit. In English and in Chinese. There were some very healthy numbers in the profit and loss account and the balance sheet. Lai was doing all right.

The centre pages were devoted to a montage of photographs of Lai's operations, the office buildings he owned, an interior of one of his grocery stores, an up-market Chinese restaurant, a gorgeous film actress at work on a film set, and a hotel. The hotel was a metal and glass tower, typical of many in Hong Kong, but this one was familiar. It was the hotel where Sally had been swimming, late at night when the pool should have been closed. It was the hotel where Sally had died.

My head swam and I gripped the accounts tightly and felt my stomach drop away. My tongue felt too big for my throat and I wished that I'd accepted the receptionist's offer of a coffee. The fact that Lai owned the hotel surely explained how Sally had had the use of the pool at night, and I wondered what other facilities they'd made use of together. I was having some pretty nasty thoughts when the door to Lai's office opened and he was there. We didn't shake hands, he just nodded and stepped to one side to let me walk through. The view was stunning, the whole wall opposite the door was glass, a panoramic view of the harbour and Kowloon beyond. Lai's desk was set in the middle of the office so that when he was working he'd have his back to the window. A smart move because the bustling waterway would be too much of a distraction. A long, low Scandinavian sideboard to the left of the desk was cluttered with a collection of crystal and a large photograph in a red frame. The picture was of Mrs Lai, about twenty years younger than the version I'd seen at the house on the Peak. She wasn't pretty, even then.

Lai motioned towards three low-backed settees arranged around a low coffee table, and we sat opposite each other, in silence.

He was wearing a dark grey suit with knife-edge creases, a light blue shirt with a white collar and a scarlet tie. He had a thick gold chain around one wrist, a wafer-thin watch on the other, and large gold cufflinks on both.

His hair was starting to grey and he had on the horn-rimmed glasses he'd been wearing in the photographs I'd seen in Sally's flat. The crooked teeth were the same too. His smile was friendly enough, but Lai was a hard man. The hardness wasn't a physical thing, it came from within. He sat with the quiet confidence that comes with having money, a lot of it. He was a man who knew he could have anything he wanted, that everything had its price and that he had enough to be able to pay it. What had he thought when he saw Sally, what was the price tag he'd seen when he looked at her? Flat? Porsche? And had she been worth it? Had he . . . God, the thoughts were back, the imaginings of the two of them together, her soft mouth, his crooked teeth. Oh God, no. I took the thoughts and strangled them slowly. I caught myself staring at Lai so I concentrated instead on watching a small freighter sail past in the harbour below. When Lai spoke it was in a brisk, businesslike voice, the arrogance lurking behind it like a mugger in a doorway.

'So you're Sally's brother. She spoke of you often.'

I bet she did. Well she said not one word about you, pal. You were a deep dark secret that she kept well hidden from me. From the brother she shared everything with.

He reached up to straighten his glasses and the sleeve of his suit rode down to reveal the watch fully. It matched the one Hall had passed on to me, Sally's watch. The one Lai had given her. Oh God, they'd had matching watches. The shared intimacy shocked me, it was as if I'd found them in bed together, laughing and kissing, her on top the way she liked it. I wondered if his had an engraving on the back, and what it said. I couldn't bear the thought of the two of them together and I tried to blot the images out of my mind.

There was so much I wanted to ask Lai, but all

that came out of my mouth was 'Why? Why did she die?'

'I don't know,' he said quietly.

The silence fell on us again and I looked at his wife's photograph smiling at me from the sideboard.

'What were you doing with my sister?' I asked.

'I loved her,' he said flatly, and I couldn't stop the snort of disbelief exploding from my nostrils.

'What did your wife have to say about that?' I said, trying to wound, to hurt.

He shook his head, sadly. 'She understood.'

'Understood what? That her meal ticket was leaving. I bet that pleased her no end.'

'Who said anything about leaving her?' he said, and that stopped me dead in my tracks. 'There was no question of me leaving my wife. She knew that.' He could see the disbelief on my face. 'So did Sally,' he added.

'Why the flat then? And why the car? And the money in her account.'

'The money was all hers. I never gave her the money. She wouldn't take it.'

'The car then?'

'The car was a present.'

'A Porsche. A fucking Porsche. What did she have to do for that?' The thoughts were running wild now, like mischievous dwarfs on the rampage, pinching and biting.

He was trying to calm me, using the voice of a parent speaking to a petulant child. 'She didn't have to do anything. I wanted to give her things. I loved her.'

'So did I,' I said with venom.

'I know,' he said quietly. Time stopped, our eyes locked as I tried to read his immobile features, tried to work out what he'd meant by that, if he really knew. He looked me full in the face as I studied him, perfectly relaxed, his lips slightly pursed, no wrinkles on his forehead. The martial arts expert at rest. Did he know? Would she have told him, would any girl ever admit to such a secret, that the love she shared with her brother was more than just the bond between siblings, that from time to time, when things really got tough, we'd seek physical comfort from each other, and had done ever since the first time, years and years ago, when our father had died and she'd crept into my bed. I knew that my half of the secret was locked away deep inside and I'd never, ever, reveal it to anyone.

Surely she would have been the same? She wouldn't have told him. And yet Lai was looking at me with an air of quiet confidence that filled me with such jealousy that I wanted to strike out at him. Instead I attacked him verbally, trying to wound him with words. Time started again.

'And your wife?'

'My wife and I have been married for a long, long time. There is a bond between us that cannot be broken. You do not understand.' He reached up to push his glasses higher up the bridge of his nose.

'You are not Chinese,' he said, as if that was the answer to everything. It wasn't, and I let him know it.

'Neither was Sally,' I said. 'Are you saying that she was happy with the arrangement?'

'Sally and I did not have an arrangement, as you call it. We loved each other. But love does not necessarily imply that we would be together, or even that we would want to be together. I have a wife, and children, a family. And with that family comes responsibilities, responsibilities that I cannot, and will not, walk away from. I have my family,

Sally had her job, her career.' He shrugged, the shoulders moving powerfully under the jacket. I remembered the photograph of him in a karate suit. At first glance he looked soft, a pampered executive in squeaky clean clothes and all the trimmings, but the stomach was flat and the legs in the tailored trousers looked strong and his hands had powerful fingers, the nails clipped straight across. He sat with them in his lap, fingertips gently touching, elbows resting on his knees.

'How long have you known her?' I asked.

'A year, maybe longer,' he said. 'We met at some construction firm's cocktail party. She stuck out from the crowd, bright, lively, intelligent.' The fingers were pressed together hard now, the tendons in the hands stretched taut. 'I want to find out what happened every bit as much as you do,' he said grimly.

'I thought it might be your wife,' I said.

He shook his head. 'My wife knew about Sally,' he said. 'And she knew that she was not a threat. At least not a threat to the things she wants, her home, her children.'

'Her passport?'

'She has that too, in her own right. And she and the children all have their own trust funds. All she was losing was my love, and that had died a long time ago.' He paused. 'Mistresses are a traditional part of Chinese life, or at least they used to be. Many of the older businessmen here still have two homes, one for the wife and one for the mistress, often with two sets of children.'

He pushed the glasses up again. 'I'm not saying that she was a paid-for mistress, don't misunderstand me. I'm trying to explain that my wife would not react in the same way as a European woman would if she found out that her husband was being unfaithful. And divorce here is not as common as elsewhere in the world. She knew she would not lose me, or my money – our money.'

'Well, if it wasn't your wife, who would want her killed?'

'I don't know,' he said, and sighed. 'I have thought long and hard and I just don't know.'

'Have you tried to find out?'

'Of course I have tried. As you know, the police appear to be certain she killed herself. They are fools. I have made my own inquiries but so far, nothing. But we have so little to go on.'

'Did she tell you what stories she was working on?'

'Rarely. She kept her work to herself, though I tried to help whenever I could.'

The door opened and a matronly secretary popped her head round and spoke to Lai in loud Cantonese.

'Would you like some tea?' Lai asked me. I said yes and he spoke rapidly to the woman. Her head disappeared and the door closed.

'I thought that perhaps it was something to do with one of the stories she was working on.'

'Which one?'

'I don't know. Everything she was working on disappeared from the system.'

'I don't understand.'

'All her stories have gone from the computer at the *Post*. And from her flat. I thought you might have had something to do with that?'

'Me?'

'There were photographs of you in Sally's flat. They've gone. And somebody searched the flat.'

'Looking for what?'

'I don't know. But there were three guys in my hotel room looking for something. Or maybe they were just there to frighten me.'

'And why do you think I was involved?' This wasn't going the way I'd planned. All the questions were coming from him. And there was a quiet authority in his voice that compelled me to answer.

I paused and looked for the signs that he was lying, the nervousness, an unwillingness to meet my gaze, a tightening of the jaw, licking of the lips, but there were none. Maybe he was telling the truth, or maybe he just had good control over his reactions.

'Yours was the last number rung from Sally's flat – after it had been searched. I figured that whoever had been there had been acting on your authority.'

'A good deduction,' he said. 'And a valid one.'

'Why search her flat?' I asked.

'Not search,' he replied. 'My men were there to repair the damage. Someone else had done the searching after you and Howard had left.'

'Yes,' I said thoughtfully. 'Howard.'

The secretary came back with two handleless white mugs on a circular wooden tray. They were filled with steaming water that had been poured onto a spoonful of green leaves. It smelt like newly cut grass. The woman knelt on the carpet floor as she served the tea. A nice touch that. I tried to imagine Andy doing the same back in London. No way. I waited until she'd left before continuing.

'Howard told you about the photographs, I suppose.'

'It seemed sensible at least not to draw attention to my connection with Sally. Late that night Berenger went back to the flat to get the photographs only to discover it had been overturned. So he called me and I sent help around to put the place in order. I am intrigued, how did you know that Berenger worked for me?'

'He had a key to the flat. I didn't think there'd be too many of them floating around Hong Kong.'

I tried sipping the tea. It tasted of freshly-cut grass. Maybe that's why they don't have tea breaks in Hong Kong factories. 'Getting into the flat obviously wasn't a problem for whoever conducted the search. But picking locks isn't exactly difficult. Did they take away the photographs of you?'

'No, they were where you and Howard left them. Howard brought them to me, along with all her papers and files.'

'Why?'

'Because I want to find out what happened to Sally every bit as much as you do.'

'And?'

'Her notes were just that, notes. And if there had been any clues among her files then whoever searched the flat would surely have taken them. I would think that they only took the files that interested them.'

'Which leaves us where?' I asked. He shrugged and sipped his tea noisily.

We fell silent, trying not to look at each other. Brother and lover, neither wanting to talk about the one common thread we had – Sally.

'How long has Howard been on your payroll?' I asked eventually.

'Several years. We have him on retainer as a public relations consultant. He helps us with press releases, our annual reports, that sort of thing.'

'Did he delete her stories from the *Post*'s computer?'

'Certainly not at my request.'

'He told you about what happened in the Excelsior?'

'He did, but from what he said I gather he spent most of the time in the bathroom.'

A phone rang and Lai got smoothly to his feet and walked to his desk to pick up a portable telephone, I guess it was the one whose number I had called from Sally's flat.

'Lai Kwok-lee,' he said, then listened as he walked back to the sofa and sat, crossing his legs. Even the soles of his shoes seemed polished. 'He is here with me now,' he said, and then mouthed 'Howard Berenger' to me.

'Yes, yes of course,' he said, and then placed the phone on the seat next to him. 'He is coming round now,' he said to me. 'Can you describe the men who attacked you? Berenger's description was decidedly sketchy.'

I recalled my attackers as best I could. Lai took notes in a small pocket notebook with a gold pen.

'I will try to find these men, but you can appreciate how difficult it will be,' he said when I'd finished.

'And if you find them?'

'Then I will ask them what happened to your sister.'

That was subtle, that, calling her 'your sister' and not 'my mistress'. Tactful.

'Can you find them?'

'Hong Kong is a very small place, and I have many friends here,' he said. 'We will see.'

He took a crisp white handkerchief out of his top pocket and began to clean his glasses, slowly and methodically. There were three blue Chinese characters on the corner of the square of cloth and they matched a set on his shirt pocket.

'I loved her,' he said, in a small voice that seemed strangely weak. 'And I miss her.'

Yeah, maybe. And what did she get in return? All his worldly goods, a nice line in patter, a quick screw in the afternoon on the bed with Woofer nearby, his big red tongue flopping out of the side of his mouth? I wanted to say something to hurt him, to find the words that would get under his skin and draw blood, but I knew that the anger wasn't rational, it was jealousy, green and acidic and eating at my heart. Not jealous of the man, or what he owned, his money or his power, but of the time he'd spent with Sally, before she'd died. Time that he'd have forever and that I couldn't touch. He missed her, well so did I, but his memories were fresher and mine were going stale and I wondered whom she'd thought of just before she died, me or him?

'I'd better go,' I said, getting to my feet. He stayed where he was, didn't even look up, didn't speak, but continued slowly polishing the lenses of his glasses, head bent down in concentration.

I'd got as far as the door when he called out my name, and I turned to see him replacing his glasses.

'I will help you find whoever did it,' he said firmly. 'But I want you to promise me one thing.'

I nodded.

'I want the life of the man or the men who killed her. I don't want you to hand them over to the police. I want them.'

'No problem,' I said. It seemed to make him feel better. The light streaming in through the large windows made his eyes glisten.

THE FIREMAN

*   *   *

The lift doors opened to reveal Howard picking his nose. He hurriedly put his hand by his side with a guilty look on his face.

'Come on, let's go back to the Excelsior and eat before we go to see Slazenger or whatever his name is,' I said.

We walked together out into the afternoon sunshine.

'You should have told me you worked for Lai,' I said, squinting under the bright sun. God, it was hot.

'I know,' he said. 'But you know how it is.'

'No, Howard, I don't think I do know how it is. The way I understood it, you're supposed to be on my side. You're supposed to be helping me, not spying on me.'

'What do you mean, spying?' he said.

'You know damn well what I mean. Why didn't you tell me?'

'Because I knew you'd blow your top. That's why. Look, firemen come and go, but Lai will always be here. The work comes regularly from him, slow but steady. The interest from papers like yours comes in waves, one day Hong Kong is flavour of the month, the next we're ignored. I couldn't live on what your paper pays me.'

'So that's what it comes down to, money?'

'What else is there?'

'How about trust,' I shouted. 'And loyalty.'

He laughed, a deep-throated chuckle that made his belly shake.

'Just remember, Howie, that when I get back to England I can do you a great deal of damage.'

The chuckle dried up but he was still smiling. 'OK, laddie, I'll remember.' His eyes were hard.

I followed him as he waded through the evening crowds, swaying with his gentle swagger as the flip-flopped through the rubbish littering the pavement. He ducked between a husband and wife frying pieces of pork and green peppers in a huge rusting wok and I knocked the man's arm as I hurried to keep up with Howard. He erupted into a tirade of Cantonese, egged on by his greasy haired wife, and I waved an apology.

Howard had turned off the main road and was heading for a bar with a garish red and blue neon sign in the window, flickering slightly. There were fewer people around, though the pavements and gutters were just as filthy. I broke into a run to catch up with Howard, who hadn't even looked back to see how I was getting on, and I fell into step with him.

Howard saw the cat first, lying on its side in the gutter, chest heaving up and down and I heard its laboured breathing from a dozen feet away. Its back had been crushed by the wheel of a car.

'Poor wee bastard,' he said, then pushed the yellow painted door of the bar as we stepped into the blackness. It was as cool and as dark as a tomb and as noisy as hell. Howard turned sharp left and we moved out of the gloom and into an explosion of red, yellow and green lights that blinked on and off in time with the Chinese pop song that blared out of a set of man-sized speakers embedded in the mirrored ceiling. The music was deafening, brain-numbing, but the dance floor was empty.

'This way,' mouthed Howard and pointed to a purple velvet-coloured bar where a Chinese girl in a yellow cheong sam absent-mindedly polished a glass. She flashed a smile the way the light goes on when you open the fridge door.

'What would you like?' she asked but I'd already made up my mind and before Howard could answer I said, 'A cardboard box,' and she looked at me as if I was mad. Maybe I was, but I told her I was serious and she bent under the bar, and reappeared with a tatty box that had been full of bags of crisps. She shook it and tipped out the last two bags, arching her eyebrows.

'Anything else?'

I didn't feel like smiling but I did and said no and then I told Howard I'd be back and went back out into the hot night, my ears ringing.

She was ginger and white and some time in the past few weeks she'd had kittens but now she was stretched out in a gutter with her spine broken. There was no blood but the bottom half of her rib cage had been flattened. She half raised her head and bared her teeth when I sat down next to her and placed the box just behind her crippled rear legs. She snarled and hissed and I loved her for that, for fighting and hating even though she wasn't going anywhere. Then her front legs scrabbled against the tarmac as she tried to get away and she pivoted around her splintered spine and she spluttered and coughed in frustration so I started talking to her quietly because I didn't want her to hurt herself, crazy because she'd be so high on her own adrenaline and hormones that she'd be feeling no pain but the words kept coming anyway.

There was movement to my right and out of the shadows stepped another cat, same colouring but bigger, tail bristling, green eyes looking me over, then the crippled cat I was trying to help. Maybe her mate, maybe her rival. A taxi horn blared and it was gone in a blur of movement back into the dark. The cat in the gutter started to pull herself along the road, claws scraping, dragging her useless back legs behind her.

'No, lie still. It's all right, it's all right,' I said, even though it wasn't and we both knew it. 'It's all right.'

An old guy on a battered bicycle pedalled slowly past, his head turning to watch. Then he wobbled to a halt and stood there, leaning on the handlebars with his finger up his nose, studying the crazy gweilo talking to a dying cat. I flared inside, a red hot anger like a parachute flare going off and I felt my shoulders tremble and my stomach tighten and I glared at him.

'If you don't get on that sodding bike and get on your way I'll ram it up your arse,' I said. Maybe he understood English but more likely he just got the drift from the way I said it. Anyway he went, almost colliding with an old lady laden with carrier bags as he looked at me over his shoulder.

There was no blood but even if there had been it wouldn't have mattered. I took my jacket off and draped it over her, gently, the way you'd cover a sleeping child.

She lay still then, purring loudly. A young couple walked past, dressed in identical denims and chatting loudly in Cantonese. He pointed and she laughed but they didn't stop, just hurried on to wherever it was they were going, arm in arm.

'Lie still, it's all right,' I whispered, kneeling forward

and picking her up, wrapping the jacket around her and putting her in the box. She shook her head once and lay still, breathing like a crotchety old asthmatic.

I sat back on the pavement, giving her time to get used to the new environment and me the chance to work out where I was going to take her. It was late evening in a city where they're more used to eating cats than caring for them, I needed a vet in a place with no livestock. The hotel seemed the best bet so I waved down a taxi and gently picked up the box, closing the flaps so that she'd be in the dark, sliding onto the back seat with it on my knees.

'Excelsior,' I said, but the middle-aged driver with a huge black mole to the right of his nose looked at me blankly.

'Excelsior Hotel,' I repeated, and this time he managed a 'Huh?' and the third time I screamed the words at him and she moved in the box, just once.

He shrugged and turned back to the wheel but at least he started driving.

I raised the flaps and spoke gently as the driver eyed me nervously in the mirror. I moved my hand to stroke her but when I pushed her head there was no resistance and it flopped sideways, her small pink tongue protruding between her sharp, white teeth.

I told the driver to stop and I got another 'Huh?' so I slapped him on the shoulder and threw him ten dollars and he hit the brakes.

I walked along the bustling road with the box under my arm, getting knocked and banged but not caring because she was dead now and there was no point in being gentle with her. The street was alive with noise, with housewives shouting at each other even though they were just feet apart, with children running between their legs and old women haggling and cackling with hawkers who'd set up their wooden stalls on the pavement, selling cheap clothes and toys, and frying food. An alley appeared on my left and I turned and walked down it, a dark place with the fetid stink of rotting vegetables, but at least it was quiet. There were stacks of wooden crates and metal bins and piles of rubbish waiting to be collected. I put the box down by the side of a black plastic bag full of what looked like fish heads and I stood there with my back against the rough brick wall and I looked up, through the network of fire escape ladders and air-conditioners, to the sky and the storm clouds above. I shook my head from side to side and closed my eyes, unable to understand how I could be so affected by the death of a cat. At least I'd tried to help, at least she hadn't died alone in the street, at least at the end she'd known that someone cared. The tears came then and I slid down the wall until I couldn't go any further and my arms were folded across my knees and I cried. She was my sister and I should have been there.

By the time I'd felt ready to go back to the bar Howard was on his fourth or fifth drink and was being entertained by a tall, willowy Chinese girl with long hair and a mouth wide enough to swallow a frisbee. He didn't mention my absence, or ask about the box, and seemed more concerned with the zip on the back of the girl's skin-tight tigerskin patterned jump suit. Almost as an afterthought Howard told me that Seligman had left a message – he was going to be late and could we go to his flat instead. Howard seemed to be in no hurry to leave so I got the American's address from him and left him to it.

Seligman lived in a basement flat a couple of hundred yards from the FCC in a ramshackle three-storey colonial building tucked away at the end of a narrow, twisting cobbled alley.

Grey clouds lay thickly across the sky, unmoving, waiting to pour down and wash the air clean. Above my head the gap between the houses was criss-crossed with washing lines, bare of clothes as the housewives prepared for the coming downpour. Windows began shutting and air-conditioners buzzed into life as the first drops of rain began to fall. I climbed down the roughly-hewn sandstone steps to the green wrought iron gate that guarded the entrance to his flat. There was a metal bell-pull set into the wall and when I gave it a tug there was a dull thud from somewhere in the bowels of the dark corridor that lay beyond the gate. A young Chinese boy wearing white shorts and nothing else padded out of the gloom and let me in.

'Tod won't be long,' he told me over his shoulder as he led me down the corridor to a gnarled oak door at the opposite end. Uneven beams ran along the length of the ceiling and the floor was bare concrete, so I guess it used to be the cellars of the building, or maybe the servants' quarters.

The boy looked to be about sixteen or seventeen but he had the sort of pretty face that made guessing his age difficult. The body below it was hard and muscled as if he lifted weights, yet he moved like a ballet dancer, gliding along on the balls of his feet. He pushed the door into a large room, surprisingly light and airy considering it was below ground. The walls had been painted white, the ceiling grey, and a large metal-bladed fan kept the air circulating. The light in the room came from a series of spotlights dotted around the walls, mainly used to illuminate a series of black and white prints of 1940 movie stars. One wall was lined with bookshelves, the books, almost all of them, Chinese, and the ones with titles that I could read dealt with Chinese political figures or analysed the mainland's economy. Deep, deep, deep.

The electrical stuff was all top quality, TV, video, full stereo system and a respectable collection of CDs, light on pop, heavy on the jazz. I found Winelight and after I'd slid it into the player and hummed along to a few bars I started to feel at home. I was pretty sure I'd like Tod Seligman, CIA rump-rustler or not. I think it was the bottle-filled drinks cabinet that won me over.

I turned to find the boy watching me like a tailor eyeing me up for a suit.

'Tod rang to say I should look after you,' he said, stretching his arms up to the ceiling and standing on his toes. I had a sudden vision of the fan slicing through his wrists and the blood jetting over the virgin walls, but then he put his hands on his hips and began lifting his knees to touch his shoulders, left, right, left, breathing deeply like a sprinter warming up. I couldn't place his accent, it wasn't British but it wasn't American either.

'Can I get you a drink?' he asked.

'Gin and tonic, please.'

'Ice and lemon?'

I nodded and smiled a thank you, wondering as I did if he took it up the arse and if it was Seligman who gave it to him. Homosexuality is still a crime in Hong Kong, even between consenting adults, but that's like saying you can't get a drink in Riyadh or a bonk in Brunei. It's done, but behind securely closed doors.

The drink he gave me had all the qualities I admire in a gin and tonic – it was long and cold and it came in a glass that didn't bang the end of my nose when I drank from it. And he used a fresh bottle of tonic.

Dotted around the floor were large blue and white chequered bean bags, the sort that are supposed to mould themselves to your body and do terrible things to your back. The boy was touching his toes now, and keeping his legs straight while he did it. I was impressed. He'd be able to tie his shoelaces without bending at the knees. I wondered when was the last time Howard had seen his knees, or his feet for that matter. He was probably now lying flat on his back while the Chinese girl did terrible things to him with her generous mouth. I asked the boy if I could use the toilet and when I got back he'd re-filled my glass.

I was just getting into the third track of Winelight when footsteps rang along the corridor and a soaking wet Tod Seligman walked into the room.

'I forgot my umbrella,' he said by way of apology.

I raised my glass. 'I'd never have guessed,' I said.

Seligman spoke quickly to the boy in Chinese and he scurried off to return with a large green towel that the American used to dry his hair.

'Have you been here long?' he asked.

'Long enough to go through two gins,' I said. He took the hint and gave me my third, pouring himself a vodka and tonic at the same time.

'Is it raining?' the boy asked Seligman. Who said beauty and brains don't go together?

'Pouring,' he said. 'There's a typhoon close to the

207

Philippines and it looks as if it's heading this way. It'll be raining on and off for the next couple of days.' He turned to me. 'Excuse me while I change.' The shoulders and trousers of his light blue suit were dark with water stains and his white shirt was translucent, a gold medallion on a thin chain showing through. When he came back he was still wearing the chain, but the wet shirt and suit had been replaced by a black kimono with a red and gold motif on the back and black kung fu slippers. His hair was neatly combed and he carried with him the smell of a freshly cut Christmas tree. He picked up his glass and flowed down into one of the bean bags. He actually looked comfortable. I was even more impressed than I had been when I'd seen his friend touch his toes.

'I'll leave you two alone,' said the boy and he flounced out of the room. Seligman did look like the archetypal CIA agent, with his steel-framed glasses, crew cut and intense blue eyes.

'Howard told you what I wanted?' I asked him. He nodded.

'He said you wanted to talk about what happened to Sally. I'm sorry. She was a good friend.'

There were those words again. Sorry. And was.

'When did you go to China with her?'

'About a week before she died. There was a diamond mining operation on the Yong River she wanted to look at.'

'In Hunan province?'

His eyes narrowed. 'Who told you that?'

'Barry Fender.'

Seligman relaxed and grinned. 'That'd be right. Once he's outside Pat Pong or Wanchai he's lost. No, Sally and I were in Zhejiang province, on China's east coast.'

'Where was this mine?'

'Mine probably isn't the right word, they were dredging up mud from the river bed and sifting through it.'

'How did you get there?'

'We flew to Shanghai on a scheduled service and hired a small plane to fly us to Hangzhou. From there we paid a taxi to take us to the mine. The journey took about six hours in all.'

'And what was she looking for?'

'She didn't say.'

I raised my eyebrows and gave him the look that said, 'Come on, we're both men of the world, you can tell me', but he looked me right in the eye and said, 'No, seriously. She was very secretive when it came to work.'

'So why did she want you to go with her?'

'She would have preferred to have gone alone, but she couldn't speak Mandarin. I was useful, that's all. But she was a friend so I could put up with being used.

'I wasn't being completely altruistic though. The mine isn't far from Ningbo, the fishing town where Sir Y. K. Pao was born. I'd never been before and I wanted to see it so I decided to kill two birds with one stone.'

I could see he regretted using the word 'kill' by the way he looked away and carefully studied a crack in the wall by the television set.

'The story was to do with diamonds, but from what her news editor told me it was just an advertising feature, a free puff for the diamond industry and the bourse,' I said.

I could see the word 'puff' didn't cause any resentment, maybe it's not a word that Americans understand. 'I don't see how an advertising feature would merit a trip to the middle of China,' I added.

'Ningbo isn't actually in the middle of China,' said Seligman. 'But I hear what you're saying. She paid for all the expenses, too.'

Winelight came to an end and he leant over and instead of slotting in another CD he just pressed the replay button. Maybe he was a Washington fan, too, or maybe it was because the pile of CDs was just out of reach and he knew he couldn't get out of the bean bag with as much grace as he'd sunk into it.

'So who would have reimbursed her?'

'I don't know. I suppose it would depend on whether the editorial was being supplied by the paper or by the advertisers.'

'I think John Healy said the advertising department of the *Post* had asked her to do it.'

'They'd have picked up the tab, then.'

The door opened and the boy walked in with a Sony Walkman clipped to his shorts and earphones plugged in, buzzing like a trapped fly. He walked over to the drinks cabinet, clicking his fingers softly to a tune we couldn't hear, picked up a can of 7-Up, smiled at Seligman, and waltzed out of the room.

'You see, I can't see why a paper would pay hundreds of pounds for the two of you to fly to a diamond mine when she could churn out a feature in Hong Kong on the back of a few phone calls. Did you take any pictures?'

'She had a camera, one of those autofocus, auto-exposure jobs. She used up a couple of rolls of film while we were there.'

'Maybe that was it,' I said. I swirled my gin and tonic around in the half-empty glass and watched the melting ice cubes bump together. 'Maybe they were planning to use a spread of pictures.'

'It's possible,' said Seligman, folding the kimono primly across his legs. 'But you're right, it's not very likely. Sally was always contemptuous of advertising features, she only did them for the money.'

I tried to read his eyes, to see if he knew about Lai because if he knew about him he'd know that Sally didn't need money so there was no reason for her to be selling her soul to the advertisers. If she was doing a story on the mine then it was because it was something that interested her, a story that would give her a kick. That's why most of us do the job, not for the money or the freebie trips, or to see your name in print, but for the knowing, the putting together of individual facts and opinions until you have the complete picture. The kick comes from having the story before anyone else, and being able to reveal it to the world. Look dad, no hands. Look what I found out. So what had Sally found out that had made her so keen to go to China?

'Will you take me to see the mine?' I asked Seligman, and I could see from the look on his face that he was going to say no, so I decided to appeal to his better nature and offered him money. A lot of money.

'When do you want to go?' he asked.

'Tomorrow.'

'Do you have a visa to go into China?'

I shook my head. 'How long will it take to get one?'

'Normally takes two days, but I have a contact who can get it done within a couple of hours, at a price.'

'How much?'

'Three hundred bucks – Hong Kong.'

'OK, we can get it tomorrow and go straight to Ningbo.'

'There's no problem getting to Shanghai, but it might be difficult arranging the flight from there to Hangzhou. We won't know until we get there. And you'll need cash, your credit cards won't get you anywhere in Hangzhou or Ningbo.'

'That's easy enough, I'll draw cash on my Amex card tomorrow morning.'

He leant back in his bean bag and ran his fingers through his short hair. 'You'll need to change the Hong Kong dollars into FECs – foreign exchange certificates. You can do that at the Hong Kong Bank, or at the airport. You can't use Hong Kong dollars on the mainland. And foreigners aren't allowed to use the renminbi, the Chinese currency.'

'Anything else I need?'

'How long do you plan to go for?'

'I just want to follow Sally's route, see what she saw, do what she did. In and out.'

'That's it then, passport, visa and FECs. I'll meet you at the Star Ferry terminal, Hong Kong side, at ten o'clock tomorrow morning. That'll give you time to get your money sorted out and for me to get the tickets. Then we'll go to Tsim Sha Tsui and sort out the visa and go to the airport from there.'

I stood up and as the muscles in my stomach tightened I felt the bruises where I'd been hit.

'Thanks, Tod, I really appreciate it,' I said, though I was well aware of the fact that he wasn't doing it for me, but for my money. Still, when you get down to it I suppose we're all mercenaries at heart. Take the money and run. 'I'll see you tomorrow.'

'Sure,' he waved his glass in farewell. 'See yourself out.' Just as I figured, he knew he'd have trouble getting out of his bean bag.

As I walked down the corridor his voice followed me, telling me to borrow one of the umbrellas hanging there if it was still raining. It was, an avalanche of water pouring from the heavens. An old woman hobbled along the pavement, seemingly oblivious to the downpour, so wet already that a few hundred gallons more didn't matter. Other pedestrians sheltered in doorways, watching the skies for any sign of a respite. But there was no break in the cloud cover above, and the air was thick with moisture, warm and clammy. The rain didn't make the pitter-patter of an English rainstorm, it came down in one solid sheet, like Niagara Falls, and the noise was the same, a single roaring note that went on and on. A taxi drove slowly past, the windscreen wipers totally ineffective against the mass of water. I put up the umbrella but it was no use because the wind was driving the rain horizontally. I got soaked.

The following day the sky was bright blue and cloudless and the air felt cleaner, all the pollution and impurities washed out by the storm.

I wanted to phone Jenny but realized I didn't know her number. I dredged up the name of her company from the dark recesses of my memory and used the telephone directory in my room to look up the number. She wasn't in the office but a secretary there took my name and said she'd pass on a message. Five minutes later Jenny rang. I had been in the shower and stood dripping onto the carpet as we talked.

'Good morning,' she said.

'Hi. How are you?'

'All the better for hearing from you. How's the face?'

'Only hurts when I laugh,' I said. I always seemed to be using clichés with her. She made me nervous. 'Seriously. I'm healing nicely. I'm going to China.'

'You'll hate it,' she said. 'When?'

'Today.'

'Have you got a visa?'

'A friend is going to fix one up for me.'

'Is it business or pleasure? Cancel that, stupid question. Nobody but nobody goes to China for pleasure. How long will you be away?'

'A day or two at most. I'm following in Sally's foot-steps.'

'Well take care. And call me when you get back.'

'Of course,' I said, pleased by her concern. 'Can you do me a favour?'

'Anything,' she said, and she sounded as if she meant it, as if I was a friend she'd known for years.

'Can you get hold of Dennis Lai and ask him to see if any of Sally's files were about diamonds. Diamond prices, diamond supplies, diamond mining. Especially diamonds in China.'

'OK, sounds very mysterious.'

'Could be something, could be nothing. I'll explain when I get back.'

'OK, bye for now.' I was the one to hang up first.

Tod was early or I was late, because when I arrived at the ferry terminal he was looking in a bookshop window. He saw my reflection and turned to give me a half-wave. He was wearing baggy linen trousers and a white shirt without a collar and he was carrying a small red nylon rucksack.

'You OK?' he asked, looking at my suit. I didn't look so bad. At least my FCC tie looked clean and new.

'Only outfit I've got,' I said. 'Did you get the tickets?'

He raised the bag. 'All arranged,' he said. 'Come on, we'll go second class.'

He took me to the turnstiles and gave me a bronze-coloured coin to drop in the slot. At the far end of the walkway was a traffic light, red and green but no amber. As we walked the green light winked off, the red light came on and a hooter bellowed. Seligman walloped me on the shoulder and shouted 'Run'. We rushed through a green-painted metal barrier just before it closed and down to the lower deck of the departing ferry. Seconds after we had sat down on a hard wooden bench gasping for breath the ramp was raised by a Chinese boy in a dark blue sailor's outfit pulling hard on a thick hemp rope.

Three-quarters of the bench space was taken up, mainly by middle-aged ladies with bags of shopping and old men reading Chinese newspapers.

'The tourists are upstairs,' grinned Seligman. 'This is one of the best views in Hong Kong,' he added, nodding towards the towers of Central. I'd seen it before from the Hong Kong Bank's junk, but I made all the right appreciative noises. While the ferry chugged across the harbour Seligman prattled on like a demented tour guide, frequency of trips, number of passengers, how cheap it was, how profitable, how it was ultimately owned by Sir Y. K. Pao's family firm which also ran the trams that clattered through the main streets of Hong Kong island. I let it wash over me, at least I didn't have to speak, there was no conversation to join in, just a one-way flow of information.

The seven-minute crossing ended when the ferry bumped into the huge wooden beams of the Kowloon terminal. The sailor released the rope, the ramp thumped down and we joined the flood of passengers that poured into the terminal. Packed together as we were, it didn't seem particularly crowded because Seligman and I were a head taller than most of the crowd. We swept through the building and out onto the pavement like a river widening into a lake.

The crowds were too thick to walk side by side so I followed in his wake, past shop windows crammed with televisions, videos and expensive electronic toys. Every second shop seemed to sell cameras, and the rest sold watches. There was a scattering of fashion shops, but nowhere sold food or drink or household stuff. The area was mainly for tourists and it was full of them, mostly middle-aged, overweight and sweating like pale-skinned pigs. The only customers inside the shops seemed to be tourists sitting on stools while assistants flitted around them like moths about a flame, pulling equipment from boxes, offering to do them a deal, latest model, best price.

None of the goods in the windows had prices on them, and the shoppers were doing their best to haggle in pidgin English, no matter where they came from. Walking past the open doorways it sounded like a United Nations economics conference, with British, American, Japanese, French and German accents all spouting numbers and discounts.

We crossed a main road and ducked under bamboo scaffolding that crawled over a modern shopping centre that was having its signs repainted. No space was wasted; even the alleys between the tall buildings were lined with open air shops, small barrows selling T-shirts with 'I love Hong Kong' or compact discs or toiletries. In front of a hi-tech computer shop an old man had set up his shoe-shine business, squatting next to a line of well-used brushes and cans of Kiwi polish as a customer stood with one foot on a small wooden box. The old man leant forward, spat noisily onto the gold-buckled shoe, and then vigorously worked in the saliva and polish with a yellow dust cloth.

'This is it,' said Seligman, and led me through a shopping arcade to a lift lobby.

'What's this place called again?' I asked him as we waited for a lift to arrive.

'Chung King Mansion,' he said. 'It's a rabbit warren of cheap guesthouses, Indian restaurants, tailors and shops. It's one of the cheapest places to stay in Hong Kong, so long as you can put up with the rats, insects and bloodstains. There's usually at least one stabbing here over the weekend.'

We were joined by a group of Indian teenagers as the lift doors opened and we all crammed in. As the doors began to close a Chinese family, mother, father and three children slipped in and we were shoulder to shoulder as the lift jerked up, a constant shuddering motion that did nothing for my nerves. My nose was about two inches from the head of one of the teenagers and the smell of spices and garlic on top of the aftershave and sweat was playing havoc with my stomach. I looked at Seligman and grimaced. The lift juddered to a halt, the Chinese family squeezed out and then we were off again. There was a typewritten certificate Sellotaped above the panel of floor buttons saying that the lift and its safety mechanisms had been inspected two months earlier and I wondered who had looked after the inspector's guide dog while he'd checked this one over. Seligman and I got out on the ninth floor and he took me down a dingy corridor to a door with frosted glass. Beyond was a small waiting room with half a dozen blue plastic bucket seats facing a wall in which was set a small serving hatch. The American took my passport and handed it along with his to the man sitting on the other side of the hatch. He passed through a handful of red notes and then asked me if I had two photographs of myself. I did, in my wallet, and I gave them to him. They too went through the hole in the wall.

'Now we wait,' he said, and we sat and watched the hatch. Not a lot happened for an hour and a half during which time Seligman did little else but talk, about his college days, how much he loved China, the politics of Hong Kong, where you could get the best Peking duck (I asked him if that was Cockney rhyming slang but he didn't seem to have a sense of humour) and where the best hi-fi bargains were to be had. Time dragged. A young couple, Germans or Dutch, I couldn't tell which, came in and handed their passports and money through the hatch and then sat down and began talking together quietly. I was just toying with the idea of introducing them to Seligman so that I could leave the three of them to it when a hand appeared in the hatchway clutching our passports. Seligman took them, spoke to the man in Chinese and then we left.

'How does he do that?' I asked.

'Do what?'

'Get the visas so quickly?'

'Normally you go to China Travel Service but the little guy back there has a cousin or something in the visa department. Saves a lot of time. Hong Kong's built on the principle of it's not what you know, it's who you know. Or even better, who you're related to.' He flagged down a taxi and we drove to the airport, getting there just half an hour before the Dragonair flight was due to leave for Shanghai.

Shanghai airport was basic, surly immigration officials, clumps of inert porters and damp-eyed relatives. It was missing a few things, like signs pointing to the exit, but Seligman knew which way to go. Outside it was every bit as hot and clammy as Hong Kong, and I took my jacket off and slung it over my shoulder. We walked alongside the terminal building and turned right, across a grass strip to a line of four hangars. All were empty. The American spotted a mechanic in oil-smeared blue overalls and he went over to speak to him. I stayed in the shade while Seligman got into an animated conversation, pulling out his wallet, waving notes around and at one point seizing the man by his shoulder. It didn't seem to be doing much good because the mechanic kept on shaking his head and shrugging.

Eventually he gave up and walked back.

'No can do,' he said. 'All charters are out and they won't be free for the next two days.'

'Shit,' I said. 'How long will it take by road?'

'To Ningbo? Three and a half hours, maybe four.'

'What about hiring a car?'

'We could, but I'm not sure of the way.'

'Let's take a taxi then.'

'I doubt if one of the airport taxis will want to go all that way. I'll ask, though.'

We went back to the taxi rank and when we had reached the head of the queue Seligman stuck his head through the passenger window and spoke to the driver. When he pulled his head back out he was smiling. 'He says he has a cousin who'll take us. Get in.'

The air-conditioning was full on and my temperature soon got back to normal. Shanghai was noisy and dirty and packed with people and cars. There were none of the tall glistening skyscrapers that gave Hong Kong its impressive skyline, just grubby store buildings that looked more like Aberdeen than how I'd imagined a Chinese city would be. The cars were constantly honking at each other and swerving to avoid pedestrians who were forced off the mobbed pavements and into the rubbish-littered gutters. We drove alongside a river that was every bit as busy as the roads, with barges, steamers and pleasure boats all jostling for space among the floating garbage.

I made the mistake of asking Seligman what the river was called and he launched into a geography and history lesson, starting from its beginnings as a fishing village on the Huangpu River in 262 BC and working up to its present fourteen million population. I lost interest when BC became AD. God, he could be a boring fart at times.

He was giving me a breakdown on the twelve urban districts when we stopped in front of a rundown garage with an old-fashioned petrol pump in front of it, like a sentry on guard duty. Our driver sounded his horn three or four times and a wooden door creaked open to reveal a worried-looking middle-aged Chinese, bare-chested and wearing the bottom half of a green track suit. The door he'd opened led to a workshop with a table full of car parts and tools.

THE FIREMAN

Seligman paid off the taxi and began talking to the garage owner. Again there seemed to be a lot of head shaking and shrugging and I was expecting the worst until Seligman turned to me and said, 'He said he'll take us, it's just a matter of how much we pay him.'

'Whatever he wants,' I said, impatiently.

'That would take all the fun out of it, for both of us,' he said, placing his rucksack on the ground. They argued fiercely for a few minutes and then the deal was obviously done because the American turned round and gave me the thumbs up.

'Way to go,' he said. 'He says he'll drive us, but he wants his brother to come as back up. The two of them will take it in turns.'

'Can we leave now?'

'Straight away. By the way, his name's Wah-yim, his brother's called Elvis.'

'Elvis?'

Wah-yim shouted into the workshop and Seligman didn't have to explain because the boy who came out carrying the top half of the track suit was obviously Elvis. His hair was lacquered into a backswept quiff that bobbed as he walked and he'd been trying to grow sideburns but without much success. His jeans were skin-tight and over a white T-shirt he wore a black leather jacket with the collar up, like something out of *Rebel Without A Cause*. As he threw the track suit top to his brother the sun glinted on the lines of chrome studs that spelt out 'ELVIS' on his back. The kid had style all right. He was chewing gum and trying to sneer at the same time as Wah-yim explained the deal to him.

They led us through the workshop and out into a courtyard beyond, where chickens pecked at the floor, a pig wallowed happily in a mud bath and an old dust-covered Mercedes Benz estate sat in the sun and brooded.

It looked like a clapped out pile of scrap in a breaker's yard but the tyres had plenty of tread on them and the engine started first time when Wah-yim turned the key. The exhaust came out black for a few seconds and then the engine purred quietly while Elvis opened a pair of wooden gates that cut the yard off from the road.

The chickens scattered noisily as Wah-yim guided the car out. Seligman and I walked by the side and Elvis closed the gates behind us. Wah-yim set the wipers going and jetted water onto the windscreen until the dust became mud smears and then disappeared. Elvis took a couple of red metal petrol cans and a tin funnel out of the back of the car and took them to the pump, returning five minutes later smelling of petrol. The cans and funnel went back into the car, next to a crate of local beer and cartons of Marlboro cigarettes.

Elvis got into the front passenger seat and shoved a cassette into the player as Seligman and I slid into the back. The real Elvis began belting out of four speakers that *You ain't nothing but a hound dog*. Our Elvis began backcombing his quiff with a steel comb while Seligman lay back and closed his eyes as he tapped out the tune with his fingers against the door. *And you ain't no friend of mine*.

It took about ten minutes to drive out of the city and we were soon on a four-lane road that cut across the countryside through flat fields and sparse woods. Elvis turned round in his seat and pointed at the crate of beer in the back and I handed a couple of bottles to him. He smashed off the metal caps on the dashboard and handed one to Wah-yim before draining his in two swallows. He dropped the empty bottle on the floor and then settled back in his seat and was soon snoring loudly. I dozed in and out of sleep for two and a half hours until the car turned sharply to the left and the hypnotic vibration of the tarmac road was replaced with the rough rumble of a cobbled road that wound its way between two granite-topped hills. Seligman opened his eyes and rubbed the sleep out of them like a small boy. 'Nearly there,' he said. Elvis was still snoring, his knees wedged up against the dashboard. Wah-yim spoke to him a couple of times, but getting no reply he banged him on the top of his head with his fist.

Elvis shot upright in his seat, his hands reaching for his head, and he yelled at the driver. I couldn't understand the words but I got the drift – 'Lay off the hair, sonny, or you'll be eating hospital food for a month.' He began pampering his quiff as if he was preparing a Yorkshire terrier for its first show.

When he was satisfied he gestured for another two bottles of beer. He smashed them open but this time made to keep them both until Wah-yim grabbed him by the ear and pulled hard. Elvis thrust one of the bottles at him and grinned.

The air was thick with the smell of beer and sweat and fumes from the petrol-filled cans behind us so I wound down the window and sucked in some warm air from outside, though as we were driving past a sprawling pig farm at the time it wasn't much of an improvement.

The road we were on linked a series of small villages like pearls on a chain, and as we drove through children and dogs would watch us go past. One small boy scraped a stick alongside the Merc as Wah-yim slowed to let a sunbathing dog haul itself to its feet and amble off. Wah-yim yelled at the boy and the boy screamed back and the dog barked. It reminded me of the Gorbals.

Seligman was fully awake now and looking intently through the side window. 'There's a turn off somewhere near here,' he explained. 'It's very easy to miss.' We were rattling through rice fields now, women in circular straw hats standing knee deep in brackish water were doing something with wooden hoes but they were too far away for me to see what. Seligman pointed and spoke to the driver in Chinese and we turned off the cobbled road onto a raised mud track that cut between two massive fields. Looking sideways gave the illusion of the car driving across the surface of the water as it lurched from pothole to pothole. Wah-yim slowed right down but even so the rear wheels kept sliding as they lost traction on the slippery surface. Elvis wound down his window and threw his empty bottles out one by one, doing his best to hit the farmers but all he managed to do was splash a young girl with pigtails that reached to her waist. She stood glaring at the car, her hands defiantly on her hips, and it was obvious even at a distance that she was cursing us loudly. Elvis threw his head back and laughed, and then waggled his leg out of the window.

After half a mile or so we slid down off the track and back onto another cobbled road, this time a single track that twisted and turned through hills dotted with spindly ill-nourished trees.

Seligman leant across and tapped the driver on the shoulder and we slowed to a halt.

'Why here?' I asked.

'The site is about a mile further along this track, but we can get a better view from the top of this hill.'

We left Elvis and Wah-yim opening another couple

of bottles and lighting cigarettes, oblivious to the smell of petrol.

The hill wasn't too steep, but even so I had to reach forward with my hands in a few places to steady myself. Sir Edmund Hillary I'm not, and I gave up any exercise that involves wearing shorts when I was eighteen so I took it slowly, while Seligman scampered up to the top. He looked the sort who'd do five hundred push-ups every morning before taking an icy shower. I could have kept up with him if I wasn't still feeling the effects of the kick in the stomach. That's what I told myself anyway.

Seligman got to the top of the hill some thirty seconds or so before me and he waited next to a large bush with thick, oval-shaped leaves. The air was cooler there, and as I joined him I could see why. About a quarter of a mile away flowed a wide, murky river and the wind was obviously blowing across it and up the hillside. The bank on the far side was just a greenish smudge with grey mist-shrouded mountains behind. The river could have been half a mile wide, or a mile, or more, there was no way of telling. There were two modern boats close to the shore on our side, white hulls with bright orange superstructures. One was heading towards us, one away. The incoming boat turned to sail alongside a wooden pier that jutted into the water, showing that most of the deck space at the rear was filled with mud. At the back was a crane-like object with a ribbed metal scoop at the end like the jaws of bulldozer.

At the base of the hill was a cluster of wooden huts and between it and the river was a corrugated iron shed, three storeys high and covering an area equivalent to a first division football pitch with room for the police to surround it to keep the crowd back. Linking the shed to the pier was a conveyor belt, an endless rubber strip that moved on stainless steel rollers suspended ten feet above the ground by wooden poles set in threes like unfinished campfires. Just before it reached the shed it veered up and disappeared into a hole on the top floor. As we watched, the boat began to dump its load of mud onto the belt, scoop by scoop.

'What happens inside the shed?' I asked.

'The mud gets washed through a series of metal screens to separate out all the stones and rocks and stuff. Then they use some sort of filtration system to separate out all the mud and smaller bits of crud.'

'And that just leaves diamonds? Sounds simple.'

'Well, there's a bit more to it than that, but basically it is simple. Sally said it was like panning for gold but on a bigger scale.'

'How big are the diamonds?'

'You can hardly call them diamonds, it's more like diamond dust, very fine particles. They use them to coat drills, grinding machinery, that sort of thing. Every ton of mud produces a gram or two, but they sift through mountains of the stuff every day.'

The long, thin heap of mud had reached the hole in the shed and it poured through like a worm burrowing into the earth.

'They ever find any big stones, diamonds I mean?'

'Sally said no, she said they never found anything that could be worn in a ring, industrial quality only.'

The huts and the shed were contained in a triangular compound, bounded on each side by a ten-foot high wire fence topped with rotating metal spikes. The base of the triangle ran alongside the river bank and the apex touched the bottom of the hill on which we stood. There was only one way in, a gate that blocked the road and which was guarded by two men in dark blue uniforms holding what seemed to be rifles, or shotguns. By the side of the gate was a Portakabin with the windows blocked off with sheets of plywood.

A group of workers, their overalls covered in the red mud, walked out of the shed towards the Portakabin. One of the guards opened the door and they trooped in.

'Was security as tight last time you were here?'

'Yes, but they didn't have guns then.'

'What's in the cabin?'

'They check out the workers before they leave the camp, there's an X-ray machine in there, or an ultra-sound, or something. They put them all through it before they let them out.'

'They X-ray them every day? I thought X-rays were dangerous.'

'Not every day,' he said, pulling one of the leaves off the bush and rolling it between the palms of his hands. 'They live in the huts down there most of the time.'

'How close is the nearest town?'

'There's a village about a mile down the road, round the hill.'

'But the workers live on the camp. Why would they do that?'

'I don't know,' he said.

'And why such tight security, if all they're producing are industrial diamonds? Why go to all the trouble?'

I sat down next to the bush and watched the men come out of the cabin one by one and pass through the gate. Padlocked to the outside of the fence was a line of twenty or so bicycles and before long the group had ridden off down the road.

The dredger had finished unloading its cargo of mud and it sounded a piercing whistle before heading back to the middle of the river.

'Who owns this place?' I asked.

'It's a joint venture between a government geological institute and some British company, I'm not sure of the name. It shouldn't be too hard to check.'

He sat down next to me in one smooth movement, one moment he was standing, the next he was sitting cross-legged on the grass. Graceful was the only word to describe it.

The two dredgers passed by each other. The crews didn't wave or anything, it was obviously a journey they'd made many, many times, just part of the job. The last of the mud vanished into the shed and the belt was clear again.

'What happened when you came here with Sally?' I asked.

'We just drove up to the front gate and asked if we could look round, it was as simple as that.'

'They let you in?'

'Sally showed them her press card and the guards fetched a manager, a Shanghainese who'd been to college in Vancouver. He wanted to practise his English so he took us into his office and gave us tea. He couldn't stop talking. He'd studied geology and then returned to Hong Kong with a Canadian passport. Jumped at the chance of helping China exploit its natural resources, but after a straight three months in the camp he said he was starved of conversation.'

'And he showed you around?'

'Sort of. He showed us everything except what went on inside the shed. He said that was off-limits.'

'But he let you look inside the Portakabin?'

'No, we saw inside on the way out. We saw one of the workers being scanned and then they shut the door.'

'What's the point of it?'

'I suppose to make sure they don't smuggle any diamonds out. It's standard practice in diamond mines, Sally said. It's so easy for someone to swallow a stone and let it pass right through his system.'

The second dredger arrived at the pier, and its scoop began unloading more mud.

'Seems a lot of trouble if all they're getting out of that mud are industrial diamonds.'

'I hadn't thought of that,' he said. No, pal, you hadn't, but I bet Sally had.

'Did she tell the guy who she was?'

'Of course, and left her card with him. He said he wanted to give her a call next time he was in Hong Kong.'

'What about you?'

'Huh?'

'Did you leave your card with him?'

'No, but he asked my name. Sally just said I was a translator.'

He'd rolled the leaf into a small ball which he flicked into the air. His fingers were stained green.

'What are you thinking?' he asked.

'I'm not sure,' I said.

'You think she died because she came out here?'

'I don't know. Maybe you both saw something you shouldn't have.'

'So why invite us in in the first place?'

'I don't know. Perhaps the Canadian was new to the job. Perhaps he didn't know what was going on.'

'And what is going on?'

I shrugged, and pushed myself to my feet. Graceful wasn't the word to describe it. The seat of my pants felt damp. I didn't want to say 'I don't know' again but that was the only answer I could think of. The sun was setting now, the evening light streaking the river orange. Lights began to go on in the huts.

'What are we going to do?' asked Seligman.

A hole appeared in one of the leaves at my eye-level and almost simultaneously we heard the crack of a rifle and Seligman and I dived flat, though he did it with a darn sight more style than me. He rolled behind the bush and then got up into a crouch and scuttled back down the hill. A second bullet whined overhead. Once over the brow of the hill he stood upright and shouted.

'They're firing from the camp. We're shielded on this side.' That was all right for him to say, I was lying spreadeagled on the wrong side of the sodding hill. A dribble of something wet trickled down my leg and I just hoped it was sweat.

'Move,' screamed Seligman.

My eyes were tight shut and my teeth clenched. There was another crack and I felt rather than heard the bullet thud into the ground a few inches to the left of my head.

'Move, move,' he yelled, and this time I didn't need any encouragement, I was on my hands and knees and scrambling over the edge. By the time I caught up with the American I was moving too fast to stop, and I stumbled, rolling over and over till I came to the bottom. Seligman came after me and helped me to my feet. I was shaking, my breath coming in ragged gasps. He grabbed me by the shoulders and shook me hard, my head jerking backwards and forwards.

'What the hell is happening?' I asked him. Seligman looked as shocked as I was, his eyes were wide and his mouth open. He rubbed the bridge of his nose and then started pulling at his lip.

He shook his head in confusion. 'I don't know. We weren't doing anything wrong.' He was starting to shake.

I crawled on all fours to the brow of the hill and nervously peeked over the top. There were three armed guards standing by the gate. They'd stopped firing and were scanning the hillside, jerking their rifles whenever they thought they'd seen something. One of them took aim and fired at a spot about fifty feet to my right. Another group of guards ran out of the shed, shouting at the men at the gate, and another two came out of the Portakabin. They stood together, yelling and cursing, two of them pointing in my general direction. Two open-topped, dark green Land-Rovers appeared from behind the shed and drove up to the gate where they stopped with a squeal of brakes in a cloud of dust.

The men with the guns climbed into the back of the Land-Rovers as another guard unlocked the main gate Jesus, they were coming after us.

I scampered down the hill again. Seligman was where I'd left him, staring at me in bewilderment.

'We have to go, they're coming after us,' I said, and pushed him towards the Mercedes. The windows were all open and *Jailhouse Rock* was on full blast. Wah-yim and Elvis hadn't even heard the shots, they were sitting with bottles of beer held between their knees, handjiving away like a couple of kids.

Seligman wrenched open the door and practically threw me in. He leant forward and began talking earnestly and rapidly to the two of them. My mind was clearer now and I reckoned that we had anywhere between one and four minutes before the guards got to us by road.

Wah-yim started the engine and did a three point turn, the road was too narrow to make it in one go. As we reversed the rear wheels slipped off the road and spun uselessly while Seligman swore and pounded his seat in frustration. He was sweating and red and a vein was pulsing in his temple, he looked as if he was about to turn green and split his shirt. I probably didn't look any better because I was shouting at Wah-yim too, begging, pleading, threatening, just wanting to get the hell out of this place where men with rifles were trying to kill us.

The wheels suddenly found traction and the car sped forward. Round the bend behind us hurtled the two Land-Rovers with wire mesh screens over the windscreens and large metal bumpers fixed over the radiators. Standing up in the back of each were two men pointing their rifles and struggling to keep their balance.

Wah-yim stamped hard on the accelerator, but there was a limit to how fast he could drive the Mercedes on the country roads and the Land-Rovers were already driving at that speed.

A bullet pinged through the rear window, passed through the middle of the car and out through the windscreen leaving a perfect hole about the diameter of a cigarette. Elvis cursed and dropped down into the footwell among his empty bottles while Wah-yim hunched low over the wheel. The American and I were lying on the back seat like a couple of canned sardines.

'What the fuck are we going to do now?' I asked his ankles.

'Shit, I don't know,' he gasped. 'But if they hit the petrol cans we're dead.'

I peered over the back of the seat to see the first of the Land-Rovers coming round a corner after us. On the straight and flat we'd have left them far behind but on these winding roads the four-wheel drives had the advantage. Wah-yim was throwing the Mercedes from side to side, and the stuff in the back of the car was rolling all over the place.

'Tell Elvis to pass his empty bottles over here,' I told Seligman's knee.

'What?' he said. There was the loud smack of a bullet hitting the bumper. Wah-yim made himself even smaller in the driver's seat, like a schoolboy in his father's car.

'The bottles,' I said. 'Get him to throw the bottles here.'

Seligman spoke to Elvis, who gave me a look that said I was crazy. Maybe he was right.

'Now what?' Seligman said.

I took off my tie and thrust it at him. 'Start pulling it to bits,' I said, and risked another look over the seat as Wah-yim took a right curve. The short section of road behind us was clear so I lunged over and grabbed the funnel and one of the petrol cans and with a grunt hauled it back. As I did the two Land-Rovers roared around the bend and one of the guards got off a shot but it went wide. I dropped down, this time with my head the same side of the car as Seligman's. He was using his teeth to shred the material, gnawing like a beaver with a branch. Elvis had started shoving bottles through the gap between the two front seats muttering to himself. There were six in

233

all, but if that wasn't enough I could always get him to drink some more.

I knelt down on the floor, keeping my head low, and unscrewed the top of the petrol can. The vapour made me feel light-headed as I filled one of the empty beer bottles, slopping the fuel into the tin funnel and trying not to spill any.

'OK, give me a piece of the tie,' I said to Seligman, and he handed me a scrap of blue and yellow cloth. I pushed half of it into the neck of the bottle and let the rest dangle down the side. It was soon damp with petrol. I went through the whole business again as the Mercedes lurched into a swift series of turns and I slopped a pint or so on the floor. By the time I'd finished I was close to passing out. I gave them to Seligman to hold while I took another look at our pursuers. They were gaining, fifty feet or so behind us, and the guys with the rifles were trying to aim, but the wind was making their eyes stream and the vehicles were bucking up and down on the uneven road. Wah-yim threw the car into a sharp right turn and they disappeared from view.

'OK, here goes nothing,' I said, and took one of the bottles off Seligman.

Elvis started talking to the American, who reached out and held my arm. 'He says he wants to do it.'

'Yeah, well I've seen his aim and I'm not impressed.'

'He says he was only trying to scare the farmers.'

'Jesus Christ, give him one then. And tell Wah-yim to slow down once he takes the next bend.'

As the car began its turn Elvis flicked his lighter into life and we both lit our fuses. He was giggling like a girl as he leant out of the window, the flaming material waving in the slipstream. Wah-yim started to brake and I joined Elvis, keeping a tight grip on the bottle. The first Land-Rover came hurtling around the bend, and I drew back my arm and threw, hard and high. The second bottle followed half a second later.

Mine went spinning wide and burst into flames by the side of the road. Elvis's hit the windscreen full on, smashing open on the metal grille and spraying burning petrol over the glass. The two armed men standing in the back were splattered with the liquid and they began hitting at themselves, trying to beat out the flames that were eating at their uniforms, screaming in high-pitched, terrified voices. The vehicle began to swerve from side to side and then one of the wheels clipped the edge of the road and it flipped over on its side and then was lost from view as we screeched around another corner. Elvis whooped for joy, punching the air with a clenched fist.

The remaining Land-Rover was more cautious after seeing the fate of the first and it dropped back, well out of throwing range. As soon as we reached a straight section they'd be able to start shooting from a safe distance.

'Now what?' asked Seligman. I got down on the floor again and began preparing four more of the Molotov cocktails.

'We'll get them to come to us,' I said, fumbling with the petrol can again. 'Tell Wah-yim to step on it and get as far ahead as he can. Then when I yell to stop he's to slam on the brakes, stop dead and let me and Elvis out. Then he's to drive a hundred feet or so and stop again.'

Seligman relayed the message to the driver, who was still sitting hunched over the wheel. He nodded furiously. Then I told the American what Elvis was to do.

He was grinning viciously and holding both of his bottles

in one hand, idly flicking the lighter as he waited. The real Elvis was singing at the top of his voice that we should lay off his blue suede shoes.

The road was straighter now, and two shots whined past the car. The hillsides were quite thickly wooded, so I told Seligman that Wah-yim was to get ready. There was a curve coming up so I nodded at Elvis and the lighter sparked into flame. We held the four pieces of petrol-soaked cloth over the lighter and they soon caught, black smoke curling up to the roof of the Mercedes.

The car hit the curve around twenty feet into it and I shouted 'stop.' We all pitched forward and the wheels skidded and Elvis and I had our doors open before we'd stopped. He ran straight for a tree half a dozen paces from the road, I dashed behind the back of the car, heading in the opposite direction.

As the doors slammed shut Wah-yim shot off and the Land-Rover came careering round the bend. It started to brake as the Mercedes accelerated, then picked up speed again. Wah-yim hit the brake pedal again and the car's red lights flashed and the Land-Rover slowed to walking pace, the driver obviously confused by its antics. The two armed guards took aim and then Elvis's first bottle hit the floor between them and they disappeared in a sheet of flame. They fell off the back howling in pain, and I threw mine at the tyres, front and back, then ran along the side of the road back to the car. Elvis was standing by the side of a tree, eagerly watching the inferno, he'd obviously forgotten about the burning bottle in his hand. I shouted and pointed and he looked at it, blew it a kiss and heaved it at the door which the driver was trying to open, then he too was running. We got in the car at the same time and Wah-yim roared off. Elvis was laughing and slapping the dashboard with the palms of his hands. I was shaking and Seligman was sitting there with a look of horror on his face. I gulped in deep breaths and tried to steady myself. Wah-yim was laughing too now, and Elvis began frantically handjiving as he enjoyed the emotional high he'd worked himself up into. I just sank back into the seat and hugged myself as I tried to wipe what I'd done from my mind. I felt sick.

It was some time before the American spoke.

'They were trying to kill us,' he said quietly. 'Why?'

'They've obviously been told to tighten security since you and Sally were last here,' I said, stating the obvious. 'Are you sure she never told you what she'd discovered? What about when you were back in Hong Kong?'

'The last time I saw her she wasn't in any fit state to say anything,' he said.

'What do you mean?'

'She'd been celebrating at the KCC, drinking champagne and telling everybody that she'd got a scoop. God, I'd forgotten about that evening. She was blind drunk but wouldn't say what the story was. Just kept repeating over and over again that she had the proof. I took her home and she was sick in my car, all over her briefcase.

'Briefcase?'

'Yeah, I had to carry it for her.' He looked at me, eyes widening. 'Shit, it's still in the car, under the front seat. She passed out in the car and I had to carry her upstairs to her flat. I couldn't manage it and her. I never got the chance to return it.

'I rang her the following morning but she said there was nothing important in it and said she'd collect it from me some time.'

'And she didn't?'

'It wasn't long after that that she died,' he said. 'I'm sorry, maybe I should have mentioned it earlier, when you were around at the flat. It'd completely slipped my mind. I'd have returned it eventually, she often used to stay over anyway, and she was used to leaving things in the flat. Half of my wardrobe is taken up with her clothes.'

I must have looked shocked because he started speaking quickly to cover his embarrassment. 'I thought you knew, I assumed Barry had told you, but you never mentioned it so I thought you were just being cool. She'd been stopping over at my place on and off for a year or so, I got the impression that she came to see me whenever she was bored.'

So Sally had used Seligman, too, and not just as a guide and interpreter. Was there anyone in Hong Kong she hadn't taken advantage of?

When we eventually reached Shanghai, Seligman decided that we'd better avoid the bigger hotels 'just in case' and after an animated conversation with Wah-yim and Elvis we began driving through a network of quiet back streets. 'They have a cousin who runs a small guesthouse,' he explained. Seligman looked calmer now, but he was still a little twitchy and every now and again he would look over his shoulder to see if anyone was following the car. Of course they couldn't be, I'd seen only two Land-Rovers and we'd stopped both of them.

The incident near the mine seemed totally unreal now, the shots, the petrol bombs, the chase, it was like a dream and I found it difficult to remember the order in which things had happened. But every time I thought back to the second Land-Rover and how Elvis and I had run from the Mercedes to attack it, my heart raced.

THE FIREMAN

The crazy thing was, we hadn't seen anything, just the mine and the boats. Their violent reaction to our being there could only have been because of something that had happened earlier, and that something could only have been Sally's visit. And her death. Nobody had got close enough to see our faces so I was sure that once back in Hong Kong we'd be safe, but China was a different matter, especially when we were driving around in a bullet-holed Mercedes. Luckily it was dark, but even so I was as jumpy as Seligman and after a while I was looking out of the rear window, too. The men with the guns hadn't been firing warning shots, they hadn't bothered. They just wanted to kill us.

'We're in the clear,' I said to him, twice, and he nodded. But we kept looking anyway.

Wah-yim parked the car in the garage and we walked a couple of hundred yards to a long brick terrace, midway along which was a door with a wooden sign above it, yellow Chinese characters on a dark blue background.

Elvis back-kicked the door with his heel until a light came on in an upstairs room, then a window opened and a head appeared. After a short and obviously money-orientated argument the head disappeared and a few minutes later we heard the sounds of bolts being drawn back.

It was a dump. A real dump. Seligman and I had to sleep on two rotting camp beds on a bare wooden floor in a room that smelled damp and which was alive with ticks and cockroaches. I got bitten almost to death and I was scratching all the way from Shanghai to Kai Tak. Elvis and Wah-yim had cost us a small fortune, for their time, their silence, and new windows for the Mercedes.

I felt dirty and dog tired when we finally reached Hong

Kong island. It was dark and we were both practically asleep when the taxi dropped me in front of the Excelsior.

'Shit, the briefcase,' said the American. 'Don't forget Sally's briefcase. Do you want to come and get it now?'

I didn't know what to say. Part of me wanted to see what was in the case, even though Sally had told Seligman that it wasn't important. And part of me just wanted to sleep forever.

Seligman decided for me. 'You're dead on your feet,' he said, reaching for the taxi door. 'Get some sleep. I'll meet you in the FCC at ten o'clock tomorrow morning and I'll bring the case with me.'

By the time I'd started to nod my head in agreement he'd driven off.

I was sitting on a ledge, high above a busy shopping district, my legs dangling into space above crowds of shoppers below. I could see for miles, the air was clean and fresh and I was so high I couldn't hear the traffic or people, just the wind. The ledge was wide enough so that it supported me from the base of the spine to the back of my knees, solid and comforting, and I could feel the rough concrete through the back of my trousers. If I leant forward I could look directly down through my knees, down onto a sea of heads that moved like shoals of fish crossing each other.

A few of the heads stopped moving and looked up, and then the patch of white grew larger and larger as more tilted back. Then cars began to stop and the occupants got out and pretty soon the streets below were full of people looking up and pointing at me. I could see a police car, blue light flashing and siren whining, pull up at the kerb, and then I heard an ambulance or fire engine in the distance, its clanging bell getting louder and louder until it filled my head. It was the telephone and it was four o'clock in the morning which meant it was 8 pm in London.

'How's it going?' asked Bill Hardwicke. I pictured him in his hamster's cage, surrounded by an ever-growing pile of page proofs.

'Not so bad,' I said. 'What's up?' The line was clear, it sounded as if he was calling from the next room.

'We were wondering when you were coming back?' Bill seemed embarrassed, as if he was asking for repayment of a long forgotten debt.

'We, Bill? Who's we?' I was wide awake mentally, sitting up in the double bed, though physically I was still wrecked.

'It's just been mentioned that you have been away from the office for almost a week now and that it was perhaps time you came back.'

'I'm sure the paper can manage without me for a little while longer, Bill.'

He paused, and I could almost hear him thinking. The line began to crackle and then went clear again. I was determined not to make this easy for him.

'Where were you yesterday?' he asked.

'China,' I said. 'I went with a friend of Sally's, an American. And I'm supposed to be meeting him in six hours' time and I'd like to get some sleep. Do you know what fucking time it is?'

'China?' he said. 'What the hell's happening in China?'

'I'll tell you when I know myself,' I said. 'I'm still trying to find out what happened. Just give me some time. Look, I have to sleep. I've got to go and pick up Sally's briefcase later this morning and someone else is going through her notes. There could be a clue there. Let me get back to you, please.'

He paused again, and the line squarked loudly.

'Have you been drinking?' he asked eventually.

'Tonight or generally?'

'You know what I mean.'

'Not to excess, Bill. No need to worry. Look, I'll be back as soon as I can. I promise. I have to arrange to get Sally's body back to Britain. There's talk of an autopsy.'

'I thought that had already been done.'

I jumped on that one straight away. 'How did you know? Have you been talking to Howard Berenger?'

'We were trying to get hold of you and you weren't in the hotel. Of course we rang Berenger. Why shouldn't we?'

'I don't trust the old bastard, that's all.'

'What's that supposed to mean?'

'Oh, I don't know. I'm getting paranoid, that's all. Look Bill, I'll be back as soon as I can, OK?'

'OK,' he said, and he seemed to say it reluctantly, as if he really wanted to increase the pressure, but couldn't, because of Sally or because we went back a long way. Maybe I was reading too much into it. Maybe.

We said our goodbyes and then the line clicked and clicked again and I put down the phone and wondered if Bill had any idea at all about what was going on and who, if anyone, had asked him to call me.

I knew now that I was on the same trail that Sally had followed, what had happened in China had proved that. I was getting close, but to get any closer I had to find out the name of the company that ran the mine. And with that thought I fell asleep.

After I had showered and dressed I rang the *Post*. I'd decided against phoning Howard. After being shot at I reckoned it best to deal only with those people I really trusted. I trusted John Healy, and to my surprise he was at his desk already. I told him what I wanted but I didn't say why. He put me on hold while he went to the cuttings library and when he came back he said there had only been two very short pieces about the mining operation.

'Funny that,' he mused. 'You would have thought they'd want more publicity for it. Most of these joint ventures seem to end in tears.'

He gave me the name of the only non-Chinese company mentioned and I thanked him from the bottom of my heart.

'Piss off,' he said, so I did. I called Jenny and I wasn't too surprised when she said there had been no reference to diamonds in Sally's files.

'Dennis was asking me what was happening, and I said I didn't know,' she said.

'Good girl.'

'Well I don't know, do I? I haven't a clue what's happening.'

'I'll explain tonight. What little there is to explain. Do me a favour, can you run this name through your computer or whatever it is you research people use?'

I gave her the name of the firm Healy had given me.

'And bring along any information you've got on the diamond industry. Anything at all.'

'Bring along where?'

'What do you mean?'

'I mean you haven't even asked to meet me yet. Or asked me how I am. Or told me how you are.'

'Whoops. Sorry.' Already I was taking her for granted. She'd quickly become a reassuring and comfortable part of my life, so much so that it hadn't even occurred to me that she wouldn't see me.

'How are you?' I asked sheepishly.

'Fine,' she said. 'Thanks for asking. And you?'

'Chagrined,' I said. 'I don't suppose you're free for a drink tonight?'

'Hmmm. I'll have to check my diary,' she said, and then burst into laughter. 'Where?'

'How about the Dickens Bar again?'

'We'll become known as regulars.'

'I'll risk that. Eight o'clock all right?'

'Perfect. How was China by the way?'

'Action packed. And you were right, I hated every minute of it.'

'I'm not surprised. Oh, I almost forgot, they finished the autopsy while you were away.'

'And?'

'And nothing. Death consistent with the fall, no evidence of drugs or drink.'

'Which leaves the police no further on.'

'I'm sorry,' said Jenny. 'This is a horrible business.'

I didn't reply, there was nothing I could say.

'I'll see you tonight,' she said. 'Bye.' Then she was gone.

THE FIREMAN

* * *

I used the anti-perspirant liberally before catching a cab to the FCC.

The smell of frying bacon greeted me as I opened the door and walked up the stairs to the bar. The area to the right where the telex machines were was now filled with cloth-covered tables topped by stainless steel trays of bacon, sausages, fried potatoes and tomatoes, and a young waiter in a blue and white striped apron was busy cooking an omelette.

Scattered around the tables in the dining section were assorted businessmen in twos and threes, talking and eating. I couldn't see Seligman there so I walked around the bar. Howard was sitting on his own at the far end, a tumbler of whisky in front of him. I pulled up a stool and joined him.

'Not eating?' I said, beckoning to a barman.

'Too early for solid food,' he said.

'Gin and tonic,' I said to the barman. 'Fresh tonic,' I added, just in case his memory was bad. Across the bar sat the hunchback, reading a magazine as he shovelled forkfuls of scrambled egg into his bearded mouth. I smiled and raised my glass to him, but he just glared sourly. What the hell, some people just aren't friendly in the mornings.

'How was China?' asked Howard.

'Nice place to visit etc, etc. Have you seen Seligman?'

'Today? No. Were you expecting to see him?'

'Yeah, he's got something for me.' I took a mouthful of the gin and tonic and let it wash around my mouth before

245

swallowing it slowly and enjoying the feeling of coldness spreading across my throat.

'Did you find anything in China?' he asked.

'A bed full of cockroaches and bad food.'

'Just like home,' he laughed, but he got the message and didn't bother asking again.

'Have you got much on today?' I asked him.

'It can wait,' he replied. 'I'm working on some PR stuff for a local agency, rewriting press releases and a couple of chairman's statements, that sort of thing.' I suppose that the retainer from Lai meant that he wasn't over concerned about his workload.

'Much happen in Hong Kong while I was away?'

'Financial Secretary said there was no question of revaluing the Hong Kong dollar, a couple of legislative councillors want to repatriate all Vietnamese refugees, and there's a chance that Michael Jackson might be giving a concert here. In other words, nothing doing. Nothing to write home about, anyway. Oh, and there's supposed to be another typhoon on the way.'

'Yeah, I felt the wind on the way in. Is this one actually going to hit Hong Kong?'

'Maybe.'

We both jumped as a crack of thunder split the air outside, a resonating bang that actually made the glasses on the bar tremble. A framed copy of a back issue of the *New York Times* with the headline 'Kennedy slain' tilted on the wall and the eating sounds stopped dead as forks halted in mid-air. The only noise in the bar was that of sizzling fat as the breakfast chef put the finishing touches to a fried egg.

'What the fuck was that?' I asked. All the windows

were blocked by louvred shutters so there was no way
of looking out.

Howard shrugged. 'Sounds like thunder.'

'I've heard bangs like that before, in Belfast, and Beirut,
and they don't have many typhoons in Northern Ireland,'
I said. 'Come on.'

By the time we were out on the street a siren was whining
in the distance, only this one didn't turn into a ringing
telephone, it was a real ambulance, and it screeched past
us, swaying madly as it turned a corner. I started running
after it and within fifty yards I was drenched in sweat and
Howard was puffing and panting at my shoulder. We were
overtaken by a fire engine, its bell clanging wildly, and by
the time we got to the road where Seligman lived they were
unravelling their hoses and connecting the engine to a red
fire hydrant. I don't know what sort of car Seligman had
had, but now it was just a blazing hulk, the bonnet open
like a gasping mouth, the windows blown out and the paint
bubbling and blistering from the fiery heat. What was left
of the American was lying under a rough blanket on the
pavement surrounded by green uniforms. Like all accidents
it had drawn a crowd, and the windows of the surrounding
houses all had curious faces peering down for a better look.
Most of the windows were broken or cracked.

'Fucking vultures,' I said under my breath, but another
part of me remembered that I'd chased enough fire
engines in my time. Worse, I'd stood by groups of
firemen at motorway pile-ups with my notebook in my
hand, waiting to see if the drivers they were cutting out
were dead or alive and just wishing that they'd get on
with it so that I could file the story and go back
to the pub. Name, age, address, job, dead on arrival

or condition. See one five-car smash and you've seen them all.

Howard moved forward and tried to lift the corner of the blanket but a couple of the uniforms held him back, faces impassive.

I knew it was Seligman, and I knew then that I was in real danger. They'd tried to make Sally's death look like a suicide but now they obviously didn't care, they'd brought it out in the open, killing a man in broad daylight. They'd killed Seligman and now surely they would be after me. And yet I still didn't know who, or why. That's what made it so frightening, the fact that they knew who I was and they were just shadowy figures moving at the edge of my vision. I shivered. A fight in a hotel room was one thing, a car bomb in a Hong Kong street was something else.

Plumes of thick, black smoke streamed into the sky and the burning car crackled and hissed and cracked. The driver's door was open, sagging on one hinge so I guess Seligman was just about to get in the car when the bomb went off. I wondered about the briefcase, but if the American had had it, it had surely been destroyed.

'What the hell's going on, laddie?' asked Howard in bewilderment, his face flushing from the heat of the fire.

'It's Seligman,' I said.

The hoses thickened and twitched like awakening snakes and then the firemen were dousing the inferno with foam as Seligman was rolled onto a stretcher by two young ambulancemen.

One of the cops holding Howard by the arm asked him who we were and he told them we were the dead man's friends and they bundled us into the back of a navy blue van and took us to a police station.

THE FIREMAN

They held us for five hours, maybe six, as we helped them with their inquiries, as they say. Most of the time we sat in a waiting room on a slatted wooden bench and looked at a recruiting poster Sellotaped to a whitewashed wall.

Who were we, who was Seligman, did he have any enemies, where did he work, how long had we known him, when was the last time we'd seen him, did we know anyone who'd want to kill him? I didn't tell them about going into China with him, and they didn't ask. I didn't know who to trust in this God-forsaken town and I wasn't going to start baring my soul to Hong Kong's finest until I'd got my own head straight. The explosion and the phone call from England seemed too close to be a coincidence, like a warning to get on a plane before the going really got tough. It just felt wrong, that's all, and I didn't want to complicate matters further by telling them about throwing home-made Molotov cocktails out of the window of a taxi. Howard obviously realized what was going on because he kept quiet too, confining himself to what he knew about Seligman's personal life.

They fed us once, a bowl of rice with some meat in a lumpy khaki-coloured sauce. They gave us chopsticks and I asked for a fork. We were given mugs of tea with strange-shaped leaves in the bottom and then the questions started again, each answer meticulously written down on report sheets.

This time they split us up. I was surrounded by six police officers, all of them Chinese, and they took turns to fire questions at me as I sat there and tried to disguise the fear I felt inside. The questions came thick and fast, a flurry that was designed to confuse rather than to elicit information. Eventually they gave up and one of them left the room, returning five minutes later with Hall. The

Chinese inspector sitting behind the one desk in the room gave up his seat to the British copper. There was no look of resentment on his face but I wondered how he felt inside.

'So,' said Hall, just the one word. I was tempted to add, '. . . a needle pulling thread' but I didn't because this was serious. He let the word hang there, reading the report in front of him line by line. He looked up. 'You were not a friend of this Mr Seligman,' he said.

'No, I've only known him a few days.'

'And the reason you were on the scene so quickly?'

'I was in the FCC, just round the corner. We heard the explosion and went to see what had happened.'

'The natural curiosity of the journalist,' said Hall, his expression blank. 'Very well, then. I see no reason to detain you further. Or Mr Berenger. You are both free to go.' He paused, then added: 'I think the time has come for you to leave Hong Kong. The autopsy was completed yesterday, and I understand a friend of yours has already made arrangements to have your sister's body flown back to the UK.'

'I'll stay for the inquest,' I said.

'There will be no inquest. Your sister's case has officially been classified as suicide and is now closed. As such there is no need for an inquest.'

I stood up, a hot wave of anger coursing through my veins. 'What the fuck do you mean, closed?' I shouted. Two of the policemen moved forward and stood on either side of me, ready to intervene if I made a move against their boss.

'The case has been closed. You should now leave Hong Kong,' said Hall.

'And if I don't?'

He gave me a half smile. 'You will,' he said. 'Far better you go of your own accord.'

And that was it. Two minutes later Howard and I were outside, blinking in the afternoon sun. Howard said he had a meeting to go to but he wasn't fooling anybody, I think he simply wanted to get away from me. I knew how he felt, I wanted to get away from me, too. He walked off like a galleon in full sail, and I headed down towards the harbour, legs moving on autopilot as my mind whirled. It had been easy to concentrate inside the police station as I mentally ducked and dived and kept them away from the events of the previous two days. Freed from the incessant questioning my mind just ballooned and chased random thoughts like a dog snapping at wasps.

There were three of them, one to my left, one to my right and one in front of me. That meant I could have turned and run for it if my back hadn't been against a stone wall. They were all smiling so that anyone who passed by would think we were just four friends, three Chinese and a gweilo chatting on a hot summer's day, the gweilo sweating in the unaccustomed heat.

'You will come with us,' said the tall, thin one in front of me, his face so close I could smell his sour breath and count the blackheads on his nose. When he smiled it was through yellowed teeth and when he spoke I felt spittle pepper my face.

'Please,' he added as an afterthought. He looked left and right as if checking that his pals approved of his English.

He seemed satisfied and then pushed his head towards me like a chicken pecking corn, nodding back and forth. 'You now come, yes?'

They were all dressed in jeans and expensive training shoes. Rotten Teeth wore a leather jacket over a dazzling white T-shirt with 'Fit Sport' splashed across the front in red. The ones on either side wore matching baseball jackets and they could have been twins. All had their arms swinging freely and were close enough to punch or kick or hurt me in a whole host of different ways.

The twins were nodding now, and the one on the left took my arm and pulled me gently away from the wall. A young boy cycled by on a small bike, whizzing past Rotten Teeth as close as he could without touching. Then my other arm was being held and I was being led gently to a large blue Mercedes. It felt as if I was gliding across the pavement. I resisted once but both twins tightened their grips so I just flowed with them. They sandwiched me into the back of the Merc and Rotten Teeth slid into the driving seat. We moved off, through Causeway Bay where the stink of the junks in the typhoon shelter streamed in through the air-conditioning and didn't fade until we were halfway through the harbour tunnel. When we came out at the Kowloon side I sat quietly in the back as Rotten Teeth handed over a note at the toll booth to a bored attendant plugged into a Walkman.

So why didn't I try to run, why didn't I fight and shout and maybe scream, to attract the attention of the police, why just let them lead me like a seaside donkey? Because there were three of them and three against one wasn't fair, or possibly, because I wasn't getting any nearer to finding out who'd killed Sally, and maybe the three musketeers were a piece of the puzzle. And Rotten Teeth had said 'please' so maybe he'd been told to be polite because he'd made an effort when his English obviously wasn't up to it.

As we headed into Tsim Sha Tsui I asked Twin One where we were going but he just smiled and nodded and gave me a thumbs up. We drove along Nathan Road and its lines of jewellery shops and boutiques and its forest of brightly coloured signs clinging to the sides of the tower blocks, red and green and gold.

I didn't know Hong Kong well enough to work out where we were going, but I knew we had our backs to the harbour and so we were heading north. Soon we left the upmarket commercial centre behind us, the blocks got closer together, public housing towers with washing sticking out on poles from most of the windows like scruffy flags fluttering in the wind. The road stayed the same, a dual carriageway that could have been in England, but the shops on either side were smaller, none of the big supermarkets or department stores that crowded into Central and Kowloon, small family shops with televisions and fridges stacked on top of each other, cheap and cheerful clothes, and everywhere the cramped housing of the workers who filled the local factories and sweat shops.

We were overtaken by a green taxi, a Toyota exactly like the ones I'd caught on the island, only the colour different, then I saw another, and soon all the taxis I saw were green so I guess that meant we'd left Kowloon and were now in the New Territories.

We started driving through an industrial area, past huge towering vertical factories with bulky air conditioning units squatting on the outside like cancerous growths.

The driver jabbed at the buttons of the telephone in

the gap between the two front seats, the electronic tones sounding like a child trying to make music. It started to ring and a voice answered in Chinese.

Then a hand grabbed the back of my neck and forced my head down between my legs and I was kept doubled up for five minutes or so, the smell of expensive leather and my own fear making me want to retch, until the car bumped over a ramp or something. Then we pitched forward, turned left and stopped.

The pressure on my neck disappeared and when I sat up, blinking and twisting my head from side to side, we were in an underground car park, fluorescent lights glinting off an army of assorted cars and vans.

'Come with us,' said Rotten Teeth in unsteady English, and they led me to a goods lift. There was something green and brown and unsavoury in one corner and I tried to keep my eyes off it as we rumbled upwards. They'd pressed the button for the twelfth floor and as a small yellow light counted off the numbers I tried to relax and steady my breathing.

We lurched to a halt and the doors opened to reveal a long, low-ceilinged room, about as long as a five-a-side football pitch. The windows had all been boarded up and the only light came from a row of bare light bulbs that bisected the room. It was filled with metal tables like school desks, each topped by an old sewing machine, wires trailing upward to sockets in the ceiling like dodgem cars waiting for the music to start. The walls were lined with empty shelves and the floor was littered with scraps of material and lengths of string, an abandoned sweat shop. Sweat was the right word because the room was steeped in the bitter smell of perspiration, an acrid tang that I could taste on my tongue, mixed with the oil that had been used to lubricate the sewing machines. There was something else, the sweet smell of roast pork, the residue of a nightwatchman's snack maybe, or the leftovers from some long forgotten lunchbox.

The experts might wax lyrical about the economic miracle that is Hong Kong, about its booming exports and hard working population, but at the end of the day I guess this is what it comes down to – a dirty, foul-smelling factory halfway up a tower block where women slaved away over old fashioned machines under artificial light.

We walked in single file through the lines of tables, heading for a door at the far end of the room, which had Chinese characters stencilled on it in white. Rotten Teeth held the door open for me and I led the way, to be greeted by Dennis Lai cradling a white portable telephone in his left hand. In his right was a small butane cylinder with a brass attachment on the top, the sort of thing Hampstead do-it-yourselfers use to strip pine. Lai was wearing a dark blue pinstripe suit but over it he had on a white butcher's apron that went down below his knees.

He fumbled the telephone and the blowtorch together and held out his right hand. He smiled as we shook hands, his grip firm but warm and wet. The smell of cooked meat was almost overpowering now, and at first I thought we'd walked into the factory's kitchen but then I heard a muffled whimpering and when Lai stepped to one side to put the telephone and cylinder on a small folding table I saw a man suspended from the ceiling by chains tied to his legs, his head six inches from the ground. His arms were tied behind his back and he'd been gagged with a leather belt which was wet and slimy with saliva and he was swinging to and fro slowly, his hair brushing backwards and forwards through a damp patch on the concrete floor.

His eyes were tightly closed but he wasn't dead because his chest was rising and falling slowly and his nostrils flared in and out as he sucked in air.

He could have been the guy who'd kicked me in the back in my room at the Excelsior, or the one who'd kicked me in the head. He could have been the waiter who'd poured me a flat tonic water at the FCC. With half of his body covered in third degree burns it could just as easily have been my Uncle Michael who'd disappeared from his office when I was twelve years old taking just his Ford Escort and his secretary with him. Rumour has it they're running a pub in Benidorm but as he was the black sheep of the family nobody bothered too much about him. Except my aunt, of course, but even she didn't seem too upset.

The man was naked except for a pair of grubby Y-fronts, navy blue and covered with red sailing boats. Most of the burns were on his legs but for at least some of the time Lai had played the blowtorch along the man's chest because there were huge blisters bursting from the hairless skin. I suppose Lai couldn't be bothered to bend down for long so he'd concentrated on the legs, which looked like steak that had been left on a grill for too long, ugly black streaks running from the ankles to the thighs, the skin puckered and burnt, with blood dribbling out from the wounds that hadn't been cauterized by the heat.

I tried to be cool. I knew Lai was on my side but it was so glaringly obvious that I was dealing with a very, very dangerous man, a man who could smile while he tortured and who was methodical enough to wear an apron so that he wouldn't soil his suit.

'Who's the barbecue?' I asked.

'He's a red pole in the Wo Hop To triad,' said Lai, gently swinging the blowtorch. He could see by the look on my face that didn't mean a thing to me so he continued. 'Wo Hop To is one of the bigger and nastier organizations in Hong Kong, and they've spread into Europe and America now. They're into drug smuggling, prostitution, gambling, anything that turns a quick profit.'

'And red pole?' I tried not to look at the swinging body, or the blood that trickled down to the floor and mingled with the sweat and saliva.

'A red pole is a fighter, one step up from a rank and file soldier. The triad system is based on a pyramid, with a boss at the top. Below him are three under-bosses. Each under-boss has three men directly reporting to him – a fighter, a negotiator and a recruiter.

'Mr Yip here is a red pole, a kung fu master in fact, not that his knowledge of martial arts is doing him much good at the moment.' He chuckled at his own joke.

'He killed Sally?' I asked.

'He says not,' said Lai. 'But he has an amazing tolerance to pain, as you can see for yourself.'

He brutally punched the hanging man in the groin, the fist buried up to the wrist in the sweating flesh, but there was no scream of pain, just a tightening of the teeth on the gag and a muffled grunt.

'Why would the triads want to hurt Sally?'

'He says they didn't mean to kill her. He says she struggled, ran and tripped and fell through the window.'

'They? Who was with him?'

'One of the Wo Hop To under-bosses by the name of Ho Chi-kwong and a soldier called Li Wing-kei.'

STEPHEN LEATHER

'She got away from three men? Doesn't seem likely, does it?'

'My thoughts exactly. That is why I feel it necessary to talk to him a little while longer.' He toyed with the blowtorch, caressing it like an expensive piece of jade.

'I still don't understand why the triads would want to hurt my sister. She wasn't working on any crime stories other than cocaine-taking amongst the gweilos here. And according to the ICAC she wasn't getting anywhere with that.'

'Money,' he said. 'You can get practically anyone killed or maimed in Hong Kong for just a few thousand dollars. A bit more if you want to hurt a policeman. But Mr Yip says there wasn't a contract out on her. If there had been it would almost certainly have been discussed at the last council meeting, and I am sure that if it had been it would have been made clear that she was under my protection. That at least adds credence to his claim that he did not intend to kill her.

'Also it would be unusual for a triad to do its own dirty work in Hong Kong. When a killing is sanctioned the assassin is usually brought in from China, Taiwan or the Philippines. The triads here hire out their own assassins to gangs in other countries. Free movement of labour, you might say,' and he laughed again. Jesus, this guy had one hell of a sick sense of humour, but I guess you couldn't be completely sane and do the sort of things that he'd been doing with the blowtorch.

'Do we know who hired them?'

'Mr Yip says no, he says the only one who knows for sure is Mr Ho. And he is apparently playing mah jong in a tea house in Mong Kok, I have just discovered.'

'Well, let's go and pick him up,' I said.

THE FIREMAN

Lai smiled again, and tapped the air with his blowtorch. 'I have work to do here.' I obviously looked horrified because he added: 'Do not feel any sympathy for this filth. He is the cause of your sister's death and he also helped plant the bomb that killed the American this morning. He has forfeited the right to live.'

He took a gold Dunhill lighter from his trouser pocket and used it to ignite the torch, then he narrowed the flame to a thin cone of blue heat.

'There is one thing you should know,' he said.

'What's that?'

'Mr Yip here thinks the orders came from overseas, from Europe. And he says the same connection ordered the American to be killed.'

'The triads have connections in Europe?'

'The gangs are no different to anyone else in Hong Kong,' he said. 'They are getting nervous about 1997 and what Communist control will mean. Many have already moved to Amsterdam where they mastermind the importation of Golden Triangle heroin through the EEC. Every major city has its Chinatown, and every Chinatown has its triads. It would not be difficult for anyone in a European city to make contact with the triads, believe me. They are a fact of life.'

'You seem to know a lot about them,' I said, as he replaced the lighter in his pocket. The blowtorch was six feet away but I could feel the heat on my face.

'It is impossible to do business in Hong Kong without coming up against them. The larger ones consist of more than twenty thousand people, men and women, bigger than many companies. Very well organized, too. Look at this, for instance.'

He took a radio pager off the table and held it out to me. I took it, a small plastic bleeper with a built-in speaker. 'Most of them carry pagers, and some of them even have portable telephones now.'

'Dial-A-Villain,' I said, but he obviously didn't understand, so I just shrugged and put it back on the table next to his telephone.

'There are very few of my businesses that don't deal with the triads,' he continued. 'They're into construction, distribution, and of course protection. And like everybody else, I pay. On occasions they are even useful.'

A thought struck me. 'Why did the European connection want Seligman killed?' I asked him.

'You miss the point,' he said. 'The bomb in the car wasn't just meant for the American. The idea was to kill you both. They expected you to be in the car as well.'

'All that means is they knew I'd been into China to see the mining camp. We were making them nervous.'

'Perhaps,' said Lai. 'But Mr Yip here says that before Mr Ho planted the bomb he removed a briefcase from the car.'

'A Gucci briefcase?'

He nodded. 'Sally's,' he said.

'What are you going to do with him?' I asked, and nodded towards Yip, whose eyes were wide with fear now as he tried to swing away from Lai and the torch.

'What do you think I am going to do?' Lai replied. 'I am going to find out everything I can from him. I have yet to find out why they were ordered to kill you and the American. He says he doesn't know why, but I have yet to be convinced.'

'And then?'

'Then I will kill him.'

'And if the police find out?'

Lai laughed out loud at that, and he spoke quickly in Cantonese to the three men who'd brought me in the Mercedes. They joined in the laughter, their guffaws echoing around the room.

Eventually Lai decided that it was time to let me in on the joke. 'What on earth makes you think the police don't know?' he said, and pointed at Rotten Teeth, who reached into his jacket and pulled out a laminated warrant card which he waved gleefully in front of my face. 'It isn't only the triads who have friends in the police,' said Lai, grinning widely.

'The best police force money can buy?' I said.

'Not money,' he said. 'Favours. Favours given and favours owed. That's why they came to me when they'd traced Mr Yip, and didn't just throw him in jail.'

'How did they find him?'

'Hong Kong is a very small place,' he said. 'Sally's death and the bomb in Central attracted a great deal of attention. A lot of police have spent a lot of time asking a lot of questions of a lot of triads. With all this fuss it has been hard for either side to get on with business. The other triad organizations have been particularly upset at what happened, and it was one of them who tipped off the police, and they in turn came to me. Together we will bring this to its conclusion.'

He turned his back on me, a signal that I was dismissed.

'They will take you to find Mr Ho,' he said over his shoulder. 'Mr Yip here says that he has the case. You will take it, I will have Mr Ho.'

I didn't wait to hear any more, I fled the room, eager to get away before the screams started and the air filled once more with the stench of burning flesh.

The three coppers followed me into the lift and we were soon back in the car, heading God knows where. Mong Kok, Lai had said, but that meant nothing to me. A hand grabbed me by the scruff of the neck and once again my head was thrust between my legs for five minutes before they allowed me up again. Sometime later the green taxis became red so I knew we were out of the New Territories and back in Kowloon.

We parked the Mercedes on a single yellow line and the driver took a handwritten notice out of the glove compartment and shoved it on the dashboard where it could be seen from the outside. The four large Chinese characters on the card could have said 'Doctor on Call', or 'Broken Down', or 'Back in Ten Minutes' or 'For Sale', but to me they looked for all the world like a man with an axe chasing a three-legged horse towards a thicket of trees. You ought to see me taking the ink blot test – I'm a riot.

All around us there were large open-topped lorries piled high with cardboard boxes. They were being loaded by young men wearing boxer shorts and training shoes, all were marked with tattoos and all had the ubiquitous bleepers attached to their belts. The tattoos ranged from small daggers on their shoulders to huge red and green dragons that rippled and waved as their owners worked, moisture glistening on their bodies. They worked noisily, shouting and cursing in Cantonese, a constant barrage of chatter like monkeys in a zoo. Once the lorries had been loaded as high as was physically possible the boxes were lashed down with rope and then the vehicles would back into the road, the loaders banging the wooden sides with steel hooks to sound a warning. Most of the drivers had their radios on and their windows wide open, and all seemed to be tuned to different stations, so as we walked along the road there was a wall of incomprehensible sound as each programme merged into the next.

While the lorries were loaded the drivers slept sprawled across the front seats of their trucks, feet sticking out of the windows. They even snored at full volume.

The road was a mixture of factories and shops, and at one point we walked past a restaurant with plastic-covered tables spilling out onto the pavement. Most were occupied by men sitting on small stools, shoving in meat and rice with chopsticks from bowls lifted close to their chins, chewing with relish and then spitting the bones onto the table top. Even as they ate they were talking, shouting, and arguing. The food was ladled from huge steaming vats by a lady with a weightlifter's forearms into blue plastic bowls held by two old men in stained white T-shirts and what looked like pyjama bottoms held up with string. The two were well past pensionable age and could have been twins, the years wiping away most of the distinguishing features and leaving them bald, wrinkled and toothless. They smoked as they worked, ash scattering across the tables as they leant over and clattered the food down in front of the customers.

The shop next to it was a butcher's, where a team of men with bloodstained T-shirts hacked away at fresh carcasses with cleavers, ripping out the offal and throwing it into wicker baskets where it lay steaming. As they cut off individual joints these were speared on hooks and hung from the ceiling. A young housewife with a small child strapped to her back with a strip of bright yellow cloth poked at a pile of tripe and one of the men wrapped it in brown paper for her. The child giggled and played with its mother's pigtail.

At the back of the shop was a large brazier and a boy sat next to it with half a pig impaled on a wooden stake, turning it slowly above the flames as it blackened and the fat hissed and smoked. The smell made me want to throw up.

In front of the shop was a line of cages raised off the ground, full of clucking chickens. A housewife opened a hatch on the top of one of the cages and reached in to pull out a bird by its wings. I'd seen the SPG use a similar grip on a student protesting against apartheid in Trafalgar Square a few years back, in the days when students were more concerned about politics than whether or not they'd get a job after graduating. It squawked angrily and tried to peck her as she squeezed its breast between her bony fingers. Satisfied with her choice, she deftly swung the bird upside down and held it by the legs before paying one of the butchers with coins from a small purse.

One chicken had managed to escape from its cage but it stayed close by, pecking idly at grain on the pavement as it waited to be returned to its mates.

The next building was a tall factory, and water dripped down from the air-conditioners high above and then trickled along the pavement and into the rubbish-filled gutters.

The space alongside the wall wasn't wasted, though, hawkers had pulled up their barrows and were selling British Home Stores shirts and Charles Jourdan belts and silk ties, their wares displayed on circular trays the size of dinner tables, protected by umbrellas to deflect the falling water.

A key-cutter had set up his grinding machine and was

idly exploring his mouth with a toothpick as he waited for a customer. Down on the floor by his side sat a woman of indeterminate age with short frizzy hair and a purple birthmark the shape of a lizard stretched across one cheek, the tail nestling against her upper lip. In front of her was a low-sided wooden box, about three feet square, filled with small cars with red flashing lights that buzzed around, reversing each time they hit the wall. They seemed to be making more of an attempt to escape than the chickens.

The factory building curved around to the right and we followed the bend past the last of the shops and turned into a narrow alley, dark and dank despite the heat. Twenty feet into the passage was an open doorway which led to a flight of stone stairs. As we climbed them in single file the air was filled with clicking noises, like a geiger counter gone mad.

The stairway led into a hall and at the end of the hall was an ornate wooden entrance that opened into a room the size of a small tennis court pitch packed to the edges with small square tables and men and women playing with small ivory tiles. Around the edge of the arena were dozens of private rooms with their own games going on.

A great deal of effort was being put into making the games as noisy as possible, the players were banging and crashing the tiles onto the tables, rattling them around, or just tapping them together while they planned their next moves. There were four at each table, but three times as many spectators crowding round, chatting to each other and by the look of the wads of notes that were being handed around, gambling furiously. Old men shuffled around pouring tea or brandy into glasses, emptying ashtrays into metal buckets and sweeping the floor with battered brooms. Just like a casino there were no windows and no clocks, no sense of time passing.

I looked at Rotten Teeth and he shrugged. He didn't have to put it into words – we didn't have a hope in hell of spotting Ho among the hundreds of mah jong players and spectators. Even assuming he was one of the three men who'd beaten me up – I was getting past the stage of thinking of it as a fight – I would be hard pushed to pick him out of the crowd, especially as most of the players had their heads down scrutinizing their tiles.

I motioned towards the door and this time we left with me leading the way. The three cops were talking quickly among themselves, but I guess they realized I knew what I was doing so they kept up with me.

Back in the car I managed to explain to the driver that I wanted him to call Lai and when Lai answered there was a disappointed edge to his voice as if we'd taken him away from a good meal or a favourite film.

I explained the problem and I asked him to persuade Yip to give us Ho's bleeper number.

'No problem,' he said, and he left the phone switched on as he went back to the hanging man. I heard the blowtorch roar and then a far-off scream before Lai picked up the telephone again. 'I have it,' he said, his breathing even, completely calm. I thought I could hear moaning in the background but it could have been my imagination.

'Give us ten minutes and then call the paging company,' I said, and rang off.

We went back to the mah jong club and spread out among the crowds of spectators, trying to cover as big an area as possible so that hopefully one of us would be within earshot of the bleeper when it went off. The three cops attracted no attention at all as they stood and watched the games but I was on the receiving end of a lot of sidelong glances as we waited. I guess it wasn't the sort of place that gweilos normally went, and it probably wasn't helped by the fact that I looked like a policeman myself. That's partly deliberate. After working the crime beat for a while you start to look like you work in CID, you dress in the same clothes, have a similar hair style, talk the same slang. You have to if you want to be accepted, it's the camouflage that lets you get in close. Some papers take it even further, and make sure that their office cars are the same colour and model as their local CID uses, even down to the same aerial configuration. It makes it a lot easier to get to the scene of a crime, and with the right look on your face you can often get waved through roadblocks and the like. I've had more than my fair share of salutes from zealous uniformed cops, too.

Looking like a copper also helps when you're sniffing around an accident asking questions. If you don't identify yourself everybody assumes you're a cop. People talk to the police whereas they might tell a journalist to go fuck himself. Camouflage.

But looking like a cop in a triad haunt probably wasn't too smart a move, a bit like being disguised as a turkey on Christmas Eve.

The bleeper when it did burst into life was on the belt of a young Chinese guy at the table next to the one I was standing at, and as I turned my head towards the sound he looked up and we recognized each other immediately. The last time I'd seen him he'd been lying flat on his back in the Excelsior Hotel, clutching his balls and squealing. He jumped to his feet, his chair tipping back, hands moving up to grab the table. I started to move towards him but he heaved the table over, and the spectators scattered, falling backwards to avoid being hit. The tiles slid against each other and then avalanched to the floor. I was bumped and jostled, maybe because there was so much confusion but more likely because they realized that I was an enemy after one of their own.

Suddenly I was in the middle of a crowd, not hostile, just passively blocking my way. There was no point in shouting 'Stop' or 'Wait' or anything, but I yelled anyway, to express my anger and to get my three little helpers over to where the action was. I tried to push through the human wall but the more effort I made the more resistance I met.

'Immigration,' I screamed at the top of my voice. That seemed to do the trick. I immediately knew how Moses felt when he waved his staff over the Red Sea. The crowds began to pour out of the doors and within seconds all that were left were the staff, my three helpers, and Ho. Yeah. OK. So I lied. The cops were laughing and Rotten Teeth clapped his hands together to show his appreciation, but they stopped when Ho reached into his jacket and pulled out a knife. I recognized it. The look on his face was pure hate as he stepped forward waving the knife, his feet crunching on the fallen mah jong tiles and broken brandy glasses. One of the old men was busily sweeping up the breakages with a straw broom, head down and seemingly oblivious to the conflict. He cleared his throat noisily and spat, a white, frothy blob hitting the ground about six inches away from my left foot. I grabbed the brush from his hand and it was like stealing a rattle from a baby. He saw my anger and backed away, wiping his nose with the back of his hand. I hefted it in my hands, felt the weight and swung it gently from side to side as Ho moved in. Rotten Teeth and the other two kept their distance, hands on hips as they watched Ho weighing me up. Rotten Teeth was laughing gently, as if refusing to take the fight seriously.

I had the advantage when it came to reach, but if it came to a choice between being stabbed in the stomach or belted on the head with a stick, I knew which I'd go for. He kept the blade low, holding his free hand out towards me with the fingers twitching up and down as he made a hissing noise through pursed lips. He got to within three feet of me before Rotten Teeth pulled a pistol out of the back of his trousers, pointed it at Ho's head and spoke to him in rapid Cantonese. I could appreciate the joke now, and saw why they hadn't rushed to help me.

Ho grunted and threw the knife onto the floor and raised his arms above his head. I stepped forward, dropped the broom to one side and kicked him in the crotch, hard. I got a round of applause from the three cops for that and they helped pick Ho up off the floor, his hands once again clutched to his private parts, and carried him back to the Mercedes.

I sat in the front passenger seat while Rotten Teeth drove and the twins worked Ho over in the back, nothing serious, just enough so that he'd tell them where he lived. It didn't take long and, to be honest, I would have been quite happy to have given them a hand. Or a foot.

He lived on the twenty-eighth floor of a high-rise block five minutes' drive away from the mah jong hall. Ho sat on a grey plastic sofa and gently rubbed his groin, his eyes full of resentment. I wanted to make a joke about red poles but I knew he wouldn't understand so I helped the cops rip the flat apart instead. The kitchen walls were thick with grease, and as I went through the cupboards I was watched by a lazy cockroach which stood on an unwashed wok in the sink. Nothing, just bottles of strange vegetables, packets of freeze-dried soup and a big polythene bag of Australian white rice with a red kangaroo on the front. There was a small fridge rattling away in the corner but all it contained were cans of San Miguel and a half-empty bottle of Kowloon Dairy milk.

Back in the small lounge Ho was screaming at Rotten Teeth who was merrily pulling everything out of a teak veneered wall unit and throwing the contents over his shoulder. By the time he'd finished the floor was littered with comics and dirty magazines. The twins had started on the main bedroom, grabbing all the clothes from a closet set into the wall and going through the pockets. One discovered a roll of red notes and he pocketed them without a word.

They started on the bed then, slashing the mattress with a wicked-looking carving knife from the kitchen. The air was soon filled with white fibres that made them cough and wheeze. I closed the bedroom door and left them to it.

I found the briefcase under a small bed in the second bedroom. I carried it into the lounge and showed it to Rotten Teeth, who smiled, nodded and dropped an ornate glass vase onto the floor with a crash. He kicked over the television set and overturned a large fish tank that was standing in a corner by the window. Ho's colourful collection of exotic fish flopped around on the floor and then lay still among the bits of broken glass and plastic castles. The bedroom door opened and the two cops came out like a couple of asthmatic snowmen, trying in vain to brush the white stuff off their clothes. They helped Rotten Teeth turn over the rest of the flat, not because they were looking for anything, just for the malicious fun of it. I helped smash up the stereo.

By the time we'd finished Ho's shoulders had slumped forward and he was holding his head in his hands and moaning. The cops picked him up and took him back down to the car while I followed with the briefcase. We parted company then, I caught a taxi to the Excelsior while they drove off with Ho. I guess they were taking him to see Lai. I didn't care. The briefcase was empty.

She looked good enough to eat in a black sleeveless dress with a thick brown belt that sat on her hips. She was carrying a black briefcase.

'Hi,' she said, and kissed me on the right cheek, close to my lips.

'Hi yourself,' I said. She smelt fresh and clean, no trace of perfume.

'You look shattered,' said Jenny, climbing onto the stool next to mine.

'Vodka and tonic,' I told the barman.

'You remembered,' she teased, pushing her hair behind her ears. She looked suddenly serious, I guess the look on my face showed that something was wrong. 'What's the matter?'

'I have to go back to London.'

'You what?' she said, flustered. 'Why?' she put both her hands on my knee, obviously worried. My heart lifted, despite the fact that I was going to have to leave her.

'I'm being run out of town,' I said, with a grin.

'By whom?'

'The sheriff,' I said.

'Be serious.'

'I am. Inspector Hall.'

'Why?'

I told her about Seligman, and as I did she sagged on the stool, hunched up like an old woman. 'God, I knew him,' she said in a whisper. 'I heard about the explosion on the radio. I never dreamed it . . .' She mumbled the rest and so I missed it. I put my arm around her and held her close.

'I'm sorry,' I said.

'We used to work together, he was a sweet, sweet guy.'

'I didn't know,' I said. Part of me wanted to ask if she knew about Sally and Seligman, but I didn't think it would serve any purpose. Another part of me wanted to ask her how well she'd known the American, but I killed that thought, too.

'Tell me the rest,' she said, and I did. I told her about going to the mine, the chase, the shitty hotel. I told her about arranging to meet Seligman to collect the briefcase, about the bomb, and being hauled in by the police. And I told her about meeting Lai, and finding the empty briefcase. I didn't mention Lai's torture chamber, I didn't think she could handle that, not after she'd just heard about Seligman's death. I'd leave that part of it for later, and maybe I'd never tell her.

When I'd finished she took some notes out of her case, along with a handful of photocopies of newspaper cuttings. There were tears in her eyes.

'This is the stuff on the diamond bourse you wanted,' she said. She sniffed and reached into a side pocket and pulled out a small packet of paper handkerchiefs, and used one to blow her nose.

She looked down and shuffled the papers with unsteady hands. She wiped her eyes with the tissue.

'Do you think they killed Tod because you went to see the mine, or because he was going to give you the briefcase?' she asked.

'I don't know. It was no secret that we were going to China. And I know now what a small place this is and how quickly news gets around.'

'But they took the briefcase from Tod's car, you said.'

'Yes, that was strange. How did they know about it? Seligman said it was under the front seat, they couldn't have come across it by mistake. Unless they put the bomb there. But why take the case?'

'Well, suppose it was the case they wanted. Who could have tipped them off?'

'That's the crazy thing. Seligman himself only mentioned it in China. He'd forgotten all about it. I suppose he could have told somebody when he got back to Hong Kong, but I don't see that he would have had the time.'

'Did you mention it to anyone?'

'Of course not. I went straight to bed.' Alarm bells went off in my head. It must have shown on my face because she leant forward.

'What?' she gasped. 'What's wrong?'

I told her about the early morning phone call from Bill Hardwicke. I'd told him about the briefcase, but I couldn't remember whether or not I'd told him that Seligman had it.

'Do you think this Bill might have told someone else?'

'No, I don't. Not intentionally anyway. But the line was really strange and there were lots of strange clicking noises. I assumed it was the satellite link, but it could just as easily have been a tap on the line. Somebody listening in. And if that someone also knew I'd been to China with Seligman it wouldn't have been too hard to put two and two together.'

'What time did he phone you?'

'Early, very early. Four o'clock I think. Plenty of time for someone to go round to his flat and put a bomb in the car. They could have planned to search his flat later and get the case. Probably came as a surprise when they found it in the car. A bonus.'

Her drink arrived and she clasped it with both hands. 'If they killed Tod because of what he knew, or what they thought he knew, then they might try to kill you.'

'I know,' I said. 'But as I'll be leaving first thing tomorrow morning, that won't be a problem.'

Jenny began tracing patterns in the condensation that had collected on the outside of her ice-filled glass. 'I'm so frightened,' she said, looking down into her drink.

'It'll be OK. Tomorrow I'll be back in England.'

She tilted her head to look at me. 'That's what I'm worried about,' she said.

I smiled, and it was a real smile, not the boyish version that I used on secretaries or the confident one I used when I was interviewing, I just smiled at her because she made me feel warm inside.

She pointed at the papers lying on the bar in front of me. 'They'll explain how the Hong Kong Diamond Bourse works, but I can give you a quick rundown.' She was very businesslike now, I guess that was her way of dealing with Seligman's death, so I let her talk.

'The bourse is in the Hong Kong Diamond Exchange Building and is now the fourth largest trading centre for diamonds in the world, after the US, Tel Aviv and Bombay. More than $6 billion of diamonds are bought and sold in Hong Kong each year, three-quarters of them weighing less than one carat.' She was warming to the subject now, confidently reeling off the facts and figures.

'Where do the big stones come from?'

'Mostly from New York, and they're usually cut and polished there. The smaller stones are cut in Israel.'

'And they all go through the Diamond Exchange?'

'No, a lot come into Hong Kong in the form of jewellery. The bourse handles only the stones.'

'You have done your homework,' I said, and stroked the back of her head. The hair was smooth and soft, like a cat's. 'What about uncut stones?'

'Mostly from South Africa, they produce about fifteen per cent of the world's output. But they're found all over Africa, plus Australia and Russia. The amount of uncut stones going through Hong Kong is usually quite small, probably not much more than one per cent of the total. Most of the stones in Hong Kong have been cut and polished somewhere else.'

'What about prices?'

'That I couldn't get.' She handed me a handful of photocopied cuttings. 'But prices have been going up because of a miners' strike in South Africa. It's been going on for several months, and although De Beers and Russia have big stockpiles, supplies have been falling.'

I studied the cuttings, most of them from the *Post*'s foreign pages.

'And the British company?'

'I've sort of got something. Although it's supposed to be a British firm that linked with the Chinese authorities, in fact the deal was done through a Hong Kong shelf company which is in turn owned by a British company. But that British company's sole assets are the shares of the Hong Kong company.'

'What about the directors?'

'They're all solicitors based in Jersey, obviously just token directors acting for the real owners.'

'And who owns the British company?'

'That's where the trail stops cold. All the shares in the British company are owned by another company in Panama, so there's nothing you can do to find out who is behind it, you can't get through their secrecy laws. And even if you went over to Panama yourself you'd probably just find a plaque on the wall of a barber's shop.

'So that's that,' I said gloomily.

'Not necessarily, let me keep working on it. I have some contacts in Beijing, let me ask around.'

We'd both finished our drinks and I asked if she wanted another. She said no, she was tired.

'Do you have to go?' I said, trying to make it sound like a joke in case she took offence.

'You hardly know me,' she said, and my heart sank. She smiled at my obvious discomfort.

'I'm sorry, I don't know what I was thinking about. Forget it. I'm sorry.'

'Hey, I was only teasing. Can I stay?'

'But you hardly know me.'

'But I want to,' she said. 'I mean, I want to know you. Don't give me a hard time, boy. Just say yes.'

'Yes,' I said.

'Thank God we've got that out of the way,' she said.

'I thought you Chinese were supposed to be more inscrutable,' I said.

She laughed. 'I've already told you. I'm not Chinese. I'm American.'

It had been some time since I'd been in bed with a girl. Months rather than weeks. Not so long that I'd forgotten what she looked like, but long enough so that I couldn't remember her name.

I was nervous with Jenny, lying next to her on the double bed and trying to work out whether I should take my shirt off first and then attack the brown belt around her waist, or if that would be too presumptious. And at what point was I expected to remove my shoes and socks? God, I hadn't been like this since I was in my teens.

Her lips were soft and warm and I let the kiss go on and on while I tried to get my act together. I really, sincerely, did not want to spoil this by rushing it, though the fact that she was there in the first place, on my bed with her shoes off and the curtains drawn, did suggest that I didn't have much to worry about.

I'd just plucked up the courage to slide my hand from behind her neck and begun undoing the buttons down the front of her dress when the phone rang. I flinched with shock and she giggled. 'You'd better answer it,' she whispered, pressing her fingers to my lips. 'It might be the office.' She rolled off the bed and skipped to the bathroom.

It was Lai. No introduction, he got straight to the point. 'Mr Ho was a little more forthcoming,' he said. I just bet he was.

'The briefcase contained a roll of undeveloped film, a cassette tape and numerous papers. Unfortunately the papers were in English, a language which the late Mr Ho was not particularly familiar with.' Subtle chap Mr Lai. The late Mr Ho. 'But he did recall that there were pictures of diamonds, and some literature from the diamond bourse. Bearing in mind your earlier indication that Sally might have been interested in diamonds I would suggest that you appear to be on the right track.'

The taps in the bathroom started to run and I heard the swish of the shower curtain being pulled back.

'Where are the papers now? And the film and cassette. Do you have them?'

'That, I am afraid, is the bad news. Mr Ho followed his instructions and destroyed them.'

'Damn. Damn and blast.'

'Quite. And according to Mr Ho those instructions came from Europe. But he knew no more than that. What are you planning to do now?'

I told him that I was leaving, and why. He said that he would do what he could in Hong Kong and that he would be in England for Sally's funeral. The line clicked twice and he'd gone. Only then did I remember my previous fears that the line might be tapped, but Lai hadn't identified himself so I didn't think there would be any problems.

I replaced the receiver as Jenny came out of the bathroom. She'd solved the problem of who was to get undressed first. All I had to do was to remove the white towel she was wearing, and it wasn't difficult.

*   *   *

She took me to the airport the following afternoon.

'You don't have to go,' she said. 'You're a Brit, Hall can't have you thrown out.'

'He could make life very difficult for me, though. And I think he'd put a lot of pressure on if I didn't go now. There was something in the way he said it. I don't know, just a feeling that he'd been told to get me out. I think someone else is pulling his strings.'

We were standing outside the entrance to the departure lounge, surrounded by clusters of Chinese families saying their farewells and taking group photographs.

'Besides,' I said, 'you'll find it easier to keep digging if I'm not around. And there's a lot I can do from Britain.'

'I want to come over for the funeral,' she said, slipping her arm through mine. Jenny had already made the arrangements, or rather had put it all in the hands of a local funeral firm who were experts in sending corpses around the world. It seemed there were very few expats who wanted to be buried in Hong Kong and there was quite an industry devoted to making the transfer as smooth as possible. They'd collect the body from the mortuary, fly it to London and then the undertakers in London would do the rest, they'd handle everything from the coffin to the paperwork, all I'd have to do was sign the cheque. I was relieved, because I'd had visions of having to check the coffin at the baggage department or clear it through customs. I couldn't have taken that.

'I want you to come over anyway,' I said. 'But I would like you to be there.' I kissed her on the forehead and walked away. I hate long goodbyes.

* * *

I arrived back in the office to find Simon Kaufman tearing a strip off Bill for missing deadlines. Bill was blaming the computers and young Kaufman wasn't having any of it. Bill was on a losing streak because the guy spoke with the authority of his father, Warren Kaufman, and we all knew it. Warren Kaufman got a kick out of owning a newspaper, but the day-to-day running, the hiring and firing, he left to his son. And recently Simon Kaufman, he of the pinstripe suits, blue shirts with white collars and cuffs and the ever-present calculator wristwatch, had been doing more firing than hiring.

Warren Kaufman was the boss of Kaufman Industries, the firm that was the eventual owner of our paper. Son of a refugee couple who'd fled from Hungary during the '56 revolution, he'd inherited a small chain of newsagents' shops when he was nineteen years old and through sheer hard work and greed he'd built them up into a worldwide group of interests in oil, mining, trading and publishing. The original chain of five shops now numbered one hundred and thirty two and he'd recently announced it was expanding into the east coast of America. Warren Kaufman was big, big money. He'd made no secret of the fact that he had political ambitions, too, and held select dinner parties every Friday night where he bored the pants off peers of the realm and top industrialists with his views of what was wrong with Britain and how he'd go about putting it right, given the chance.

As a way of giving himself a higher profile he acquired

an ailing London evening newspaper and revamped it into the capital's first twenty-four-hour paper. Then he began printing it in Glasgow and Birmingham and to his great surprise it made money. That wasn't his original intention, mind you, he just wanted to see his face, and his views, in print. I met him once as he toured the offices, shadowed by a photographer as if it was a Royal visit. Kaufman sitting at a terminal, Kaufman in the caseroom with a scalpel in his hand, Kaufman watching the presses roll. I didn't get to speak to him, though Roger did. Rank has its privileges, though I don't suppose meeting your boss's boss's boss actually counts as a privilege. I'd rather have had the car.

I remembered Kaufman as a greying, charismatic, snappy dresser who always talked as if he had a Cup Final ticket and it was five minutes before kick-off. I doubt he would remember me. His son did, though, and he scowled at me as I walked past. He had obviously told Bill to give me a hard time because I was immediately sent out to cover a tedious fraud trial that stood no chance of getting into the paper. Or maybe Bill had just decided that it would be better to keep me out of the office while young Kaufman was on the warpath.

As I sat on the press bench, doodling in my notebook, I tried to make sense of what had happened in Hong Kong, but I kept coming back to the shadowy figure who was controlling it all, the person who had killed Sally and Seligman, who'd sent triads to beat me up and who'd put pressure on Hall to get me out of Hong Kong. I had almost all the information that she'd had, but I couldn't make the final jump, I couldn't find the missing piece that would complete the picture. I was so close I could taste it.

The case dragged on and on and when it was obvious that it was going over to the next day I left and phoned Bill. He said I might as well call it a day and go home.

Home is a two-bedroomed house on the Isle of Dogs that I'd bought four years ago before the developers had laid the first brick. It had trebled in value, and I hated it, but it was within walking distance of the office and that was a big plus at the time because they'd taken my driving licence away. The door opened straight into the sitting room and the front window looked out over a scrap of garden about the size of a boy scout's groundsheet on which grass stubbornly refused to grow. The area around our enclave of brick-built houses was still very seedy, decaying tower blocks of council flats, abused and neglected and a far cry from the towering homes of Hong Kong, where I'd never seen any graffiti or vandalism. On the Isle of Dogs our fences and walls were regularly spray painted with 'Build homes for the people, not for the City' and all that rubbish. The locals were still sour about what the eastward expanding City had done to property values here, but what the hell, the locals weren't the sort who'd ever want, or be able, to buy their own homes whatever the price.

The developers had wisely built a twelve-foot wall around our settlement of middle-class boxes, giving it the air of a fortress surrounded by enemy territory. They hadn't put broken glass or barbed wire on the top yet, but I was sure it would come. The wrought-iron gate was opened electronically by a guard who sat in what looked for all the world like a concrete pillbox, without the machine gun. In time, that would probably come, too.

A black cab dropped me off outside the gate and I waved to the guard as he opened it for me.

THE FIREMAN

It was Robbie Brady, a forty-year-old ex-copper with short greying hair, a square jaw and a Spanish-style moustache that he'd started growing after he'd left the force. He was a good guy, and in the days when I'd been drinking heavily he'd often carried me into the house after I'd been poured out of a car. He understood, he usually had a bottle of Scotch tucked away somewhere in his little pillbox.

As the taxi drove off, a white Transit van screeched around the corner and braked heavily. The back doors were flung open and four Chinese youths jumped, or fell out, shouting and screaming, waving cleavers, faces contorted with fury and hate. They ran towards me, no planning or forethought, just a random charge that was terrifying in its ferocity. I slipped inside the gate and screamed at Robbie to close it but the mechanism was so slow that two got through before it clicked shut. The two trapped outside threw themselves at the gate and began to climb up, but at that point I was more worried about the two young thugs facing me.

They came at me with the cleavers raised above their heads, mouths open and shrieking. Robbie came out of his den, uniform immaculate, buttons shining, and a three foot long truncheon in his hand. I ran towards him and he stepped to one side, then dropped low and swung the stick like a baseball bat, catching one of my pursuers in the stomach. He grunted and pitched forward, the cleaver clattering along the ground, sparking on the paving stones.

I moved to pick it up but the second attacker was too close, and I ducked away as his cleaver sliced through the air missing my shoulder by inches. I backed away, towards the aluminium dustbins lined up behind Robbie's pillbox waiting for the rubbish to be collected. I grabbed one of the dustbin lids and held it in front of me like a shield as the guy kept on coming, forcing me back against the wall. He chopped down and I raised the lid to block it and it clunked down hard, banging the lid against my head. I lashed out with my foot and caught him just above the knee as he raised the cleaver again. Behind him I could see his two pals reach the top of the gate, then another car pulled up and four more Chinese got out, shouting and waving. Reinforcements. Christ, what the hell was going on? Everybody was screaming now, including me, and even Robbie was bellowing like a bull, charging towards my attacker as he slashed left and right, each time connecting with the edge of the dustbin lid. Each failure to cut me to the bone seemed to increase the fury of his attacks and I was sure I wouldn't be able to fend him off for much longer, when Robbie cracked him on the back of his head with his truncheon and he fell to his knees and then keeled over with a long, low groaning wail. Robbie was breathing heavily, but he was smiling and I could see he was having fun.

'Takes me back to my days in Notting Hill,' he said, and we turned to face the gate. The four Chinese who'd arrived in the car had grabbed the two gate-climbers and were pulling them down by their legs. Once on the floor they started a pitched battle, four against two. The two with cleavers stood back to back while the four late arrivals surrounded them. They had a mixture of weapons, one was using one of those two bits of wood joined by a chain that Bruce Lee used to whirl around his head in kung fu movies, while another had two small swords with curly bits around the handle that he was using to try to trap one of the cleavers every time it came within reach. Another was twirling a staff around his head while the fourth had what looked like a hockey stick. Shit, it was a hockey stick.

'I think they're on our side,' I gasped to Robbie, and we ran to join them. Robbie opened the gate and we spilled into the street just in time to see my two would-be attackers fall to the ground under a hail of blows. Even when they'd dropped their cleavers and curled up into fetal balls with their arms wrapped around their heads and their knees up against their chests, the four assailants continued to kick them and hit them, they didn't stop until there was no sign of movement.

The newcomers picked them up one by one and threw them into the back of the Transit van. They came inside the gate to collect the other two while their leader, a thickset Chinese wearing an olive leather jacket and brown cords, came over to speak to me.

'I am sorry about thet,' he said, in a Cockney accent that took me by surprise. 'Mr Lai told us to keep an eye on you, but I didn't realize they were so close.'

'What is going on?' asked Robbie, swinging his truncheon by the side of his leg.

'It's OK, Robbie,' I said. 'These guys work for a friend of mine.'

'I'm calling the police,' said Robbie.

'No, no, it's OK, honest. Let them sort it out.'

He agreed reluctantly, and went back into his den. I could hear a bottle being opened.

'This will not happen again,' said the Chinese. 'We will not let anyone get that close again. Besides, having failed so dismally they are unlikely to have another go. But if they do, we will be better prepared.' He bowed slightly, the action totally out of character with the accent.

'One thing . . .' he added.

'I won't mention it to Mr Lai,' I said. He grinned, realizing that I understood.

'Thank you,' he said. 'Do not worry if you do not see my men. They will be around.' He bowed again, and then got into the car which drove off, the van following with its cargo of four unconscious thugs, now firmly gagged and tied. I didn't know what they planned to do with them and I didn't care.

I was more concerned about how the triads had found my home. Jenny and Lai had both explained how the triads were active in London, but someone must have told them where I was and there weren't too many people who knew where I lived.

Deciding where the funeral should be hadn't been a problem. My mother had wanted Sally buried in the churchyard near her home in the West Country and had already chosen a coffin and a plot near a middle-aged oak tree by the time I was back in England. Jenny had made all the arrangements, just as she'd promised, and she arrived in London two days after me. She stayed at my house. I didn't mention the attack in London, I didn't want to worry her. Besides, the Chinese Cockney had been right, having been so soundly beaten they would be unlikely to try again. That's what I told myself when strange noises woke me in the middle of the night and I strained to hear more over the sound of

Jenny's gentle breathing. If Lai's men were still around, I never saw them.

I suppose my mother was used to funerals, having seen off two husbands, and at first I was a little surprised that she wanted Sally buried so close to home because she'd had no qualms about having my father cremated and I don't think she gave a second thought about his ashes. Then I realized that the death of a spouse is different from the death of a child, and that she probably still had a lot of grieving to do.

I phoned Lai and told him when and where the funeral would be, and asked him to bring something with him, something that I hoped would solve the riddle of Sally's murder. He said he'd be there.

It was Sunday when I called him, and the funeral was Wednesday. I spent the time showing Jenny the London I knew, treating her like a tourist and just enjoying the warmth of her company.

Not all the time, though. I got the name of a tame Hatton Garden diamond merchant from one of my pals on the Met, and we collected a stack of information about the diamond business from him, technical stuff like world prices, fluctuations, stocks held by the different diamond-producing countries and so on. He was able to supply just what I needed, including tables of average prices on a daily basis for the big diamond exchanges around the world.

He'd run the charts off from a computer and the graphics weren't so hot but the figures were clear. Jenny and I spread them out on the kitchen table and looked at them.

'So what are we looking for?' she asked.

'That, for a start,' I said, and pointed to a drop in the diamond prices on the Hong Kong bourse about nine months earlier. It lasted for about a month and then the line picked up, it was a small dip but it came at a time when the graphs for London, New York and Tel Aviv were all on the rise.

She looked confused, so I explained. 'Everywhere else in the world diamond prices were going up then. But in Hong Kong they were falling. Why? Because somebody was dumping diamonds in Hong Kong, increasing the supply so that prices dropped.'

'So why did they stop?'

'They didn't stop,' I said. 'Look at the graphs. The prices of diamonds rose in Hong Kong, sure, but not as fast as elsewhere in the world. They obviously realized that selling too many at a time would attract attention, so they controlled the flow. Maybe they started selling them on other markets. But this is the giveaway. See how prices really started taking off when the miners' strike started in South Africa. In New York, London and Tel Aviv, they shot up. But in Hong Kong, nothing. When the supply from South Africa was cut back, obviously more Chinese diamonds were put on the market. Not a huge amount, nothing compared with what De Beers produces, but enough to distort the prices in a small exchange like Hong Kong. Then after a few weeks prices start to rise again. See?'

'But didn't the dealers notice?'

'Maybe they did. Somebody must have mentioned it to Sally, this isn't the sort of thing you stumble across. I suppose she came across it when she was doing her interviews for the advertising feature. In fact, thinking about it, I bet most of the dealers would be pretty pissed off about what was happening, seeing what it was doing to diamond prices.'

'Perhaps not,' said Jenny, looking at the graphs. 'Diamond trading is an international business . . . what if the dealers were buying in Hong Kong and then reselling them overseas? If whoever was mining them in China was dumping them in Hong Kong at prices below New York and London, surely the local dealers wouldn't miss out on the opportunity of making a quick profit. They wouldn't care where they were coming from. Just so long as they had a piece of the action.'

She looked up from the graphs, her eyes sparkling because she knew she was right. Then she frowned. 'But why didn't whoever was mining the diamonds simply sell them in New York and London themselves?'

'How would they have got them there?' I answered. 'It's one thing to get them from China to Hong Kong, but it'd be a different matter to get them unnoticed into the United States. By doing it through Hong Kong they could spread the diamonds around the world without attracting attention to themselves.'

'Until Sally found out.'

'Yes,' I agreed. 'Until she found out.'

'What now?' she said.

'Now we wait for Lai.'

On the day of the funeral Jenny stood next to me, her arm through mine, and she cried softly. She was on my right, my mother on my left, in the front pew of the sandstone church where my mother went every Sunday. Behind us were a scattering of relatives, a couple of dozen at most, mainly elderly, and several that I couldn't put names to. Bill Hardwicke was there, and I was grateful to him for that. He hardly knew Sally, but he came anyway. We listened to a service given by a vicar who didn't know the deceased but who did his best to persuade us that it was all for the greater good. We sang a couple of hymns and bowed our heads and then we stood in the graveyard and watched her being lowered into the ground.

I hadn't seen Lai in the church but he was there in the cemetery, a grey wool coat draped over the shoulders of an expensively-cut black suit, flanked by two Chinese heavyweights. One of them I recognized because he'd helped save my life a few days earlier. The three of them stood to one side of the grave, about twenty feet away, close enough to intrude. Lai stood with his head bowed, his hands clasped just below his groin, deep in thought.

I knew that the Sally he was remembering wasn't the same girl who filled my thoughts, the chameleon that was my sister had left behind a jumbled set of memories, and I doubt that any two of her friends would have seen her the same way. But that didn't make any of the faces of Sally any less real, that much I knew.

When it was all over I walked over to him, with Jenny still on my arm. He shook my hand, saying nothing. I guess I knew what was on his mind, and he knew what I was thinking, so there was no need to put any of it into words.

He said hello to Jenny and she reached out to touch his arm. Lai's two bodyguards stood by impassively. They were wearing dark suits but were obviously uncomfortable and they both kept moving their shoulders around as if they felt trapped.

'Thank you for coming,' I said, more to fill the silence than anything.

My mother walked along the tarmac path that led to the road, supported by my aunt. They looked curiously at Lai and I as we stood together on the grass, but said nothing.

'You're welcome to come back for a drink,' I told Lai. 'My mother has arranged something.'

'Thank you, but no,' he said quietly. 'I have merely come to pay my respects to Sally. I will leave you now.'

'Did you . . .?' I started, but he nodded his head before I finished the question. He took an envelope from his pocket and handed it to me. 'You can check the numbers?'

'No problem,' I said. 'And once I know who we are looking for I'll call you.'

'How long will it take?'

'A few hours at most. I'll do it when I'm back in London tomorrow morning.'

'I'll be at the Inn on the Park,' he said. 'I'm staying over for a few days to attend to some business. Call me there.'

'I will,' I promised, and Jenny and I walked with Lai and his two minders down the path in silence. Before they left in a dark blue Jaguar I gave Lai Sally's watch, mumbling something about being sure that Sally would have wanted him to have it.

'What's in the envelope?' Jenny asked. I opened it and showed her.

'Sally's phone bill?'

'Yeah. What I originally asked for was a list of all overseas calls from her flat, but I didn't realize that Hong Kong telephone bills are all itemized, with every telephone number and the time and cost of each call. And as the flat

291

was in Lai's name it was no problem getting an up-to-date copy of the bill.'

'And?'

'And then I'll be able to track down every number and find out who she spoke to in England before she died. Because I think that she rang up someone here on the diamond story, and I think that whoever it was, was worried enough to have her killed, ordered Seligman's car to be bombed and tried to have me killed too.'

She shivered, and I knew it wasn't the cold. 'Come on,' she said, 'let's go talk to your mother.'

There were only fifteen overseas numbers on the phone bill, and nine of those were in Peking, spaced out over the three weeks before Sally had died. The remaining six were all UK numbers.

Jenny and I had sat on the floor in my lounge on the thick red-dyed sheepskin rug that hid the wine stain on the carpet. The CD player was on, digitally playing Louis Armstrong singing something deep and meaningful. It was eleven o'clock in the morning but she was still wearing my light blue bathrobe and her hair was damp, fresh from the shower. I wasn't due in the office till three but I'd put on number two suit, the one where the zip in the trousers was starting to go, and my Glasgow Press Club tie, green with a yellow quill. Who says journalists have no sense of style?

Of the six UK numbers, one I recognized immediately, it was my office number, the main switchboard. She'd phoned two days before she'd died and been on the line for forty-five seconds which meant she'd tried to leave a message and I cursed Roger the fucking Dodger or Handy fucking Andy or whichever bastard had been too lazy to tell me she'd called. Or maybe she'd phoned late at night and a cleaner had answered, and if she'd got through to me maybe she wouldn't have told me what she was up to, she probably just wanted to pick my brains. If she'd had anything really serious to tell me she would have rung back, but that didn't stop the ache in my heart and the horrible gut-wrenching suspicion that if we had talked there might have been something I could have done to have saved her life.

Before she'd phoned me there were three London numbers, one of them she'd dialled twice. The sixth call I noticed with a jolt like an electric shock was several days after she'd fallen to her death and then I realized it was our mother's number and it had been me that had made the call when I'd gone back to the flat to use the recall button.

That left three numbers.

'What are you going to do?' asked Jenny.

'I've got a contact who works for British Telecom who'll trace numbers for me, but there's no harm in trying the direct approach first.'

First I dialled the number that Sally had called twice. Both times she'd been on the phone for about half an hour, and when a voice answered 'London Diamond Exchange' I realized why. She'd been getting background information on the diamond business, the sort of facts and figures that Jenny had scattered on the floor around us, production, prices, exports and so on.

The second number was De Beers, and that made sense because she'd be asking questions about the strike, the miners' walk-out described in the cuttings that Jenny had got for me in Hong Kong, how diamond production had been hit and how there were still no signs of the miners going back to work, despite two of the miners' leaders being killed in mysterious, and violent, circumstances.

The adrenaline was starting to flow and the hairs on the back of my neck were starting to stand on end because I could feel we were getting close, I felt as if I was on the trail with Sally, closing in for the kill. Except that when Sally had gone in she'd probably been her normal headstrong self and gone charging in without a second thought. I hit the seven digits and there was a pause and then the ringing tone. Six, seven times it rang and I was starting to think there was nobody there and then the receiver was picked up and a woman with a crisp upper-class accent said 'Mr Kaufman's office' and then it all clicked into place like the jaws of a steel trap springing shut.

'Mr Kaufman's office,' the voice repeated, this time with an impatient edge to it.

Jenny looked at me and mouthed 'What's wrong?' but I shook my head.

'That is Warren Kaufman's office isn't it?' I said.

'It is,' said the voice. 'Who's calling, please?'

'Is he there?' I said.

'I'm afraid he's in a meeting at the moment. Can I get him to call you back?'

'No, no, that's all right. I'll call back later. Thank you,' I said, and put the phone down.

'Jesus Christ,' I said. 'Jesus H. fucking Christ.'

'What's wrong?' said Jenny, reaching for my hand and holding it close to her chest. I told her.

I told her that Sally had called my office but hadn't spoken to me because she'd been trying to get Warren

Kaufman's number and had obviously found someone to give it to her. And I told her that the reason Sally hadn't told me what was going on was because the man who was behind the diamond operation in China was the same man who owned the newspaper I worked for. And that explained a whole stack of worries that had been gnawing away at my insides. Like why she hadn't called me. Why Bill had managed to track me down to my home. Yeah, the fact that Warren Kaufman was behind it explained a lot.

'Are you sure it's him?' asked Jenny.

'It was definitely his office, and other than De Beers and the diamond exchange his was the only UK number she called. You can see from the phone bill.' I handed it to her. 'She was on the line for twenty minutes so she must have given him a real grilling. And I reckon she told him more than she should have done. You know, fools rush in where angels fear to tread. She probably said she'd been to the mine in China, seen the security arrangements, and somehow she managed to trace the ownership of the mine to him.'

'What are you going to do?'

'I promised Lai I'd give him the name.'

'You must be sure first.'

'I am sure.'

'Let me check it out first. It'll be easier starting with Kaufman's name and working backwards. Let me see if I can connect him to China. Just give me one day at Companies' House.'

I agreed, reluctantly because in my heart I was already sure, but I told her everything I knew about Kaufman and his company. She dressed while we were talking and fled the house.

She phoned me in the office later that evening, her voice excited and her breath coming in short gasps.

'God, you were right,' she said. 'One of Kaufman's mining subsidiaries has an offshoot which has its head office in Panama, the same address as the company that's involved in the mining joint venture. And I've rung one of my contacts in Beijing who says yes, Kaufman was there three years ago talking about exporting industrial diamonds. And I found out why Kaufman wanted to keep it all low key.'

'Because he's ripping them off to the tune of millions of pounds a year,' I said.

'No, there's more to it than that. Both he and the Chinese wanted no publicity right from the start because he's also in partnership with the Taiwanese in a computer manufacturing company in Taipei. Some of the equipment he's making there has military applications and when Kaufman first started dealing with China there was a lot of tension between the two countries. They're still technically at war and there was no way the Chinese could be seen to be dealing openly with a man who was such a good friend of Taiwan. So it suited everybody not to announce details of the mining venture.'

'But I thought relations between the two were warmer now?'

'Sure, but that's a recent phenomenon, there's no problem these days for companies doing business with both. But a few years ago it was a very different story.'

'We've got him,' I said, elated.

'Yes, boy, we've got him. You can tell Lai, now. See you soon.'

I phoned Lai at his hotel and we talked for the best part of an hour. I was all fired up to dish out the same treatment to Kaufman that Lai had given the triads in his factory. I wanted Kaufman to suffer. I wanted him to scream. And I wanted him dead.

I know a better way to hurt him, Lai said. Trust me. We will have our revenge. He told me what he wanted to do, revenge Chinese-style.

'We'll do it your way,' I said, when he'd finished.

'Good,' he said. 'I'll be in touch.'

It was just four days after the funeral when it started. A couple of paragraphs on a left hand page of the *Financial Times* saying that a Kaufman Industries construction subsidiary had been awarded two prestigious hotel contracts, one in Shanghai and one in Peking. Jenny pointed it out to me over breakfast. I was getting used to having her around. Already her clothes were hanging next to mine in the wardrobe and her toothbrush seemed like it had always been in the bathroom. She'd taken two weeks' holiday to stay with me and I wasn't looking forward to the time when she'd have to go back to Hong Kong. Neither of us could work out what the significance of the hotel contracts was, but the following day the shares nudged up a couple of points.

A week later the office was buzzing with the news that a group of the paper's executives were flying to China to advise on the setting up of a new English language newspaper in Peking. The rumours hit fever pitch just before Kaufman called a press conference confirming the deal. Kaufman Industries was to build a newspaper publishing plant just outside the Chinese capital using state-of-the-art technology. In return for a US$40 million investment the British company would get free advertising space which it could then sell on to other companies. The paper was pitched at an initial circulation of five hundred thousand but Kaufman had also agreed to build another ten plants in provincial centres with pages transmitted across the country by satellite. Within five years sales were projected at nine million in a country that was eager to learn English and take its place in the modern world. Kaufman himself led the team that visited China and for several days our paper was filled with pictures of him, Kaufman at the Great Wall of China, Kaufman in the People's Palace, Kaufman meeting top Chinese dignitaries. At the end of his four-day visit to the mainland the Chinese announced that Kaufman would be the main contractor in a new superhighway linking Peking to Guangzhou. But the revelation that really started the share prices soaring was that there would be no restrictions on foreign exchange, the Chinese would pay in American dollars.

Kaufman was hailed as the man who had finally cracked the China market, one of the heavy Sundays ran a centre-spread profile on him and Tony Wilkins, one of our best feature writers, was seconded to ghostwrite a book by Kaufman on doing business behind the Bamboo Curtain.

Jenny and I watched and waited, spectators unable to take part, not even knowing what Lai had planned. Jenny had extended her stay, using up her full quota of paid leave. When I asked her what would happen when her holiday entitlement ran out she just laughed and made a joke about unpaid holiday. I wanted to ask her to start looking for a job in London, maybe ask for a transfer within her company, but I was frightened of showing her just how much I cared. Frightened of showing her how much I needed her.

In the two weeks after Kaufman's China visit it seemed as though the industrialist could do no wrong, contract after contract was signed, with more and more of his finances and management being committed to the mainland: a soft drinks bottling plant, a power station, several office blocks and a stake in a new container terminal. It looked as if Tony was going to have his work cut out for him.

Kaufman became the darling of the Stock Exchange and in less than one month since I'd left Hong Kong the shares rocketed forty per cent. There was talk of the shares being listed on the Hong Kong Stock Exchange, a sign of Kaufman's faith in the colony and in China. According to the guys in the City office Kaufman was stretching himself a little too far, and there were market rumours that the group was planning a rights issue to raise more capital. Not that that was reckoned to be a bad thing now that Kaufman Industries had the support of China to what appeared to be an unprecedented extent and the big institutions were queuing up to grab a piece of the action. Their hopes proved to be stillborn when Kaufman called a press conference to announce that a Chinese investment bank was taking a nine per cent stake in his company. Admittedly they were paying a bargain basement price but it was evidence of a further strengthening of the links between the conglomerate and the mainland and the City lapped it up.

I started to worry that Lai had been all talk, I couldn't for the life of me see how he could be behind all these deals or how it would help us to get back at Kaufman when all that seemed to be happening was that he was going from strength to strength. Jenny told me not to worry, to trust Lai. The holiday problem had been solved, temporarily at least, because her company had agreed on a temporary attachment to their London office. I suppose they didn't want to lose her, better to have her working for them in London than not at all. I still couldn't get over how easily, how casually, she'd slid into my life and become a part of it. Losing her now would be like losing an arm or a leg.

It was early September and I'd been on the wagon for six weeks when the shit hit the fan. Without warning and with the bare minimum of explanation the partners in all of Kaufman's Chinese ventures began to pull out, one by one. The Chinese Government said they were cutting back on their spending on infrastructure, the highway and the power plant were being put on ice, and the newspaper project was scrapped despite Kaufman having committed several million dollars to the deal. The hotels were declared surplus to requirements as was the container terminal. Roland Harper, the paper's dapper diplomatic correspondent, came in one afternoon bursting with the news that the Chinese were now making it unofficially known that Kaufman was about as welcome in China as an AIDS carrier with a nosebleed.

'See,' said Jenny. 'I said you could trust him.'

The bottom fell out of Kaufman Industries shares, and when the China-backed bank announced it was selling its nine per cent holding to a Hong Kong company for substantially less than they'd paid for it the news made the front of the *Financial Times* and, on the back page, one of the writers of the Lex column wrote an authoritative and totally wrong analysis of what was behind the change of heart and what it meant to the company. All the crap about gearing,

price-earning ratios and Chinese hesitancy to open up fully
to Western capitalism just didn't apply. The company that
now held a major stake in Kaufman Industries was Dennis
Lai's. He had Kaufman by the balls and he was starting to
squeeze. The share price hit rock bottom the day before Lai
bought into Kaufman Industries and then it started to climb
again, slowly but steadily, putting on a couple of points
each day. According to the City reporter who threw the
stock market report together, buying orders were coming
in from around the world: Toronto, Sydney, San Francisco,
and London. Nothing big, nothing that passed the five per
cent mark at which point the buyer would have to reveal
himself, just steady acquisition of the group's shares by a
number of mystery buyers.

The call came two months to the day after I'd left Hong
Kong, two months during which I hadn't touched a drop
while I'd hungered for revenge and wondered time and time
again what the hell Lai was up to and if he'd be able to pull
it off, whatever it was. It was the white phone on Roger's
desk that rang, but he made no move to answer it. He was
up to his eyes in an expense sheet, his most creative work of
the week. The paper was making it harder though, there'd
been a clampdown on all expenses, and they'd got shot of
a number of casuals.

'Nothing I can do, lads,' Bill Hardwicke had told us.
'Pressure's coming right from the top this time, it's not
just a question of lying low until it blows over. This is
serious – Kaufman's in trouble and every part of his empire
is coming in for some pretty drastic belt-tightening. We're
just going to have to grin and bear it.

In the good old days of Fleet Street it would have been
a union matter and the NUJ heavies would have gone

in and a couple of days of working to rule would have sorted the matter out, either that or they'd have lost a few million copies. But new technology, the new generation of newspaper barons and the high wages had taken the fight out of the unions so we just sat at our terminals and tried to be more creative, substituting taxi fares for hospital bills and signing each other's restaurant receipts.

The line from Hong Kong was clear as a bell, only the slight satellite delay giving any indication of the thousands of miles between us. His voice was flat and emotionless and he didn't bother with small talk as if he was worried about the cost of the call.

'I will be meeting him in the Grill Room of the Mandarin Hotel in three days' time. Can you make it?'

'Try and stop me,' I replied.

'Thursday, one o'clock,' he said. 'It might be better if you arrived slightly later, it might scare him off if he sees both of us waiting for him.'

'I'll be there,' I said. 'God, I thought you'd never ring.'

'You should have had more faith in me. And you should have realized that this is not something that can be rushed. I will see you on Thursday.' He cut the line and I held the phone to my ear for several seconds as waves of relief, pleasure and excitement washed over me, an adrenaline kick that tightened my stomach and set the hairs on the back of my neck standing as straight as soldiers on a parade ground.

'What's up?' asked Roger.

'Nothing,' I said. 'Just a friend.'

'You're grinning like a Cheshire cat. Rich relative just died?'

I smiled at him and imagined pushing a lighted cigarette into his left eye. It made me feel better.

'Here, sign this for me,' and he threw over a blank receipt from one of the more upmarket wine bars on the Isle of Dogs. 'That Kaufman is a bastard.'

'Yeah, isn't he just.' I scrawled a spidery signature on the yellow slip and scribbled in a few numbers.

'Fifty-six OK?' I said.

'That'll do nicely,' he said, and I handed it back. I hoped he didn't look too closely at the signature because his sense of humour had nose-dived since they'd taken his car back. Seeing 'M. Mouse' might just drive him over the edge. I thought of pushing a broken bottle into his throat and I positively beamed at him.

'I have to go to Hong Kong again.'

'Not on our budget.'

'I'll take some days off. I'm owed enough.'

'You'll have to check with Hardwicke.'

'Will do.'

Bill just nodded and said sure, take as long as you want. He seemed to be frowning all the time now, and he looked older. The paper was in profit, with new technology you had to try really hard to lose money in publishing, but the parent company had pulled out most of its cash and saddled it with a hefty debt. He was having to make do with fewer reporters, a reduced wire service, and his travel budget had been cut to the bone.

'Problems with the Hong Kong cops?' he asked. His hair seemed greyer, too, what little he had left.

'No, just a few loose ends to tie up.'

'OK. Get back as soon as you can. You know how short-staffed we are.'

'All hands to the pumps.'

'With the rats queuing up to jump ship.' Two of the paper's feature writers had already handed in their notice and it was an open secret that another half dozen reporters were looking for other jobs. 'I hear Roger is after a move.'

'He's been whispering into the phone a few times,' I admitted. What the hell, I didn't owe Roger any favours.

'It's to be expected,' he said, stacking together the heap of page plans that forever seemed to be strewn across his desk. 'This isn't a particularly happy place at the moment.'

'It'll pass, Bill,' I said. 'Swings and roundabouts.' He looked smaller, too. In all the years I'd known him I'd never seen him look so defeated, so hurt. The word around the office was that his son was dying of cancer, but he'd never mentioned it and it wasn't the sort of thing you could bring up in normal conversation. Professionally we shared everything but on a personal level he was a virtual stranger. Hell, I didn't even know his wife's name.

'Are you OK, Bill?' I asked.

He nodded and rubbed his nose with the back of his hand. 'I've got a lot on my plate, at the moment,' he said, and shrugged his massive shoulders. 'That's all.'

'If I can help . . .' I didn't finish the sentence because what the hell could I do? I left him with his page plans and whatever was troubling him.

Roger was still filling in his expense sheet when I got back to his desk.

'Bill says it's OK,' I told him.

304

'So it's OK.' He didn't look up. I took an axe and hacked off his head and watched it roll across the floor. 'When are you going?' he asked.

'I'll fix up a flight tomorrow.'

'Any idea how long you'll be away this time?' The arrogant runt still didn't bother to look up.

'As long as it takes,' I said in a quiet voice, wanting to rile him, to pick an argument so that I could unleash the bitterness and resentment.

'Don't be away too long.'

'Afraid I'll miss your leaving do?'

That made him look up sharply and I was pleased that at last I'd touched a nerve. I logged off and waved goodbye to Katy.

'Do you want me to speak to Robbie?' she said.

'No thanks, love. This one's on me.'

I booked into the Excelsior and they made the same spelling mistake on the matches but what the hell, I don't smoke anyway. The mini-bar was well stocked and my fingers played over the gin bottle before I took out a can of Sprite, more to kill time than to quench my thirst. It was Thursday, half past twelve, and the Mandarin was just ten minutes away in a cab. I paced the room, drinking from the can, my heart thumping in my chest. I had a headache, a dull pain that filled my skull and I'd drawn the curtains to keep out the blinding midday sun. All night I'd tossed and turned but at least I hadn't had any 'I'm back' dreams. When I thought of Sally now it wasn't with a gut-wrenching feeling of loss but with a gentle sadness. I missed her. I missed Jenny, too. She was staying in London, thinking of moving there permanently. She'd wanted to come with me to Hong Kong but I told her I wanted to see this through on my own. She understood. Now I wished she had come.

It was exactly five past one when I walked into the cool grandeur of the Mandarin Grill and asked the maitre d' to take me to Dennis Lai's table. It was in the far corner and he led me past a long table that groaned under an elaborate display of seafood. A crowd of green crabs with their claws tied with string scuffled on a pile of ice chippings, and a couple of large lobsters slowly waved their antennae, sensing movement. Kaufman had his back to the entrance so he didn't see me until I was standing next to the table and a funereal waiter pulled a chair out for me.

The restaurant was a masterpiece of plush opulence, subdued lighting and subdued conversation. The tables were far enough apart so that diners couldn't eavesdrop and there were so many waiters about that no matter when you reached for a cigarette a light would be held in front of you before you could get it out of the packet.

Kaufman's eyes didn't register recognition when Lai introduced us, and my name didn't seem to mean anything to him. He might have been playing cool because I was pretty sure he would have pulled my file from personnel at some point during the last few months. And he must have known who I was because he'd put pressure on me through Bill Hardwicke to get me back to London. I'd had a couple of sleepless nights once I'd gone back, thinking that perhaps Kaufman would set out to get me, but after the attack outside my home I'd been left alone and after a while I'd got out of the habit of looking over my shoulder when I unlocked my front door. I guess he thought that without evidence there was no way I could hurt him. He was wearing an immaculately tailored, grey pinstripe suit, a spotless white shirt and an MCC tie. His steel grey hair looked as if it had been welded to his head and shaped with metal cutters and a blow torch. He looked cool and unflustered which I guess was to be expected because he'd booked a suite in the Mandarin and had only had to take the lift down to the restaurant. I was wearing my number three blue Marks and Spencer suit with the cigarette burn by the middle button and I was sweating. Wiping my hands on the crisp white serviette that was every bit as dazzling as Kaufman's shirt didn't seem to help. Lai asked me what I wanted to drink and the little demon in me that craved alcohol asked for a gin and tonic but I pushed him back into his cell and ordered a ginger ale. The first couple of days on the wagon I'd tried drinking neat tonic water but it brought back too many memories of its constant companion so I'd packed it in.

'Cheers,' I said, raising my glass to Lai, who nodded without smiling. He made no move to explain my presence to Kaufman, who spent a few minutes fishing for a hint from me before giving up and consoling himself with polite social chit-chat about the hotel, the weather, British politics and 1997. We'd just started on the way AIDS was spreading through Asia when a waiter appeared with voluminous leather-bound menus. He was followed by a wine waiter in a gold waistcoat with what looked like a silver ashtray hanging from a chain around his neck, so we got on with the serious business of choosing the food and wine.

Lai and Kaufman seemed to treat it seriously, anyway, scoring culinary points off each other at every opportunity as they discussed methods of preparation and presentation. Kaufman chose oysters and a mixed grill while Lai asked for smoked salmon and beef from the trolley. I wanted soup but the way my hands were starting to tremble, I knew I had little chance of getting any from the bowl to my mouth with a spoon and asking for a straw was out of the question. Without thinking I asked for the same as Lai and Kaufman raised his metal filing eyebrows but what the hell, there was no doubt whose side I was on. The choice of wine turned into a battle of wills with Lai eventually conceding and agreeing to try the Nuits-St-Georges, letting Kaufman have his way with a curt smile.

The conversation moved towards China and by the time the main course arrived the two businessmen were discussing the problems of doing business with the mainland.

'You seem to have been having more than your fair share of problems there,' said Lai, cutting a piece of beef with the careful precision of a Harley Street surgeon opening up a peer of the realm, and spreading it thickly with mustard. English mustard at that, he must have had an asbestos mouth.

'It's an ill wind, Mr Lai,' said Kaufman.

'I don't follow you,' said Lai, using a scrap of beef to wipe through the gravy and the yellow smear on his plate.

'It was my problems in China that allowed you to buy into my company,' said Kaufman, placing his knife and fork together and then dabbing his napkin on his lips.

'You were very unfortunate, Mr Kaufman,' said Lai. He stopped eating, too. Perhaps he'd lost his appetite.

'And you were lucky. Very lucky,' said Kaufman.

'Oh, I think there was more than luck involved.'

'I'm sure there was. I should have realized that the Chinese contracts fell into my lap too easily.' Kaufman rested his arms on the table and toyed with the salt cellar as he talked. 'I should have seen what was coming.' A waiter unobtrusively removed our plates. I'd hardly touched mine, and now I was sitting in silence as the two adversaries squared off for battle.

Lai leant back in his chair and folded his arms across his chest. 'You were impatient,' he said. 'You saw the chance of a lifetime and you grabbed it with both hands.'

Another waiter arrived and handed out dessert menus. Kaufman ignored his but Lai idly flicked through it as he talked. 'You weren't to know it would go sour.'

'But you did, Mr Lai?'

Lai smiled. 'Of course. And now you must pay the price of your greed.'

'So now we get down to it,' said Kaufman. 'What is it you want, Mr Lai?'

'Oh,' said Lai, looking up from his menu. 'I rather think I will have the lemon meringue pie.' He chuckled quietly at his own joke.

'If it's a fight you want, Mr Lai, you've got one. And I'll take you apart, piece by piece,' Kaufman said, and for the first time there was a note of menace in his voice.

Lai slowly placed his menu down in front of him, and waved the approaching waiter away. He smiled at Kaufman, showing teeth but no warmth. They'd forgotten I was there, their eyes were locked and their minds were focused on each other.

'Oh, I don't think there will be a fight, Mr Kaufman,' he said, and leant forward, resting his elbows on the table. Kaufman looked at him quizzically.

'What do you mean?'

'Mr Kaufman, I already have your company in the palm of my hand.'

Kaufman snorted with impatience. 'Nine per cent won't even get you a seat on the board,' he said.

'I don't have nine per cent, Mr Kaufman.'

'You have the shares that I placed with China,' said Kaufman.

'I have bought more.'

'How many more?' The eyelid was twitching now, and his breathing was heavier.

'I now own twenty six per cent of your shares, Mr Kaufman.'

'What is this, greenmail? You expect us to buy out your shareholding, is that it?'

'Hardly, Mr Kaufman. Not the way your shares have been performing recently. They have been rising steadily and I doubt that you could afford to buy me out.'

'So you want a seat on the board, is that it?'

'No, Mr Kaufman, that's not what we want.'

Kaufman picked up on that quickly, like a terrier pouncing on a rat. 'We?' he snapped.

'My friends and I,' said Lai.

'Friends?' asked Kaufman, his hands clenched around the salt cellar. 'What friends?'

I knew the answer to that one. The recent buying orders for Kaufman's shares had been coming in from San Francisco, Sydney, Toronto and London, the boys in the City Office had said, all places with their own Chinese communities, cities where Lai was sure to have friends and relatives who could buy shares in small batches without attracting attention. I was certain that Lai would have made sure that there was no way anyone could prove he was acting in concert with the other investors, and that to an outsider and, more importantly, to the regulatory authorities, it would seem to be totally unconnected buying.

'Suffice it to say that as of today I control fifty four per cent of your company, Mr Kaufman.'

Kaufman's eyes widened in disbelief, and he swallowed several times before he spoke.

'I don't believe you.'

'I directly own twenty six per cent of your firm,' said Lai. 'The remaining twenty eight per cent are in the hands of people who are sympathetic to my aims.'

'Your aims? What is it you want? My company?'

'I already own your company, Mr Kaufman. On Monday morning I will announce to the London Stock Exchange that I am making a bid for the shares that I do not already own. My allies will announce at the same time that they are accepting my offer. You, I believe, personally control some twelve per cent and a further six per cent is held by a trust for your children.' Lai smiled and held his palms up at shoulder level like a conjurer showing he had nothing up his sleeves. 'I really don't see how you can stop me.'

Kaufman's teeth were clenched tightly and he was breathing heavily through his nose, his eyes tense with hatred and anger. The waiter reappeared at Lai's shoulder and he ordered his lemon meringue pie.

'Anything for you, Mr Kaufman?' he asked, and when he did not reply Lai looked at me, eyebrows raised.

'Just coffee,' I said, and when I heard my voice I realized that I hadn't spoken for a full ten minutes and that my mouth was dry with anticipation.

'Three coffees,' said Lai, ordering for Kaufman.

'I built that company from nothing, Mr Lai. It's mine, 's part of me. I won't let you take it from me.'

'You cannot stop me, Mr Kaufman.'

'It's my company, you won't be able to run it without me. And I'll never work for you '

'I don't intend to run your company, Mr Kaufman. I sincerely hope that by this time next year there will be no trace of Kaufman Industries left.'

'What?'

'I shall be breaking your company into its component parts one by one. As soon as I have full control of the group China will announce it is reinstating all the projects it has so recently cancelled. Then I shall begin selling off the company piece by piece. Most are already promised to my friends. You have built up a world-wide empire, Mr Kaufman, and I have friends around the world. I am going to dismember your company, and it will be as if you never existed. No one will remember Kaufman Industries or you. You will not even be history.'

His dessert arrived then, along with the coffees. Lai cut into his pie with the edge of his fork and delicately tasted it. 'Delicious,' he said to no one in particular. 'You really should try some, Mr Kaufman.'

'Why?' asked Kaufman quietly. 'Why?'

I thought Lai was going to joke again, but he looked coldly at his adversary and rested his fork carefully on the plate. The time for joking was past and I watched with morbid fascination as Lai moved in for the kill, like a snake mesmerizing a rabbit.

'Why? You want to know why, Mr Kaufman?' He nodded slowly. 'Very well, I shall tell you.'

He paused, on the surface he was as unruffled as a

stagnant pool but I knew how much Sally had meant to him and he was fighting to control his anger, but his voice when it came was level, flat and emotionless.

'You, Mr Kaufman, are a greedy man.' He made it sound like a schoolboy insult. 'Your mining operation in Ningbo was a sound investment, it was generating perfectly reasonable profits and showed every sign of continuing to do so. But you decided that you wanted more.'

Kaufman leant back in his chair and sighed deeply, lowering his head onto his chest and frowning as he studied Lai. Lai looked at me, and I picked up the story. I'd done the digging and so I wanted to tell it. But as I spoke, Kaufman looked only at Lai.

'The deal you had with Peking was that you would pay them a proportion of the value of the diamonds that you mined,' I said. 'Diamonds were examined in Ningbo before being flown to Hong Kong by two valuers acting for the authorities. Their job was to check on your production, value the diamonds and send back a monthly report to Peking. But the arrangement wasn't good enough for you, was it? You wanted more. The initial surveyor's report suggested that most of the stones would be small, industrial quality diamonds, but when you started finding more and more large stones you began to resent the percentage you had to pay to China. So you began to hide the good stones from the valuers and showed them only the low-grade industrial diamonds.

Then just before the diamonds were put on the plane you replaced the big stones.'

Still Kaufman refused to look at me.

'You couldn't release those diamonds onto the open market because that would have depressed prices and people would start to wonder where the new supply was coming from. Am I right so far?'

Kaufman said nothing, I guess he wasn't used to being lectured and he just stared broodingly at Lai from under half lowered lids. He was gripping the silver salt cellar with one hand and his knuckles shone white. Lai smiled thinly, acknowledging his adversary's discomfort, relishing it.

'So you stockpiled the diamonds, and after a year or so began releasing them in small batches through the Hong Kong bourse,' I continued. 'But again your greed got the better of you, you wanted too much, too soon and the price began to move. And it began to go down at a time when a miners' strike in South Africa should have sent the price soaring. Dealers started to talk and a young girl reporter writing an advertising feature on the diamond exchange listened. And then she went to Zhejiang to see for herself what sort of diamonds you were coming up with. All she had to do then was run a cross check with the authorities in Peking and she'd find that you were short-changing them to the tune of millions of dollars a year. What did she do, Kaufman? Type the story into the *Post*'s computer where somebody read it and tipped you off? Or did she telephone you to see if you knew what was going on?'

Kaufman still didn't reply. His lips were clamped together, locking in anything he might have wanted to say. He looked like a trapped wild cat trying to work out which way to jump.

'Whatever, you had her killed,' Lai broke in. 'And when you killed her you killed a part of me.' I nodded in agreement. 'She was my sister,' I said, but Kaufman didn't even look at me. As far as he was concerned I didn't exist, it was between Lai and him and I wanted to shake him and force him to face me, to admit that I was there.

'It was an accident,' Kaufman said quietly, talking to Lai.

'She was thrown through a window fifteen floors above the street, Mr Kaufman. How was that an accident?'

'They were supposed to keep her quiet, that was all.'

'And how were you going to buy her silence? With money?' Lai smiled, his eyes sad and soulful as a sick spaniel's. 'She had all the money she could ever want, Mr Kaufman. She could never have me but she knew I would give her everything else.'

'Sally couldn't be bought,' I said, to both of them. To Kaufman because I wanted him to know she was a reporter, and that the story would have meant everything, and to Lai because I wanted him to know that even he could not buy my sister and then the car and the flat flashed into my mind and I realized that maybe he could. But still I was ignored like a young child sitting at a table with squabbling adults.

'But as far as you were concerned, she knew too much,' Lai pressed.

'You don't understand,' said Kaufman, exasperated.

'I understand perfectly,' said Lai.

Kaufman snorted, and banged his hand down on the table, hard enough to rattle the vase and its carnations sitting dead centre. He glared at Lai.

'It wasn't what she knew, it was what she planned to do,' said Kaufman.

'She was a reporter, she was working on a story,' I said.

'Oh really?' said Kaufman. 'Is that what you think? That your precious sister was in pursuit of the truth. It's a pity you weren't in my office when the little bitch rang me up.'

'What do you mean?' asked Lai, beating me to the question.

'She tried to blackmail me,' said Kaufman. He sounded more confident now, he straightened his back and looked down his nose at Lai, the look of a man who thought he had right on his side.

'She phoned me in London. Asked me a lot of leading questions about the mine, about the diamonds and about the financial arrangements. As you can imagine, I was not exactly truthful in my replies. I admit I had a lot to hide.'

He paused, as if planning what to say next. 'Then she told me she already had the story. It was already written, it was ready to be published.'

'And?' asked Lai.

'And she asked if I wanted to buy it. Exclusively.'

'Balls,' I shouted, loud enough to turn heads.

'For half a million pounds I could have exclusive rights to the story. And it was up to me whether or not it ever appeared in print.'

'Bullshit,' I said. 'She wouldn't have done that.'

He looked at me coldly. 'You have my word,' he said. 'I am telling the truth. Your sister was a blackmailer.'

'And so you had her killed?' said Lai.

'No,' said Kaufman. 'I have contact with some of the less savoury elements in Hong Kong. I arranged for them to go round and speak to her, to persuade her to drop her price. To accept a more reasonable amount. I swear to you that I did not want her killed.'

'Sally did not need money,' said Lai.

'Maybe she didn't need it, but you can take it from me she wanted it,' said Kaufman.

Lai shook his head in emphatic denial, but I felt a terrible coldness spreading through my belly, the numbing realization that maybe, just maybe, he was telling the truth.

'Why did she die?' I asked. 'If the heavies you sent were only to frighten her, why did she die?'

'I don't know. I don't know why they went to see her at the pool instead of at her flat. I suppose they thought she would be more vulnerable, on her own, at night. The way I heard it they switched off the lights and she started screaming before they even had a chance to talk to her. She got out of the water and started running. She was hysterical.'

'Of course she was hysterical, she was naked and three strange men had turned off the lights and were chasing her,' I said.

'One of them, Ho I think, grabbed her but she was wet, slippery, and she pulled away and slipped and fell. Through the window. It was all a mistake, a tragic mistake. I can only repeat, they were not trying to kill her. That is not what I wanted.'

'Whatever you wanted, Mr Kaufman, that was the end result,' said Lai.

Kaufman fell silent again, pondering like a grandmaster planning his next move.

Lai leant forward, his upper body curved over the table. 'And let us not forget Tod Seligman. Was the bomb in his car just your way of asking him to keep quiet, Mr Kaufman?'

'And what about the men who tried to kill me in London,' I said, but once more I was ignored.

Kaufman took the salt cellar and tapped it gently against his cheek before placing it on the tablecloth.

'Let's cut the bullshit, Lai. It's time to put up or shut up. I might not be able to stop you taking over my company but I'm fucked if I'm going to grovel in front of you. If I lose the company the Ningbo operation doesn't matter one way or another. So what are you going to do, Lai? Go to the police? You can't prove a thing.'

Lai nodded thoughtfully, as if considering Kaufman's outburst.

'I do not need proof, Mr Kaufman. All I need to know is what happened. And now we know everything.'

Kaufman said nothing, he just looked Lai straight in the eye and waited for him to make his move. The two sat staring at each other, locked in a silent tableau of hate as the restaurant hummed around them. It was Lai who broke first, but it wasn't because he had weakened under the other man's menacing stare, it was to reach for a thin burgundy leather briefcase by the side of his chair. The gilt locks cracked open together and he removed a large manila envelope which he put by the side of his plate before relocking the case.

'That's your proof, is it?' asked Kaufman.

'No, Mr Kaufman. My proof is a conversation I had with two men in a factory in the New Territories.' He rapped the envelope with the knuckles of his right hand. 'No, this isn't my proof.'

He bared his teeth and his eyes gleamed with naked hostility and it was suddenly obvious how much he was enjoying making Kaufman wait, like a cat tormenting a mouse.

He slowly opened the envelope, his eyes never leaving

Kaufman's face as he drew out a sheaf of papers interspersed with black and white photographs. He took the top sheet and handed it to Kaufman. As it passed in front of me I saw there was a picture of a smiling blonde girl clipped to one corner of what appeared to be a CV, ordered lines of type detailing her career.

Kaufman frowned as he read it and studied the picture. 'Am I supposed to know her?' he asked, genuinely puzzled.

'Elizabeth Richardson, your second cousin. You've never met her. A sweet girl, she's studying to be a PE teacher at Loughborough.'

Before Kaufman could speak, Lai handed over the next sheet and photograph. A balding middle-aged man in a tweed jacket. His CV was about twice as long as the girl's. Now Kaufman looked even more puzzled. 'You've never met this one, either. Roger Wolfendale. Another distant cousin. His computer business in Ireland is about to win a big order from Germany, I understand. He seems to be doing well.'

Lai started giving Kaufman the rest of the reports in quick succession, summing up each one in a few words, a shop assistant, a lawyer, a Jaguar salesman. There was one common thread, they were all related to the tycoon, starting with distant relatives like the blonde girl and the balding man on the outskirts of his life and working steadily to the core, to his mother in Newton Abbot, his son, Simon, and two daughters, his five grandchildren, and finally his wife. By the time Lai had finished there were thirty-one people's lives laid out in front of Kaufman on the white tablecloth. He looked down at the faces of the men, women and children who meant the most to him in all the world, the human beings who carried in their cells the same genes that made him what he was. He looked down and he understood and when he finally raised his eyes they were filled with haunted fear, the look of a loser who knew he had lost.

Lai didn't have to say anything else, he didn't have to take Kaufman by the scruff of the neck and rub his nose in it like you would a dog that had soiled the carpet. He didn't have to, but he did, slowly and methodically, his eyes fixed on the industrialist.

'I want only one thing from you, Mr Kaufman. I want your life.' He paused, and it was for dramatic effect, no other reason, and I remembered the look of satisfaction as he lit the blow torch in the New Territories.

'You have exactly two weeks from today to take your own life or I shall begin to hurt every single one of your living relatives. Then I will kill them. One at a time. And when I have finished with them I will start on you.'

Kaufman began to shake his head slowly from side to side, he was breathing so heavily it sounded as if he was snoring and his cheeks were reddening.

Lai leant forward and pointed his right forefinger at Kaufman's sweating face, jabbing in time with his words. 'You have no alternative, Mr Kaufman. No alternative.'

Lai leant back in his seat and held out his arms, palms of his hands upwards and shrugged his shoulders.

'I don't care how you do it,' he said. 'But let me make one thing abundantly clear. I don't want the police to find charred ashes in a burnt out car or a pile of clothes and a wallet by the side of the Thames. Do you understand, Mr Kaufman?'

Yes, Kaufman understood, and so did I. Lai wanted a

life but more importantly he wanted a body, and maybe even a grave to dance on.

'My company will announce its bid for Kaufman Industries within the next forty-eight hours. If you are still alive twelve days after that . . .' He let the sentence hang and shrugged again, the Marlon Brando school of theatrics. I'm gonna make you an offer you can't refuse.

Kaufman was sitting ramrod straight in his chair and from the look on his face it was obvious that his mind was racing, running through all the various combinations and permutations that might lead to a way out, a grandmaster trying to come up with a lifesaver with checkmate only one move away, plenty of options available but all leading to the same result. For a fleeting second his mouth opened as if he was about to speak, but then he clamped it shut.

You want to know what terror is? I'll tell you what it isn't. It isn't being chased through a dark, empty house by an old lady with a carving knife, or walking through a misty graveyard on a moonless night and hearing a tomb creak open. Terror isn't creatures from the deep, or monsters from outer space, that's fantasy, teasing your imagination with things that might happen but never do.

You want to know what real terror is? It's when a middle-aged Chinese businessman with a half eaten piece of lemon meringue pie in front of him and crumbs on his upper lip tells you that you are going to die and you know there's not a thing in the world you can do to prevent it, to know that you are going to be dead in two weeks' time, and that if you are not then every member of your family will be killed and then your life will be taken anyway.

Terror is when you look into the cold brown eyes of a man who wants you dead and you know that he means it, that the eyes aren't going to crinkle into a smile and tell you that he's joking.

That's real terror, and that's what was facing Kaufman as he sat in the Grill Room of one of the world's top hotels amid padding waiters and clinking cutlery. I thought he was going to say something, to beg or to threaten, but no words came. He stood up abruptly, and his chair keeled over backwards as he leant across the table and slapped Lai across the face, hard, the sound cutting through the restaurant like a pistol shot. Heads whirled round and a waiter scampered over to retrieve the chair and Kaufman was the centre of attraction as he walked quickly to the door, head held high.

Lai sat in silence, seemingly oblivious to the curious stares of the customers and staff as he slowly gathered up the photographs and slid them back into the envelope.

'Would you really do it?' I asked him.

'Do what?' He replaced the envelope into his case, avoiding my eyes.

'Hurt his family. Would you do it?'

He smiled. 'I won't have to.' His left cheek was flushed from the slap, and he reached up to stroke it gently. 'It's enough that he believes I will. And you saw yourself that he knows I am not bluffing.'

'But did you mean it? If he doesn't . . .' I couldn't finish the sentence, I was as terrorized as Kaufman, though I doubt that I could have managed the same aloof exit that he'd made, my legs were shaking under the table.

'Does it matter?' he asked.

Yes, you cold callous bastard, of course it fucking matters, I thought. It matters that you could threaten thirty-one people you'd never met and who had never done you any harm. That was what I thought, but I just pulled a face and said no, I guess not, and finished my ginger ale as Lai gestured for the bill. I left before it arrived and I didn't say goodbye.

Kaufman's body was found two weeks later, in the bedroom of his Suffolk farmhouse. He'd sent his wife to London on a weekend shopping expedition and retired to bed with a bottle of twelve-year-old malt and a bottle of sleeping tablets. There was no note.

In a way I suppose it was poetic. It started with a suicide that was obviously murder, and it ended with a murder that actually was suicide. But I didn't want to think about that too closely, it was a train of thought that would rush me into a dark tunnel where I was afraid to go just then. I went out and got drunk. Two months, one week and six days. A record. Jenny was not amused, but she forgave me. Eventually.

STEPHEN LEATHER

THE DOUBLE TAP

'Masterly plotting . . . rapid-fire prose' – *Sunday Express*

'A fine tale, brilliantly told' – *Oxford Times*

The assassin – the world's most successful contract killer –
ice-cool, accurate and elusive. An anonymous professional
with a unique calling card – one bullet in the head and one
in the chest for each of his targets.

The Judas goat – an ex-member of the SAS, Mike Cramer
is the perfect sacrificial bait. When the FBI discover the
next name on the assassin's hitlist, Cramer is set up to take
his place.

The wild card – Cramer's past has caught up with him.
Ex-IRA extremist Dermott Lynch blames Cramer for his
lover's death and he's out for revenge.

As Cramer trains for the most dangerous mission in his
career, Lynch hunts down his sworn enemy. And the
unknown assassin silently closes in on his target.

The players are in position for the final deadly game . . .

HODDER AND STOUGHTON PAPERBACKS

STEPHEN LEATHER

HUNGRY GHOST

'Very complicated. Fun' – *Daily Telegraph*

'The sort of book that could easily take up a complete weekend – and be time really well spent' – *Bolton Evening News*

Geoff Howells, a government-trained killing machine, is brought out of retirement and sent to Hong Kong. His brief: to assassinate Chinese Mafia leader, Simon Ng. Howells devises a dangerous and complicated plan to reach his intended victim – only to find himself the next target . . .

Patrick Dugan, a Hong Kong policeman, has been held back in his career because of his connections – his sister is married to Simon Ng. But when Ng's daughter is kidnapped and Ng himself disappears, Dugan gets caught up in a series of violent events and an international spying intrigue that has run out of control . . .

Tough writing, relentless storytelling and a searingly evocative background of Hong Kong in the aftermath of Tiananmen Square make *Hungry Ghost* a compulsive read.

HODDER AND STOUGHTON PAPERBACKS